Three Days in Ashford

Three Days in Ashford

Ty Tracey

Published by Ty Tracey: **www.tytracey.com**
ISBN: 978-0-692-19079-1
First Printing: 2018
Printed in the United States of America.

This is a work of fiction. Names, characters, businesses, places, events, locales, and incidents are either the products of the author's imagination or used in a fictitious manner. Any resemblance to actual persons, living or dead, or actual events is purely coincidental.

For Jessie and Nellie

Prologue

I would rather be dead than go back there. Back to Ashford—the town that Satan calls home.

I am chronicling my experiences in Ashford, all these years later, because it is part of my assignment, part of my rehabilitation, and part of my never-ending "healing process."

For all intents and purposes, Ashford took my life from me. I am writing this because I must and because I haven't given much of a shit about anything since I left there. I am writing this because according to my personal parade of psychotherapists, if I don't let this out, it will eventually kill me—not that I would care in the least.

My name is Daniel Hallowell. I am forty-five years old and the father of a twenty-two-year-old daughter and the ex-husband of a forty-one-year-old wife.

I was married when I got locked in here, as happily married as any realist might expect. But a few years in this hellhole, teamed with my vehement refusal to accept the subjective opinions of the quacks that oversee me, drove Ellen away, and we eventually divorced.

Most of my family-related correspondence comes to me in letters from my daughter, Annie. She is the most hopeful soul I will ever know, still cheering me on all these years later, believing that I'm just going through a "difficult" phase and at some point, will be poised for some sort of comeback. I still love her and Ellen with all my heart, but they've moved on from me, and I can't blame them.

I left on a routine trip one night, and the man Ellen had married, and the father Annie had grown to love never came back. My watch has been one day ahead ever since. There is your elusive, Freudian justification for all my problems. You can call off your search for some singular, elegant solution and simply accept the fact that I don't care anymore. I don't even care enough to try caring. I am the five-time gold medalist in the apathy event.

My team of psychological "professionals" were kind enough to offer me a choice. I can either chronicle my time in Ashford or I can accompany a group of them back there to "face my demons" head-on. I chose the former. You'll never get me back there—not on your life.

You wouldn't care about much either if you knew what I knew or had seen what I've seen. Whether you choose to believe me or not, this is what happened. The story starts at the airport.

1
Cleveland Hopkins International Airport – 1:00 a.m.

"Holy shit! It's that guy from that show!"

If I only had a nickel for every time I'd heard that. How is it that nobody ever knows the name of a show but can immediately recognize a character from it, even when that character is standing in the third row of a hoard of people surrounding a luggage carrousel? And that character is cloaked in a hoodie, Red Sox cap, and aviator sunglasses?

Here we go, I thought. It only takes one jackass to recognize you, and the rest of the lemmings all follow suit. I called them the Oh Yeah's. One person points you out, and not even a second later, half the other people in the room say in near unison: "Oh yeah..."

Suddenly, they all recognized me as though they had all along. It's a juvenile effort to not look like the one person in the room who hasn't seen your show. Even though our ratings clearly illustrated, on a weekly basis, that approximately two people out of the fifty or so Oh Yeah's around that carousel would have watched my show more than once throughout the course of their entire life.

It's not like I didn't welcome the attention back then. Hell, I ate it up most of the time. There were just certain times that I would have preferred to be left alone. One o'clock in the morning in the Cleveland airport after a two-hour, twice delayed, bumpy flight from Boston qualified as one of those times.

I obliged, swallowing my pride. I shook all their post-flight filthy hands and let the girls get their smartphone pictures with me. I scribbled my name on whatever pieces of paper they could find for me to autograph—mostly boarding passes and luggage tickets that night. I guess I was famous, although it was not something I had ever asked for. At least I was famous for something I loved doing and because I was good at what I did.

I was thirty-nine years young at the time, but I was the good kind of thirty-nine. Some thirty-nine-year-olds look like they're fifty, but I could've still easily passed for twenty-nine. I still had a full head of my dirty-blond hair. I would let it protrude underneath my signature ball cap, which rarely came off. If there was ever one thing that gave away my real age, it was my eyes—especially my eyes at 1:00 a.m. following a flight. I wore my aviators everywhere to hide the crow's feet on the sides and circles underneath my baby blues.

That was at least thirty pounds ago. I used to love going to the gym of whatever hotel the network was paying for that week. I still had a formidable muscle tone for someone who was very nearly on the wrong side of forty. My height never helped me disguise myself with the crowd very well, at six foot four. I would have had to be surrounded by a basketball team to blend in.

"OMG," said the teenager who could never find the time or energy to vocalize the first three words of any sentence. "I cannot believe I am getting my picture taken with Daniel Hallowell. I watch you like every week. Like, I never miss an episode."

"I appreciate that, sweetheart," I managed. "Did you watch the show this week?"

"Umm, yeah, I watched this week," she replied with a bubbly giggle.

"Fantastic. Well, I am glad to have had a chance to meet you and so many other fans. Everyone, please make your ways home safely, and have a great night."

There was no show that week. There hadn't been a show or a rerun on television for over a month. We were in the middle of filming our fourteenth season. It's not as though I was vacationing to Cleveland and landing at 1:00 a.m. by the graces of my own scheduling standards. Obviously, I was there to work.

I shook the last few hands, smiled and waved, grabbed my luggage, and got the hell out of there. Thankfully, the shuttle to the rental-car park went without any further recognition.

My hotel was about five minutes from the airport. I think I had to make one turn to find it from the rental parking lot. I got there, parked my Chevy Malibu, and checked in. I shared a brief back-and-forth with the cute girl at the front desk, verified with her that the rest of my crew had already arrived, set up a wakeup call, and retired to my room.

I was asleep by 1:30 a.m.

2

I remember lying there in my hotel bed. I was thinking about how it seemed that hotel beds always managed to be more comfortable than whatever bed you had at home. Thinking about things like that had always been how I fell asleep. Eventually, such thoughts evolved into deeper, more critical thoughts about life and the times we lived in and eventually into that mental solace that comes with deep sleep.

As I write this, I find it incredible that I can tell you exactly what I was thinking about as I drifted off to sleep that night. I couldn't tell you of such things from many other nights of my life, but that particular night registers incredibly clearly to me, as it was the beginning of the most profound three days of my life. It was my ticket to my destiny of waking nightmares that would haunt me to this very day.

I could hear the howl of a train in the distance and the subtle rumbling of its mass as it thundered along down the track, occasionally interrupted by its blaring horn. I remember thinking as I drifted off:

Why in the hell do they have to blare their horns? Doesn't a fifteen-thousand-ton train with metal wheels screeching against a metal track at forty miles per hour make enough noise? Shouldn't that be enough of a warning to anyone or anything in the way? I suppose they are legally obligated to sound their horns anytime they rumble through a stretch that intersects with human beings. But why? Human beings are far more likely to be hit by a car in their lifetime than they are a train. And people driving cars are not legally obligated to blare their horns every time they drive over a crosswalk. Thank god for that. Could you imagine how noisy the planet would be if every driver laid-on his or her horn every time they drove over a crosswalk? It would create such a public nuisance that people would begin losing their minds within a week. The very fabric of our society would become utterly shattered.

Before I could think about it any further, I fell into a deep slumber. I remember being chased in my dream. My specialized line of work invited the darkest of phantasms into my subconscious. I have made my life their playground, and the ghouls and poltergeists I'd studied and hunted my entire life had a way of sticking with me.

I don't remember what was chasing me. I can remember hiding from it, though, and I was in grave danger. If my unseen stalker were to find me, I would soon be joining it in its supernatural oblivion. I was holed up inside of a train boxcar in a desolate stockyard in a post-apocalyptic wasteland. I was aware that I was hidden from my pursuer but pigeonholed at the same time. I came in through the one door in or out. If I were to be found, there would be no avoiding whatever hunted me.

Bang!

The thirty-ton boxcar rattled violently as a massive amount of force slammed into the steel door directly across from me. I crouched near the ground, struggling to maintain my balance. My pulse raced. This car was empty, therefore there was nothing to hide behind. Maybe it was just testing the car, slamming into it to see if it could elicit a reaction from me, attempting to expose my position.

Bang! Bang! Bang!

My eyes opened, and I gasped for air as reality rushed back to me. Someone was knocking on the door of my hotel room. The inconsiderate, over-aggressive knocking had seeped into my dreams and manifested as the devastating crashes into my hideout. I glanced at the Hyatt-provided alarm clock to my left. It was 2:15 a.m. I had managed a whopping forty-five minutes of sleep prior to the unwelcomed awakening.

Pissed off, I tripped about five times on my way to the door. Upon my arrival, I had not mastered the unique nuances of that particular room, and the walls and corners seemed to be jutting out into my way at every turn. I looked through the peephole to find my equipment tech, Gary, along with some other dingus I didn't recognize. I opened the door a crack, allowing the safety catch to prevent the door from opening farther. I tilted my head into the crack and addressed my unwanted guests.

"The fuck do you want, Gary?" I barked.

"Danny!" he replied in a tone that suggested surprise that I had come to the door. "We need to talk to you right now. Let us in."

"What? No. Who in the hell is this with you?"

Gary Jenkins was a simple man. And by simple, I mean stupid. Don't get me wrong, you could not find a better equipment tech in the business. Our show required us to venture to some of the most desolate locations in all weather conditions imaginable. Gary always seemed to keep a handle on everything we needed technologically. Everything stayed dry, powered up, and working. Cameras rarely malfunctioned, and the sound equipment was always tuned perfectly to whatever acoustic conditions surrounded us.

Otherwise, Gary was, for lack of a better description, horrible at life. He was thirty-three at the time, divorced twice, in jail once, upside-down with the IRS, in debt up to his eyeballs, and whatever level of alcoholic it takes to still manage to function in your job. When he wasn't drunk, he was stoned. I never understood how he managed to score pot no matter what part of the world our show brought us to. I always hated driving around with him for fear of being pulled over at any moment. There was never any doubt that he had little baggies of weed and his various paraphernalia stashed all over our van. You would think he would have taken some of his "pot money" and paid off the IRS. I guess he just didn't care. The network and various sponsors paid us handsomely, but Gary never managed to have any money. You couldn't go to Burger King with the man without everyone having to chip in to pay for Gary's lunch.

"Danny," he said again, "I assure you, you will not regret letting this guy in and hearing him out."

They reeked of that half-vomit, half-liquor smell of stale, already-ingested whiskey. If you have ever been in a men's room on St. Patrick's Day, you know the odor, and you can't ever un-know it. They didn't have to tell me that they had met each other at the hotel bar. Gary never met a hotel bar that he didn't absolutely love.

"I don't know who the hell this person is with you. How do I know he isn't some sort of deviant who just wants a chance to get into my ass as soon as I let him in my room?"

They both laughed. Up until that remark, the strange man Gary had brought to my room in the middle of the night had just stood there, smiling silently. His high-pitched, nervous, stupid-sounding laugh was the first noise he had made.

"This dude is cool, man," replied Gary, slurring. "He is going to change our entire assignment here and probably going to make all of our careers."

I gave the stranger another visual once-over and came to the realization that he was about the size of one of my legs. There would be no chance of this man overpowering me unless he was some sort of Judo master. His nerdy sensibility suggested otherwise.

I undid the safety latch and let them both in.

3

They entered the room, and Gary immediately entered the bathroom, no doubt having to relieve himself of whatever lethal combination of alcoholic cocktails he had poisoned himself with that evening. I was left alone with the strange, drunken dwarf-man. He was for some reason ogling me up and down.

He broke the ice. "I cannot believe I am in Daniel Hallowell's hotel room right now."

"Is this like an achievement for you or something?" I asked him.

Shaking off my previous remark and talking over the Niagara River that had begun flowing out of Gary, he continued, "I've watched your show. I cannot believe how good you guys are. I mean, compared to all the other teams of guys who do what you do, you're a real cut above everyone else. You care about the science, and that gets you the best evidence of anyone."

"Look," I replied, "we aren't the Beatles. We are a bunch of parapsychologists and one overweight lush of an equipment technician who likes bringing strange dudes to my hotel room in the middle of the night. Why don't you just tell me your name and what is so important that it is going to 'make all our careers'?"

"Sorry, sorry, sir," he replied. "My name is Lance Filner, and I am just a huge fan of yours. I am so sorry to barge in on you here. But I think I have a suggestion for you that will change your life."

"How old are you, bud?" I asked. "You barely look old enough to be drinking."

With a note of dejection to his voice he replied. "I am twenty-six years old, sir."

"Christ," I replied, "you look about nineteen."

Just then, the toilet flushed, the door to the bathroom opened, and Gary returned. It was obvious that he had elected to skip the entire hand-washing, personal-hygiene, public-health portion of the exercise. I sat on the corner of the bed and responded to Lance. "Have a seat, buddy. Sorry to be a dick. I have just been so busy trying to replace my equipment tech with someone who is not a complete low-life."

I had one eye on the rotund, brown-haired Gary the entire time I was talking about him as he approached from the bathroom. For someone who never had any food money, Gary never managed to lose weight. He was the same round man I had known since college. His hair was the equivalent of a C-student in the hair world. It had all the potential—it was all there—but he just never seemed to be able to get it together. It was always the perfect portrait of average. Something was always glaringly wrong with it. On that night, his double colic was jutting out in all directions like antennae from Sputnik, yet the front of his hair was still parted on the side and fairly well brushed. He was basically Bluto from Animal House but without any of the charm or wit of John Belushi.

Assuming I had been joking with him, and I was, although I was genuinely pissed off, Gary flipped me the bird as he sat in the desk chair. Our new friend Lance sat in the uncomfortable hotel chair that always seemed to be parked in an odd part of the room that is good for nothing but sitting in and staring off into the middle distance like some kind of a vegetable. Everyone was just sitting and looking at one another while smiling awkwardly.

"All right," I announced. "Now what? Pillow fight?"

Gary interjected, "Lance, tell Danny what you told me in the bar."

I looked over at Lance. The young man was still gawking at me like I was the pope. He finally cleared his throat and initiated his attempt to justify his being there. "Have you ever heard of the town that Satan calls home, Mr. Hallowell?"

"You mean Cleveland?" I asked.

Gary and I chuckled at the remark. My eyes were still fixed on Lance, who was not laughing. He showed no emotion whatsoever. He held a small brown book in his armpit. It looked like a journal of some sort, but I could not read any inscription on its face or spine. It was a small volume—its brown-leather body approximately the size of a steno notepad.

"There is a town," Lance said in a stormy tone. "It's about thirty miles east of here, called Ashford. What if I were to tell you that this is the most haunted town you will ever come to know as long as you both shall live?"

I replied, "Well, Lance, I would ask—what makes Ashford so haunted?"

Lance was staring off into space. He had gone pale, bordering on lethargic-looking. He didn't seem to care that I had asked him a question. His voice went soft and raspy as he continued, "There is a creek that flows through Ashford. It flows peacefully into town and peacefully out of town. But while the water is there, it is dark and cloudy. It quenches the blood lust of the town."

I looked at Gary, perplexed. "What the hell is this guy talking about?"

Lance interrupted me, carrying on with his story in a more authoritative tone. "What I am trying to say, Danny, is that the town itself is haunted. The entire town is evil; every micron of matter is cursed within its borders."

"Lance," I replied. "Every rube in the world can find reasons as to why their little dot on the map is haunted or evil. I need specifics."

"Ever heard of Melissa Keeler?"

"Nope."

"Dr. William Sharp?"

"Nope."

"Samuel Liston?"

"Nada."

He took a deep breath and continued, "These are all citizens of Ashford who have gone missing in the past five years alone. The list goes on and on—these are a mere drop in the bucket. The FBI has spent more time in Ashford over the past twenty years than they have in Quantico.

"These people literally vanish. One moment, they're watching television and they run to the bathroom during a commercial and are never seen again. Samuel Liston is a fitting example. He took the trash out one morning. His wife was helping him. They both went to the end of the driveway and dropped off the bags of trash. She turned back toward the house first and didn't get a quarter of the way back up the driveway before realizing she was totally alone. Her husband was just gone. Nobody has seen or heard from Samuel Liston since."

"Sounds like you have a serial killer on your hands, son," I suggested.

He shook his head. "This has been happening over the course of at least eighty years. It is estimated that throughout that time frame, at least a thousand have gone missing. That would have to be one highly motivated, persistent, incredibly elusive and elderly serial killer. The bodies are never retrieved, so nobody can even prove that these people are being murdered. How and where do you hide a thousand bodies in an eight-square-mile town?"

I looked at Gary, who was looking at me with an ear-to-ear grin on his face and his eyebrows raised. I knew that grin, it was his *I am intrigued, and I know the feeling is mutual* kind of grin.

I remained skeptical. "And what does the FBI have to say about all of this?"

"Nobody is even sure how many disappearances there have really been. Nobody really started documenting anything prior to circa 1935. Don't you find it strange that you've never heard of Ashford?"

"Well, if what you say is the truth, then yes, I do find it strange. I would think that such a systemic run of unexplained disappearances would have found its way into the news by now, absolutely."

He thrust his finger into the air as though he had just reached a spiritual breakthrough with me. "Bingo, Danny! The FBI doesn't know shit except that there is no human explanation for what is happening in Ashford. They aren't even trying anymore. They've gone into contain-and-control mode. The only thing they do know for sure is that they can't have something like this getting into the news. Imagine if the people of this great country were suddenly made aware of something like this being a possibility? The FBI has done everything they can to quarantine us—to keep us out of the public light. You can't find Ashford on a map anymore. The roads on your GPS or phone applications will never take you through it. Every single person who has gone missing there is off the grid. You won't find a record of their deaths anywhere—or their births, for that matter. None of them ever existed.

"Seven years ago, everyone was given an option to leave—to be relocated out of Ashford on the government dime. Everyone left, except for a few hundred of us. All that are left there now are the people who are sworn to secrecy and legitimately care about figuring out the meaning behind the disappearances. It goes without saying that we aren't supposed to leave town unannounced, and we absolutely should not be having this conversation. I am here because I snuck out along the creek bed for eight miles until I hit Huntsfield and managed to call a cab. I assure you that my being missing is causing quite a stir back home. Half the town has probably written me off as the next victim. Nobody leaves unless there is a dire emergency, and even then, they're monitored."

"Cute story," I replied. "So, we just take this at face value? No records to consider, and no proof of any of this happening? What do you want from us? Should we just go to your town and hope someone spontaneously combusts? If we could even get in, that is."

"There is a heart. There is an epicenter. The townspeople know of it, and the feds won't go near it. You should investigate it. You guys are the best hope anyone has to crack this thing."

"A heart?" I asked.

"I call it a heart because there is an evil that can be felt throughout Ashford and no more strongly than at this epicenter. Everyone knows about it, and if you spent five minutes there, you would feel it too."

"How do you suggest we get into your town?" I asked. My level of intrigue had begun to rise the more I listened to Lance. At first, I had been humoring him but now I genuinely wanted to know more.

"I have discovered a fairly substantial gap in the ability of the FBI to surveil a key point of entry into town," he replied.

"What kind of a gap?"

"I know the guy who patrols the main road into town tomorrow morning. I know that he parks his Yukon down the road, about three miles from my house, every single morning between eight o'clock and noon, and sleeps. You can walk up and shake the car, and he doesn't wake up. The man could sleep through a category-five hurricane. During those hours, every day, the only presence the feds have patrolling the main road into town is this guy, who clearly doesn't care enough to stay awake."

Finally, Gary chimed in, "Lance, why did you have to walk eight miles through the creek to escape? Couldn't you have just waited until your guy was asleep and driven right passed him and out of town?"

"My guy was off last night, and a different patrol was on duty. This was the only night I could get to you guys in this hotel, so I had to come tonight. I had to make tonight work at all costs."

I was still confused as to what he was expecting of us. "Well, what do we do once we're in town? I don't feel like dodging the feds all weekend. Surely there are more agents skulking around other than your slumbering sloth-man."

"It's not like there are roadblocks or anything. They can do everything in their power to decrease the likelihood of anyone wondering into town, but people do from time to time. It is not against any sort of law to accidently drive into Ashford. Just tell anyone who asks that you are headed to my place to look at antique camera equipment; you won't have any issues. I have an ad on Craigslist, so the story will check out."

I looked over at Gary. "What do we have on the agenda for tomorrow?"

He looked at me like I had just asked him to solve the riddle of the Sphinx. "Umm, well, we're supposed to go and meet with the proprietor of the Carnegie Steel Mill. Then we got some equipment checks and an interview on some radio station."

I shook my head, knowing that those menial tasks could be accomplished by my understudy, Rick Voss. "Get Ricky to handle all that shit. We're going to Ashford in the morning. I'll meet you in the lobby in five hours. Now, both of you, get the hell out of my room."

4

The rest of the night was spent tossing and turning as I replayed Lance's story in my head. Very little of what he had said made any sense to me. I had a powerful sense that we weren't getting the full story out of him. It wasn't like Lance was the first fanboy to approach us and try to pitch his town as a hotbed of paranormal activity. It was hard to go a day back then without some kid coming up to us and begging for us to visit because they saw the ghost of their dead grandmother in the backyard or they were convinced there were demons residing in the walls of their home or one day they stepped out of the shower and found a spectral, shadowy man standing in their bathroom. Most of the time, they ended up being drunks or were recalling an unpleasant experience while tripping on shrooms.

But every now and again, their yarns proved to be fruitful for us. By now, you have likely been able to deduce my previous profession. I was a paranormal investigator and a damn good one at that. I hold a PhD in psychology and a master's in parapsychology. I have been published in *The Journal Nature* on several occasions—the first such publication of any parapsychologist. *Time* magazine once described me as "the man who proved the afterlife."

I authored my autobiography, chronicling my life leading up to Ashford. It spent nearly a month at the top of *The New York Times* Best Seller list. It was called *The Ethereal Hunter*. I didn't pick that name. I thought it was stupid. I wanted to name it: *The Autobiography of Daniel Hallowell—A Paranormal Trailblazer*. But a bunch of really good marketing folks convinced me to go with their harder-hitting name. Not a month has gone by in the years since it was published where I didn't get a check in my mailbox from its sales, so they must've done something right.

When I started in the business, you could count on one hand the number of universities that offered programs in parapsychology. Now, thanks in large part to my efforts, it is hard to find universities that don't. My goal had always been to take my research from the doldrums of the hobbyist basement to a general acceptance as an actual scientific field. Over the years that I spent on it, I took every step to disprove my own evidence, only presenting the findings that had absolutely no possibility of any rational explanation associated with them. If I had to put a finger on the one aspect of my work that set me apart from the rest of the community, it was that sort of manic meticulousness. I absolutely, vehemently refused to publish anything that I could not prove without a shadow of a doubt to be paranormal in nature.

After making a name for myself in the community as, dare I say, a hobbyist, my friends and I were approached by a representative from the Museum Network. We jumped at the opportunity to be featured on our very own television show. I was all too happy to take their funding, so I could use it toward better paranormal research. Independent, amateur ghost-hunting is not a particularly lucrative enterprise, so if you can get some bloated, ratings-starved network to steadily pay you for it, you count your lucky stars and sign that paperwork.

The rest is history. Our show, *On the Other Side—Featuring Daniel Hallowell,* was born. It lasted thirteen seasons and quickly grew into the Museum Network's personal cash cow.

Most of the assignments for the show were dictated to us by the suits that ran the network. In the early years, they insisted we investigate locations that would in some way tie in to other Museum Network programming. For instance, they once had us investigate a wing of the Smithsonian because that week was Smithsonian Week on the network. Shockingly, allowing marketing people to decide what locations to send us to, proved to be a dubious venture. Tourist locations are typically not haunted. The paranormal rarely reside amongst the living, let alone somewhere that accommodates six million people a year, like the Smithsonian. Our fans noticed. It didn't take long for the complaints to start rolling in. Turns out, people don't want to watch some bunch of paranormal investigators trying to investigate a location that isn't haunted.

The Museum Network pivoted their strategy and placed much of the control over what locations we would investigate back into our hands. Most of those locations became known to us through word of mouth. Some fanboy or fangirl emailing us and telling us about how haunted they thought someplace was. We would make a few calls to corroborate their yarns, and after a bit more research and a bunch more paperwork, we would schedule an investigation. One such story from a fan ended up leading us to our most compelling evidence to that date.

We were in West Virginia and scheduled to investigate some estate on the Ohio River near where the Point Pleasant Bridge had collapsed. It was the day before the investigation was supposed to get underway, and we were having our typical eight to twelve beers at the hotel bar before we turned in for the night. I was younger—my liver was far more functional in those days. We were sitting and talking shop when the couple in the booth next to us overheard our conversation about one of our previous investigations. The woman turned around and announced to all of us, "I know where you guys can get some of the best evidence you've ever seen."

I was eight beers deep at that point, and I replied before realizing that she had been sitting with her enormous, bald-headed husband. "Yeah? And where would that be, Hot Pants?"

I turned slowly to find her hulking, bearded, mountain of a spouse eyeballing me murderously from about seven inches away. I stared back at him for what felt like a minute before his intense gaze suddenly shifted into a welcoming smile. He had at least realized that I had made an honest mistake and was willing to shake it off.

We shook hands, and his grip was so firm that I swear I still have nerve damage. "I am Sam Millbury, but my friends call me Big Bear. Hot Pants over here is my wife of ten years, Daphne."

"How do you do, Big Bear?" I asked.

"Better than most. Now, you guys are some sort of ghost researchers or something?"

"You could say that. We're a group of paranormal investigators from New England. We're here to investigate the Allen Lotus estate, down on the river."

I was driving the entire conversation, as the other two men who were with me were too busy gawking at Big Bear, preferring to remain in the background for fear of blurting out something stupid that might piss him off.

Daphne spoke up: "We live just outside of town here, out near the quarries over on Speen Road."

I always loved how locals just assumed that they lived in the center of the universe and that everyone could somehow identify with their vague descriptions of where they lived. Obviously, we weren't from around there. Speen Road, near the quarries, meant absolutely nothing to us. But I shook my head in approval, as though I had lived there my entire life.

She continued, "Well, the whole area around here sits atop a network of old coal mines. You're sitting above them right now. It's a goddamned miracle that half of West Virginia hasn't sunk into a crater considering how many tunnels and caverns have been dug out over the ages. The main entrance to Old Foolish just happens to be on our property. It's just about an acre off our backyard, into the woods."

"Sorry, Old Foolish?" I asked.

"That's right," she replied. "Old Foolish is the name the miners gave to one of the biggest systems in the state at the time. They named her Old Foolish because there were so many incidents there over the years that it just seemed foolish to keep having men go down there. It has quite a history—fires, collapses, and incidents with explosives. It was finally shut down in the '50s after a massive fire in the caves burned twenty-seven men alive."

My ears perked up at that revelation, knowing that this fact likely validated their claim that we might find good evidence there. The most highly active locations for investigating the paranormal tended to center around locations where tragedies had taken place. Spirits who died unexpectedly horrible deaths had a greater tendency to remain earthbound. Obviously, such tragedies should not be celebrated in any way, but from the sense of what we did for a living, they were, not to be insensitive to the dead miners of Old Foolish, a veritable goldmine. This was the sort of tip we would take seriously. There being actual history behind an alleged haunting was always a great sign.

"What sort of stuff have you experienced personally?" I asked.

Big Bear jumped back into the conversation. "I poked around when we first bought the property about six years back. I won't go back there anymore though. I don't even go in the woods near it." He looked around as he spoke, as though he was concerned about giving away classified information.

Naturally, I was getting excited. I was a kid in a candy store at that point. Anything that could scare Big Bear's pants off had to be absolutely terrifying to the common man. I was ready to head out even before Daphne continued, "We have seen and heard just about everything you can think of. The activity is not contained to the mine entrance; it spills over into our yard and into our house even. We woke up one night to a man at the end of our bed. He was covered in coal dust with a hard hat on. He was dripping wet like he had just walked in out of a rainstorm. He was not so much standing as he was hovering over the end of the bed. Sam jumped up to confront him, and he just vanished into thin air. That is just the tip of the iceberg. Any given evening, you can stand in our backyard and hear moaning and sometimes screaming in the woods. You can always kind of half-see people walking around back there. You know what I mean? Like, you will see someone walk from behind a tree in the distance and then disappear behind the next one. Leaves you unsure if anyone was there at all. That is, until it happens again the next day and the next and so on and so on. You get the point."

My lead investigator, Ricky, dropped his beer glass and spilled all over himself as Daphne continued her story. She had a way of telling it. You could tell she wasn't making it up. The look on her face and her husbands was that of genuine horror. I remember almost being saddened to see a man like Big Bear that afraid. This man had no reason to be afraid of anything living but seemed to have met his match when he came up against the undead.

As Daphne finished up her story, I glanced around my table and asked, "Road trip out to Speen Road, boys? Who is the least drunk?"

Ricky volunteered to drive, as he had only had about two and half beers at that point. We left the bar and followed the Millbury's back to their place. I can remember the ride. Even it was creepy. None of the roads within five miles of their place were paved, and none had any sort of lighting as we traversed them in the wee hours of the night. The parcels in that part of the state were enormous. As we wound around the hills on those roads that were barely wide enough to accommodate our van, we only passed about three identifiable residences throughout the twenty-five-minute drive to their home. We followed them down another "road" that ended up being their driveway, which led about a quarter of a mile into the pitch darkness of the surrounding forest.

All our moods were anxious. We had all seen plenty of horror movies that started with some group of unassuming nitwits following some stranger home for some reason only to subsequently become trapped and tortured to death.

When we finally arrived at their home, we were immediately relieved. Their property was the antithesis of what we had been expecting. It was a rather large and modern log-cabin-style home and by far the nicest place we had seen since arriving in the state. The surroundings were well lit. The front of the raised home was a massive deck that backed into floor-to-ceiling windows that wrapped around the entire perimeter of the home. We exited the van and rallied with Daphne and Sam in the driveway.

"Holy shit, Big Bear!" I said, my eyes still trained on his beautiful home. "This place is incredible. What is it you said you do for a living?"

He smiled and chuckled a bit. "I am in the security business. I take care of VIPs, mostly when they come down to rub elbows with one another at the various mountain resorts we have in the area. If you require protection, I'm a pretty good guy to have around. I learned the ropes in a little group called the Navy Seals."

Suddenly, Big Bear's entire persona began to make a lot of sense. I smiled at him, and we chuckled together. I remember being relieved to find out that these were people we could trust, yet all the while being even more anxious about what we were there to investigate. These people had no reason to be lying to us. They obviously weren't in need of a payday or attention. This man could likely kill anyone he wanted with his bare hands, so that ruled out anyone who might think about playing tricks on him and his family. Yet I saw how scared he became as his wife described their run-ins with the paranormal. What could be so horrifying that it could evoke that level of dread out of a Navy Seal?

We loaded up, prepped a few cameras and electronic voice recorders, and headed into the backyard. It was also well lit, and the landscaping was striking. There was at least a full acre of well-manicured grass that terminated at a dense tree line. We ventured into the trees, and Big Bear immediately began to sweat. His eyes became intense, and his senses appeared ultra-heightened.

I tried to lighten the mood. "How far you think we are from the entrance to Old Foolish, soldier?"

He kind of smiled at me and wiped it away as fast as it had come. "Not far, it's just through these pines."

We walked quite easily through a series of seemingly perfectly spaced pines. Our steps made very little noise, as the straw cushioned our feet. When the trees ended, we entered a clearing.

It was a dumbfounding sight to see. The woods ended and started again about a quarter acre ahead of us. In between was an old, overgrown access road that was once used to transport coal from Old Foolish. The pitch blackness of the pines gave way into the relatively well-moonlit clearing. To our left and right, we could see the long-abandoned roadway with woods on either side as it cascaded through the landscape. It stretched as far as we could see in either direction. The clearing consisted of waist-high grasses and brush, but I could still feel the stony remnants of the bygone road on my feet as I walked along.

"There it is," announced Big Bear, pointing to something ahead of us.

"There is what?" I asked, unable to acquire what he was pointing at.

"That's the entrance to Old Foolish. See it?"

I squinted my eyes and finally managed to make out what he was speaking of. Cut into the tree line across the clearing from us, there appeared a seemingly normal rock formation, but upon second and third looks, I could clearly see how it was man-made. To an everyday passer-by, it might've just looked like a cave, but to the ones who knew of it, it was obvious. I could see how the earth graded downward into it with like-sized rock walls blasted out on either side. Old, rotted, oak planks were positioned inside of the cave walls to help reinforce the load. I could visually follow the beams as they ran down into the cave until the moonlight ran out, leaving a perfectly rectangular patch of pitch blackness. As we got closer, we could see remnants of the old steel tracks coming from the mouth of the mine, once used to transport coal cars into and out of Old Foolish.

About halfway through the clearing, Big Bear stopped dead in his tracks, refusing to get any closer. Gary, Ricky, and I pressed on. It was, after all, our job to collect any kind of evidence we could. As we got closer, we were able to see into the mine itself and noticed that the entrance had been blasted shut, likely long ago. Once we were about thirty feet in, we would be met by an impenetrable rock wall. I told Gary to set up a night-vision camera pointed into the mine and to fire-wire it into a hard drive. We would then let it run throughout the night and come back to collect and review whatever we caught in the morning.

Throughout the entire journey back there, we had all been recording on our electronic voice recorders. The paranormal do not typically speak to humans in such a way that can be heard by using our naked ears. They tend to speak within frequencies that only our recorders can capture. Such frequencies are often described as "the white noise." We tested the audio and video on the night-vision camera, ensured that we were getting a quality recording into the hard drive, and left.

The entire time I had been in that forest, I couldn't help but feel like something was wrong. I don't know how to explain it, but everything just seemed . . . off, like it was not part of the same world I was accustomed to. I knew that feeling, and I was excited about it. That feeling of uneasiness usually led to quality evidence.

We spent about another hour with Big Bear and Daphne, enjoying a nightcap on their deck and they allowed us to take up residence in their guest rooms for the night. To be honest, I felt nothing while in their home that suggested a haunting. It seemed welcoming, free of any sort of dark spirits. I fell asleep easily.

I woke up to a knock on the door about two hours later, jumped out of bed, and swung the door open. It was Ricky, and to that day, I had never seen a more horrified look on his face.

"What the hell, Ricky. You look like hell," I said.

He was holding his voice recorder that he had taken with him back to Old Foolish earlier that night. Without saying a word, he hit play. At first, there was nothing but the familiar static. Then, in the deep background of the white noise, we began to hear a high-pitched banging sound. It sounded something like a sickle striking rock repeatedly. This sound got louder and persisted to a point where it resembled that of a man hammering metal to rock, mere feet away from where Ricky's recorder had been. Suddenly, multiple voices began to come through.

Spirit voices, for those who are not familiar, only vaguely resemble human voices. They do sound like people speaking, but there are unmistakable electronic undertones to them. They are of a completely different wavelength and often come through on our recorders either much slower or much faster than any normal human vocal tempo. They are more harmonic—almost synthesized. They often sound like someone speaking while rushing by at an incredible rate of speed. The first time you hear one that you have captured is an unforgettably terrifying and thrilling experience.

Suddenly, one of the voices boomed, "GET THEM OUT OF THERE!"

I jumped back from Ricky, unable to believe my ears. To that point, this was the clearest electronic voice phenomenon (EVP) I had ever heard. It was what we call in the business a "class-A EVP." The thumping of the sickle stopped with that voice and was replaced by the sound of multiple men screaming. It started off as a distant sort of moaning and groveling.

Neither of us recalled hearing anything with our naked ears on our trip back there besides crickets and the mountain wind. The shivers crept from my shoulders all the way down through my toes, as nothing, to that point, had tempered me for anything like what we had just heard. Most EVPs are a sentence here or a phrase there and barely audible. This was clear as day, as though we were reliving one of the many catastrophes that had taken place at Old Foolish.

The distant moaning elevated in volume until the voice produced actual feedback into the recorder—another first for any EVP I had ever heard or captured. This would indicate that the source of the disembodied voice was right next to us when we were back there. The moaning escalated into screaming. At least five distinct vocal tones could be heard simultaneously. Something awful was happening to them. They were enduring some level of incredible agony that none of us would likely ever know. One of the screaming voices suspended itself into an unnaturally consistent high pitch. Then an earth-shattering explosion could be heard underneath it, somewhere close by. Then another blast, and another. They seemed to register closer to the recorder as they went off, one by one. One of the voices could be heard rapidly hitching for air for a moment. Then there was dead silence. The event ended as quickly as it had begun.

Ricky and I looked at each other, both horrified but excited. We knew we had just discovered what amounted to the Holy Grail of all electronic voice phenomenon. My hands were shaking. I barely slept the rest of the night, which was but a couple of hours until sun-up. Birds could be heard cooing and cawing already as the pitch blackness of the night had again lost its battle against the soft-tangerine dawn.

As soon as I could clearly see the forest out of my guestroom window, I was out of bed and pacing on the deck outside. Ricky, sharing in my excitement, was not far behind. Big Bear joined us about fifteen minutes later, having heard us marching around on the deck outside of his bedroom window. None of us had gotten any reasonable amount of sleep. We had all just woken up but appeared more as though we had just arrived home from an all-night bender.

On the way through the backyard and into the pines, Ricky played the EVP from the previous night. I honestly just needed to make sure I hadn't dreamt the entire thing the night before. If anything, it was more impressive to listen to on the other side of the night. We were a bit fresher and had had a chance to piss some of the night's beer out of our systems. This was the first time Big Bear had heard the EVP, and he was just shaking his head, almost appearing angry that Ricky had chosen to play it for him. Even as a former member of the Seals and in the luminous morning sunlight, Big Bear would have found the walk back to Old Foolish much more favorable not having listened to it.

The fire-wire and hard drive assembly was exactly how we had left it. The night-vision camera, however, had been knocked over and had slid across the ground, uphill, approximately four feet from where we had left it. This might sound creepy and curious; however, finding one of our cameras moved or on its side was not all that uncommon in those sorts of circumstances. There was wind to contend with. The tripod rarely sat with all three legs sturdy on whatever ground we could find to place it on. The possibility of animals knocking it over was always there. Not to mention the fact that it was pitch black and we were drunk when we set it up. There were a lot of factors working against us.

I could still feel that sense of unease, like I had committed an unforgiveable cardinal sin and I was finally backed into a corner with no way to escape. As soon as I entered that forest, I felt that way. I felt hunted, guilty, and terrified. I lived for that feeling; I basked in it.

Hoping that the camera had at least lasted through a decent portion of the previous night, we packed it up along with our other equipment and headed back to Big Bear's house. Within minutes, and before Daphne had had a chance to greet us with a fresh pot of coffee, Gary had the hard drive mounted on Big Bear's laptop and was streaming the footage from the mine on his twenty-seven-inch monitor. Everyone was gathered around, watching and listening intently.

Ricky controlled the software, stepping through the footage at four times the real-time clip but careful to stop and examine anything that might seem out of place. For the first hour or two, there was nothing but the familiar darkened mouth of the mine—lined with its ratty, oaken pillars as they plunged clumsily into the mound of rock that had sealed the entrance to Old Foolish decades before. The only sounds were crickets and the occasional rustling of grass that had been whipping around directly to the left of the camera audio.

Things began to get interesting as we reached the third hour of our footage. The night-vision camera amplified any level of light tenfold, into a greenish-bluish hue. Under normal definition, it would have been impossible to see anything at that time of night aimed into a blackened mine shaft. The night vision allowed for us to see things that could not have been seen even with the naked eye.

At exactly the 192nd minute of our captured footage, three quick but distinct shadows flashed from the right side of the camera and darted directly into the rocks at the mouth of the shaft. We rewound and reviewed the event at least thirty times trying to make out any human characteristics to the anomalies. There were none. They were all solid black and perfectly rectangular shadows that came one after another from somewhere behind the camera. They traveled along the wood-lined walls of the mine and disappeared into the oblivion below the rocks. They were timed perfectly—each nearly an exact second after the other. These were all important aspects of the phenomenon, as they all but ruled out anything natural. Nature doesn't operate on such a perfect schedule or produce such perfectly linear shapes.

The look on all our faces was pure elation having caught such compelling visual evidence. I looked over, and even Big Bear was smiling back at me, thrilled that we could capture such a high level of paranormal footage on his very own property.

We both gazed down at Ricky, expecting him to be sharing in our jubilation. Ricky's eyes were still trained on the monitor, his jaw hung open, his eyes wide in pure awe. He had taken a sip of his coffee, which had begun dribbling back out of his gaping mouth and into his mug. To be honest, I didn't even want to look at the monitor having absorbed Ricky's reaction to whatever it was. Over the previous years, we had both seen our fair share of video evidence of the paranormal, but I had never seen that look on my colleague's face.

My eyes finally wandered back to the monitor as my jaw immediately joined everyone else's, hanging wide open. Down into the shaft, within the stones that sealed Old Foolish off from the natural world, there were arms—human arms, clear as day. They appeared as yours or mine, only slightly transparent, brighter than ours would look in that situation. They were all thrashing about—reaching, lurching, some grasping the rocks below them, their owners desperate to escape the mine. My last count was over twenty distinct arms jutting from the jagged rocks. It resembled something from an ancient Greek painting of the fourth level of Hades.

Your typical ghost that you catch on camera will appear and then disappear as quickly as it would manifest. Often, they would loosely resemble human form, but only in one or two facial or bodily features, and the rest of them would appear as a murky, iridescent haze. These arms, however, looked far too real. The thought crossed my mind more than once that perhaps there had somehow been actual, living human beings trapped last night and that we should rush back to help them.

The event lasted upward of three full minutes, which is still completely unprecedented for any sort of video evidence of the undead. You could hear a pin drop in the room as the audio began to crackle into a rhythmic pounding. The noise accompanied the arms as they thrashed about more wildly and desperately with every passing thump. The noise was similar to the metal-on-rock noise Ricky had captured on his voice recorder, only much closer and far crisper. It was as though some sort of hypnotic hammering had been taking place directly behind our camera position.

A moment later, the rock wall that had pinned all the flailing arms into submission appeared to crumble inward. As it did so, the night vision lost focus for about ten seconds. The camera readjusted, and we were suddenly able to see far deeper into the mine than previously possible. The blast wall had collapsed, revealing a massive fire so bright that our night vision could barely map it. The arms were gone, but the reason for their desperate thrashing had become grievously obvious to us. We had been watching the final, frantic attempt by those miners to save themselves from that blaze and the certain, indescribably agonizing death that accompanied it.

We watched, unable to believe our eyes, as the flames were suddenly sucked back into the mine shaft. The metallic pounding abruptly stopped. There was total and complete silence for a moment. Then a high-pitched screeching, whistling noise rose from a distance into a thunderous roar. As that noise reached its crescendo, the flames reappeared, streaming at an impossible velocity from the bowels of the shaft. The roar grew deeper and deeper as the flames shot out of the mouth of Old Foolish. The shockwave reached the position where our camera had been placed, knocking it over and propelling it four feet, uphill, onto its side, exactly how we had found it earlier that morning.

Then it was over. We could still make out the rock wall from the angle that the camera had fallen. It was suddenly absent of any jostling appendages or walls of flames. The very rock wall that had fallen moments before was back in its original ordinal position. Crickets again became audible, along with the fluttering of the tall grasses as they tossed in the midnight breeze.

Big Bear was sweating as though he had just completed a half marathon. Ricky and I had a smile from ear to ear on both of our faces. As terrifying as it was, we knew it was the kind of thing that would compel a vast audience. And it did. The footage was broadcast on every local news outlet from Point Pleasant, West Virginia, to Frankfurt, Germany. CNN and *60 Minutes* lined us up for specials a week later. Every special-effects geek in Hollywood took turns failing to figure out how we could have doctored that footage. None had any luck. To this day, it is roundly accepted as the best paranormal evidence that any human being has ever captured.

That chance meeting in some bar in Nowhere, West Virginia, turned into the night that made all our careers. Following that day, Big Bear and his wife, Daphne, were hired by us and began acting as our private security. They couldn't wait to find a reason to leave that property after that night and after watching our footage.

Since then, I had always been willing to listen to "crazy" stories from our fans. I would often take them up on their offers to show me wherever they believed our world met the mysterious plains of the afterlife. Most of the time it led to disappointment, but every now and again, it led to Old Foolish. None of us ever thought we would see anything like that again. Then we took another chance. Then we went to Ashford.

5
Cleveland Airport Hyatt – 6:00 a.m.

I awoke again, no more than three hours later. Who the hell needs sleep anyway? Glancing at the alarm-clock, I quickly found it to be 6:00 a.m. I had exactly two hours before Gary and I headed to Ashford. I wandered half-coherently over to the window opened both sides of the curtains, letting some natural light into the room. I marveled for a moment at the sunrise as it had begun dancing up the distant horizon in the form of a ruby-red blanket, warming the cool October streets.

Northern Ohio in the fall is a beautiful place. For years, I had watched innumerable late-night talk show hosts and had read countless articles and blogs in financial and sporting publications ostracizing the Greater Cleveland area. But I came to find that people tended to fall in love with the place having visited there, even once. It's some ubiquitous combination of the people, the landscape, and the energy in the atmosphere that breeds their culture. The people are at home in cooler months—a community of kids who grew up wearing orange and brown football jerseys before they knew how to dress themselves and girls who grew up as tough as their Midwestern charm could allow. All their parents knew what it meant to work a day in their lives and the irreplaceable pride that came with earning everything they have.

Two million souls representing the human embodiment of the fall— each born to wear their hooded sweatshirts and boot-cut jeans—each embracing the cool breezes that had begun to swoop into town off their great lake like an annual rite of passage. I stood for another moment, watching the gray-blue skies chasing the night westward, riding the crest of the dawn sunlight. I had to take a shit.

I headed toward my Hyatt-issued restroom when I noticed Lance's small, leather-bound book on the corner of the television stand. He must've left it in the room by accident as I shuffled him and Gary out the previous night. I picked it up, still finding no evidence of its contents anywhere on its face or spine. I assumed it was Lance's journal, which brought about a snicker and a shake of my head. I could only imagine what sort of *fascinating* subject matter that a journal kept by the twitchy weirdo I had met in my room the previous night might contain. I took it with me into the bathroom and dove right in.

My assumptions were immediately sent to their grave as soon as I flipped open the dingy, worn hardcover. The opening page was neatly printed in some sort of fancy font—far from the handwritten mess I had expected to see out of Lance. The age of the volume alone suggested that he could not have penned it. Still, I couldn't imagine why Lance would have been carrying such a book around with him. My brief, however profound, first impression of him suggested to me that he should have possessed the literary enthusiasm of the average seagull. Nonetheless, I continued to the prologue.

The Medical Memoirs of Kenneth Harvey
Text copyright 1931
Huntsfield Publishing:

Prologue

My name is Kenneth Harvey, and I am, for lack of a better term, a brain doctor— a neuroscientist by all formal standards and trades. One could say I have forgotten more about the human brain than the human brain has the capacity to forget.

Having graduated from The University of Virginia at Charlottesville many moons ago, I returned to my hometown of Ashford, Ohio, to assist with a series of cases that I found interesting, to say the least about them.

I had made my money earlier on in my career in the big city, and I had long been starved for something to pique my specialized interests. I knew that there was a need for me back in Ashford, and I was willing to do everything within my vast power to meet that challenge.

In this prose, you will find a multitude of information relating to my ongoing study of the human brain and the resulting human condition as the physiology of our most fascinating organ is manipulated and damaged.

Moreover, you will find how my journey into these fields of science has changed me for the better.

To be able to manipulate the animal brain is to gain the ability to mold reality——is to become . . . God.

I slapped the book shut. "Fucking quack," I uttered to myself as I stood from the porcelain throne and flushed. I was, however, interested in delving deeper into the story, as I suspected it might contain some insights into Ashford and the problems that Lance had described. This was the only reason I could think of that he would possess such an anomalous memoir. My time was limited, as I was due to meet my colleagues in the lobby.

I quickly packed up a change of clothes and my toiletries, along with my newfound literary masterpiece. I silently hoped that I wouldn't be gone long enough to need the clothes or sanitary products, but I had been burned before by ill-preparedness. I tossed everything into my backpack, grabbed a quick shower and shave, and headed down to the lobby to meet Gary, Lance, and Big Bear for a free hotel breakfast.

6

Not halfway between my room and the elevator, I could feel my phone vibrating in my jeans pocket. I pulled it out and read the name on the screen—Ricky. His name was accompanied by a picture of a massive pile of dinosaur shit, cropped out of a scene from *Jurassic Park*. You see, Ricky was my number two, and everyone referred to him for years as "Number Two." Therefore, it became a nickname of sorts. I never felt like it was my fault that the act of defecating shared the same nickname. It was merely an unfortunate break on Ricky's part. And how else was I supposed to celebrate that coincidence, other than having a huge pile of cretaceous-era shit appear on my phone every time Number Two called me? It just felt too right.

All joking aside, Ricky was one of the best that I had ever encountered at capturing paranormal evidence. Rarely would we visit a location anywhere on the planet where he wouldn't capture at least one piece of terrifyingly compelling evidence of the undead. He had a gift and still does to this day. Even within the first few weeks of working with him, I knew the kid had a bright future in the business.

He was just an arrogant kid then—seven years younger than me and constantly testing my patience. It took a good year or two before I accepted the fact that what I perceived as his unorthodox and ill-advised investigative method ended up producing some of our best results. I don't know when it happened, but at some point, I took the leash off Ricky, and it never went back on.

I would often split our team into two separate crews, sending half with Ricky while I would manage the other half. We effectively doubled our coverage of any location that way. We did our entire third season under this format, and the audience loved it. It added a completely new and exciting dynamic. I was still the face of the franchise, but Ricky helped us reach a younger, more difficult-to-please demographic. We began seeing a lot more college and high-school-age kids taking an interest in the show. We decided to maintain that format, and it remained that way clear to the end.

Ricky was the kind of guy that seemed to be able to get any girl, even though he never bothered to comb his hair or wear anything but a plain black t-shirt and jeans. He had that rare quality about him where he was always able to attract women despite absolutely no effort on his part.

I pushed the answer button on my phone. "Number Two, I presume?"

"Hey, buddy." Ricky reminded me of a used car salesman anytime he spoke. The words and names he used with you might suggest that he was genuinely excited to be speaking with you. But his drab, effortless tone always suggested otherwise. You could tell he was just going through the motions of sounding excited, but in his heart of hearts, he couldn't really care less about the entire conversation. Anyone who has ever worked in a large office environment knows this type of speak, and Ricky was a Jedi Master at it.

"What up, dog?" I replied, trying to sound fresh and relevant to our token member of the younger generation.

"What is this shit I hear from Gary about you guys taking the day off and going to some town to meet up with some hick about antique camera equipment?"

Just typical, I thought to myself. I was not at all surprised that Gary had managed to provide Ricky with what amounted to an uncontained tire-fire of an explanation into our plans for the day. He had obviously mixed up our cover story with the real story of what we were about to undertake and had managed to relay his confused, nonsensical mess to Ricky.

"Christ," I replied. "We are going to a town called Ashford for the day to investigate what is potentially a paranormal connection to a series of disappearances that have been taking place in the town. Gary and I met some guy named Lance last night. He and Gary showed up at my room, and he explained everything to us. Apparently, the place is crawling with feds, so we are using the camera equipment thing as cover in case we are accosted by the authorities."

Ricky was laughing into the phone as he replied. "Wow! That is a much different story than what I got out of Gary. I don't know how he manages to dress himself sometimes. So, what the hell? You want me to handle everything down at the Carnegie Mill?"

This was not the first time that something had creeped up prior to an investigation and I had to send Ricky somewhere to cover for us. We would always spend three days on location of wherever we were shooting our show. The first half of the first day was a shitload of paperwork. Ricky and I, along with a few suits from the network, would meet with whoever was the owner of the location. We would, as quickly as humanly possible, negotiate the contract terms to essentially have our run of their haunted location for twenty-four hours. We would then sign the contracts, pay them, and spend the rest of the day soliciting interviews with people who might possess any sort of intimate knowledge of paranormal occurrences there.

After that, we would typically go back to the hotel and have a Google/Wikipedia cram session focused on the location, learning everything we possibly could about its history and previous paranormal events. The places we would go were not exactly tourist attractions, so we had to do a lot of deep digging to uncover the facts. Had anyone ever died there or had anyone ever been murdered there? Who all had owned, operated, or, in some cases, lived there? These are but a few examples of the key pieces of information we would arm ourselves with before going into an investigation. Our job required us to travel to the most haunted locations in the world on a weekly basis. Over time, such infamous locations would spawn a colossal amount of local rumor and legend. Separating the facts about a location like that from the folklore can be an incredibly painstaking challenge.

Day two on location consisted of a lot of operational planning for the third day, which was our actual investigation. This is when Gary and the producers would walk the entire location, figuring out the best shots and where to setup cameras and audio equipment—basically anything they could do technologically to provide the best end result for the audience. The creepier you could make a location appear, the better. And Gary was an absolute horror virtuoso. With a few cameras, a few boom-audio microphones, and some lighting effects, he could turn the main drag through Disneyland into *A Nightmare on Elm Street.*

And, of course, day three was the investigation itself. Ricky and I would walk around the place with all the power, except to our own equipment, cut off, and do our best to capture evidence of the paranormal.

In this case, we were investigating an old steel mill on the outskirts of the south side of Cleveland—the Carnegie Steel Mill. It had been shuttered in the mid-1980s and unsuccessfully repurposed several times since. The building had done nothing for the previous two decades besides sit vacant. The main draw, which brought us to the location, was something that the locals referred to as the blood room.

Supposedly, there was a room on the second deck where twelve men perished in a massive fire that destroyed a quarter of the facility in the 1960s. Legend had it that the blood room was a last resort for the men as they were hunkered down there trying to escape the flames. The room had been designed specifically for that purpose. It was airtight and flame resistant. But those characteristics, combined with a ludicrous design oversight, were what ultimately doomed the men.

There was one massive vent in the room that led to the deck above them and into another airtight, safe room that was identical to the one they were in. Suddenly, the flames somehow reached the room above them, which the employees had (dubiously) been using as a pseudo-storage location for several liquid oxygen tanks. The tanks inevitably burst with impossible intensity. The explosion produced an immediate and unfathomable area of low pressure just above the men. Since the blood room was doing what it was designed for—keeping the men in a completely airtight space—the explosion above them and the massive pressure change invoked an unimaginable amount of suction through that single vent, from their room into the exploding room above. The sheer velocity and violence of the event instantaneously liquefied everything inside of the twelve men's bodies and subsequently expelled it out of their mouths, ears, noses, eye sockets, asses—basically any hole they had. Their insides were sucked at a hundred miles per second toward that one vent, coating the entire room in gore. Hence the locals calling it the blood room.

There are allegedly still stains and remnants of their fluids splattered about in there. It is said to be impossible to spend an hour in that room without coming into close contact with one lost soul or another. We planned to spend a good amount of time in it during the investigation.

I replied to Ricky. "Yeah, just day-one stuff. Get everything worked out with the owner. Get a few interviews done—preferably stuff about that blood room. Dig a little into the history of the place. Take a few notes, and that's it. I don't see us being in Ashford for more than a half-day. We should be back to the hotel by the mid-afternoon. I am on my way to breakfast now to meet Gary and Big Bear, and we should be in Ashford in about an hour and a half."

"I can handle that," he replied. "Let me know if this thing in Ashford turns into something. I can come meet you after I finish up here."

"Will do, buddy. Just text me whenever you finish up, and I will let you know what we've got going on out there, if anything. I don't know why I agreed to this. I have a feeling it's going to turn out to be a monumental waste of time. I think I just wanted Gary and his weirdo friend out of my room so badly that I would have agreed to anything."

Chuckling again, he replied, "Yeah, you never know, could turn into another Old Foolish. Hey, I'll talk to you later, bro. I'm pulling into the mill parking lot."

"Later, bud. Have fun."

I hung up the phone, got in the elevator, and made my way through the lobby and into the dining area. I piled an assortment of horrendously innutritious breakfast items onto my Hyatt-issued, white breakfast plate and sat down next to Gary, Lance, and Big Bear.

7

Everyone else was mid-meal by the time I arrived. Once Big Bear started eating something, he was basically dead to the world until it was completely devoured. Gary, as usual, was taking full advantage of the complimentary hotel breakfast. It was nearly impossible to see his three pancakes, as they had become buried somewhere below a heap of bacon and eggs.

I remembered hearing on some news show that scrambled eggs from a buffet were one of the riskiest food items to your health that you could possibly ingest. I think it was Anthony Bourdain who likened it to playing Russian Roulette with salmonella, and salmonella usually won.

Gary would never heed that kind of warning. As far as his health was concerned, he trended toward the exact opposite of what normal, god-fearing humans would do to take care of their bodies. The fact that he remained nimble enough to navigate the places we would investigate in order to set up the equipment was nothing short of a medical miracle.

"What's that?" Gary asked me through a mouth full of lukewarm disgustingness.

He was pointing at the little brown book I had brought down from my room. "Lance left this in the room last night," I replied, tossing it to Lance across the table.

With a sideways grin, Lance tossed it right back to me. "You need to read this, Mr. Hallowell. I left it up there for a reason."

"All right. Firstly, it's Daniel, Dan, or even Danny. Mr. Hallowell is my father. Secondly, why in the blue hell would I be interested in reading an eighty-year-old novella about neuroscience?"

"Oh, it's about a lot more than just science, Daniel," replied Lance, that stormy tone from the previous night having returned to his voice. "Yeah, sure, there is a bunch of guff about neuroscience, but intertwined within all of that is the first documented research about the problems in Ashford. Even then, they were dealing with all of it. That book that you hold there is one of the hottest commodities in Ashford. The feds have been trying to get their hands on it for decades."

"Well, goddammit, Lance. I don't want to be carrying around your contraband!" I shouted.

"I will take it back if you want," he replied. "But if you're truly interested in Ashford and what is going on there, it's a must-read. I told you before that there is a heart to all the hauntings in town. That heart is halfway down Whistler Road—an old abandoned psychiatric facility. Now, I will give you three guesses as to what area Kenneth Harvey was investigating when he was in Ashford."

"Halfway down Whistler Road?" I asked in the most patronizing tone imaginable.
"Precisely, Danny—1552 Whistler Road. Nobody in town, including the feds, have been near it in decades and come back with their life or their sanity. Nobody even goes near it now. It's just not worth it."

"Lance," I said condescendingly. "Let me ask you this—why in the world does anyone stick around this hellhole of a town? And don't feed me anymore of that civic pride bullshit. Nobody has enough pride in their town to put up with three generations of their friends and neighbors inexplicably vanishing."

His breath was beginning to grow frantic as he started to respond. I cut him off before he could even start. "I know you are lying to me about certain aspects of this. You have already contradicted yourself several times. If but one person a week disappeared in Ashford as you have professed, and this has been happening since 1931—again your words—then that means that over 4,400 people would have gone missing by now."

Lance's eyes began to wander.

"Look at me, Lance." He again mustered the gumption to look me in the eye as I continued, "There is no fucking way that the world could have remained ignorant to over four thousand people going missing in an American town over the last eighty-five years. Now, you better take that dainty, little, camera-fixing hand of yours and put that fork down and start telling us the real fucking story. If you don't, then I am taking this goddamned book straight to the local FBI office and you can get it back from them. I don't know how to be any clearer. You are playing games with my emotions and my money, and you don't want to do that."

Lance exhaled; he looked shaken. "I understand. I might not have been completely transparent with you guys last night. I am not *from* Ashford, and there isn't really a few hundred of us there anymore. I was born and raised in West Cleveland and heard horror stories about Ashford from my grandparents, who really did live there. At first, I didn't believe them. I thought they were just trying to scare me. One day, my dad comes up to my room, and he's crying. He sits me down and explains to me that my grandparents are dead, and it was 'that piece of shit town' that killed them. I was ten at the time, so I had no idea what he was talking about. That day, combined with the fact that there was never a funeral for either of them or any record of their deaths, really spurred my interest. Whenever I would ask my father about it, he would just tell me: 'We're not allowed to know the truth.'"

Lance was starting to look pissed off as he carried on with his revised story. "He didn't *want* to know anything else. But I did, and that is why I went there. My dad was too scared to ask any questions, too worried about Ashford somehow knowing that he had found out too much and punishing him for it. To this day, I still don't understand where that fear in him came from. It was totally irrational."

Lance's face had gone beet-red. I could almost taste his anger as he continued, "Screw that, people can't just die and that's it. My grandfather fought in a world war. My grandmother raised five kids. They lived through so much history, and we're all just supposed to forget them and act like they never existed? No way . . . not me. I am never about to treat my family with that kind of disrespect. An entire existence cannot be allowed to be swept under the rug. It flies in the face of everything that makes us human.

I went to Ashford and have been there ever since, trying to unravel the mystery. And I will stay until I do. Apart from five federal agents, there are fifteen of us, at last count, who take up residence there. Other than that, it is rare to see a car pass through our town, and even if they do, there is nowhere worth stopping. Everyone there has a story like me. Everyone *needs* to figure out the truth for some personal reason. We just can't talk to anyone outside about it for fear of the feds finding out."

Gary had finished eating and was finally able to take air into his mouth, regaining the ability to speak. "Goddammit, Lance, that's not at all what you told me at the bar."

Shaking his head, Lance replied, "I wanted the town to sound more welcoming to you guys because, let's face it, I am trying desperately to get you there. I thought if I made it sound like a real town, with real people, then I might have a better chance of bringing you there."

He was noticeably upset as his entire ploy unraveled before his eyes. I spoke up: "This sounds awful risky. There is no way we're blending in with only twenty people in this entire town. And the feds are sure as shit not going to think we're there to look at antique camera equipment when we roll into town with all of our state-of-the-art camera equipment."

"Guys, please," Lance begged. "You're the only chance anyone has of figuring out what is happening there. You're the only crew on the planet who can handle this kind of thing. It would mean everything to a lot of people if you just tried. Danny, there is something happening there. If I could tell you what it was, I wouldn't be here pleading with you. The god's-honest truth that I have told you still stands. There is something in that town, and whatever it is isn't something that humanity has ever encountered. It is not something of this world."

Big Bear had sat silently until that moment but finally broke his silence. "What the hell are we waiting for, guys? I say we do this damn thing."

"Have you even been listening, Big Bear?" I asked, half laughing.

"Been listening to myself eatin a shit-ton of bacon," he replied with a belch.

We all stopped and laughed a moment. It was a necessary break from the tension that had built up. I was still on the fence about the whole thing and pissed off that we hadn't gotten the full story initially from Lance. I don't know why I ever decided to go there. Not a day has gone by since that I haven't wondered what my life would be like now if I had just told Lance to get lost. If we had just stuck with the original plan to investigate the Carnegie Mill, then I might still have my wife and a real relationship with my daughter. I might still have a life.

"Lance, I want to know how the hell we get into Ashford without becoming detained by federal officials. You have until I am done eating to come up with a plan that sounds to me like it will work and does not involve us all going to jail or being shot.

"Gary, do me a favor and get Ricky back here. If we do this, we're going to need everyone on it."

8

I knew I needed Ricky with me if I were to embark on such a project. As good as I was when it came to the paranormal and psychological aspects of our investigations, Ricky was just as good with the real-life, investigative aspects. He had always seemed able to piece together all the little clues that the rest of us would overlook. He seemed to have an innate ability to paint a clear picture out of any situation, however disjointed it may have appeared. Put it this way, anyone can go and *investigate* a haunted house. How well you investigate that haunted house is completely up to how prepared you are for your investigation. Every location we'd investigate would be mired in rumor and old wives' tales about what had happened there to make it so haunted. Ricky could sort out, through historical research and his seemingly innate investigative ability, what was a real clue and what was hearsay. The information he came up with would ultimately lead to better and more fruitful investigations because we would go into them armed with a clearer picture than anyone else about what had led to the haunting. Disembodied souls, believe it or not, are more adept to revealing themselves to people who have some idea of what in the hell they are talking about.

Ricky had graduated with a master's in criminology and investigation from the University of Rhode Island. The kid should have gone into the CIA or FBI or with his abilities—some covert, black-budget, government outfit. But he'd always had a passion for the paranormal, which was how he found us. The fact that he was handsomely compensated and got to travel around the world, never having any sort of difficulty hooking up with chicks, certainly kept him around as well. His job was not without perks.

He never worked out, yet he somehow maintained a near perfect physique. Back then, I used to run five miles three times a week just to maintain a crappier body than his. Ricky had some sort of magical, freak metabolism, and I was jealous of it, and it pissed me off. He was shorter than me at about six feet with short brown hair that I had never seen him touch, brush, or comb in my life, but it was always just the right kind of messed up. I don't know how he managed to always have that perfectly shaped five-o'clock shadow, but he did. He wore jeans and a black t-shirt everywhere and in all seasons. In the winter, he added a black Carhartt coat on top of it all.

I could always tell that I was gradually losing the audience to him, and I really didn't care. I was still the best talent in the crew when it came to anything and everything pertaining to the paranormal. I sensed that he would eventually become the face of the show. As the seasons dragged on, he would get more and more camera time, and I would get less and less. All our commercials were basically Ricky looking as sexy as possible while he searched for ghosts while the rest of us goons lurked in the background. I didn't care because it got us more viewers, and more viewers meant more money. Hell, I knew what I was getting into with Ricky the first time I interviewed him, and he told me how he had originally become intrigued by the occult.

Ricky was fifteen years old when his parents left for the airport one morning. His father was dropping off his mother at T.F. Green Airport in Rhode Island for a flight to Chicago on business. It was a stormy morning, and her trip was nothing unusual. She worked for a major pharmaceutical firm that demanded she travel often to meet with various business interests.

His parents had left an hour prior, and young Ricky was sitting on the couch watching the television and listening to the thunder as it rode along the horizon with the sheets of downpouring rain. He decided to get up from the couch and look out the sliding door into the front yard to observe the storm. At that time, he had something of a passing interest in meteorology.

The wind was a persistent growl, thrusting the rain sideways into the door, distorting the outside world. He blinked a couple of times, trying to improve his ability to see through the wet window. There was someone in the front yard. It was a woman, and she was sopping wet and slouched over. The saturated window had become a nuisance, making it impossible for Ricky to identify the trespasser. She was about thirty yards away, near the tree line that separated their property from the next. She seemed in distress or possibly injured as she hunched over and pulled her arms into her stomach, facing the ground. Her saturated brown hair draped in front of her, masking her face.

Just as Ricky began to turn, ready to toss on his shoes and head out into the storm to assist her, a gust of wind raged to life outside. It was so strong that the glass from the sliding door in front of him vibrated. He could hear it whistling as it exploded through his property. A barrage of leaves and sticks rode the burst of wind, suspended in mid-air from left to right before him. To his recollection, he couldn't remember ever having experienced such a sudden and turbulent burst of atmosphere.

There had already been a thick cloak of unease hanging over Ricky. The woman was still crouched out there, and the fact that the storm was gaining intensity by the second only added to his anxiety. The only positive that had come from the raging storm was that the wind had become so powerful that the water on the outside of the window had beaded and mostly run off, allowing for a much clearer view of her.

Just as the wind began to die down, the woman stood straight up. In the same motion, she tossed her soaked hair backward, away from her face. Ricky finally had a clear view of her. He stood frozen in place, unable to understand what he was looking at. The woman standing in the yard, sopping wet, in the grips of the worst storm to hit Rhode Island in a decade, was his mother. She was in the same clothes she had left the house in an hour before.

Instinctively, Ricky looked around for his father, but he was nowhere to be found, nor was the family car that they had left for the airport in. Why would his mother be out there alone in such violent weather? Had she missed her flight? And where the hell was his father? He had, after all, driven her to the airport an hour ago. Where was her luggage?

He banged on the glass, trying to get her attention, needing an explanation for what she was doing out there. His mother turned slowly to face him, a somber, stoic look on her face. He explained to me that the look on her face was nothing he had witnessed previously from her. Anyone close to their mother grows intimately familiar with any and all of her facial expressions over the years. That look, he explained to me, was as though she was in shock but accepting of it, yet terrified, all in one facial expression. Clearly the person standing in that yard was his mother; he did not doubt that. But he was startled by that look. Ricky's entire body shuddered as the sight of her face shot a cloying tinge of dread clear down to his bones. He knew something was wrong about her. There was something more than wrong with her; there was something terrible about her. He took a step back from the window as she began to walk slowly toward him.

Her steps along the ground were not in tune with the progress she was making over the distance. She would only travel a couple of feet having taken several full steps. She seemed to be wet, but no water dripped from her. It was as though she were a wet person in a photograph and not directly affected by the still downpouring precipitation. The trees behind her whipped and yawed back and forth in the gale, yet his mother's hair remained stagnant, completely unaffected by the wind. After a few unnerving moments, Ricky was face to face with his mother as there was but a single pane of glass separating them. She had formed an unusual, forced smile toward him. Her posture was still hunched and her movements lethargic in nature. Ricky kept on blinking, not accepting the fact that he could clearly see the edge line between the driveway and the grass directly through his mother's face. Slowly, she made a full turn, looking over the entire property, taking it all in. When she came back around to face her son, her expression had returned to that chilling look of melancholy and dread. She stayed there like that for several minutes, just gazing into the house, mostly at Ricky but occasionally beyond him and into the living room. Every moment that went by, her face became impossibly more haunting in appearance. It was something depressed and confused, angry. Previously, she seemed to be fighting it, but it had since evolved into a despondent expression of melancholy of which she no longer had a choice but to project.

Ricky could feel an electrified charge of frigid air within feet of the window. His hair stood on end along with the hairs on his arms as he looked on at his mother. They both found themselves enveloped in an invisible fog of electrostatic energy that had not been present before her approach. She began phasing in and out like a weak analog signal. She would completely disappear and return an instant later, a few inches to the left or right of where she had previously stood. Sensing that his time was wearing thin with her, Ricky, overcoming his horror, stepped toward the window and extended the palm of his hand to the glass. He looked her in the eyes and shouted, "Mother!"

Without making a sound, she mouthed, "Ricky—my little boy. I will always love you."

Then she put her head down and broke eye contact with him. A fleeting moment later, she vanished into thin air. Ricky stood in agonizing silence, expecting her to come back again at any moment, but she never would. The unnerving siren of a special news bulletin interrupted his show on the television. Completely mortified and confused, Ricky stumbled backward from the window and faced the television just in time to see the headline: "Flight 862 from Providence to Chicago has crashed shortly after takeoff. Survivors unlikely."

9
Cleveland Airport Hyatt – 8:00 a.m.

I could hear music playing outside as we rolled underneath the marquee at the entrance of the hotel. It was something of a trance, hypnotic, easy-listening sound—barely audible. It was the kind of high-society hotel music that you hear constantly in such places. It exists to provide patrons with that false sense of entitlement that goes along with staying in a nicer place of lodging. From my experience however, it didn't matter what kind of music they played. The bathrooms were veritable cesspools of virus and bacteria, the sheets were saturated by years of previous patrons' fluids, and the absolute last thing you ever wanted to do was put that hotel room phone to your ear.

I stayed at a well-known, five-star hotel once in Pittsburgh and found an entire bag of rotten Cheetos smashed inside of a built-in Kleenex dispenser in the bathroom. Do you have any idea how long it takes a bag of Cheetos to rot? They basically are, in and of themselves, preservatives. They must've been smashed into that cubby for months before I was unlucky enough to find them. That high-society, bullshit, trance music just sounds hilarious after you find something like that in your room.

The sun was at eye level and warming through the side window as we left the hotel parking lot on our way to Ashford. I watched the sea of buildings whip by. I thought to myself about how unique of a city Cleveland truly was. It was unusual but inviting, sprawling but quaint. A modern city with modern architecture folded into a post-industrialized landscape and peppered with a few monolithic, art deco skyscrapers and bathed in a thin sheen of morning sunlight that glistened like diamonds atop an immense and wild lake to the north. Having lived my entire life in Boston, I had grown accustomed to the bustle and masses of humanity that came along with the major East Coast population center. Cleveland, while large enough, lacked that level of commotion that went along with a booming, properly diversified economy. Whether that's a good or a bad thing, I suppose, is a matter of opinion.

Big Bear was driving, and Ricky and I were packed into the front seat of the tow truck. Gary was in the far back seat that faced awkwardly and uncomfortably sideways. Lance was sitting in the driver's seat of my rental Chevy Malibu as we towed it behind us. That morning, as far as anyone who might ask was concerned, we were a tow-truck crew, and we were towing Lance, who had rented a car which had subsequently broken down, back to his house in Ashford.

This plan had good and bad points all over it.

Firstly, we had to be the only four-person, single tow-truck crew on the planet. The overhead of such an operation would quickly put any reputable tow-truck company out of business. This immediately made our shell-vocation profoundly unconvincing.

Secondly, we had wrapped all our research equipment that wouldn't fit into the back seat or trunk of my rental car in a tarp and strapped it to the tow-housing with bungee cords. We just kind of hoped nobody would notice it.

Thirdly, and worst of all, this tow truck was owned by one of Gary's buddies who lived in the area. Again, I have no idea how he knew this guy intimately enough for him to loan us a tow truck, no questions asked, at the drop of a hat. I am, however, certain there were other shady dealings going on between them.

Fourthly, none of us knew anything about the towing business or how to drive a truck that size. We would be lucky to get to Ashford without driving off a cliff or ramming Lance and my rental car up against the side of an embankment. None of us were dressed the part—I was wearing a three-hundred-dollar Egyptian cashmere sweater, a fitted Red Sox cap, and my six-hundred-dollar, designer aviator sunglasses— hardly appropriate attire for a job that often entails crawling around on filthy roadways underneath defunct vehicles. If we were suddenly thrust into a situation where we were, for any reason, forced to prove our towing credentials, it would quickly become laughable.

There was, however, some authentic craftiness mixed into the plan. At the forefront, my car was coming with us. That way, we had a way to leave easily whenever we wanted. Lance's friends were going to take our place in the tow truck after we got to his house and drive it back to the hotel to get it back to Gary's friend. So, anyone paying attention would assume we came, dropped off Lance and *his* rental car, then left—never knowing that we were still there and the guys in the truck were completely different people than those who had driven it there. I had been involved in worse plans in my life up to that point, just not very many.

Ideally, we would just get into town, nobody would notice, we would get to Lance's place, and everyone would be fat and happy. Worst case, we would get stopped and questioned, quickly recognized as the fraudulent tow-truckers we were, and thrown in some cornpone, country jail on a charge of illegally operating an industrial vehicle or something of that sort.

I shook my head as I glanced into the rearview and saw Lance with a shit-eating grin on his face, giving us all the thumbs-up as he dragged along behind us. It was shaping up to be a gorgeous day. It was fall, and the early morning was the kind of brisk that you somehow knew would evolve quickly into milder, more tolerable weather. It was cool when the wind blew. In the sun, however, one could still easily break a sweat.

I smelled it one second and immediately knew what was going on the next. Gary had begun smoking a bowl in the back seat, completely unannounced. Like most pot smokers, he thought that if he blew whatever he sucked into his lungs out of his window, it would somehow magically prevent the entire cab of the vehicle from smelling, never realizing for an instant that most of the aroma comes from the dope that is on fire inside of the bowl in your hand. Also, like every single person who has ever habitually smoked pot, he just assumed that because he was comfortable with it, everyone else in the general area must also be all right with his illicit drug use.

"You're such a dipshit, Gary. Just what we need!" I shouted back at him.

He gave me a look like I was somehow the one being a complete asshole. "What's the problem, Danny?"

"Well, Gary, the problem is we're all in a tow truck that Big Bear is struggling to operate and that none of us are registered to be inside of. Not even one of us knows a goddamned thing about towing. We have an idiot, who you introduced us to, inside of my rental car behind us. You've got upward of twelve grand worth of our network's equipment strapped to the outside of this death trap. The network already chewed my ass this morning about this whole unplanned excursion, and now you're just sitting back there, doing drugs, like we're at Burning Man."

Gary began laughing at my description of the situation. It quickly evolved into that uncontrollable, hysterical, inappropriate-for-an-adult sort of laughter that one becomes familiar with by spending time around pot smokers. Ricky began laughing his ass off as well at Gary's laughter, and I was pretty sure Big Bear was just chuckling about the entire unfortunate situation we'd found ourselves in.

Gary handed Ricky the bowl, and he quickly dove right in. Once Ricky was finished with his puff, he handed it back to Gary and so it went until the bowl was spent. At that point, any hope for intelligible conversation between us went up in the proverbial smoke. Ricky and Gary were both stoned out of their minds, and Big Bear was laser-focused on the herculean task of not killing us all as we hurtled down the highway in our ridiculous, unauthorized transport.

My phone vibrated three times in my pocket in rapid succession, indicating that I had received a text. I pulled it out of my pocket and slid my finger over the screen to unlock it. It was my wife. "Call me ASAP! Need to pick your brain about Annie's homework assignment."

I texted her back. "Talk in a bit, babe. Right in the middle of a shoot."

I wasn't in a texting mood. My brain was too wrapped up in my own self-involved problems at that moment. I was mainly trying to keep my crew and myself out of jail. I made a mental note to get back to her as soon as we got to Lance's place and the situation became a bit less ridiculous.

I was smashed in between Ricky and the unforgiving door like a sardine. I could feel something digging into my ass from my back pocket. I reached back and pulled out the little brown book that Lance had given me.

"Hey, Ricky," I shouted. "How long is this ride?"

"According to Lance, it's about an hour," he replied. "Maybe a little more, depending on traffic. His directions were confusing, so who knows, man. Hey, are we okay with the network? They don't approve of this trip?"

"Don't worry about the network," I shouted back to him over the roaring diesel engine. "You have seen the latest ratings, right? The Museum Network has less viewership than the religion channels. Then every week, Friday night at ten rolls around, our show airs, and their ratings for our one-hour block light up like NBC primetime. They need us a hell of a lot more than we need them. They can dock me for one day."

I flipped open the little brown book and began reading. Ricky and Gary had drifted into a marijuana-laden, vegetative state and were just kind of gazing out through the windshield as though they were watching the greatest movie they had ever seen in their lives about a truck barreling down a highway. Big Bear had seemed to have figured out the many nuances of operating the rig and appeared a bit more comfortable. I put my head down and again began reading *The Medical Memoirs of Kenneth Harvey*.

The Medical Memoirs of Kenneth Harvey

Background

Shortly after completing my studies at university, I made my way north to New York and began my internship, working under the great and gifted Dr. Elliot D. Striker. I accredit much of my knowledge to him; however, the years and subsequent technological advancements since did allow me to eventually overcome his, at the time, distinguished level of expertise.

I took care of many of his samples of brain matter. They came from various species of which had descended from various backgrounds. It was under Dr. Striker that I first accrued my firsthand experiences with the animal brain—mammalian (including human samples), reptilian, as well as amphibious.

Together, we were able to piece together many of the striking similarities between the brains of various species. This intrigued me, it astounded me, and it motivated me to know more. It so piqued my curiosity, and that curiosity quickly birthed creativity.

Dr. Elliot Striker died abruptly a mere eleven months into my internship. One of his lasting requests was for me to carry on his work. I have done so, and I have made it my life's passion.

I inherited his practice and lab in New York and continued with our research. I received grant money on a tri-annual basis from his alma mater, Princeton University, in exchange for conducting a once annually, neuroscientific workshop for the medical students. They never received an argument from me.

I spent the next decade there as my research continued to amaze me on a daily basis. I eventually determined, in theory, how one might be able to manipulate certain lobes and hemispheres of the human brain so as to completely transform that person into something better.

I surmised that people could become better at comprehending arithmetic by enhancing the parts of the brain responsible for logic and memory. People might be able to experience better sleeping habits if I managed to manipulate the brain chemicals to force circadian rhythms into their proper order. Soldiers could be molded into greater hunters and killers if one could overstimulate the reptilian portion of their brains, responsible for violence and aggression.

Ashford

One pristine summer day, I was going about my business when the postmaster arrived. He had a telegram for me, and it had been marked on the envelope as "most urgent." I glanced at the sender on the envelope and quickly found it to be from the sheriff's office of Ashford, Ohio.

I mentioned previously that I had grown up there. To be perfectly honest, I had all but forgotten about Ashford by that point in my life and my career. I had not seen the place in years, and that parcel represented the first such correspondence from Ashford I had received since leaving, outside of the occasional letter from my since-deceased parents.

As soon as the postmaster left, I tore open the top of the envelope and read.

Dr. Kenneth Harvey,

Firstly, I want to express how very proud everyone back here in Ashford is of you and all that you have achieved since leaving. Word has made it back here about your accomplishments, and everyone is, deservingly, looking at you as an example of what someone from lowly old Ashford can achieve with a good education. I do hope this letter makes its way to you, as I do not have your formal mailing address. I write this to you at a time of great distress that is afflicting our town and its residents.

I am struggling to write this to you, as it will sound completely ludicrous. Our problems here started in the late summer of last year: 1930. The leaves began to change colors, same as always. Only last summer, every one of the like turned a deep red. Most found it concerning; some thought it beautiful—a rare treat of the natural world. I didn't much care for it myself—far too much red. Standing atop the Exchange Station, it looked like the hills outside of town had been drenched in blood.

Accompanying the curious color changing was a collective breakdown of the very social fabric of our community. Not having one killing in the last decade, we endured three such that autumn and early winter alone. Don't know if you're old enough to remember him, but Morris Cole—should've been about your age—drowned his wife in the northern edge of his pond. He took his own life with the noose not an hour later up in his barn over on Mulberry Street. But only after he had slaughtered his entire sheep flock, looking like he did in the whole lot—some thirty-seven animals— with his bare hands.

Every single person I've talked with in Ashford since them leaves started changing two years ago now has had a sense of hopelessness about them. It's like something came through here that fall like an invisible storm and sapped the spirit from everyone. Most cope with it; some like old Morris Cole could not. There is nothing behind anyone's eyes here in Ashford anymore. As if the unbearable sense of unease around here wasn't enough, I fear the final straw has just been drawn. Last week, over on Whistler Road, the Ashford Hill Lunatic Asylum went up in a blaze. Fire brigades from three towns were sent over there, but I am afraid it was far too late by the time the first one had arrived. It burned so hot at one point that much of the brick structure shone as a blue arc of scolding flames clear above the tree line. People claimed they could see the glow from it clear over in Baines Township and Hunters Valley. I would give a sizeable portion of what's sacred to me to know what could have been in that place to produce an inferno like that. Took two full days to bring the fire under control enough for me and my deputy to enter the remains of the building. We only found the remains of one body and have identified it as the chief doctor of the facility, Dr. Roderick Crowe. Not a single other shred of human remains could be found anywhere on site. By our records, there should have been, give or take, 160 souls committed to Ashford Hill at the time of that fire. To not find a single one of their bodies was curious, to say the least. We should've found teeth and bones no matter how hot that building burned.

There are three known survivors who were outside of the main building at the time of the fire and managed to get themselves to safety before the inferno ensued. All three are useless to me as of now. These three . . . well, you can tell that there was no better place for them than that lunatic asylum—that is for sure. My deputy and I have been busier than a couple of three petered monkeys trying to get anything at all out of them. They can barely speak; hell, they barely blink. One is a male, and the other two are female. They are borderline incontinent, and personal hygiene seems to have all but been forgotten about. Thus far, we have not been able to nail down an identity on any of them. Only one of the females has spoken a single word to any of us, and all she talked about, in an incredibly incoherent rant, was Dr. Roderick Crowe. She, for some crazy reason, calls him The Divine Father. I told her that he had perished, and she immediately began thrashing her head into the brick wall next to her bed, howling and cussing up a storm. We've since provided more adequate facilities for them.

Already, not six days since the fire, two people have gone missing. Jed Dallinger and Ruth Adkins have vanished, seemingly into thin air in both cases. Jed went out in broad daylight to get his horses brushed. His family watched him walk into the barn, and he hasn't come back since. Ruth walked down into the basement of the grange to pick out some eggs for her family breakfast that weekend. Went down the stairs—never came back up. There is no other way in or out of that cellar—been down there a thousand times myself.

Folks, including myself, fear that the escapees from the lunatic ward are behind these disappearances. The fire and our inability to locate any of the bodies have thrust many of our citizens into a persistent state of hysterics. Ashford Hill contained a great many notorious characters. The idea that the rapists and murderers and deviant types of mental-inept could now be at large is more than many of our people are able to cope with.

I fear this is the spark that we've been dreading since them blood-red leaves that autumn, and it is something I need to stop.

We need to get answers out of these survivors, however vegetative their states might be. Far as we know, they weren't supposed to have been outside at that hour of night. Perhaps they knew the fire was coming; perhaps they're even responsible. Mostly, I want to know why we can't find any evidence of the patients who should have burned to death there.

I am hoping this is where you can assist us. Your reputation precedes you as far as knowing the ins and outs of the human brain. You're far and away the best psychological mind that has ever come from our neck of the woods. I am hoping that you still have some loyalty to Ashford and are willing to help your old home in this time of great sadness and great need.

Sincerely, and desperately awaiting your response,
Sheriff Fredrick K. Williams

I snapped the book shut, as I had begun to get a headache. I sat silently, collecting my thoughts and thinking about how Lance had explained to me that I "must read it." I was not far enough into the volume for it to make any kind of sense to me or to understand its relevance. From what I had read to that point, Kenneth Harvey seemed like a total crackpot who today would have likely been stripped of his medical license. But back in his heyday, I suspect the rules and regulations were far more liberal. I began questioning if the book was even real. I found it odd that nobody else seemed to have ever heard of Ashford, seeing as all this horrific stuff had been going on there for the past ninety years. Lance had offered up his explanation—the feds were concealing everything.

I sat in that van, allowing the pot smoke to soak in and saturate my three-hundred-dollar sweater, wondering what could have been going on in Ashford if what Lance was telling us was indeed true. I wondered what it all had to do with Dr. Kenneth Harvey and an insane asylum that burned down in 1931.

10

I had long since grown bored. We still had at least a half hour of the ride left to go, so I decided to call my wife back. After all, Annie needed help with her homework, and who better to help her out than a guy on the phone while stuck in a tow truck and in the middle of a nasty contact high?

The phone rang a couple of times before Ellen answered.

"Hello, Daniel."

"Hey, baby," I replied. "I am stuck out on the road with my infantile crew at the moment and have a few free minutes. What's up with Annie's homework?"

"Well, aren't you so kind to find a few spare minutes for your family."

"Look on the bright side; you're in Boston right now. I am on my way to Podunk, Ohio, in a tow truck that may have very likely been reported stolen by its owner. To boot, I am crammed in here with three stinky dudes."

Ellen had begun laughing into the other end of the phone. "Yeah, that sounds pretty terrible. Why are you in a stolen tow truck?"

"Don't ask. It's not really stolen but might as well be. It's a long, long, stupid, stupid, ignorant story. So, what's up with this homework problem?"

She let out an exhausted sigh. "Some creative writing assignment that she needs to get done by tomorrow. Her teacher gave it to her a week ago, and of course it didn't occur to her to get to it until today and it counts as her midterm. I tried to help as best I could, but apparently she takes after me and also sucks at creative writing."

I sighed. I had always been the creative parent—the one who helped with these sorts of projects. Ellen helped with math and science, which was weird because I had more schooling in those subjects. I have always had a passion for writing, though. I genuinely enjoyed helping Annie with those types of things.

"We all have our unique talents, baby. Writing is but one of my many. Can I talk to Annie?"

In the most conniving tone imaginable, she replied, "In that case . . . Herman Melville . . . here is your daughter."

Ricky looked at me through stoned, bloodshot eyes, knowing that I was about to talk to Annie. "Ask her what she is wearing."

Annie was seventeen at the time and had recently come into a more adult figure. Ricky knew it bothered me and took every opportunity to exploit that fact. "Ricky, remind me to never invite you within a hundred yards of my family, you goddamned deviant."

Everyone in the truck laughed.

"Hey, Dad, what's up?"

"Hey there, baby. Your mother says you have some homework assignment that is due tomorrow?"

"Yeah, it's for English. I have to write an essay on something I feel passionate about. At the same time, referencing a historical character."

"That's easy," I replied, chuckling. "Just write it on your father."

She snickered into the phone. "Has to be a real historical character, not a pseudo-celebrity. Otherwise, I would've just done it on Lady Gaga."

"Pseudo-celebrity—that hurts," I replied. "Well, give me some examples of things you feel passionate about."

Again, Ricky made eye contact with me. "I know something I feel pretty passionate about right now." He licked his lips in a suggestive manner. I immediately punched him in the arm. I held nothing back. The thud sent him hurtling sideways into Big Bear, causing him to lose control of the truck for a moment.

"What the fuck!" shouted Big Bear. "Cut it out, you assholes. It's difficult enough to drive this enormous hunk of shit without people banging into me!" He quickly regained control, but the stress of operating such a foreign vehicle was clearly getting to him.

"Is that Ricky?" asked Annie in an exited manner.

"Just answer the question; this isn't that hard. What do you feel passionate about?" I was beginning to lose patience.

"That's just it. Like, what am I supposed to feel *passionate* about? I mean, I'm seventeen. Like, I don't even watch the news."

"What about those dog commercials?" I suggested. "The ones where they're all in cages, looking pathetic and lonely and wanting someone to adopt them? Every time one comes on the tube, you start whimpering. So, you must feel passionate about animals?"

"I do, but it has to involve a historical character," she replied, with a note of whininess.

"Go online and look up someone named Dian Fossey. I have a feeling you'll appreciate what she did," I told her.

We shared that passion, which is how I knew it would spur her interest. Dian Fossey spent her entire adult life trying to save mountain gorillas from poachers and authored *Gorillas in the Mist*. It happened to be one of my all-time favorite novels.

"Sure, I'll check it out. Thanks, Dad."

"Now, baby, you do understand that the entire point of school is to teach you how to do your own critical thinking? There is going to come a point in time in the not so distant future when you won't be able to call me and get an answer."

"I know. I'm just so stressed," she replied. "Like, he didn't tell us this was our midterm until yesterday—two days before it's due."

I let out another slow, disappointed-sounding breath. "You should have done it last week when it was assigned to you and not waited until it became an emergency."

"I know I should have done it last week," she insisted. "Sorry, Dad, I just couldn't think of anything to do it on."

"Remember what I've always told you, Annie. It is up to yourself and only yourself to choose the world you see."

"I know, Dad, you tell me that like every day."

I sighed. "Put your mother back on the phone."

"Okay, thanks again, Dad."

"You are welcome, baby. Love you."

Ellen returned to the line. "Thank you, Ernest Hemingway."

Chuckling, I replied, "Hardly. My pleasure. How is everything else over there?"

"Good. We miss you, but what else is new?" she replied.

"Yeah, I'm sorry. I would love to be there. I'll be back in a couple of days."

We exchanged a few more pleasantries and hung up. Annie did do her report on Dian Fossey and got an A minus. Little did I know, I would never return to that home again.

11

I remember wondering if I might be causing permanent damage to my legs. They had been so numb for so long, packed into that truck like some sort of a Japanese subway car at rush hour. A massive blood clot would have been no surprise to me whatsoever. Every time Big Bear shifted, his arm would hit Ricky's leg next to me; then Ricky's other leg would inevitably smash into my legs as he tried to move out of Big Bear's way. At first, I was annoyed by it, but over the course of the trip, I'd just stopped caring. I wanted out of that truck. I craved physical freedom like some sort of a caged animal.

We had been on the road for an hour and a half. Clearly Lance hadn't provided us with an entirely accurate estimate as to how long the ride should have taken. I glanced behind us in the rearview and saw Lance in my rental car giving the thumbs-up to all of us as we finally exited the highway. From that point, it was only a couple of miles and we were essentially in Ashford, at least from what I understood of the directions.

"Why is this asshole giving us the thumbs-up?" I asked everyone around me.

Gary, who was now in some sort of drowsy yet functional state of stoned, answered, "Dude, Lance said he would give us the thumbs-up when we got close to Ashford. Remember, there are no signs for it anywhere?"

It occurred to me at that point that we had done an incredibly piss-poor job of planning out the entire operation.

"What is this? *Top Gun*? Are we taxiing a jet on an aircraft carrier right now? Why are we relying on hand signals from a hillbilly to know where the hell we're going?"

"He doesn't have a cell phone," announced Ricky, chuckling.

Big Bear chimed in, "Would you relax? He gave us detailed directions. If we stay on this road for another mile or two, we should hit County Line Road; we take a right, and we're in Ashford. Then we make another right onto Hazelton Street, and we are basically at his house."

I apologized. The tense atmosphere and inability to feel my extremities had heightened my temperament. Like clockwork, three minutes later, we reached County Line Road and took a right. Almost instantaneously, we found ourselves thrust into a darkened, desolate woodland. There was nothing there but the road we were on and the dense thicket to either side. We had driven for about a mile on the semi-paved roadway and didn't see any sort of distinguishable residence. The trees there were enormous—wild and unchecked. Their limbs jutted out over top of the road on either side, forming a domelike canopy above us. There were no utility lines of any kind. There hadn't even been a speed-limit sign since the turnoff.

Everything I had heard from Lance and had read in the memoirs of Kenneth Harvey began to flood into the forefront of my mind. It suddenly seemed more real. There were, of course, no signs announcing our entry into Ashford, but we all somehow knew we were there.

I glanced down to check the time on my phone. There was no signal. "Anyone got any bars?" I asked.

Everyone looked, and nobody had any service. I found that fact incredibly off-putting. Between the four of us in that truck, we represented three separate cellular carriers. The fact that none of us were getting a signal, so suddenly, suggested that service was cut off intentionally. I told myself that we must have just driven into a cellular dead zone and put my phone back in my pocket.

When I think of the general color of Ashford now, the only color that comes to mind is gray. The foliage had color to it, but it seemed less defined than anywhere else we had seen on our way. Most of the trees appeared to be in their death throes, holding one another upright for their dear lives. It was fall—the trees should have been saturated in red and yellow and orange hues. Most were just barren, and those that did have leaves looked like they were holding onto them begrudgingly, counting the moments until they fell. The ground below the trees was coated with knee-deep brush, dead leaves, twigs, and low-lying shrubbery. The foliage made it nearly impossible to see more than a few feet into the forest on either side of the road.

I rolled up the window next to me. The warm autumn day did not seem to exist there. Mind you, we had driven most of our way on the interstate with the windows down and the air billowing through the truck. It had been warming and pleasant. In Ashford, however, we hadn't broken twenty-five miles per hour, and the air had become chilling, uncomfortably cool. It made absolutely no sense from a meteorological standpoint. The sun-drenched streets of Cleveland seemed a world away, as though we had driven into a different country that had a completely different climate. I knew the same warming sun was probably above the overgrown trees that had enveloped us since our arrival, but it certainly was not doing us any good at that point.

We reached a point where all effort to maintain the roadway had broken down. We passed a guardrail that had rusted completely through, leaving only a brittle skeleton of the structure behind. You could tell County Line Road was not a high-traffic thruway, as our path had become covered nearly completely by various forms of brush. We sort of had to guess the nature of the pavement (or lack thereof) below us, as we could no longer see it. It seemed to be paved, but every now and again, we would hit a massive crater, forcing all our numb asses downward against the already uncomfortable seats. I only hoped that all our equipment was intact and undamaged from the turbulence.

I glanced back and saw Lance still giving us the thumbs-up with that familiar, dumb-looking grin on his face. Then I looked beyond him down the road to our rear. There were headlights in the distance. It was another testament to how dark it was on that road—a vehicle needing their headlights at ten in the morning. My heart sank. I could feel my throat go dry in an instant. "We've got company," I shouted.

Big Bear shifted his attention to the rearview. "Goddammit," he whispered. He had started sweating, as he always did in stressful situations. "Where the hell did they come from? We haven't passed a driveway or road since we turned onto this goat path."

Nobody answered. Everyone faced backward as the vehicle began to come into view. Lance, having seen us all looking behind him, had since taken notice of it as well.

"Please just be the mailman or some lost pizza boy or something," I said.

The vehicle was still well off into the distance behind us, probably a solid mile, but we could already see it blowing the leaves and twigs to either side as it closed the gap on us. There was no doubt that it was moving a lot faster than we were. As it came closer, we saw that it was a large SUV. A black GMC Yukon to be exact. Having been around my fair share of federal officials, as we had investigated numerous *official* sites throughout our careers, I knew that a blacked-out Yukon was not an ideal type of vehicle to find behind yourself while trying to dodge the feds.

"Goddammit—it's the feds!" I shouted.

"What do you want me to do?" asked Big Bear. He had begun to panic.

Before I could respond to him, I had a miniature nervous breakdown. I thought of my entire career and how it might be compromised. I thought about how we were in a borderline stolen tow truck and how none of us knew the first thing about the towing business. I remember thinking that the entire situation would have been far easier to explain had we just driven there in my rental car and left that tow truck in the realm of terrible ideas where it clearly belonged. I thought of my wife and daughter and how I might have to explain to them that their father was in jail for being a moron and how that would subsequently go over with the suits at the Museum Network. The same suits who, oh, by the way, signed all our paychecks and had sternly expressed their disapproval of our present venture not two hours prior. Worse, the entire vehicle still reeked of pot smoke, potentially adding drug charges to whatever sort of rap sheet we had accumulated that morning.

"Just keep doing what you're doing, Sam," I told him calmly. "Doing anything drastic now will only make us look like a bigger bunch of dickheads than we already do." Everyone already knew that something was very wrong, but the fact was reinforced when I referred to Big Bear by his first name. I hadn't in years prior.

The vehicle worked its way right onto our ass. The bastard had his high beams on in the middle of the day. I could have torn the paneling off the door next to me as hard as I was gripping the handle. Every muscle in my body puckered and flexed. I could feel my abdominals twitching with the anxiety, knowing that at any moment I was going to see those familiar blue and red lights flagging us down from behind.

The Yukon was completely blacked out, making it impossible to see anything inside of it. The tint on the windows didn't even allow silhouettes of those inside to bleed through. The headlights and blinkers were covered in black plastic. The license plate was a generic-looking, black-and-white rectangle consisting of only a four-digit, alphanumeric code—a far cry from any state-sanctioned license plate. Those characteristics, along with an exorbitant number of antennae, left little doubt that it was indeed a very *official* vehicle.

Out of nowhere, the Yukon gunned its motor and pulled up directly next to us. I turned to look at it over my left shoulder. I noticed Lance sort of half slouched over in the front seat of my rental behind us. He was looking over at the SUV. I couldn't be sure, but he appeared to smile at the vehicle as it passed by, giving it a kind of nod of his head. Perhaps this was his idea of a futile attempt at looking innocent and docile toward the officials. As the vehicle pulled directly next to us, I looked beyond Ricky, who was leaning as far back as he could against the seat, refusing to look over at the vehicle. Big Bear was sweating profusely—his hands had begun trembling atop the steering wheel. It was taking everything he had left within him to maintain control.

The passenger-side window of the GMC began to roll down. I caught a glimpse of the passenger. It was a woman in black sunglasses. I could see the topmost indication of her clothing—a navy-blue blazer. She had a white earpiece in her left ear, and she appeared to be staring directly at me. She had blond hair pulled back into a ponytail, and she was stunningly attractive—high cheekbones, full lips, everything perfectly symmetrical in her face. If I had to estimate, she was likely early to mid-thirties. She was chewing gum on one side of her mouth and gazing at us intensely, sizing us up, getting a read on everyone. It reminded me of how professional athletes eyeball members of the opposing team during the opening coin toss. I couldn't see the driver from my angle, as the woman's head and body were blocking my view deeper into the Yukon.

"What the fuck are these clowns doing?" yelled Gary from the back, unable to control himself any longer.

I replied to him through my teeth, trying to avoid allowing the woman, whose stare was burning a hole into my soul at that moment, from reading my lips. "Hey, Gary, how about you shut the hell up back there? Maybe you shouldn't have clam-baked our truck on the way here. At least then we wouldn't have to worry about getting pinched on drug charges on top of everything else."

Just as I concluded my insult to Gary, the woman rolled up her window and disappeared again behind the tinted glass. A moment later, the GMC's engines roared to life and the vehicle raced ahead of us, throwing a cloud of leaves and dirt into our truck in its wake. It moved away at twice our rate of speed and was gone, completely out of sight, in less than a minute.

A collective sigh of relief from all of us cascaded throughout the truck.

"What was that all about?" asked Ricky.

"I don't know, man. But I'll sure as hell take it," announced Gary from the back seat. He had begun tossing the remainder of his weed out the window, along with his associated paraphernalia, for fear of a sudden return by the feds. We continued down the desolate roadway for several more miles. Our nerves were shot to hell from the encounter. We sat in silence a while, attempting to regain our bearings.

We had still not passed a single residence, driveway, or intersecting road. We had still not seen any type of street or speed-limit sign. There were no telephone poles, wires, or phone or electrical lines. It was a town completely forsaken of all modern infrastructure. The cliché way to describe where we were then would have been: "the middle of nowhere" or, perhaps, my favorite: "Bum-Fuck, Egypt." Even those descriptions failed to do that raw sense of desolation justice. That road with so much foliage atop it looked completely out of place, as though it had been digitally superimposed into the middle of a dense forest. It was uncomfortably flat and straight, allowing us to see for what felt like an eternity ahead and behind.

I couldn't help but feel like County Line Road was something more than just your average thoroughfare. The farther we drove, the more uncomfortable we all began to feel. Over the years, I had grown highly sensitive of the supernatural. I knew all the metaphysical warning signs to look for—out-of-place, unexplainable smells and odors, the sounds of water dripping from an unknown source, the chills, the hairs on your arms and legs standing on end, the unexplained sixth sense that we all have which allows us to sense a presence that we cannot see, often kicking in when there are no other humans present. What I felt on that road, was far worse.

It no longer felt like we were in a tow truck careening down that roadway. It felt like we were in a diabolic vessel, slowly transporting us, against our collective will, into an alternate universe. Every inch that we progressed onward, I could feel it grow stronger. My bones began to hurt, and the hair on my head tingled. I looked on at my colleagues, and their emotions seemed to mirror my own. My teeth began to chatter. I felt pure dread.

I had been in similar states of fear before. It's that feeling you get when you get inside of your own head. That feeling when you are in the cellar alone at night and you begin to imagine a stalker—someone or something lurking in the shadows around you or just around a corner that you're unable to see around but inevitably must walk past. That feeling that propels you to get the hell out of wherever you are as quickly as possible. That horrible feeling of total fear had swept over me like a blanket made of fiberglass. Instead of sensing an entity observing us from an unseen location, I felt completely engulfed by an unexplainable energy. It felt like the very ground we drove over that day had somehow been tainted or spoiled by a force that could not have been anything earthbound. What I felt there was demonic.

About a year prior, we had investigated an abandoned convent outside of St. Louis, Missouri. It had sat empty for the better part of thirty years prior to our visit. Through numerous paranormal investigations, it had been labeled "The Demon House." It turned out to be one of our most-watched and, subsequently, syndicated broadcasts. One major reason for its popularity was the fact that it was the only investigation our entire crew had ever refused to finish.

The moment we laid foot inside of that place, there was no doubt in any of our minds that the rumors we had heard about it were true. A demonic presence is a completely different and far more terrifying animal than your typical ghost-haunting or poltergeist event. There is a certain sense of evil that can immediately be felt when in the presence of a demon. It is widely accepted that ghosts, even ones who have a tendency toward violence and aggression, are simply earthbound spirits of deceased human beings. A demon, on the other hand, is an earthbound presence whose origin has no reasonable explanation. Every major religion throughout history has taken a crack at trying to explain where they come from. The Catholics and Christians call it Hell. More ancient cultures like the Mayans believed it to be an alternate dimension known as Xibalba. The Islamic religions refer to it as Jahannam—a place of fire where you are broken to pieces.

A demon has an ability that other spirits do not. Not only can they affect the natural world around you, they can also attach to you. And when they do, they can take over your thoughts and your body. They can essentially replace your entire sense of being with their demented spirit—that of incredible rage bound to crippling hopelessness. We all began to sense such a presence as we investigated The Demon House.

When everyone in your group unanimously begins to sense the same unnatural, overbearing evil that floods the atmosphere while in the presence of a demon, there is a certain responsibility you must possess. If you ever plan to investigate the paranormal, you must be able to see the signs of a demonic presence coming. And when you do, you leave as quickly as you possibly can. A demonic presence is something that can bind to a person. You can leave a house that is merely haunted, and in all but extreme cases, everything goes back to normal. Demons are a different story. They can follow you home and if provoked in the wrong fashion, they can and will kill you.

It is a common misconception about the paranormal. People, for whatever reason, assume that spirits can only scare the shit out of us but are powerless beyond that ability. Nothing could be further from the truth. In many ways, they're just as, if not more, powerful than we are as humans. They can scratch you; bruise you; push you down stairs; levitate objects and turn them into projectiles; even reach inside of you and crush your organs, forcing you to join them in the afterlife. You must know when to stop. Provocation and aggression toward the paranormal often does bring about the best recordable evidence, but one must understand the potential consequences and when not to use such techniques. It truly can be the difference between life and death.

Knowing this, and only after getting an incredible amount of compelling evidence of the presence at The Demon House, we decided to pull the plug and get the hell out of there before investigating the entire premises. The risk to our entire crew far outweighed the benefit.

Whatever it was that we were feeling then, on that road felt similar, even stronger and even more sinister. I could feel my teeth chattering. I could feel the adrenal glands in my back pumping a cocktail of nervous intensity into my body. It felt like my soul had become bound to the place that we drove farther into that day. Suddenly, I became a part of the zeitgeist of unbridled intensity and rage that seemed to saturate that road. In one horrible instant, I felt a flood of a new kind of anger wash over me. It was a rage that should only be reserved for the most diabolical killers the world tends to occasionally produce. I could feel hatred and misery stronger than I had ever felt any previous emotion in my life. I felt like I could jump out of that truck and rip the world apart with my bare hands, and I would have enjoyed every minute of it. I wanted to inhale oxygen and exhale death upon everything and everyone. I didn't want to just dispatch my enemies—I wanted to ingest their souls—I wanted to eradicate their very existence from the known universe.

Without any warning, I reached into the back seat to my left and, in one motion, grasped Gary by the hair on his head. I ripped him forward, off his seat, toward my face, and screamed. "You and your fucking drugs. You're the one who brought me here! You're the one who has interrupted my slumber, and you will pay dearly." I screamed into his terrified, cowering face. My eyes bulged. I showed all my teeth. I wanted to peel his face back and eat whatever tissue was left on his skull afterward. I wanted to dominate. I wanted him bleeding—dead at my feet. I opened my mouth to take the first bite. Gary screamed and tried to pull back but was helpless to break away from my adrenalin-laden grasp.

Big Bear reached across his body with his left hand. His incredibly precise and devastating punch caught me just above my left eye, knocking me completely unconscious.

12

I can remember feeling a sense of perfection. I was drifting through space, one with myself, yet connected to the rest of the universe at the same time. My mind began to race. I was moving forward, but I was putting forth no effort. It was as though I were consciously floating through space but no longer in command of my own body. I knew I wasn't awake but also not asleep. Some part of my inner ear was still functional enough to allow me to feel the tow truck moving, ever forward and deeper into the belly of the beast.

I could faintly still hear Ricky, Gary, and Big Bear conversing around me. I knew I was still in the truck, as I was completely aware of my surroundings. My mind, however, was in a different place altogether. I was drifting; the viewpoint presented before me consisted predominantly of a blackened yet distinctly visible landscape.

If there was ever one positive takeaway from my trip to Ashford, Ohio, it is the fact that I gained an incredible sense of self-realization in that place. I acquired a sense that I have not since lost, even now, as I sit writing about the most terrifying experience of my life.

I could see fractal shapes at first—incredible geometric patterns that were transforming at an impossible rate as I moved into and through them. It was difficult to tell if I was moving through a series of these fractals or if it was simply one pattern changing over and over again, creating the illusion of forward motion. It was beautiful—like nothing I had ever seen. The colors associated with the shapes were luminous and somehow melted into one another. I felt like I was observing another realm of reality. It was as though I were swimming through a fascinatingly complex sea of molten stained glass, backlit by the light of an exploding star.

I had not forgotten that I had been punched. Even in that state, I had the wherewithal to consider that I might simply be experiencing the consequences of a sudden and jarring blow to the head. I doubted that was the case, though. What I was observing and conscious of was something that my brain should have never had the ability to produce. I have always been decent with mathematics—slightly above average— but the calculus necessary to produce the impossibly abstruse fractal images that I observed then was far beyond my aptitude. Their complexity—their incredible elasticity and ability to evolve from one impossible mathematical figure into another—is not something I could have conjured up on my own.

It felt like I had traversed a great distance, a distance that could only be measured in cosmic terms. I came out of the fractals and into something of a clearing. The background was a brilliant red with what appeared to be a city skyline in front of it. All the buildings were made of blackened glass. It was a magnificent, distant skyline. The city was enormous—at least twice the size of Manhattan or Chicago. I was at least five miles from the heart of it, yet the buildings stretched from left to right as far as I could see in either direction.

I hovered there for several moments, taking in the majestic scope of the shimmering, black city when I suddenly felt a presence. It was that same feeling you get while in bed and you become overwhelmed by that sense that there is someone or something there with you, someone who shouldn't be in the house, something observing you next to your bed. I turned slowly away from the city. In my periphery, I could see the edges of the luminous shapes I had ridden on my way into that realm. I completed my turn and came face-to-face with the entity that had followed me there.

It was decidedly not human. It was comprised of arm-like bands of energy that fired and whipped around a central mass of glowing, purple, plasmatic material. Its torso bore the shape of a human form— a waist, chest, and head-like structure on top. Its face was completely featureless. It floated and listed in the space above and in front of me. It looked to be flying, but in such a way that seemed indigenous to that higher realm of reality.

I looked on at it, trying to figure out what it was and what it wanted from me, when suddenly I was overcome by a tremendous sensation of déjà vu. The apparition that floated in space in front of me was as foreign an entity that could possibly be imagined by any member of humanity, yet it somehow registered as familiar to me. Inexplicably, I knew I had met it before.

Suddenly, it all made sense as I continued to watch the massless figure float about before me. Its structure resembled that of a plastic bag floating about in a steady breeze. I was supposed to be there. Everything I was observing—the entity, the darkened city, the impossible fractals—were . . . me. I can't explain how I felt it. The best I can figure was that the sudden, overwhelming sense of familiarity I began to feel at that moment was the dead giveaway. Suddenly, everything I looked at had lost its mystery. As quickly as the fractals would flash by, they took on a new meaning and told a new story. Every one that would change in front of me was like peeling back another layer of myself as I progressed deeper into the depths of my own psyche. This was a journey into my own soul. Every shape I was seeing was the mathematical simplification of what made up my sense of being. What I was seeing then, in those shapes and patterns and in the ghostly mass that accompanied me, registered as clearly to me as my own reflection in a mirror or my most beloved memories.

A hand suddenly grasped my shoulder. I could feel my heart rate immediately elevate as the total peacefulness of my journey was abruptly extinguished. I was being pulled backward, toward the black city. Everything had spoiled; the light had been erased from the patterns. Everything, in mere moments, had atrophied into a static, darkened, green canvas. It was then that I realized I had previously been in my own personal sense of nirvana. But that had been brought to a swift and unwelcomed end.

A second hand dug into my other shoulder. There was now one on each, and I was moving backward at an impossible velocity. The serine, white figure that had danced so gracefully before me seemed miles away. It had molded into a defensive stance—a posture of protective aggression as it watched me being ripped away. I could feel its concern for me, yet I also understood that it was somehow powerless to help me. I fought to turn around, desperate to see who or what was thrusting me away so quickly. I needed to confront the imposter. I managed to dislodge one of its hands from my right shoulder. Its hands were human-like yet elongated and boney. I could see massive, blue veins throughout them all leading to its filthy, yellow, razor-sharp nails.

I struggled and squirmed, exhausting every possible effort, and with my last semblance of energy managed to twist my head around to confront the imposter. I began to scream before the face of the phantom could fully register to me. It was human, but everything about it projected wrath—something born out of pure evil. Its face was the personification of unbridled hatred. It had an astonishingly sinister intensity to it. Its eyes were a picture of death that allowed me to see straight through and into the nightmare that ravaged behind them. It had a distinctive face and hands, but the rest of it appeared like the malevolent, white figure from before, only this creature glimmered a brilliant, shimmering red. Radiant bands of energy exploded out of it in all directions.

It didn't belong there. I couldn't help but feel like it had somehow broken in and overtaken my reality against my will. Everything about it was hopelessness, shame, guilt. It was a cancer. It opened its mouth, and I felt my ears violently pop. I felt the pressure pulling my eyes unnaturally out of their sockets as I witnessed it sucking the color out of the realm around us and into the soulless vacuum that no doubt existed at the core of that abomination.

Just as I established the horrible realization that I was moments from my demise, it spoke to me. It, in a terrifyingly disconcerting fashion, possessed a distinctly high-pitched, childish voice: "Telal ma alal ma buzar nasahu su anna ki-gal."

I had no idea what it was saying and didn't feel that I had time to engage in a dialogue with it. I fought vigorously to escape, knowing I had mere moments before it literally sucked my entire soul into whatever hell it had come from. I closed my eyes and pushed away with all the force I could muster. I felt a sensation of free fall, and I was suddenly jolted awake, just as my full weight landed me flat on my back onto the rock driveway outside of Lance's house.

I was immediately blinded, as the gray skies of Ashford had suddenly invaded my retinas with their unexpected brilliance. I looked up a moment later, and through the blur, I saw Gary and Big Bear standing over me. They had been attempting to carry me out of the tow truck. I staggered back to my feet, caught my breath, and regained my bearings on reality.

Big Bear shouted at me as though I weren't three feet away from him. "Hey, bud. I'm sorry I hit you. But I'm pretty sure you were about to eat Gary."

I completely blew off his statement. My mind was still racing back through the impossibly bizarre vision I had experienced in the moments prior.

"Yeah, sorry about that," I managed. "We've got some goddamned research to do. Let's get inside."

13
Lance Filner's Residence – Ashford, Ohio – 10:15 a.m.

I turned just in time to see the tow truck pulling down the street, having just left the driveway. Lance's friends had taken over and were already on their way with it back to Cleveland. Their mission to return it to Gary's stoner friend was underway. I was happy to see it go; it represented the last reminder of the horrible plan that had brought us there. Thankfully, they had remembered to leave my rental Malibu in the driveway before dragging it away with them. Lance's friends were going to use the return of that truck as an excuse to sneak out of Ashford for a while. Nobody expected to be seeing them back anytime soon and certainly not with that miserable tow truck. It all allowed a sense of relief to wash over me like a warm, fleece blanket, fresh from the dryer.

I had my first chance to observe Ashford up close and personal. The ground smelled wet from the rain the night before. The entire back of my body was chilled from the dampness that had seeped through my jeans and sweater. Everything seemed wet. Even the trees glistened in what appeared to be a brand-new sheen of moisture from a barely visible mist that saturated the air. Around us, it felt like we were immersed in a thick fog. It felt heavy—like claustrophobic humidity. The undulating landscape around us was filled with mature maple trees that cascaded up and down the rocky slopes for as far as I could see. Lance's house sat in a bowl surrounded by dense patches of maples and enormous pine trees along with a few towering white ash. They formed a forest around our entire perimeter. When the sun would momentarily break through the clouds, it became an annoyance, as it would boil up more moisture from the ground, adding more fuel to the already heavy atmosphere.

"Lance, why is everything so wet? I don't remember rain being in the forecast yesterday," I asked.

Lance chuckled. "Right now, you are standing in the lowest point in three counties. My house sits twenty feet below sea level, so pretty much half of northeastern Ohio drains into my yard. It's an absolute bitch to keep my basement dry. Every passing rain shower is a damn emergency around here."

I nodded, accepting his answer. I was somewhat happy that this yard was the exception and not the rule. The minimal supplies I had brought with me were woefully ill-equipped for such a swamp-like environment.

We all headed down his white-rock driveway toward his cornflower-blue, bungalow-style house. It was two stories, appearing to have a single room on the second floor, sitting atop the middle of the much-wider first floor. There was a detached garage ahead of us, adjacent to the back corner of the house. The house itself was sided with cedar wood which had been painted, yet it appeared to have begun peeling at some point during the Ford administration. The first floor had white shutters around the windows that complemented the blue tone of the house well and appeared to have been painted relatively recently. The driveway was full of sparse, white gravel with massive potholes and ruts from where years of tires had dug into it. It wasn't so much a driveway as it was simply the absence of the weed-infested lawn in that strip of property. There had been some landscaping relatively recently, but the frost must have hit Ashford early that year. A couple of rose bushes sat in front of the home, but their familiar green leaves and pink flowers had all gone yellow. Along the drive were scattered a few neglected and quickly dying hydrangea. On the other side were equally neglected hosta. The property with even a little effort could have been so much more, but it was obvious that Lance had other priorities, was not handy by any stretch of the imagination, and absolutely did not possess a green thumb.

We made our way through the muddy, faded grass onto the concrete stoop. Lance opened the front door, and we all entered his home.

The first thought that came to my mind as I observed the inside of Lance's house was: *Good god, we've just entered the home of a serial killer.* The décor seemed to have been molded around a deep-seated mental illness. The odor of rotting food and garbage was as pungent as it was unmistakable. It was nearly impossible to observe the floor plan of the place, as it was packed wall-to-wall with clutter. Where there weren't clothes strewn about, there were bags of trash. Where the trash wasn't bagged, it was strewn about. There were couches and a television in one of the rooms, but newspapers and other random documentation had been stacked on top of them, nearly obscuring the furniture from view entirely. There was one yellow-fabric recliner that remained uncovered and sat directly in front of an old, tube-style television. The walls were dotted with newspaper clippings, many of which had little notes written on them or circles around a particular paragraph or blurb of text. The only way to get around the place was to follow Lance through the pathways that had been cut through the mountains of nonsense.

I've nearly blocked the kitchen from my memory and for good reason. All I can remember as we passed through that room were maggots in the sink, slithering around a stack of filthy dishes that had grown beyond control and taken over all the available counter space. The stench in that room nearly knocked me out. Gary began dry-heaving. That is literally all that I can describe of that room.

Ricky broke what had been an extended period of queasy silence among all of us. "So, let me venture a guess, Lance. You're single?"

We all shared a brief laugh, although humor of any kind would have been dulled as we traversed such deplorable squalor.

Lance replied, "I know. The place is kind of a mess. Sorry, guys."

This brought about a much larger laugh from all of us. I finally caught enough of my breath to speak. "'Kind of a mess'? That's like calling a hurricane a passing rain shower."

"I spend most of my time in here in my workshop," he replied, ignoring my insult.

Lance motioned us toward a door that led farther toward the back of the house into what was obviously a later addition to the original structure. I fully expected a blacked-out room with chains hanging from the ceiling, connected to various torture devices. At that point, a room full of bodies, stacked floor to ceiling, would have brought about little surprise.

Lance swung the door open, and we all stumbled down one step onto a shimmering, pristine, hardwood floor. The stench from the rest of the house was quickly replaced by the delightful aroma of pine-scented floor cleanser. The room was a rather large addition; it had to be a solid sixteen by eighteen feet. It had four windows that were providing a fair amount of light which supplemented the three rows of track lighting that lined the ceiling above us.

I was momentarily floored by the contrast of the room in relation to the rest of the house. It was like stepping from a war zone into Disneyland within a matter of seconds. It was somewhat off-putting and only added fuel to the idea that Lance might have been a few fries short of a happy meal. It seemed impossible for a man who was mentally stable to be able to maintain such an incredibly variable level of cleanliness from one room of his house to another.

There was a nice desk that faced the rest of the room. It was modern—likely something from IKEA, a black slab held up by two, white, screw-on legs on one side and a series of drawers on the other. A very formidable and relatively new Mac Pro, complete with a giant flat-screen monitor, sat on top of the desk. The matching Mac keyboard and wireless mouse sat in the middle of a well-organized array of pens and pencils, post-it notes, and a perfectly stacked set of notebooks. On the far side of the room was a perfectly maintained, black, leather, wraparound couch with reclining seats. It faced a wall-mounted fifty-five-inch flat-screen television. The walls were painted a kind of gun-smoke gray which contrasted the light hardwood on the floor perfectly. Every corner and angle of the room had been finished with white crown molding. Several potted, well-manicured fig trees sat in front of the windows. In between the windows were framed portraits of various people whom I assumed to be Lance's bygone family members.

I could have laid down and passed out for a good ten hours. I had a lump above my eye the size of a golf ball. I was likely in the preliminary stages of a concussion from Big Bear's strike to my face. It hurt, but I had certainly been in worse pain in my life. This was more of a throbbing annoyance than anything debilitating.

"Yep, this is my little slice of heaven," Lance announced.

"How can you keep this room up so well while the rest of your place is in such dire straits?" Big Bear asked.

Lance seemed genuinely taken aback by the question. "Do you guys really think it's that bad?"

We all shared another laugh until we realized Lance was serious. It was obvious that he had no idea what depths of squalor he was living in.

I spoke up. "Let me put it this way, Lance. The dumpster behind a Chinatown butcher and fishery is easier on the eyes and nose than the rest of your house."

Nobody laughed at my remark, sensing Lance's growing sensitivity to the topic.

"Okay," he said, sounding somewhat dejected. "I'm sorry, guys. I guess my whole life lately has had me wrapped up in Ashford and the disappearances and trying to figure out what happened to my grandparents. This was their place until they went missing one day like all the others. I moved in with all my stuff and never got rid of their stuff. It's always just been me, and I rarely have company, and I guess I just never learned how to take care of things."

"You know what you need?" Ricky suggested. "Some pussy—you need a nice woman to come in here and show you how to keep the place. You, my friend, are suffering from a bad case of bacheloritis." Ricky looked at me; it seemed like he was seeking my approval. I think he sensed that Lance was feeling a little picked-on. He put his hand on Lance's shoulder and continued, "Seen it a thousand times. I have had similar problems of my own. I have always said—a man without a woman will inevitably have his living conditions devolve into a huge pile of shit. We are basically still just cavemen, you know? Without the possibility of a vagina showing up, why even bother picking up the place—am I right?"

Lance began to blush as we all chuckled at Ricky's rationale. I had been to his place, and even between steady lays, it was pristine. He lived in a four-thousand-square-foot flat in the wildly expensive Back Bay neighborhood of Boston. It could not have been further from the total shithole we stood in on that day. We all knew he was just trying to liven Lance's spirits.

"I had a girl once, a couple years ago," Lance replied. "I was in love with her. I never felt that way about anybody. I used to get butterflies just thinking about seeing her. Back then, the place was in great shape. She told me one day after we had kind of a fight that I was too caught up in my research and I was obsessed with this town and needed to learn to take care of myself. Then she left." His voice had taken on a bit of a tremble. "I called and called. I sent her flowers. I even tried talking to her friends, but she never spoke to me again. God, that was two years ago, but it feels like two minutes. I couldn't believe that someone who I know loved me could just leave like that and never speak to me again. The hurt turned to hate, and the hate turned to depression. Here I am, I guess. I just don't care enough to take care of myself or this house."

We stood with our heads down. I felt legitimately bad for him, to an extent. On the other hand, pretty much every guy I knew had been through a horrible breakup in their lives and had never let their home devolve into a landfill. I was still more confused than I was sorry for him.

"Why do you keep this room so nice?" I asked, trying to get him off that topic.

"My grandparents had this house built in the 1940s. My grandfather always talked about building a study. He went to a trade school to learn carpentry for a year. He saved up the money and put this addition on himself. When he would talk about it, his eyes would light up. He fought in World War II, lived through the Great Depression, and traveled all over the world, but he never talked about anything as favorably as he talked about how he built this addition himself. He poured the concrete slab, stick-framed the entire thing, drywall, electrical, the works. I feel like I owe it to him to keep this room how he would have liked it."

I nodded, accepting his explanation. My fear that Lance might be a raving lunatic had subsided, having found out that he was just a depressed, confused, heartbroken slob. We all made our way over to the black, leather wraparound and sat.

"So, let's get down to brass tacks here," I announced. "What does 'telal ma alal ma buzar nasahu su anna ki-gal' mean? And what the hell language is that?"

14

Lance headed over to his desk and sat. He fired up his computer.

"You get internet here?" I asked.

"Nope, not for a long time," he replied. "I have software installed locally that should help with the translation, though."

"How do you have power at all? I didn't see any lines on the way in," I asked.

"There is exactly one working circuit left in town. We are sitting on top of it. Everyone who remains in Ashford has congregated along it. The only other option is to live Little-House-on-the-Prairie style."

Gary chimed in, "We did begin to see some power lines along the way as we got closer to Lance's place, Danny. You must have missed them while you were unconscious."

"That's right," Lance added. "The circuit along County Line Road is the only one intact anywhere in town. Interesting thing about it—I've never gotten a bill. I sort of get the feeling like it isn't *supposed* to work but somehow does. I'm sure the officials have some sort of a hand in keeping it running—surely, they need power. Kind of like we're all splicing someone else's cable."

"Hey, did you hear that, guys? Free power, plenty of move-in ready homes, and plenty of law enforcement," I declared. "Anyone who thinks Ashford is lacking amenities has clearly never spent an afternoon here. If I didn't know any better, I would call this the Paris of Wahoga County, Ohio."

"Very funny, Danny," Lance replied. "Why don't you take us through what you experienced, and I will see if I can translate this phrase."

I described the vision I'd had while knocked out on the way into town. I told everyone how I had felt so at one with myself, how I had journeyed within my own mind and into the essence of my own being. How I had been shown a vision—a snapshot of a portion of my own soul. I went into detail about the fractals and what I thought they represented. I told of the black city and its unimaginable vastness. Everyone was most interested to hear about the beings I had encountered. The purple-and-white, faceless specter was interesting enough, but when I began telling of the being that had dragged me toward the black city, everyone was on the edge of their seats. I struggled to describe it to them, how it had the presence of a powerful man, yet it registered to me as more of an emotion than as an image I could paint for them. It had a face, eyes, nose, ears, and a mouth, but it seemed elastic or artificial—a mere cloak for whatever true evil lurked underneath. It allowed me the ability to see inside, deep into its infernal hatred. It allowed me to become one with its sheer hopelessness. It projected an affectation of ancient menace—one that it had built up for far longer than we as humans could possibly fathom. It had cloaked me in that feeling with it, letting me in, enveloping me in its despair. I told of its juvenile-sounding, high-pitched voice and how it had barked the mysterious phrase to me that Lance was researching.

I described to all of them how I'd screamed and how that scream was reactionary and compulsive, almost instinctual and completely involuntary. I had screamed more from the shock that I felt in that situation and less from any kind of fear I was feeling. To me, the most disturbing aspect of the ordeal was how familiar it all felt. Even the most vine-ripened wrath that was imposed in those dire moments felt like something I had experienced before. I was struggling to describe how such passionate malice could have seemed native to me. I was at a loss as to what could have invoked those feelings of familiarity. There was nothing I could think of from my past that approached that level of depravity that I could have been subconsciously drawing from.

The closest example I could muster was from when I had been in an awful car accident when I was much younger—still in college. I spoke of it in detail in my autobiography. It seemed to gain a lot of fanfare and enquiry from the media and critics as I had described it as one of the most profound, important things that had ever happened to me. It was one of those incredibly rare experiences that shaped me as a person, rewired certain fundamental parts of my brain. But at the end of the day, it was a car accident. Pretty much everyone gets into several throughout the course of their lives. It was hardly anything that should have prepared me for that vision and certainly not to a point where arriving face-to-face with a demonic body snatcher should have felt like second nature to me. So, what else? What else could have happened to me throughout the course of my entire life to evoke déjà vu from such an unprecedented situation?

I got into a lot of trouble growing up. I was picked up by the Boston police on several occasions. Most of my foster parents' idea of discipline came in the form of beatings. I never knew my real parents. These are things that sucked, sure. But I reconciled my emotions with all that a long time ago. I don't remember, throughout the course of any of it, feeling the monumental level of paralyzing hatred and anguish I had experienced inside of that vision mere hours before. Yet it felt as close and familiar to me as a picture of my own daughter's face.

Lance walked back over to us from the computer. He was carrying a sticky note with some words scribbled on it. He handed it to me, and I read out loud.

"Sumerian: Telal ma alal ma buzar nasahu su anna ki-gal. English: The demon warrior, the destroyer, the master of the deep commands you unto the realm of the death gods."

15

"What in the hell is happening?" I asked nobody in particular. "Why would someone in my head be speaking fluently in ancient Sumerian? I've never spoken anything but broken English. I failed Spanish in high school."

Ricky spoke up, attempting to qualify what we had just learned. "Lance, how did you translate that? How did you figure out it was Sumerian?"

"It is a pretty rock-solid assumption, Rick. I cross-referenced it against two different translation tools I keep on my Mac," he replied.

Ricky pressed, "Okay, but isn't Sumerian the oldest-known language on the planet? Why would it be in Danny's head?"

"What am I, a goddamned linguist?" Lance replied defensively. "If you're asking me why your friend's vision was in a language that predates ancient Egypt by a thousand years, well then . . . fuck if I know."

"Let's just move on, shall we?" I announced. "Lance, regarding the clowns in the SUV on the way here. They're obviously the feds you've been speaking of, right?"

"That's correct. The woman we saw is one of the higher-ranking ones, I think. She has been here since I first arrived, and I don't know how long before. I have spoken to her once, on accident. I literally ran into her while I was taking pictures up in the old town square. She told me that her name is Victoria."

"Is she just really bad at her job?" I asked. "Why wouldn't they have pulled us over and questioned us? They know you, correct? They probably should have suspected that wasn't your car. Having gotten a good hard look at all of us, they should have deduced that we weren't your average tow-truck crew."

"I really don't know why they didn't pull us over, Danny," he replied.

"I ask you this because the whole point of our coming up with that god-awful tow-truck plan was to cover our asses in the event we were spotted by the feds. I would like to think it worked. But on the other hand, I can't imagine Victoria and whoever else was in that Yukon being that naïve. None of us planned on being spotted from three fucking feet away for two full minutes. My point is, I would hate to find out that we could have just as easily driven out here in the comfort of our own van and had a similar experience. Especially when you consider that that ride culminated in a throbbing, tumorous lump above my eyeball and likely a concussion."

"Am I being interrogated right now or something?" asked Lance. He had gone fully defensive. "We got here, didn't we? You *are* paranormal investigators sitting in the middle of a town that has so much paranormal activity that the United States government has a team of officials assigned to it permanently. All any of you have done since you got here is make fun of my home and question me at every turn. Now you want to sit here and question me more? Why don't you take a turn answering some questions, Danny? Why don't you start by telling all of us why you attacked your friend and tried to take a bite out of him? Call me crazy, but I, for one, consider attempted murder far more interesting than how dirty you think my kitchen is."

I exhaled. The bastard had me there. I still had a splitting headache, and I knew it wasn't going away anytime soon. I replied, trying to calm the mood, "I don't know what came over me in the truck, Gary. It was like a wave of anger hit me. Then another one, and another after that, over and over again. Each wave seemed to gain strength exponentially. After a few moments, it was pure evil that was washing over me. I could feel my chest tightening, my ears popping, my toes curling up. My mind was on fire. I can recall not being particularly proud of the thoughts that began to race through my head. At the same time, though, I identified with them. I felt like they were perfectly logical. I wanted to sweep over the entire planet like a global hurricane and eradicate every living thing from the face of the earth."

"Jesus Christ, man." Gary had genuine concern in his voice. "I'm pretty glad Big Bear knocked your ass out."

"Me too, actually," I agreed. "As another wave of that pure hatred slammed into me, something told me it was Gary's fault that I was in that situation—which really wasn't too far from the truth, but that's beside the point. Then I just snapped. I did want to kill Gary, and I probably would have had Big Bear here not put my lights out."

A collective groan swept over the entire group. I didn't see any point in sugarcoating anything as I explained it to them. This was something we were all up against. One item that you simply cannot underestimate as a paranormal investigator is complete and total honesty among your peers. There is a certain stigma that tends to arise within groups of men, where for some reason it is frowned upon to be transparent with one another about your feelings. But when you're dealing with the paranormal, you really don't have a choice. A group of paranormal investigators who cannot be honest about their feelings with one another is a ticking time bomb. Someone will eventually get hurt or killed because of their failure to communicate. When you're dealing with invisible beings who can attach to people and manipulate people's thoughts from the inside out, you're only hurting yourself by not being honest about it. You're only prolonging the ordeal. Human toughness doesn't earn you any points against pissed-off supernatural beings.

I have written about this very topic in various articles. I do believe that ghosts, for lack of a better term, are conscious beings. They are just on a different level of consciousness from all of us. However, they do have just as much of a grip on reality as you or me. I also believe that ghosts can remember their previous lives and are typically aware of the fact that they are no longer of the living. I'm not sure if they are generally aware that they are trapped in their earthbound state; however, I do suspect that some of them are. Either that or they have made a conscious decision not to pass on to whatever the next step may be after their deaths. I believe that spirits view the opportunity to latch on to the living as something to break up the monotony—a method of regaining a human consciousness, if even for a few fleeting moments. In that sense, they're a lot like parasites. You become their livelihood, and they won't leave until you do something about it. Imagine walking aimlessly, for hundreds of years in some cases, desperate for any sort of human interaction. What if you were finally able to find a way of getting some of that interaction? You're going to take that opportunity, and you're going to hold on to that for as long as you possibly can.

Therefore, it is paramount for people in my field to be as transparent about their feelings with one another as possible. If we can identify that you are being attached to or are otherwise under some level of supernatural control, there are steps we can take to break the attachment, to force the spirit back out of you. Otherwise, if you aren't honest, they will stay attached, and you will bring a lot more than just dinner home to your family that night.

"So, I want to know what you guys think is happening here. Ricky, with everything you know about Ashford and taking what happened on the way here into context, give me your take."

I wanted Ricky's opinion more than anyone else's. He was far and away the most analytical mind of any of us. His real-world, investigative background had always proven invaluable. This seemed like a perfect situation for him to apply his unique way of thinking.

He started in that familiar used-car salesman tone, "Well, to me, it's obvious that Lance here, while not completely up-front with us on all of the details, was for the most part telling us the truth. Unless the president is in town, I see no other reason for that kind of law enforcement presence here in little old Ashford. I got a good look at Victoria, and she was the real deal. That vehicle also—textbook CIA or FBI. Taking all of that into consideration, we can deduce, with a high level of certainty, that something serious is indeed happening in this town.

"There wasn't a single sign on the way in that said anything about Ashford. All the other towns and bergs that we drove through were documented somehow with signage. Some of the headers from the newspaper clippings that Lance has hanging on the walls in the disgusting part of his house appeared to be from a paper called *The Ashford Sentinel*. Some were from as far back as the sixties. So, we know that at some point there was indeed a town named Ashford here. I also noticed that Ashford is not labeled on any of my GPS apps on my phone. I googled as well, prior to us entering this cellular exclusion zone, and couldn't dig up anything about Ashford.

"So, you take the lack of signage; the inability to find this place on any modern map; the fact that we know, from Lance's newspaper clippings, that where we are now used to be called Ashford; the presence of the feds; and you roll it all up. To me, it seems likely that what Lance told us about the feds trying to keep a lid on this place is true.

"As far as what happened to you, Danny, I think it was classic demonic attachment. We've all seen it at one time or another—or at least heard about it happening. I felt something similar on the way in. Nothing nearly as intense as you describe, but on that road in, I did begin to feel lethargic or almost like I was going to faint. I was angry, but I've been pissed since this morning when you pulled me off the Carnegie Mill investigation that I spent the last two weeks researching. So, I can't say for sure if this town affected me or if I was just generally grumpy.

"I've heard of people having visions like the one you were shown. From a purely scientific point of view, I would suspect that you saw a movie or read a book once where someone uttered that phrase in Sumerian and you stored it somewhere in your subconscious. Then Big Bear knocked you out. Your head, in its slightly damaged state, invoked that memory and wrapped a bunch of trippy imagery around it. That's the Occam's razor explanation. As far as the paranormal alternative— well, I don't really want to talk about that."

Ricky had a way of putting complicated situations into such a clear perspective.

"Why don't you humor us all and tell me what you think the paranormal alternative is?" I asked.

He sighed again and continued, "I do believe that you were attached to by something. The reaction that it invoked from you suggests that that something was demonic, at least in its nature. I know you, and I have never seen that look on your face in my life. When you say you would have killed Gary, I believe you. I think you might have been knocked out with whatever it was still attached to you. At that point, your eyes close, your brain is no longer processing any external input from any other senses, and your only sensory input is that of your mind's eye. Your entire sense of being is limited to what you can see inside your own head, behind your own eyelids.

"So, who's to say that you weren't simply seeing what the entity which had taken over your mind and body wanted you to see? Who's to say that they can't completely take over our subconscious minds? It's well documented that they can easily take over our conscious minds. Maybe it all seemed familiar because all that shit you saw was familiar to the entity that was controlling you. Maybe the entity speaks Sumerian. Even more intriguing—what if the red figure, the one you described that terrified you so much and tried to pull you toward your black city and spoke that Sumerian phrase to you . . . what if it wasn't talking to you? What if it was speaking to the thing that was hijacking you? What if it was commanding . . . it . . . back to the realm of the death gods? Whatever the hell that is."

I exhaled as I nodded approvingly. Once again, he had come up with a perfectly formulated and clear insight into our current situation. "Ricky, as usual, that makes a lot of sense and gives me a lot to think about. How do you sleep with these crazy theories whipping around your head all the time?"

He chuckled and replied with a sideways grin, "I usually have someone's daughter to keep me awake."

"You're a douche," I replied, unable to keep myself from outwardly laughing at his retort. "Gary, why don't you go get our equipment from outside and bring it in here. Let's do an inventory on everything and make sure we didn't leave anything on the highway or damage anything expensive. I want an idea of how much life we have in that equipment. Do we have the necessary battery life? You know the drill."

Gary hopped to it. If there was one thing that he always had my full trust in, it was the equipment. I might give the guy a lot of shit, but when it came time to maintain our technology, I would hire him again in a second. There was simply nobody better.

"Big Bear, your thoughts on the situation?" I asked.

He had stood silently thus far, listening intently. He was the muscle of the operation, but he was incredibly intelligent at the same time. The Navy Seals are far from ignorant grunts. This is one of the many reasons they are so much better at what they do than any other fighting force the planet has ever known.

He stood with his thick, rock-solid arms crossed. His pectorals jutted out, clear through his hooded sweatshirt. His bald head was glistening, by choice—he shaved it daily with a straight razor. He towered over us at six foot six and easily 260 pounds. His entire body filled out his clothes. It made his appearance like something that had been carved out of a single chunk of granite. I had always said, Michelangelo himself would have had a tough time sculpting something that did his physique justice.

He looked down at us on the wraparound. His face was how he had earned his Big Bear nickname, long before we had met him. He had one of the most non-threatening faces—total baby face, thick goatee, chubby cheeks, gentle smile, wide eyes. He truly was a big bear of a man. At the same time, considering his background and level of training and conditioning, you did not want to piss him off.

He spoke up. "I think it would be advisable to stay here and come up with a plan the rest of today and then start investigating tomorrow morning. None of us knows a thing about this area. We also don't know what's going on with the feds beyond some educated guessing. I figure, we hunker in, inventory our equipment, and talk out a plan tonight. Let's focus on the big targets. Obviously, we need to find a way to get to Whistler Road in the morning undetected, to check out this doctor's place. According to our gracious host, that is the heart of this whole damned thing. I am worried you might have a concussion, Danny—I caught you solidly above the eye with that punch. Everything you guys are describing sounds like something you don't want to dive into without doing the proper preparation and gathering the proper intel. Hell, we don't investigate normal places without doing days or weeks of homework first. I would also love to find out from Lance here exactly what happens when these government officials find out what we're doing."

Lance replied, "A few people have been picked up by them. They're taken to what used to be an exchange station on the far west side of town. One guy came to town once. I assumed he was investigating the place, same as you guys. I know he got picked up by the feds and taken there. I witnessed them escort him into their Yukon and watched them drive into the exchange station after that. I saw him in town again a couple years later, so it's not like they murdered him or anything. I assumed they just asked him some questions or maybe they intimidated him to keep him quiet. Who could say what happens if they catch you? I mean, it isn't like they're storm troopers—they aren't just going to find you and start blasting."

My massive lump on my head had begun to throb, agonizingly, in perfect concert with my pulse. "There's that Star Wars reference I'm sure you've been holding back all day, Lance. I agree, Big Bear, we all need to figure out what angle to attack this thing from. Let's take tonight and regroup a bit and come up with our strategy."

Ricky agreed.

Gary had come back with the equipment and had begun to inventory everything. We explained the situation to him, and he, as usual, was not intelligible enough to care one way or another.

16
Lance Filner's Residence – Ashford, Ohio – 2:15 p.m.

We had decided to take a little break before making our plan as to how we were going to proceed with our investigation. We had spent the earlier part of the day poring over as much documentation about the town as Lance could provide. It was the mid-afternoon, and Lance had turned the television on. For some reason, the only channel it picked-up was an old-time version of the BBC, and the only program being broadcast on it was a grainy, black-and-white replay of the 1936 Berlin Olympic Games.

I took the chance to dive back into Kenneth Harvey's medical manifesto. I quickly found where I had left off and began reading.

The Medical Memoirs of Kenneth Harvey

Ashford had been selected by the State of Ohio as a top candidate to accommodate one of the new, larger psychiatric facilities. Many such units as these had begun cropping up in recent years all over the eastern share of our country. Even back when I had called Ashford my place of residence, plans were being drawn up to erect the Ashford Hill Lunatic Asylum.

I do remember the community welcoming the place. Ashford had been founded as a farming community, and it served its purpose in that respect. But that part of Ohio is not ideal for farming. The ground is rocky and often saturated, and the frost comes early because of the abundant groundwater, cutting short the time with which one has to birth and harvest his crops.

The local farmers had managed to make it work in the earlier years, but recent advances in irrigation and the elevated cost of good seed (more resilient to temperature change) had made the vocation into a far more expensive enterprise than it had previously been. Ashford effectively became a town desperate for other opportunity, which is why the people were thrilled at the prospect of accommodating a massive, state-funded asylum for the mentally ill.

I never cared for the overall idea of such places myself. When it comes to potentially dangerous mental illness, I would personally trend toward separatism. Essentially, I prefer a smaller, more personal approach when dealing with the mentally incompetent. I never understood the thought process behind allocating so many mentally unstable people into one place. I presume the idea stems from a simple consolidation point for resources that can deal with the prisoners.

I call them prisoners because that is exactly what they are. They're prisoners masquerading as mental patients. Every tenant of the Ashford Hill Lunatic Asylum had, for one reason or another, been legally deemed unfit for society. Many of the patients there had committed crimes, and sadly, others were simply inept individuals whose families were wealthy enough to see them locked away so as to no longer be a burden or embarrassment to their affluent ways of life.

Another issue that I take with such places is that they are built with the idea in mind that the people who will be locked away there are not intelligent enough to understand what has happened to them. When one finds himself to be a part of the psychiatric industry, it quickly becomes apparent that the sciences behind the illnesses are not taken into consideration by the people tasked with making the larger decisions. This, mainly, is a result of said persons not being scientists at all. Rather, they are often politicians or wealthy members of the surrounding region who possess certain lobbying abilities with the key decision makers.

This is how Ashford Hill came about. Something that politicians thought would be a good-idea for the economic growth of the community—never taking any of the science behind the eventual tenants' illnesses into consideration. Therefore, the place was designed more as a prison than as a hospital, using the naïve logic that the prisoners wouldn't even be aware enough mentally to care one way or another. The stark reality is that most, if not all, of the afflictions that the patients imprisoned therein were suffering from were likely abrupt-onset conditions—brief spells of psychosis and/or flashes of uncontrollable lunacy. Many of these unfortunate states likely only lasted minutes before they would pass, only to come back weeks, months, or, in some cases, years later. In between these spells, most of these poor souls were likely as normal from a mental standpoint as you or me—completely aware of the deplorable surroundings they had become trapped within.

For these reasons, the letter I had received from Sheriff Fredrick Williams, asking me to come help with his little problem, brought about little to no surprise from me in the least bit. In absolute honesty, the only item that surprised me at all is the fact that Ashford Hill had lasted this long before someone burned it down. Whatever might have happened there was an inevitable eventuality of what I imagine were positively tragic and unbearable living conditions for so many of those people.

The other issue I took with the sheriff's request was that he assumed I could assist simply because I worked in a similar field. While I did have some experience in psychology and acute mental illnesses, it was certainly not my capital area of expertise. I am a doctor of the neurosciences. I am far more interested in the organ and the associated systems and physiology involved with the conditions than I am in the actual persons who possess said illnesses. Essentially, I preferred the approach of allowing the psychiatrists to deal with the patients. When the patients eventually would die, I would get to examine their physical brain. All to observe any unique characteristics that could have accounted for their previously documented behavior.

I did, however, understand that he was summoning me personally because I was familiar with the area and many of the people involved. However, if he wanted to get someone who could really help, he likely could have just driven the fifty miles to Cleveland (the sixth-largest city in the country) and found dozens of psychiatric professionals who are far superior to myself in the handling of such a situation.

I had never attempted to elicit any kind of information from persons whom, according to the sheriff's letter, had been in a borderline vegetative state. My initial prognosis seemed to point to actual physical brain damage to these people and not a specific mental ineptness, per se. I am only making professional guesses, however; the mental illnesses that we know about and see most often do not manifest themselves by placing the stricken individual into a borderline comatose state of lethargy. Typically, it is the exact opposite. What the sheriff was describing to me sounded a lot more like a few people who had sustained physical damage to the frontal cortex of the brain, which is the region responsible for much of what we perceive as mental cognition in others.

I was, however, intrigued. I needed a reason to get away from the big city. A chance to return triumphantly to my old home seemed like a wonderful opportunity and an excuse to break up the monotony that had recently begun seeping into my daily life. I also did genuinely want to understand what had happened to all those people whose remains should have been found within that scorched building. I secretly hoped it would have a happy ending. Perhaps they had gotten out ahead of time and disappeared. I somehow doubted it, as many of the prisoners in such places would have likely welcomed the flames as a vehicle to finally get themselves the hell out of that asylum.

I went next door to the local post office and was able to use their phone bank. I left a message with one of the underlings of Sheriff Fredrick Williams. I let her know that I would be traveling to Ashford to assist with the case and that they could expect me there at some point in the next several days. I demanded all previous medical records and court filings associated with the patients who I would be examining.

I packed a few changes of clothes, a set of my tools, along with a few medications I thought might be useful, and I headed to Penn Station to catch the first train to Cleveland.

My head was beginning to throb again, and I was having a tough time keeping my eyes open. I leaned over to my left on the leather wraparound, laid my head on one of the armrests, and fell asleep. As I began to dose off, I kept replaying Kenneth Harvey's words in my head. I began to understand his point of view in some backward fashion. Obviously, I was not on board with his politically incorrect word usage while describing persons who suffer from mental illnesses, but he wrote it in the thirties, and that is how such people were described in those times, for better or worse. But I was beginning to draw correlations, however loose, between his story and my own. We had both been asked to come to Ashford to figure out what in the hell could be happening there. We were both highly established in our respective fields of study. We had both been summoned to Ashford by people who were expecting us to provide an explanation into the happenings there, and neither of us were particularly qualified to provide such explanations.

I remember how it occurred to me, just before I reached the full depths of my subconscious, that I really had no business being there. I had no idea what I expected to achieve by traveling to Ashford. So far, all I had to show for my trouble was a spot in the most disgusting house I had ever set foot inside of and a lump above my eye that had grown to a point where I would soon be legally obligated to name it.

The town obviously had some sort of a long-standing issue that people had been documenting as far back as the 1930s. What appeared to be highly trained, well-equipped resources of the federal government, who had been there for years before my arrival, had not been able to break open whatever was going on there. So, what did I expect to achieve? How could I have expected myself, my stoner equipment technician, my womanizing sidekick, a retired special forces operator, and a local basket case, to have had any chance of demystifying the secrets of Ashford, Ohio?

17

"I'm going to dump this glass of water on his pants. That way, when he wakes up, he'll think he pissed himself."

That's the first thing I heard as I roused from my slumber on the wraparound. It was Ricky, thinking I was still asleep. We had pulled a lot of juvenile stunts on one another over the years. Messing with one another had become something of a tradition within the group—a way to break up the overly serious monotony that managed to hang over us most of the time.

"Go ahead," I growled at Ricky with my eyes still shut. "But if you do, by day's end, I promise you will be punched, with a closed fist, square in the dick. The choice is yours, my friend."

"Dammit, he's up," replied Ricky, taking a step back. He might have been younger and more attractive, but if it ever came down to a scrap, he knew I was the superior physical specimen. It was the same reason neither of us messed with Big Bear all that often. If we, for any reason, ever agitated Big Bear, he had the know-how, training, and physical toolset to literally rip our heads from our bodies.

We would mess with Gary from time to time, but he always overreacted, sapping the fun out of it. He took everything too personally, holding grudges for way longer than any normal guy should. Gary had a way of making the everyday ribbing that occurred within a group of dudes into a depressing, irritating mess. This was why Ricky and I pretty much just stuck with pranking each other. I sat up and found Ricky, Big Bear, and Gary standing in front of me.

Gary spoke up. "Lance went into town to get us some food."

"In my rental car?" I asked, thrusting myself up and onto my feet.

"Yep."

"Awesome idea, guys," I replied, nearly shouting. "It's got Missouri plates on it, which half the rental cars on the planet tend to have for some reason. But don't worry, I'm sure none of the Quantico-trained, federal officials are going to notice that menial detail."

Big Bear chimed in. "You want to head into that kitchen and make yourself something to eat, Danny? Maybe a nice sandwich? The dipshit doesn't even have ice in this house. Literally the only thing he has in his fridge is some sort of a melon that looks like it might be getting ready to give birth to another, even uglier, more disgusting melon. It took Ricky and me a solid fifteen minutes of staring at it to even agree that it was, indeed, a melon."

"Okay," I replied dejectedly. "I'm trying to put that kitchen out of my mind forever. I am honestly considering climbing out one of these windows whenever we decide to leave to avoid having to walk through it again. Okay?"

We kind of just sat there, smiling at one another a moment. Each of us had begun to grasp how ridiculously stupid the entire situation had become. The gray skies had disappeared behind a deep-orange and navy-blue dusk. I must have been passed out for five hours. Out the numerous windows in the room, the sea of maples and ash trees were still visible, but they had begun their nightly routine of fading into the darkened distortion that came with the half light of the early evening.

Ricky broke the silence. "About these feds, Danny—I think we should just forget about them. I think we need a plan which goes right to the heart of what we're doing here. We're never going to be able to truly investigate Ashford if we have one eye over our shoulder the entire time. I just assume, if we get caught, we get caught. What exactly are we doing that's illegal? Sure, there are no signs or anything else pointing to the existence of Ashford. But there's also nothing that says we *aren't* allowed to be here. So, I just say to hell with it. I think we treat this like any other investigation. If they catch us, what are they going to charge us with? Felonious paranormal investigation? All they're going to do is question us and try to intimidate us, probably make us sign non-disclosure agreements, then send us on our way."

"I agree with you, Ricky," I replied. "I thought about that myself. I can't see a viable option around the feds while still being able to investigate this town. I do, however, think we need to protect Lance a little bit here. We need to come up with a story about how we came about Ashford that doesn't involve Lance telling us to come here. Shit rolls downhill. If we get caught, then sure, *we'll* get a slap on the wrist. But I bet they aren't as nice to Lance. Keep in mind, we get to leave and go back to Boston. He's the one who has to live here."

Gary intervened, "Why don't we just say that we were on our way through here anyway in the tow truck, since they saw us in it anyhow? We were on a deadline and in a pinch, our normal van died, and we used the tow truck as a last resort. We got lost because we didn't have our normal GPS. We ran into Lance, whose car had broken down, and we offered to give him a tow back to his place."

I nodded. There were certainly holes in it. For instance, hopefully nobody would bother to check on whom the rental car was registered to. But it was about as good as we were going to get. "I like it, Gary. Unless anyone has any better ideas, I say we stick with that."

Nobody had anything better than that, so we moved on.

Ricky suggested we wait until dark and investigate the area immediately around the house that night. We would then sleep there and delve deeper the next day. We all agreed that if what Lance had told us was true—about every tree and every rock in town being haunted—we should be able to get solid evidence anywhere we went.

We sat and waited for Lance to get back and discussed our plan. We decided we all wanted to get to Whistler Road as early as possible the next day, seeing as how Lance had described it as the heart of whatever curse hung over the town. I was chomping at the bit to get out there and dive into everything, needing some further explanation for my earlier outburst in the truck and my perplexing vision after Big Bear had knocked me out. I knew, however hard, it was best to throttle back my anxiousness. Whatever was wrong there that could cause people to disappear, out of the blue, without any trace, for all eternity, was bigger than me and my ego.

BOOM!

It sounded like an anvil had been dropped from ten feet in the air onto the floor above us. We all simultaneously leapt from our seats on the couch and faced the ceiling. The incredibly heavy thump was so loud and so sudden that it sent a quick rush of adrenalin into my system. It was as though a car had crashed into the roof of the house—a fantastically jarring strike, disorienting and violent. It felt aggressive. It immediately felt purposeful to me for reasons that, to this day, I can't explain.

Gary screamed like a frightened woman. Ricky and Big Bear simultaneously shouted the same expletive. I made no kind of noise but went from somewhat drowsy and comfortable to having every one of my senses purely concentrated and homed in on the ceiling above me in that instant. Whatever it was made the entire room shake. Several of the unfamiliar portraits tilted to either side. Even the potted fig trees swayed back and forth for a moment.

"What in the fuck was that?" shouted Ricky.

Nobody answered; everyone was still just staring at the ceiling, listening intently for any further noises—anything that might give an explanation as to what in the hell it was. When something like this happens, it is human nature to immediately begin trying to come up with explanations for it. I can remember being surprised at how quickly, in my mind, I tried coming up with something that could have explained the crash. I thought maybe a limb from one of the trees might have broken off and struck the top of the house. The idea that a meteor might have happened upon the roof did not get immediately ruled out. The problem I had was attempting to reconcile the sheer violence of the crash with anything realistic that could have caused it.

"Is there an upstairs to this room?" asked Big Bear. "Whatever that was, it was directly above us."

There were chills throughout my entire body at that point. A couple of moments had gone by since the bizarre, thundering strike had sent shockwaves throughout the entire residence. My mind had begun racing through the worst possible hypotheticals.

"There might be an attic above us," I suggested. My voice had gone intense, yet shaky. "This room was a late addition, remember? Lance's granddaddy built it. There are no stairs anywhere, so I don't think there's a top floor, but maybe an attic." I immediately wished I hadn't come up with the idea that there might be an attic above us with something lurking inside of it. Something capable of creating such a violent and sudden crash. I liked the idea of a falling branch or meteor better. You never consider how close the floor above you is until you are standing, staring at the ceiling, afraid of what might be on the other side of it. If there was an attic and there was something up there, it was not three feet from us. It would have been just on the other side of a few inches of flooring and drywall, lying on the floor, listening intently, enjoying our conversation, drinking in the terror it had thrust upon us.

"I'm going outside to look around," I announced.

Big Bear, Gary, and Ricky followed along, and we all headed back into the original part of the house. It was darker than it had been when we arrived and darker than it should have been under any kind of normal circumstances. The amount of clutter and hoarded garbage that was piled floor to ceiling throughout the residence blocked much of the normal light that should have been flooding into the place. The entire first floor glowed in a kind of dark, golden hue. The dim sunlight that was left after passing through Lance's brown drapery was all that illuminated our path. The smell seemed to have gotten impossibly worse since the last time we had passed through. Everyone was completely silent as they followed me back to the front door. This house was a terrible place to have to find your way out of. It gave off a sense that if you made a wrong turn, you could be stuck for hours trying to navigate out of the slovenly chaos.

The only sound was water dripping onto the wretched stack of dishes in the kitchen that we had put behind us moments before. I hate the sound of water dripping. It is one of the seminal signs of a demonic presence. Most, if not all, documented demonic episodes describe the sound of a dripping faucet in the days leading up to a confrontation or possession. Typically, in those cases, the source of the dripping is unexplainable and unable to be found anywhere on the premises. At least in this case, we knew for a fact that it was coming from the kitchen sink. For this reason, throughout the course of my entire professional life, anytime I would hear dripping water, I would stop at nothing and move mountains until I was able to locate the source. If I couldn't, I'd leave immediately and wouldn't go anywhere near the place again.

We were nearly to the front door when the second crash occurred. It was even more jarring than the first, as we were all silent before it happened. Our level of fear and adrenalin was already heightened. I leapt high enough off my feet that for a moment, I could feel the spackle from the ceiling brush against the top of my ball cap. We were all thrust into a panic. Again, it was a single, violent smash above the addition we had just come from. We all turned as it happened. Several piles of junk were disturbed as the thump again shook the entire house. Stacks of papers toppled over; some fluttered about briefly before scattering on the floor.

We were all facing the pathway through the filth that we had just come through, half expecting at any moment to see a shadow coming toward us. My mind raced. Perhaps whatever was responsible for the disturbance had managed to break its way through the ceiling and into the addition. Perhaps the monster was just around the corner and getting ready to pounce. I could feel my pulse hammering in my chest and temples. Big Bear had begun his typical perfuse sweating ritual. Gary was in the middle of some sort of an extreme episode of hyperventilation. Ricky, somehow, only appeared slightly concerned. For whatever reason, he always seemed, in even the most extreme situations, to have ice water flowing through his veins.

"All right, let's get the fuck outside!" I shouted, needing to get out of that house for fear of a third thump causing something heavy to topple over on top of me, burying me forever in an endless pile of rubbish. Nobody argued as I swung the door open and we all exited the house and headed back through the saturated yard and onto the sparse, white-rocked driveway. As we piled out, Lance was pulling back in, with my rental car. He had the window rolled down as he pulled up to us.

"What's going on, guys?" he asked.

I explained the situation to him as calmly as possible. I hoped he might have an explanation for the terrifying crashing sounds above his addition. Perhaps they were something that happened often. Unfortunately, Lance was just as confused and mystified as all of us by what I had explained to him. He had picked up several pizzas from a friend he had in town who apparently provided a kind of food service for the holed-up residents of Ashford. He left them in the passenger seat and got out, joining us in the driveway.

"You heard the thumps above the addition?" Lance asked. "There's nothing above the addition but a roof. There's no second floor or attic or anything."

This brought about a bit of relief. At least we knew that whatever might have caused the two mammoth thuds wasn't physically inside of the house. I guess that just proved that whatever it was, was on the roof. For some reason, that registered as less terrifying to me.

"Let's head around back and see if we can see anything," I suggested.

We all followed Lance down to the end of the driveway and around the garage into a poorly manicured but somewhat spacious backyard. It was a solid half acre from the back of the house to the wooded tree line behind it. The grass was longer and every bit as saturated as the front. The sky was still clouded, and the daylight was holding on to its last gasp before night again put it into submission. The distant maple trees had melted into a yellow-green mass that separated the yard from the rest of the world. Only a few were individually discernable in the quickly diminishing twilight.

There was no external lighting, and we knew we had maybe fifteen minutes to figure out what had caused the crashes above the addition before it would become impossible to see. We reached the addition. It jutted off the back of the house at a ninety-degree angle, directly into the center of the backyard. It had the same cornflower-blue siding and white trim as the rest of the place, but it did seem a bit newer and better maintained. It still looked shabby, just less shabby then the rest of the property. The outside was somewhat of a strange contrast to the modern and well-kept inside of that room.

My idea of a tree limb having slammed into the roof was already on thin ice once we heard the second crash. It was put completely to rest when we arrived in the backyard. There were no overhanging trees, and none in the immediate vicinity had limbs large enough to create a disturbance as violent as we had witnessed inside, let alone two of them in rapid succession.

It was not a tall structure. We walked around the entire perimeter of the addition at enough of a distance that we could clearly see from the edge of the roof all the way up to its peak. It was maybe sixteen feet above us at its highest point. There was nothing on the roof and no chance of anything hiding from us up there.

What chilled me the most was the fact that there was absolutely no sign of damage of any kind. If there was no attic and no upstairs, something had to have taken the brunt of those consecutive, incredibly jarring strikes. That something should have been that roof. Having felt the sheer intensity and violence of the events—strong enough to shake the entire residence—there should have been, at the very least, minor structural damage. There should have been a few shingles out of place, a torn stretch of felt paper, a length of gutter or two dislodged. Hell, I expected to see a full-scale crater in that roof. There was nothing of the sort. The roof looked as good as the day it was built—not a single sign of damage. We spent a few more uneasy minutes in the backyard, searching for an explanation that we would not find. Not on that night, at least.

18

Having stood around the backyard for longer than any of us were comfortable with, we decided to head back inside. It was obvious that the answer to the raucous thumping noises that had driven us out there was not to be found. It was also beginning to grow darker by the moment, and visibility was becoming compromised. Something had to have produced those thunderous crashes, and that something had to be in that yard. The idea of standing exposed with the chance of it still lurking around, now with the cover of darkness on its side, did not sound appealing to any of us.

With a deep sense of apprehension, we all headed back into the study. It was, after all, the one room in the house where one could possibly be productive in any way. We ate pizza, drank bottled water, tried to shake off our exploding nerves, and talked. After a brief discussion, we decided we needed to get right to the heart of the troubles as early as possible, the next morning. First light, we would all pile in the Malibu and head straight to Whistler Road. Lance knew a few backwoods roads we could take, avoiding the middle of town and, therefore, limiting our chances of running into the officials.

We were all still very much on edge from the crashes that had occurred on the roof. Any little noise caused us all to twitch in a defensive over-alertness. I needed to find a way to calm my nerves a bit, so I decided to dive back into Kenneth Harvey's book. I skipped ahead to his arrival in Ashford. I wanted to know what he had found out about the asylum that had burned down. Mainly, I wanted to learn more about Roderick Crowe and why the surviving patients had referred to him as The Divine Father. Something told me that that entire storyline would answer some of the many questions I had swimming around my head since my arrival.

The Medical Memoirs of Kenneth Harvey

The last thing I remember when I left Ashford was County Line Road. Not a lot about it had changed since my departure many years before. When I left, it was dirt. Now it was covered over in a hardened mixture of cinders and gravel, no doubt allowing for more traction in the harsher seasons that were not at all uncommon in this share of god's country. The road was much smoother now than I previously remembered. The sheriff had arranged my pickup at the train station in Cleveland, and this road represented the last half hour of the four-hour journey in the Pontiac police car.

Some of the familiar County Line landmarks were still there from when I had departed. The Ashford/Baines Hunters Supply Market was still in business, likely busy in this latter summer season as the deer would have begun venturing from their depleted food sources and closer to the populous. The Ashford Reserve Grain and Seed Exchange was still open down the way a bit. It looked dilapidated, no doubt a victim of the depleted farming industry in the area. There were still a few men along the side of the main grange shoveling feed into the back of a carriage, so, at least it was not completely dead in the water. It very likely though was well into its death throes.

The last time I had traveled that road, my mind and body were bursting with excitement about my chance to travel to Virginia to attend university. The University of Virginia at Charlottesville would only accept twelve out-of-state enrollees per year, and I had to lobby, with the help of my parents and local teachers, for a good year before I finally got the letter of acceptance. On my way out, I knew I would be entering an odyssey of sorts, one that would likely keep me away from Ashford for a prolonged period. I never thought I would have been away as long as I had. My parents had died several years previously, and I should have traveled back then, but I was far too focused on my work and had little means with which I could have made the journey.

What a whack job, I thought. Who doesn't even have time to go home for their parents' funerals? Yet, the bastard didn't have any problem dropping everything and heading back to Ashford as soon as they needed his help figuring out why a building burned down. They apparently hadn't taught him much about compassion or priorities or work-life balance while he was off "attending university." I shook it off and continued reading.

Completely contrary to the feeling of excitable elation that flooded me on the day of my departure was this horrible feeling of paranoia that began to overtake me on Country Line Road on my way into Ashford that day. It was as though we had driven into a fog that nobody could see but we could all feel. There was a certain point before which everything was normal. I had been immersed in some of the nostalgia of the old town. After which, however, everything went stale. I understood what the sheriff had referred to when he told of a cloud that hung over Ashford. I felt we had just driven directly into it.

I began vomiting out of the side of the Pontiac. The overwhelming terror I had begun feeling finally forced me to give in to the mounting nausea. I hadn't eaten much that day—a couple of apples on the train and a few pieces of buttered bread at the train station, so most of my heaves were empty.

The most curious thought went through my head as I finished my vomiting. I looked down at my portfolio, which I had open on my lap. I had a fountain pen tucked into it, next to my journal. A very nearly uncontrollable compulsion flooded over me. I envisioned grasping my fountain pen and thrusting it into the throat of the driver. Its point was sharp enough to break through the skin easily, and with a bit of work, I imagined pulling it to and fro in such a way that would have severed his carotid artery system into his head. I didn't care for the obvious repercussions that would have resulted in the immediate term—as in the car inevitably crashing. Or, for that matter, in the long term—as in my going to jail and likely the electric chair. None of it seemed to matter to me. I felt trapped—as though he were driving me into that town against my will, even though I had announced my intention to come, days in advance.

I had never felt that kind of rage in my life. I am not a person who has ever been described as aggressive or moody. But that one spell, that horrible fit of murderous indignation, would come to dominate my thoughts throughout my time there. After a few moments of sitting in the side seat of the Pontiac, panting, staring creepily at my driver, I managed to collect my thoughts. I was sweating and had begun feeling an awkward sense of shame toward myself. I had not done anything wrong. I had not acted on any of my compulsions, but the fact remained that I had wanted to. In the heat of my fervor, those terrible thoughts resonated as though they were advisable, as though ripping the throat of my driver out was somehow the right thing to do. That worried me. I feared that I would soon fall into another spell, and if it were but a bit stronger, I would become unable to control myself.

After another twenty or so minutes, we arrived at the town center. It had remained very similar to how I remembered it. There did, however, seem to be a noticeable lack of commerce. It had once been a bustling hub of activity. It still was compared to the outskirts of town, but much emptier than I'd remembered.

The courthouse still stood in the dead center of town. It was still the tallest structure—six stories, with its red brick, surrounded by four entrances which were flanked by two white pillars each. Its gold steeple sat atop the middle of it. I had been up there when I was in school, and you can see all the way to the next town on a sunny day. The sheriff's station was next door, which blended in with the other buildings. The entirety of the area was comprised of three-story Victorian brick buildings. They were built in two nearly identical strips along the sides of the town center, surrounding the courthouse. They were predominantly red brick when I left, and now, upon my arrival, they had faded significantly to more of a rusty, brownish hue. A singular white overhang ran along the top story of the structures, adding to the architectural ambiance of the area, neatly tying the otherwise boring brick structures into the grandeur of the white-pillared courthouse.

The flanking buildings, while attached to one another, housed numerous stand-alone establishments. All the necessary clerical and municipal agencies for Ashford and the surrounding communities called them home. There was a title agency called "Bert's Page" on one side, flanked on the other by a newspaper called "The Ashford Sentinel." There was even a pub next to the sheriff's station. None of this had been there when I left. The buildings were the same, the businesses far different.

There were, however, a few familiar holdovers from my growing up there. Harder's Grocery and Restaurant was still in its familiar location, tucked away into the south corner of the property. The old Wahoga Trust Bank still stood, catty-corner, across the way from Harder's. Behind the Victorian buildings on the west side of town, I was still able to spot the smokestack of the old Fawcett Tile Plant. It still jutted upward, tall enough to be seen from any point in Ashford Center. The familiar dark smoke of a tough day's work inside billowed out of its cap.

There was still the one road that went around in a loop and then back out the way it came in. The road formed an oval around the courthouse in the middle and along the front of the adjacent three-story buildings. It was still technically County Line Road; however, about a hundred yards before entering the town square, it, for some reason, had become Country Main Street. This was another new aspect to my hometown that had changed since I had left. I assumed it was a way to instill more of a sense of community among the long-dwindling populous. After all, what is a town without a Main Street?

We parked, and I followed the driver into the front door of the sheriff's station. I was pleasantly surprised by the general tidiness of the place. The doors and floors were creaky, which was to be expected out of a building that age. All in all, it seemed solid, well taken care of, far from disrepair. The white tiled floors were pristine and looked but a few years old at most. One thing Ashford always had were exquisite tile floors, getting the deeply discounted pick of whatever was left over from the tile plant.

I was greeted first by a woman with wild brown hair who sat at a desk next the front door. She had obviously known of my eventual arrival in advance and introduced herself before I could properly take in my surroundings. Her name was Ruth Daniels, and she was a warm, stoic, Midwestern woman—a prime example of the persona I had recalled pretty much everyone to possess from the region. She took my jacket and quickly invited me down a well-lit hallway that led clear to the back of the building. We came to a door marked "Sheriff Williams." She knocked, opened the door to let me in, and bid me adieu.

As I entered the room, the sheriff immediately greeted me. I knew instantly that I had seen him before, but I could not recall the specific context. It had been so long since I had been to town, and when I had left, he was not the sheriff. I would later recall that he was a deputy under the sheriff of my time, and he had looked familiar because he had come to our grade school and taught us a class on hunting safety once. I never became much of a hunter, so it did not surprise me that the memory did not resonate.

He thanked me for coming and again explained how proud he was of me. He explained again what a fine example I had apparently been built up as around town. It almost made me feel bad for him. At no point in my life, to that point, had I felt like I was doing anything all that special. In their sullen eyes, however, mired in an impoverished and simple community, what I did for a living seemed far more impressive than most known trades of their own.

I quickly found that the situation had remained the same as was described in his letter to me. There had really been no progress over the three days that it had taken me to make my decision to come and to get myself there. The three survivors of the blaze at the lunatic asylum were still borderline incoherent. They were still unable to elicit any kind of intelligible information from them about the fire. There had still been no evidence of any other survivors of the fire or any evidence of their remains in the wreckage. Unfortunately, they were unable to produce any sort of previous medical documentation for the three subjects, fearing that it had been burned, along with everything else inside of the asylum. They had not yet been able to even get their names. He advised me that they had been referring to the blond female as Mary, the brunette female as Rose, and the male as Fred. Evidently, the patients had even begun responding to those names. This fact called into question whether they even knew their true names.

I demanded to see them immediately, and the sheriff obliged. We headed downstairs into the basement of the building. The walls were dark—the foundation of the station was comprised of mortared, chipped bedrock. It was well lit, as was the rest of the station, and as clean as any subterranean level could be in a building that old. It was warmer down there than the rest of the station, which seemed overtly drafty to me since my arrival.

I followed the sheriff down a narrow, rock corridor which opened to a series of black, cast-iron holding cells. My heart sank for a moment at the thought of these three devastated human beings having escaped whatever deplorable conditions they knew at the asylum for another jail cell a few miles away. My worry was quickly put to rest when I saw them. They were behind bars, but only the one set that enclosed them into the entire holding area. The rest of the cages were opened, allowing them to move about freely. There were four cells in total, and Mary, Rose, and Fred were the only occupants.

The four cells in which they were contained had been crudely covered over with pillows and mattresses that lined the walls and bars. Only the basement windows were left uncovered. This was for the patients' own protection. The typical wooden-slat beds had been removed from the cells and replaced with more formal twin beds to offer a little more comfort. One of the toilets and showers had been walled off, complete with a portable, enclosed, private dressing area.

All three looked well fed and watered. This was the only positive note I could strike regarding my first impression of the patients. The good sheriff had certainly been telling the truth in his letter to me when he had described them. All three sat in a row on the floor on the far side of the room from where we had entered. The mattress behind them protruded outward, forcing their upper bodies to slouch over their lower extremities. Each sat on the ground with their legs stretched straight outward in front of them.

The sheriff explained to me that this was how they would sit in between the time they woke up and the time they would sleep. This did not bode well for any sort of cognitive brain function. The act of sitting like that for any normal human would quickly become far too painful to bear, as it would prohibit the blood flow to the lower back and keep the tendons in the legs stretched to capacity.

As we approached, the smell that wafted from them became repugnant. It was strong enough to stop me in my tracks. Each had still been unable to regain the ability to use the facilities and had instead taken to continuously soiling the ground around themselves. They were dressed in thin, fleece robes which I assumed were easier to clean and get on and off for their daily assisted washings.

There was no dignity to any of them. Mary and Rose both sat with their breasts completely exposed, out of the robes. Their legs rested far enough apart to leave nothing to the imagination. Fred was the same. His robe wasn't even tied in the front and just hung open, exposing the entirety of his nude body to anyone who might be looking.

They made absolutely no acknowledgement of our approach—not even one of them moved to look at us. This was another strike to the already-slim chance of me getting anything out of them. The very real possibility that these people were clinically brain-dead had occurred to me. It was entirely possible that they had been in this state prior to entering the asylum. For all we knew, they could have been involved in some series of horrific accidents that had brought them to this. Without any sort of formal identification or previous medical documentation, this proved impossible to know.

I was holding on to a few shreds of hope, however. If these people had been in this state at the time of the fire, they should have never been able to escape. They were found near the woods, several hundred yards from the dormitory where they belonged. They had to have gotten themselves there somehow, indicating that motor activity was not impossible. There was also the fact that the sheriff had managed to get a response from them when he mentioned Roderick Crowe's name. Mind you, it was a negative response, culminating in them referring to him as The Divine Father. But nonetheless, it was a response, indicating that there was still some level of neural dexterity taking place.

I approached Fred. I took my cigarette lighter out of my pocket and flicked it, igniting the wick. I grabbed Fred's hand and quickly ran it through the flame. He pulled his hand back from me as quickly as anyone else would have in that situation. He made no other movements or noises. None were necessary. The fact that he had a conscious reaction to physical pain meant his brain was still somewhat functional.

I repeated with Rose and got the same reaction. As I approached Mary, however, I found her looking at me and shaking. She looked terrified. I knew then that I was going to have to approach them, going forward, a bit more compassionately. I gently held my hand over Mary's eyes and counted to sixty. I released my hands, holding her left eye open. I was able to see her pupil grow back to its normal size as the light from the room flooded back into it. I knew then that she had some semblance of brain function as well.

Of the three of them, I knew that I was most likely to gain the best possible information from Mary. She was the only of the three who had showed any kind of an emotional response to my presence—cowering in fear having observed my lighter test on her colleagues. This indicated a higher level of mental competency than the other two, who had just allowed it to happen without showing any emotion, only reflex. I gently grasped the bands of her robe and closed the outsides over her exposed torso, tying it tightly so it would not easily come loose again. I did the same for Fred and Rose, yet they could not have cared less. Mary, however, had begun following me around the area with her eyes. She had even begun making subtle throaty noises and squeaks. This was clearly my subject.

I let the sheriff know that I would likely only be able to work with Mary and that I doubted anything could be gleaned out of the other two. I recommended they be transferred to another hospital immediately, where they could be properly cared for. I decided to get a feel for Mary's lymph nodes in her neck, just for a basic idea of what sort of health she might be in. In doing so, she obliged me by tilting her head backward. As I looked on at her face, I immediately removed my hands and lurched back away from her. With her head tilted back, I was able to see her nose from underneath, and I was immediately mortified and saddened by what I observed. I quickly moved over to Fred and Rose, tilting their heads back, finding the same terrible symptom.

Each of their left nostrils was significantly widened and damaged compared to the right. While the right nostril could be seen inside of, to the point that it reached their frontal sinus, the left seemed to have been bored out, allowing me to see deep into a seemingly endless tunnel, inching upward into their craniums. I had heard of this before but had never actually seen it in practice. I knew what it represented, and it sickened me. Quickly, everything that was wrong with these poor people made sense. All three of them had, at some point recently, been lobotomized.

Lobotomy is a highly invasive, surgical procedure that the Europeans came up with. Allegedly, it remedied several types of psychotic behavior. To perform one, a "doctor" would insert a sharp speculum of some sort into the patient's nostril, literally hammer it through the sinus walls, run it all the way to the brain of the patient, and detach the tissue that binds the prefrontal cortex of the brain to the skull. And it absolutely didn't work. Like so many other conceptual procedures in the psychological field, some imbecilic nurse likely cured a patient by other means, but at some point between the actual cure and anyone declaring the patient as cured, they lobotomized him or her. So naturally, being the barbarians that they are, they assumed it was the lobotomy that had resolved the issue.

I was positively staggered by what I was seeing. A lobotomy is something that a neurosurgeon might perform once in his entire career. And that circumstance would have to come about under the most extreme set of circumstances. The patient would need to have been a mortal danger to themselves or the people around them. All other remedies would have had to have been tried and retried many times over before something so extreme could be authorized. The fact that I was sitting on the floor in an otherwise respectable American town and seeing three patients who appeared to have been lobotomized as recently as a few weeks prior positively broke my heart.

I knew that there was now very little hope of getting any information out of them, even Mary. When I say lobotomies don't work, I don't just mean that they don't cure the present psychological affliction. They also inflict a tremendous amount of additional damage in the process. It is a lazy, irresponsible procedure and is something I truly wish could be denounced from the medical world for all eternity. Inevitably, as the "doctor" would insert and begin thrashing around with the speculum to detach the prefrontal cortex from the brain cavity, the patient would move. In many cases, the subject would violently shudder about in reaction to the incredibly unnatural and cruel procedure. In doing so, the speculum would not only slice through the gray material that handles the attachment to the skull, but also would inevitably cut through the prefrontal cortex itself, causing irreparable, permanent brain damage. It is widely believed that the prefrontal cortex is responsible for the vast amount of what we perceive as mental awareness—the ability to know right from wrong, the ability of a human being to be able to understand that if they are dirty, then bathing would make them clean, if they are cold then they should try to get warm. If this region of the brain becomes badly damaged enough—and it often does under such horrific circumstances—you essentially end up with Mary, Rose, and Fred.

I stood and shouldered my way through the mattresses that had been draped over the door and approached the sheriff. I was livid. I specifically remember what I said to him, but I will exclude any expletives that may or may not have been included.

"You presume to call yourself the sheriff of this town, sir. Well, can you shed some light on the egregious, illegal, irresponsible medical malpractice that quite obviously has been running rampant at Ashford Hill?"

Since it was a state-run facility, the sheriff and his department had no power over anything that went on there. To be honest, I knew that, but anger had taken ahold of me. I had to let it out somehow, and I chose the sheriff as my scapegoat. As my time in Ashford would go on, I would find Sheriff Williams to be a delightful fellow and one of the finest men I had ever worked with. At that point, however, I approached the Sheriff. I explained to him why his patients were the way they were and how they had come about such lowly states. I explained to him the procedure that brought them to it and how absurd it was to see something like that in one patient in a lifetime, let alone three in one day.

He shared in my disgust and my heartfelt sorrow for Fred, Mary, and Rose, none of whom would likely ever recall their original names. I still held out a fleeting spark of hope that Mary would be of some value. Perhaps her lobotomy had not produced the same level of damage as it obviously had in Fred's and Rose's cases.

I took the rest of the day to formulate my plan. The sheriff provided me with one of the offices upstairs. I needed to rest and figure out how I planned to work with Mary. I was barely able to stomach my dinner that night at Harder's Restaurant. I was provided lodging in the local hotel, free of charge, for the duration of my stay.

I met with Mary first thing in the morning. I found her surprisingly alert compared to her previous, deplorable state of mind. She had been brought upstairs ahead of my arrival back to the station and was waiting for me in my office, directly next to the sheriff's. I found her staring out the first-floor window with a hint of a smile, watching the birds frolic in the maple trees across the street. She had been significantly cleaned up and dressed in a relatively attractive skirt and sweater. Despite her obvious and well-documented struggles, she was an attractive woman. Her shoulder-length red hair was recently washed and reflected the morning sunlight through the window. Her eyes, while tortured and distant, were large and round, once beautiful. She had tremendous features and a striking body when she wasn't wallowing around in her own filth in the basement of a police station. She sat in the chair across from my empty desk. I sat on the other side of the desk and broke the ice, attempting to communicate.

"So, Mary," I asked. "You and your friends downstairs sure are lucky to have escaped such a horrific fire, wouldn't you say?"

I received no response, as well as no sort of acknowledgement of my presence.

I tried again. "Tell me about how you came to be committed to Ashford Hill."

Again, nothing. She sat, as she had before my entrance into the room, staring out the window with that subtle smile.

"Sweetheart, do you like those birds outside? How would you like it if we went out there and took a closer look?"

Her eyes widened subtly, but her head still did not budge. I could tell that I had hit some kind of still operational part of her brain with my offer.

"I walked over here today," I continued. "It sure is gorgeous outside. Listen, let's just start by you telling me what your real name is."

 I still received no further indication that I was getting through to her at all. I decided to take a different approach.

"You know, Mary, Dr. Crowe burned to death inside of that asylum. Yep, good old Roderick Crowe has lobotomized his last patient. It sure is a shame that he is dead and gone, never to be heard from again, huh?"

Quickly, as soon as I finished, her head snapped from the window to me, face to face. She spoke in a deep, raspy voice. Very little of her vocal tone could be attributed to anything remotely female. Had I not been able to see her speaking the words, I would have assumed they had come from an elderly man as he choked out his final remarks from his deathbed. "To think that The Divine Father is dead is heresy, and nonbelievers will agonize their judgment."

I shook off the chills that I had rush through me at such an unlikely response and voice from Mary. "So, he isn't dead? Is that what you think? Because we found several of his teeth, no longer attached to the pile of ashes that used to be his face. So, I don't feel like it is all that far-fetched to believe that Roderick Crowe is dead."

"His body," she replied, "all of our bodies, are merely the vehicles with which our senses of being have access to in this realm."

I was thrilled to be eliciting these sorts of responses from her. While the context of her responses might have been suspect, these were highly intelligent, constructive, even philosophical thoughts that she was projecting. This suggested that her brain was more than capable enough to assist us.

"What's your real name, sweetie?"

"Margaret, Margaret Peirce."

"Okay, Margaret. I really like that name, I always have. My name is Dr. Kenneth Harvey. Tell me, how did you come to be institutionalized?"

"I don't remember."

"That's okay, that's okay. How come you seem okay now, but when I saw you yesterday, you seemed so distant and lethargic?"

Every response I received from her, her voice became a bit more feminine, almost trying to work its way back to normal, likely from years of not using it. "I don't remember seeing you yesterday. I don't remember anything since the last time the sheriff asked us all of his questions and I hit my head on the wall."

"He said you became very upset when he mentioned Roderick Crowe to you. You know, he was just a psychologist, and not a very good one. Had he lived, he would have likely spent the rest of his life in prison for what he did to all of you."

"What The Divine Father gave to all of us was a gift. A gift that none of you could possibly ever imagine."

"Margaret, he lobotomized you. He performed a procedure on you that has absolutely no medical benefit whatsoever. You're lucky to be able to hold your head up straight right now."

She began to laugh. It started as a kind of a brief snicker and continued into a hearty belly laugh. This went on for about a minute before she responded, still chuckling in between words, "I have never been lobotomized, sir."

"Margaret, I can see clear through to your brain through your nostril. How can you explain that, other than lobotomy?"

As she stopped laughing, the distant look returned to her. Her attention had once again shifted to the window as she responded, "What is god aside from the ability to control reality?"

I raised my voice a few decibels. "Margaret, stay with me here. What has that got to do with the fact that you've clearly been lobotomized?"

"Reality," she continued in a hoarse shout, "was our prison. The Divine Father showed us a way to transcend our shackles. He showed us the way into an everlasting ecstasy."

"What do you mean by 'an everlasting ecstasy'?"

The subtle smile had returned to her face as she watched the birds again, hopping from branch to branch of the maples. "You said so yourself, Kenneth Harvey: The ability to damage and manipulate the animal brain, is to mold reality—is to become . . . god."

I was floored. This woman was quoting something I had said to a professor of psychology at Princeton University seven years prior. There is absolutely no conceivable way for her to have been able to quote me. Prior to this memoir, I had never documented that quote in any fashion. There was simply no way for her to quote such an anomalous statement like that back to me. Yet, here she was, doing just that.

I snapped. "How did you know I said that?"

Her gaze returned to my eyes; her faint smirk had transformed into something of a sinister grin. "You see, Harvey? The Divine Father knows everything there is to know."

I couldn't keep my hands from trembling in my lap. "And how does he come to know of . . . everything?"

Her head tilted a fraction to the right, further inflaming the sinister gaze that she had begun pouring in my direction. "Through a far superior vantage point and unimaginable power."

"Would you care to elaborate a bit on that, Margaret?"

She replied, "In your left pants pocket, right now, you have a lighter and a handkerchief. In the right, you have a cheap timepiece that is exactly eleven minutes behind."

Almost involuntarily, I began fondling my pants pockets. I could feel the handkerchief in the left as it wrapped my lighter, corroborating her description. I didn't need to examine my pocket watch, since it had been precisely eleven minutes behind for several months prior.

I stood. A look of awe must have shown thick throughout my face. I slowly backed away a few steps, her malevolent gaze following me the entire time. I needed to regroup. I tried my damnedest to mask the unmistakable tremble to my voice. "So, Margaret, if this Divine Father knows everything and he seems to have shared his gift with you, then why don't you tell me what happened at Ashford Hill? How did it come to burn down?"

She had lost any note of playfulness, and her gaze had begun burning a hole through me as she responded, "The origin of the fire is not something that could be understood by you."

"Why don't you humor me, Margaret?"

"All things have a natural timeline with which they are locked. It was simply the building's time to go."

I was growing weary of her antics. "For god's sake! How would you like it if I took you back down into the cellar and parked you next to the others again? Trust me, this is Ashford; they'll never require your cell for anyone but you. Cut out this foolishness and just explain to me how the fire started."

Understanding that if she continued her dodging of my questions, this interview would abruptly conclude forever, leaving her to enjoy a cell in the dank basement of a police station for an undisclosed period, she spoke up. There was suddenly a more somber mood to her tone. "The Divine Father spoke of a disturbance. He spoke of it for weeks prior to the fire. He never explained it in any detail, just that it would lead to our family being broken up."

"Your family?"

"All of us in the hospital, he called us his family. For most of us, it was the only family we had. So, we adopted a family atmosphere. It was nice; it was something that, otherwise, a lot of us wouldn't have ever known."

"Okay, so why was your family being broken up?"

"He never explained that to us, just said it was inevitable. He told us we wouldn't need to worry. He would defend us from the disturbance. He said that our family would be together forever. He was acting strangely—very jumpy and sensitive. The day of the fire, everyone was gathered together and given a special regimen of medication."

I let out a disgusted groan. "Did the Divine Father, by any chance, explain to you what this special regimen consisted of?"

"It was the same thing he had always given to us. He would hold our heads back and inject a blue fluid into our left nostrils. We would gag as it hit us, but after a moment, it was pure bliss. I had been given that medication for a few months, about once per week. But the one from the day of the fire seemed so much stronger. He told us it was our final passage into his realm, into his family."

I didn't think there was a way for me to be more shocked than I had already been. But every sentence she spoke seemingly added to my frustration. This man, who was trusted with these patients' lives, had instead used them in some sort of cult-like experiment. Before Margaret had explained all of this to me, I had not felt obligated to help with the situation in Ashford. I felt it was the right thing to do, as though I were doing my old town a favor, but nothing that I absolutely needed to continue. If ever I felt the compulsion to leave, I would have. But as I listened to her more and more, I became motivated. As she explained these egregious abuses of practice by Crowe, I became more than determined to get to the bottom of everything involved in this case.

"Were you ever given any indication as to what this medication was?"

"No, just that it was our key to the realm of The Divine Father."

"Well, can you explain to me a little about what it would do for you when it was administered?" I thought perhaps I might be able to deduce what it was if I could understand its effects.

"It wouldn't do much for about ten minutes except burn the inside of your nose, terribly. Sometimes the pain was too much to bear. But then, as suddenly as the pain would come, it would wash away. Most of the time, I would watch my own body, like from above. I could even hear people's conversations around me while my body below appeared to be asleep. Then I would go on a journey. Not one that would make any sense to you whatsoever. It felt like I was taking a tour of my soul, as though I were moving through myself, my very sense of being. There would be shapes—they looked like snowflakes but so much more complex. They would melt into one another as I flew through them. I could see other beings floating along with me. They looked like brilliant, glowing spirits. None of them had a definitive head or body or were male or female; they were just pure, beautiful energy. Somehow, I was able to identify them as my friends from the asylum, there with me in that realm. We would float there for a while and eventually make our way to a city. The city was so beautiful. I somehow felt like I belonged there. I so wanted to stay. The buildings were all made from glass, taller than any I have ever seen. It looked like something from a thousand years into the future. And when we would get there, The Divine Father would be there to welcome us with open arms. He was the only one with a face we could make out. He had a mouth, eyes, and ears, but his body was like ours—made of pure angelic energy, only he was a deep, indescribable shade of crimson. He would only remain that way for a brief time, so we could identify him, and then he would take his spirit form."

"His spirit form?" I asked.

"Indescribable. His spirit form represented something far more profound than anything native to this realm. There is no comparison to describe it against."

I had absolutely no idea what kind of known substance could elicit this type of psychological episode. My previous research certainly had not provided me with knowledge of anything like she had described.

"And what happened once you made it to this city with your . . . Divine Father?"

"We would all become one. He would embrace us, and we became, a part of something larger. I don't know exactly what it was, but it seemed familiar, like a place I had been a thousand times. To me, it seemed like the place where my soul belonged. It was like heaven."

"And how long would these voyages last?"

"Most of the time, they would only last a few hours, a day at the most. But the most recent dose, which was given to me the day of the blaze, only wore off a few hours ago. We were relatively new to the program; we only started on the medication a couple months ago. The others, they were further along. Some of them, who had been taking it for years, their heads seemed to grow much larger. Their foreheads would protrude out several inches more than what was natural. Even their faces would swell."

"You know what this sounds like to me, Margaret? This sounds like Roderick Crowe tricked all of you. It sounds like he wanted to drug you all, get you into a comatose state, and then burn the building down, killing everyone inside."

"Then why can't you find any remains except Crowe's?"

She had me there.

"Tell me more about the people whose heads would swell up."

"It was about, maybe thirty or forty people. They were the closest to The Divine Father. They received special privileges and had their own wing in the lower level to themselves. They had all been administered to the asylum, the same as all of us, but after a while on the medication, their symptoms disappeared. They became better than they were before being checked in. One man, I only knew him as Henry, was unable to read or write, and his brain damage was quickly causing him to lose his ability to speak. He struggled through sentences; it was impossible to find the time to wait for him to get his point across. I ran into him a few months later. His head had blown up to twice its normal size. It almost looked like the back of his skull was going to burst through the skin. His hair seemed sparse since it had become spread out over such a large area. I could see the veins in his neck had swollen, and his pulse pounded through his bloated temples. But then he suddenly began speaking to me in such a sophisticated fashion. He sounded like one of the doctors. He explained to me his entire past and how he ended up in the asylum. He told me of books he had been reading, how The Divine Father gave him a life he was finally proud of."

"Margaret, do you have any idea of what happened to all of those people? What happened to all your friends from the asylum? How come none seemed to have been in the building when it burned?"

"I remember being administered the medication that day; then I remember traveling to the city and becoming one with The Divine Father, and the next thing I can remember was when the sheriff was asking me questions in the basement of this station. I don't know how or why I was not inside of the asylum when it burned to the ground. None of us had any means of getting outside. I do have one suspicion, though."

"And what is that, Margaret?"

"The medication had some strange, unexplainable effects. There was one dose I was given in my room, which was locked from the outside. Once I was given the drug, I can clearly remember the orderly leaving the room and locking me in from the outside. I can remember lying in my bed, waiting for the drug to take its effect on me. It did, shortly thereafter. But when I came to, I was in the boiler room in the basement, which had also been locked. I have no recollection as to how I got there. I was lying on the concrete floor, inches away from the scalding-hot boiler tanks. If I had walked there, I would have had to get out of my room, which, again, was locked from the outside; passed several nurse stations which would keep watch on us, all day and night. I would have then had to have gotten into the locked basement, into the locked boiler room, and then managed to relock the door to my own room as well as the basement and boiler rooms. It absolutely defied all logic that I had managed to get in there myself. It was impossible."

"How do you think it happened?"

"I assumed someone had brought me down there in my sleep. I didn't think much of it, to be honest with you, but then I started hearing others talk of the same type of things happening to them. Some even awoke to find themselves completely outside of asylum property. It became kind of a running joke among some of us. A few of the girls would giggle about wishing to wake up in Clark Gable's bed the next time. Crowe was constantly studying it. I don't even think he understood what was happening."

"Really? A few minutes ago, you were calling him 'The Divine Father' and telling me about how he knew everything there was to know."

"He knows more than anyone I have ever known."

"Fair enough, Margaret," I replied, chuckling. "Please continue."

"There was one time when Crowe gave one of the gentleman patients a larger dose, or so I heard, and he was placed in restraints and left alone in his room. His wrists and ankles were chained to his bed, which was bolted to the concrete floor. Somehow, three hours later, he was found the next town over, in Hunters Valley, lying nude in a ditch. He was brought back and questioned but obviously had no idea how he had gotten there."

"Why do you look at this Roderick Crowe in such a positive light? To me, he seems like a complete lunatic who had no business practicing medicine in any capacity."

"Dr. Harvey, we're all lunatics. Every one of us in that asylum was thrown out with the Sunday trash a long time ago. We were labeled, called things like mentally inept, crazy, retarded. Crowe gave us a way to transcend our horrible, forgotten-about lives. Imagine going through your entire life—and for all we know, you only get one—being locked away because someone else decided your mind wasn't acceptable enough to be a part of their world? Kenneth Harvey, that is a level of hopelessness that could never be properly described. It fosters a sense of sheer desperation, rage, deep-seated suicidal tendencies. Most of us, prior to Crowe coming along, would have much rather ended our own lives, if given one chance, then spend another moment struggling to come to grips with that reality."

"What did Crowe say to you? What did he say specifically that made you believe in what he was doing?"

She smiled and giggled a moment before responding, looking down at the desk, and then back to my eyes. "It is up to yourself, and only yourself, to choose the world you see."

19

"Lance, come in here a moment!" I shouted. I slapped the book shut as a shiver ran through my body.

"It is up to yourself, and only yourself, to choose the world you see." I had been telling that to my daughter on a weekly basis, since she was old enough to know what all those words meant. I began wondering where I had first heard that phrase, but I could have sworn I had made it up myself. I remember having felt proud of myself for having made up such a profound, intelligent-sounding, deep, insightful phrase.

"What is it, Danny?" asked Lance from behind the couch I was still sprawled out upon.

"Buddy, this book is starting to creep me out."

"Told you. It's a great place to start investigating this town."

"Firstly, the woman, the patient, describes this drug she was given in the old asylum. The experience she had on the drug is a spitting-goddamned-image of what I saw when Big Bear, over here, knocked me unconscious. Secondly, the woman says Crowe told her a phrase that I swear to god I made up myself, thirteen years ago."

"I don't know, Danny. Keep reading, and maybe it will help lead us to whatever in the hell is going on around here."

"How exactly did you come by this book?"

"It was just here in this house—in the attic when I moved in. My grandparents must have acquired it at some point. Don't ask me how. I really have no idea."

I pulled my phone out of my pocket and looked at the clock. It was approaching midnight. I had exactly one bar of service. This was the first micron of cellular service I had noticed on my phone since entering Ashford. Hesitant to move from that spot for fear of losing my bar, I quickly went to "Recent Calls" and phoned home. The phone rang three times before my half-asleep wife answered it.

"Daniel," she said, "you should look out the window."

"What?" I asked, completely taken by surprise by the way she had answered. "Honey, are you asleep? What are you talking about? What window?"

"The one toward the woods. You should look out the window that faces the woods."

To this day, as I look back at those horrible three days in Ashford, I do not believe I had been speaking to my wife at any point on that phone call. It was her voice, undeniably, but it was a note deeper, a tinge more serious, alarming, urgent.

"Ellen, how could you even know that there's a window in the room I'm in? One that faces the woods no less."

What came through that phone next was undeniably not my wife. It was the most terrifying voice I had ever heard. It was a throaty, grunting gnarl—something you would imagine only being possible through the vocal cords of Satan himself. "Daniel Hallowell," it shrieked, "look out the window, and face your destiny."

The call ended abruptly and immediately turned into a fast-busy signal. As soon as it did, another massive crash erupted above us, this one far more violent than either of the ones from earlier. It knocked every picture off the wall. Everything that was in the room lifted several inches off the floor and crashed back down. Several of the clay pots that had been holding fig trees crumbled and shattered in the tremor. The power went out to the house, enveloping us all in total blackness. Everyone was jolted wide awake and positively terrified.

We were all on our feet, speechlessly listening as the clutter throughout the house slowly settled. I expected the roof to cave in. It felt like the entire house had been lifted from its foundation and dropped back into place. My heart was pounding. I gazed down at my phone again. It was still blaring the fast-busy signal. I hung up and slid it back into my pocket with my badly trembling hand. I approached the window as I tried to gain any semblance of control over the countless, scattered, cloudy thoughts firing through my head. The back of my neck felt hot, my throat dry, my hands swollen and numb. I saw nothing but darkness at first, but as my eyes adjusted, I began to make out the scene. Into the trees, about thirty yards from my vantage point, I could see a mist beginning to form, just into the edge of the woods.

I immediately knew there was something wrong about it. It was pitch black, yet this mist was a brilliantly luminescent contrast against the night. It was thicker than fog—than smoke, even. It wasn't a flat-white color like fog, more of a shimmering, phosphorescent plume. With every hitching breath that escaped my mouth, the plume would double in size; it was already five times its original footprint.

As I gazed upon it, I began to feel those horrible emotions that had haunted my mind on the drive into town creep up again. It grew closer, and the closer it grew, the more my mind became flooded with thoughts of egregious acts. The idea of cold-blooded murder became as familiar to me as my own voice, as though I had committed it previously, as though I enjoyed it.

More terrifying, I let it in. I remember allowing the blood-lust to wash over me like a warm shower. I let it engulf me. I wanted to be a part of it. I wanted to take everyone in the room by their throats and squeeze until I felt something important break. The idea of their choking aroused me. The idea of punching through the skin of their necks and ripping out their throats nearly brought a tear to my eye. But not a tear of remorse or shame—a tear of pure bliss, elation.

The mist had crept its way to the point that it was right on top of the house, licking the very window where I stood in wild fascination. My fists clenched. My jaw trembled. I was shaking but not cold as rage racked my entire being to the point that it was overloading my nervous system. I not only wanted to kill everyone in my vicinity, I wanted to rip them out of existence. They and everyone else on the planet. I wanted to know their dreams and incinerate them. While they watched their dreams burn, I wanted to burn them. I wanted to exterminate their livelihoods and destroy every memory of their bloodline. I lusted in the idea of walking the earth alone, having reduced every other living thing to hot dust. I would bathe in their blood, quench my thirst with their dying tears, and laugh hysterically into their faces as they suffocated through their final pleas for mercy.

For a fleeting instant, a picture of my daughter, Annie, flashed through my head. There was an idea of love. I felt it in my chest as sure as I had ever felt anything in my life. An instant later, my entire torso began to burn as if my body had begun reacting with hostility toward the conflicting emotion. Any thought of love was not welcome within whatever I was becoming on that night. It was far more than a mere warm sensation in my gut; it was a scorching, physical, external burning, throughout my entire dermas. It was as though something were punishing me for evoking such a sensation. I knew I had to rid my head of it, for fear of literally becoming detached from my bones and melting into a smoldering heap of guts on the floor.

I stole a glance in the direction of the others. They had all since migrated to the far side of the room, as far from me as they could possibly get without leaving entirely. All their eyes were fixed squarely on me across from them in the darkened, lightless room. A look of complete dread shrouded each of their faces. Even Big Bear did not dare look me directly in the eye. Instead, he stood, awestruck, looking on at me as though I were some deranged stranger who had manifested out of thin air.

My voice wasn't even close to my own. I fixed my view on Big Bear. My words poured out in a screaming howl, firing through the blood that saturated my sinister grin: "I think I'll start with you, big boy. You'll bleed the most."

I realized what I was saying about halfway through the statement. But I made no effort to stop myself. I reveled in the level of intimidation I saw in their eyes. A full-blown Navy Seal literally shaking before me like a child who knows Daddy and his belt are on the way up the stairs.

I slowly returned my gaze back out the window. A man was standing just outside, inches from the glass, smiling back at me. He wore a black rain slicker, black pants, and black shoes with a white button-down shirt and black bow tie. Under any sort of normal circumstances, there would have been nothing exceptional about him. But these were far from normal circumstances. I was somehow able to immediately infer that he was not human. There was something about him that was too . . . perfect.

His parted, blond hair appeared plastic. It was perfectly formed and absolutely shimmering. His clothes were pressed so perfectly that it appeared he had never moved an inch in any of them. There was a gleam about him. He had that salesman smile that represented joy just as much as it did bad intentions. His vividness seemed one with the mist that he brought with him, as though they were both part of one larger, living organism. I somehow knew that one could not exist without the other. He had blue eyes that I could not help but investigate and feel like they were reading not only my present thoughts, but my entire history.

The man stood completely still, just staring directly at me with that sinister grin. Somehow, I knew his rage was a match for mine. At that point in time, we were brothers in arms. Without a single word exchanged between us, I knew we shared the same interests. This being, this angel of death, would go to the ends of the earth with me. He would be the wrath to my plague, a guardian at my side as I swept through humanity—slicing through everything and everyone that crossed my path.

It became apparent to me that I knew this man; I just had no idea how I knew him. He was, however, familiar to me. I latched on to that thought for a moment, trying desperately to understand it. I'd certainly never seen him before, at least not in present form. But his essence, his sense of being, was as familiar to me as my own mother. A horrifying construct of a man. A man who appeared to me as more of a spectral mannequin than anything remotely human was, in that moment, as intimate a colleague to me as anyone I had ever known in my life.

His mouth closed slowly, and he began to glide backward. My ears popped as the mist began to draw away from the window with him, so dense that it began to suck the atmospheric pressure from the room along with it. I was still unable to take my eyes off him as he slowly turned. The back of his silhouette was as perfect as the front. Slowly, he made his way back into the woods along with the mist. He seemed to flow as he moved away, in parallel with the hypnotic motions of the shimmering cloud that danced along with him.

As he moved away farther, nearly out of sight, I understood something about him very clearly. This was obviously not a man. That much I had established. But he was also not a ghost. I sensed that he was a force of nature, a being only explainable in theological terms, a being who transcended my understanding—or anyone else's, for that matter. Above all, he was not to be fucked with.

20
Lance Filner's Residence – Ashford, Ohio – 11:55 p.m.

I stood, observing my petrified colleagues. Adrenalin coursed through my veins. I felt a warm, syrupy substance dribble out of mouth and down my chin. Quickly wiping it away, I looked at my hand. It was saturated with a thin sheen of crimson. A moment later I realized I had chewed a gash into my tongue. The intensity of the rage I felt while eye-to-eye with the stranger was so powerful that I had inflicted, and subsequently failed to register, trauma to my own body. I looked down at my shirt. The front of it was nearly covered with my blood. The windowsill I had been watching the action from was coated as well. At that moment, the pain finally began to register. It was a sharp, throbbing burn that shot waves of misery throughout my entire upper body. I nearly keeled over as it hit me.

"Lance, do you have any ice?" Ricky asked.

Everyone was still staring at me, wide-eyed, mouths open, unable to fully grasp what could be afflicting me. Nothing from our previous paranormal experience drew any parallels to anything that was happening to me. The situation was unprecedented on nearly every level.

"I really don't, Ricky. I wish I did. I am sorry, Danny," a jittery and nervous Lance replied.

My mind had temporarily escaped the whirlwind of horrific emotion that came with the stranger. I was, however, still fixated on Big Bear. I was wrestling with my thoughts in such a way that was as foreign to me as Sanskrit. I wanted those thoughts out of my head. I wanted to go back to thinking through the situation logically, collaborating with my team, getting organized, analyzing what had happened, formulating a plan. If I had to put a number to it, perhaps 80 percent of me wanted calm and peace.

But there was another 20 percent that wanted something else entirely. Undeniably, it was there. A loud minority voice in my crowded conscious. This was the part of me that kept my eyes homed in on Big Bear's throat so intently that I could pick out the individual follicles of stubble over his larynx. My eyes would periodically dart to the shattered glass on the floor from one of the fallen portraits that had come down in the latest crash. My mind was a fog of violent undertones. I figured I could stumble over to the glass and, in one motion, pick up one of the bigger shards and twist it into Big Bear's throat, elude him as he bled out, and after a few minutes, nobody else would be able to match me physically. I could work through the rest of them at my leisure, killing them all one by one.

I shook my head from side to side a couple of times. My fists were clenched. I could again sense the rage gaining a foothold inside of me. But there was also an undeniable sense of shame. I was quickly destroying relationships with men whom I had looked at as brothers, hours before. If I allowed it to go further, I would not only cause irreparable damage to our friendship, I would kill as many of them as I could. I knew I had to get out of there, for the safety of myself and everyone around me. I darted toward them.

"Danny, stop! Let's just get in the car and get the fuck out of here," Ricky shouted as I approached. Everyone dove to one side or the other, parting my way through the door and out of the study.

I heard them shouting various phrases peppered with expletives as I weaved through the house toward the front door. Someone was after me, but they weren't keeping up—probably Gary. I knocked over at least three distinct piles of trash as I bolted through the clutter. After a few moments, I was out the door, across the yard, and into my Malibu. I didn't even bother to look to see if I had a pursuer. I hopped in and found the keys still in the ignition from Lance's pizza run. I started the engine, jammed the transmission into reverse and was out of the driveway and onto the road in a matter of seconds.

I think about that moment from time to time. Maybe I want to think they came after me. Maybe they didn't really try. Why would they? Would you? How motivated would you be to voluntarily pursue a man who was in the grips of his second psychotic episode of the day and who had just threatened to kill you?

The night was clear and chilled, but my head was in a fog. I knew I was driving recklessly, but I didn't care. I needed out of that town. I needed on the first flight back to Boston. To hell with anyone else. It was obvious that the town was not affecting the others like it was me. That town was driving me outside of my own most basic moral ambiguity.

Trying to remember that drive is like trying to remember the first hours of a trip to a foreign country while incapacitated by jet lag. I can remember the drive enough to describe it, but it all happened in a haze, and there are missing pieces. Within the first ten minutes of the drive, I remember making at least three turns. I knew that was wrong, vaguely recalling the description of the directions to Lance's house on the way in. I, however, had been knocked out cold for the latter part of the trip, so I was unsure as to how exactly we had arrived there. The roads were thin, curvy, and unkempt, and I was not compensating for that fact with my driving. Every confused turn I took brought me to a thinner, curvier, tree-lined, leaf-covered road. I felt a sense of claustrophobia closing in, as though I were never going to get out of that town. Using my dashboard compass, I settled onto another unmarked goat path of a road. It was taking me west, which I at least knew should take me back toward Cleveland, as we had traveled due east for most of the trip there.

It was an unusually dark night. I could see about ten feet in front of my car, barely leaving enough time to responsibly negotiate the curves that would abruptly fly out in front of me. I was growing more desperate by the moment. I slammed on my brakes as something dashed across the road in front of me. The rear of the Malibu lurched sideways nearly ninety degrees.

It was a human figure that had run across the road. But there were quite a few key characteristics about it that seemed wrong. It was just out of range of my high beams, on the edge of my visual periphery. There was no doubt, however, that I saw it. It ran across in an almost animalistic fashion, hunched over, using its hands in front of itself to balance. I could only make out a silhouette—a vastly darkened one at that. It seemed to be skinny, almost to the point of malnourishment, but its head was elongated, possibly suffering a mass of some sort atop its skull—something highly abnormal. To be perfectly honest, at that moment, I was not terribly interested in finding out exactly what was going on with whatever in the hell it was. My goal was crystal clear, and my goal was singular: get the fuck out of Ashford no matter what.

Seeing no further sign of it, I jammed my foot back onto the accelerator and took off, leaving a ten-foot tread mark in the road behind myself. I had one eye on the road ahead and another in the rearview, ensuring that nothing pursued. Chills shot through me. The rage I had left Lance's house with had all but melted away. A juvenile fear of the dark and the unknown had swept in to take its place. I was caught somewhere between kicking myself for ever getting into that situation and the dread associated with the fact that I could now not find my way out of it. On top of that, I had an overwhelming sense of not being alone out there. I felt watched, stalked. There wasn't a light or distinguishable residence or building of any kind throughout the entire ride. There was only a seemingly endless maze of dark, unmarked, unfamiliar, barely passable roads.

It seemed like I was in a labyrinth. The curves I took didn't make sense. I could take three consecutive left-hand turns and never cross back over the original road. It should have been impossible. The farther I drove, the less progress I seemed to make. There were no distinguishable landmarks, only tall, barren trees canopying the road above, blotting out any moonlight or view of the stars or anything else that might have acted as a waypoint. Looking into the forest on either side of the road gave a sense of endlessness, as though if I were to venture into those trees, I could walk in one direction for centuries and never find an end to them. Worse, I had not mentally catalogued my trip to that point. Therefore, even if I wanted to go back to Lance's, I would have never found my way. I pulled my cellphone from my pocket only to find it completely dead. My charger was somewhere, buried in Gary's equipment stash back at Lance's house. I was completely on my own.

My engine was redlining as I crested a small rise in the road. I was blind to the other side of the bluff until I traversed its apex. As my headlights again pointed down upon the road, not twenty feet in front of me was another one of the things. This time it stood in the dead center of the street. It was startled by my headlights, standing straight up in an alert and defensive stance. I hit the brakes again, and my heart began to pound as it came fully into view.

A male figure, completely nude, standing no more than five foot nine. Its pale body stood, barefoot, in the street. It was looking directly at my stopped vehicle. There wasn't a solitary inch of its skin that wasn't calloused over or scarred. Slender would be an understatement. This thing looked like it hadn't seen a meal in weeks. I could see its ribs as well as lumps in its midsection that outlined its internal organs as they pressed against its paper-thin skin.

My gag reflex kicked in as I took in its face and head. I quickly began choking back bile like a kid after taking his first experimental shot of whiskey from his father's liquor cabinet. Its eyes were the normal size for a human being, but they had no lids, and I didn't get the impression that it had been born that way. Also missing were any sort of ears or lips or nose. Again, it appeared that they had once existed and were at a later point removed. Its head was completely bald and at least three times too large for its body. At first, I considered that the cranium may just appear that way in contrast of its incredibly slender torso. But the longer I looked on, the more obvious it became. I could clearly see evidence of its vascular system throughout its face, neck, and head. Its facial features, as horrific as they looked, were standard size but, in an ungodly disconcerting fashion, sat in the middle of its massive skull. It had a look of evil about it—a gaze of intensity and anger. I couldn't be sure if it was forced into that look by the obvious trauma it had undergone or if it was legitimately *trying* to look at me that way.

Its teeth were completely exposed, clear around to the third molars. Its eyes were stretched wide open, bulging two-thirds of the way out of their sockets. It remained nearly motionless, as though in a trance, but occasionally its head would tilt to one side or the other in an inquisitive fashion.

I was absolutely petrified. I had some reasonable expectations upon coming to Ashford as to what I might be confronted with. Nobody, however, could have anticipated what I was looking at on that road on that night. As a paranormal investigator, I typically dealt with ghosts and things that go bump in the night. Such things are typically invisible. This thing was clear as day and twenty feet in front of my car. It wasn't a ghost, but it indeed was something paranormal.

I decided to beep my horn at it. Perhaps that would startle it, and it would go away. As my horn blasted, its head again craned to one side. It was anything but startled. It took a step toward the car. Immediately, I jammed the stick into reverse, looking into the rearview. I tried to focus my eyes but could not see out of my rear window. Something was blocking my view. I turned my body around, desperate to be able to back away from the horrific miscreation stalking toward me.

I let out a screeching shout as I turned and was able to see the second thing, perched onto the trunk of my Malibu. The entirety of its wretched face was pressed against the rear windshield and fixated on me. As did the one in front of my car, this one suffered from the same facial deformations and cranial inflation. It bore the same intense, sinister gaze. It looked at me directly in the eyes. I was petrified beyond thought. I could feel the rear of the car lurching up and down with its weight as it shifted and squirmed atop the trunk. If nothing else, this validated that these beings were real flesh and blood. Ghosts don't have mass; therefore, they could not affect the suspension system of a Chevy Malibu.

The first one had crept its way to my side window. It bent down, revealing its horrible face to me again—only this time it was inches from mine. I lurched against the middle console, determined to put the maximum amount of space between me and it. At that distance, the horror of the being was far more pronounced. It was as much skeleton as it was man. At the same time, the shape of its skull was more alien than human. I could clearly make out a pulse, as I could see purple blood hitching through the bulging veins in its neck and temples. There was a thick layer of mucus over the area where its nose once existed. With nothing holding the sludge in place, it had free reign to bubble and dribble out of its exposed nasal cavity. Its head was still craning from side to side as though it were studying me, figuring out its next move.

Another moment later, it pressed its disgusting yet horrifyingly sharp teeth to the glass and performed an abrupt chomping motion. Its mouth opened and closed at an incredible rate—at least ten times over a couple seconds. I could hear the grisly clicks of its teeth chattering together with each spastic chomp. It wasn't trying to chew the glass or get into the car. It felt like a warning, a prediction of horrible things to come for me.

"Fuck this!" I shouted. I dropped the stick back into drive and floored the accelerator.

I observed the first thing dive toward the ditch and away from my rocketing car. I could feel the rear of the vehicle thrust upward as the second monster leapt off. I managed a brief glimpse of the two creatures in my rearview mirror. They were in the middle of the road, still watching as I pulled away into the night. Another instant later, and they were completely gone, as though they had vaporized into thin air.

Completely abashed, I returned my gaze to the road ahead and quickly slammed on my brakes once more. I came to rest on a one-lane bridge that traversed a swiftly rushing creek. Just beyond the bridge was the only road sign of any kind that I had seen on that entire bloodcurdling journey: "Dead End."

21

Wahoga County Courthouse – Huntsfield, Ohio

I am including parts of this document, as it was released to me by my legal team and is relevant at this juncture of my story. It has been all but ignored for years and dismissed in court on multiple occasions, citing a conflict of interest between myself and Ricky, which, might I add, is a total crock of shit.

I am bringing this to the forefront at this point to tell my colleague's side of the story. I am doing so to keep the story as chronological as possible, as this is the only insight I have into their very relevant perspective after we became separated due to my speeding away from Lance's house like a raving goddamned lunatic. It should be noted that I do not expect any of this to validate my side of things. I am not hoping for any sort of reprieve. As I stated earlier, I truly don't give a shit. If you think I enjoy having to document these three days, then you are sadly, sadly mistaken. But anything worth doing is worth doing thoroughly.

The Deposition of Rick Voss: (First Session):

The following is a word-for-word dictation of the legal deposition of Rick (Ricky) Voss as witness to events that the State of Ohio finds admissible in relation to incidents occurring in Wahoga County, Ohio, between October the 14th and 17th of the year 2018.

This deposition will be conducted by State (Ohio) appointed prosecutor Doug Levine. In addition to Mr. Levine, FBI Special Agent Martin Roy will be in attendance. Mr. Voss is represented by his attorney, Sarah Miles.

This proceeding is an information-gathering session. The goal is to produce an outline of events that took place around Daniel Hallowell between the aforementioned dates. This proceeding is part of the formal preparation for the pending trial: State of Ohio v. Daniel Hallowell.

The honorable Judge Randall Stokes will preside over the deposition.

Mr. Levine: *Rick, would you prefer to be called Rick or Ricky?*

Mr. Voss: *I really don't care. Either will be fine.*

Mr. Levine: *I am going to refer to you as Rick. I hope that is okay.*

Mr. Voss: *Sure.*

Mr. Levine: *Rick, what brought you and your friends to Wahoga County?*

Mr. Voss: *We were in town from Boston, preparing to investigate the abandoned Carnegie Steel Mill. But the night prior to our investigation kicking off, my colleague Gary—*

Mr. Levine: *Gary Jenkins, your equipment technician?*

Mr. Voss: *That's correct. Gary met Lance Filner at the Hyatt Downtown Cleveland Bar and Lounge. Lance convinced Gary that we should investigate his town, Ashford. The two of them managed to convince Danny . . . Daniel Hallowell that he should go there and spend time unraveling this yarn that Lance had spun to all of us. Which, by the way, was very loosely based on any sort of truth. The next morning, we drove out there, expecting nothing, and ended up getting a whole hell of a lot more than any of us had bargained for.*

Mr. Levine: *Essentially, as soon as you arrived, Mr. Hallowell began showing signs of—let's call it violent psychosis?*

Mrs. Miles: *Don't answer that, Ricky. Mr. Levine, you are leading.*

Mr. Levine: *Let's try this again, shall we. Why don't you explain to us what happened in the truck on the way into town?*

Mr. Voss: *Danny . . . kind of freaked out. We were on County Line Road for about five miles and then had an encounter with some sort of law enforcement vehicle. Shortly after that, Danny attacked Gary.*

Mr. Levine: *Care to elaborate?*

Mr. Voss: He grabbed him by the front of his shirt and tried to bite his face. Sam was forced to physically restrain him to prevent him from doing so.

Mr. Levine: And that was Samuel Millbury, also known as Big Bear?

Mr. Voss: That's correct.

Mr. Levine: Can you talk a little about what happened later that night prior to Mr. Hallowell leaving Lance's place of residence?

Mr. Voss: Sure. Danny managed to get a cell phone call out to his wife. Somehow, she knew to inform him to look out one of the back windows of Lance's house. He did what she said and saw . . . something out there.

Mr. Levine: Did you see anything?

Mr. Voss: No.

Mr. Levine: Did anyone besides Mr. Hallowell see anything?

Mr. Voss: Not that I am aware of.

Mr. Levine: Do you think anything was there?

Mrs. Miles: Objection. We are here to collect facts and not to speculate about what someone else may or may not have seen out of a window.

Mr. Levine: Let's just move on.

Agent Roy: If nobody minds, can we jump back a step here? During your time in . . . this town, were you, at any point, able to locate any physical evidence indicating that you were in Ashford, Ohio?

Mr. Voss: Yes.

Agent Roy: And what was that?

Mr. Voss: *There were old newspaper clippings all over the walls of Lance's house that had been cut out from* The Ashford Sentinel. *Danny also had a book titled* The Medical Memoirs of Kenneth Harvey *which detailed the author's time spent in Ashford.*

Mr. Levine: *I am really perplexed. It seems that nobody besides you and your friends have ever managed to set foot in this town.*

Mr. Voss: *How's that going?*

Mr. Levine: *How is what going?*

Mr. Voss: *Being . . . perplexed?*

Mr. Levine: *Well, not great, Rick. Not great at all. It's also not great for any defense your buddy presumes to organize for himself. Do you have any idea where this medical book might be now?*

Mr. Voss: *I don't know. Danny had it in his back pocket when he left Lance's house in a frenzy that night. That was the last time I saw it.*

Mr. Levine: *So, aside from a book that nobody can find, which must've been a single print—believe me, we have tried to find another copy anywhere on the face of this planet—and excluding some long-lost newspaper clippings, you have no other evidence proving that you were ever actually in Ashford?*

Mr. Voss: *Nope.*

Mr. Levine: *Did you ever see an Ashford on a map or your GPS on the way in?*

Mrs. Miles: *What are we doing right now? Are we trying to prove the existence of a town, or are we gathering information for the upcoming trial?*

Mr. Levine: *This line of questioning is crucial to our establishing a chain of events.*

Judge Stokes: *Rick, please answer the question.*

Mr. Voss: *I looked. But I was never able to find any evidence of Ashford on any map or any of our GPS units.*

Mr. Levine: *You realize that there is no known road in Ohio named County Line Road?*

Mr. Voss: *Well, I do now.*

Agent Roy: *Did you ever see a sign titled County Line Road?*

Mr. Voss: *No, we were following Lance's directions which had his road names on them.*

Mr. Levine: *Doesn't it resonate as odd to you that you are describing events that occurred in a place that the State of Ohio has no record of ever having existed?*

Mr. Voss: *Absolutely, Martin. You bet your ass that it resonates as odd to me.*

Mr. Levine: *Rick, what I'm driving at here is this: There are things in this upcoming trial that the prosecution is going to be able to prove rather easily. Things that are not going to bode well for your friend. However, there are a lot of other things we can't prove. And many of the unprovable items may be able to help your friend. For instance, if you can help us nail down a location where these events might have taken place, we may be able to collect some relevant evidence that may benefit your friend. As it stands now, our search area consists of a fictional town somewhere in Wahoga County. Do you see our dilemma?*

Mr. Voss: *Of course I see your dilemma, Doug, but what would you like me to do about it? Believe me, I have tried to find my way back there a dozen times. I can't. At the same time, I know I was there. I know how I got there with Lance's directions the first time. But that route, for some insane reason, cannot be replicated.*

Mr. Levine: *Okay, Rick, take us through what happened after Mr. Hallowell left Lance's place of residence.*

Mr. Voss: *We just kind of stood there for a while, silent. None of us knew what to make of what we had just witnessed out of Danny. He was totally out of his mind, bordering on manic.*

Mrs. Miles: *Ricky, just stick to the facts. Don't get into trying to describe what Danny might or might not have been feeling emotionally or what his mental state might have been. That must be taken as opinion and cannot be representative of fact.*

Mr. Voss: *Well, he did chew through his own tongue. From my admittedly limited experience evaluating the psychological states of human beings, people in normal states of mind don't typically do that.*

Mrs. Miles: *Short of being a licensed psychologist who has had an opportunity to thoroughly examine Danny with regards to that particular point in his life, any mention you make of his mental state may only be recorded as speculation.*

Judge Stokes: *That is correct, Rick. If you describe things like your friend's state of mind, it will be added to the record of this deposition but will not be admissible in court. You are literally wasting your breath from a legal sense.*

Mr. Voss: *Okay, fine, whatever. So, after a few tense moments, we heard Danny peel off in his rental car. We decided that we needed to get after him. In . . . whatever state of mind he may or may not have been in at that time, it behooved us all to get a handle on him. We ran next door, which, by the way, was about a quarter of a mile down the road. One of Lance's colleagues, some guy named Darren, lived there.*

Mr. Levine: *Last name?*

Mr. Voss: *Never got it. The situation was frantic. Darren takes one look at Big Bear and tosses us the keys to his single-cab 1990 Ford Ranger. Big Bear drove, and Lance rode shotgun. Gary and I sat in the bed of the truck. We were all shouting to one another through the rear sliding window. Lance was barking out instructions. We managed to get back onto County Line Road or whatever in the hell that road is really called. We headed back the opposite direction that we came into town.*

Mr. Levine: *Can you describe how you traveled from Lance's road to County Line Road?*

Mr. Voss: We took a right out of Darren's driveway, drove about a half mile, then made a left at a four-way intersection, and we were back, presumably heading east, on County Line.

Mr. Levine: Any idea why Mr. Hallowell may have had such a tough time locating what seems to have been such a trivial turnoff?

Mr. Voss: He was physically restrained for the last portion of the ride into town—approximately the last ten minutes of the trip there. He never got to see where we turned onto Lance's street. Beyond that, I really can't say why he might have missed it.

Mr. Levine: And there were no actual street signs?

Mr. Voss: There weren't even stop signs at intersections.

Mr. Levine: Okay, please continue, Mr. Voss.

Mr. Voss: It is difficult to describe what happened next. On the way into town, on that road, earlier that day, something just felt . . . off. Time seemed . . . slower. I don't know how long it took us on County Line Road to reach Lance's street. It felt like a normal amount of time, maybe twenty minutes, maybe less. For one reason or another, while traveling on that road, I felt ill, almost concussed. You are cognizant of your surroundings, but there are pieces missing. You aren't registering a complete picture. You don't seem to get a clear manifest into your memory of what's going on. The best way I can describe driving on that road that day and night was that you only exist in the present moment, without any ability to reflect on the past or anticipate the future. By past, I mean minutes prior—you live it, and a moment later, that experience fades off into oblivion. It was as though time itself was dying and it was dragging my consciousness along with it.

Mr. Levine: Did anyone have a watch?

Mr. Voss: We all had phones, none of which had a signal. Mine had long since died, as the battery had drained from searching for a signal all day, as had Big Bear's, and I'm not sure about Gary. I don't think Lance had anything. The Ranger we were in didn't even have a radio. None of us brought our phone chargers. None of us expected to be in that town for more than a few hours.

So, we are driving down County Line Road for what felt like an eternity. Nothing was changing. It felt like we were trapped in one of those old cartoons where the rabbit would run and run and run, but the background would just repeat, over and over again, forever. After a great while, maybe a solid forty-five minutes, we collectively came to the realization that we weren't making any progress. It seemed that we should have, long ago, reached the turnoff that had brought us there. We must have at least tripled our travel time on County Line Road from when we arrived into town.

Mr. Levine: *Any sign of Mr. Hallowell on this trip?*

Mr. Voss: *None. There was nothing out there but darkness and trees. Along with a dead-straight, leaf-covered, endless road.*

Mr. Levine: *What happened next?*

Mr. Voss: *We eventually thought we had made a mistake. We executed a four-point turn in the middle of the street and turned around. We went back the way we came. And in about two and a half minutes, we arrived back at the turnoff to Lance's house. Our hearts all sank. There was no conceivable way that we could have traveled for so long away from that road, turned around, and gotten right back to it so quickly. We were all absolutely petrified. It quickly registered to all of us, in that moment, that something was not allowing us to leave that place. When we pulled back up to Lance's house, there was a fully blacked-out Yukon waiting for us in his driveway.*

22
The Wooded Streets of Ashford, Ohio – 1:00 a.m.

I don't know why anyone would have put a bridge there. If the road was just going to end a hundred feet over it, why bother taking the time and spending the money to build one at all? Just end the road before the creek.

Nonetheless, it was there, and my Malibu was parked on top of it. My hands were saturated with stress-induced perspiration, gripping the steering wheel. My heart had not yet had a chance to return to any semblance of normalcy since my encounter with the things not five hundred feet behind me on that very road. My eyes were forward, unable to believe that I was looking at a dead-end sign. Beyond the sign—the only one in town from what I had seen—rose a steep slope covered underneath a dark, dense forest. Were it not for my high beams illuminating the area around the front of my vehicle, my sight would have been limited to a couple feet in front of my face.

The one-lane bridge seemed sturdy enough, but it had seen better days. The steel side rails had rusted completely, shedding the vast majority of their military-green paint. The concrete below the car was holding its own, although desperately in need of a resurfacing. I could see to my left and right a bit, assisted only by the light that my own car was producing. The bridge traversed a substantial creek. I could hear flowing water rushing below me. The drop from the bridge, at its midpoint, was no more than fifteen feet down to the water's surface. Along each side of the creek was blackness and woodland as far as I could see in either direction.

I had no choice but to go back the way I came, back down the street where I had, moments previously, been accosted by two horrible, giant-headed creatures. One of which, might I add, was threatening to eat me alive. It was so dark behind my car and the road so narrow on that bridge that I could not get a clear view behind myself through any of my mirrors. I rolled the window down and hung my head out the side. With my body turned, I managed to navigate my car off the bridge. As I grabbed the stick and prepared to put the Malibu into drive, the engine revved down, and my ears perked up.

I thought I heard a baby crying, somewhere to the left side of the bridge, down the creek some ways, in the darkened beyond. I listened for a while longer, and the longer I listened, the surer I became. There was an infant crying somewhere out there. Thousands of years of human evolution has given the youngest of us the ability to cry in such a way that demands a caretaker's immediate attention. It is an unmistakable, high-pitched, hitching sob. It is a defense mechanism. A mechanism adjusted and honed innumerable times over the centuries to become the most likely noise to wake up a human adult. It is an incredibly important and fundamental aspect of our nature and the survival of our young.

There was no denying it at that point. I couldn't believe what I was hearing. What sort of lunatic would have a baby outside in this godforsaken hellhole of a town? What if it was lost or what if someone had left it? I couldn't live with myself knowing that it was out there, freezing and hungry. I had to, at the very least, attempt to find it.

Taking a last look out my rearview and seeing no further evidence of the monsters that had harassed me earlier, I turned off the car and got out. With the engine completely cut off, the crying of the baby was clear as day, several decibels louder. The only other sounds competing with it were the wind rustling through the mostly dead trees and the babbling creek water rushing out of town as quickly as possible. Who could blame it? I wondered for a moment if this was the creek that Lance had allegedly followed as he snuck out of town to find us. If that part of his story was even true.

No doubt, the infantile sobbing was coming from my left. I proceeded to that side of the road. There was an incredibly crude pathway cut into the forest about fifty feet up the street. I couldn't tell if it had ever been a real trail or if it was simply the lack of a tree in one spot. Regardless, I walked into the woods, still listening intently to the crying. My idea was to follow it, locate its source, assist if necessary, and get the hell back to the Malibu as quickly as humanly possible. I would then do everything I possibly could, stopping for nothing, moving mountains if they got in my way, to drive back to Lance's house and regroup with my crew.

Mentally, I was back to reality, albeit a horrible reality that, to this day, I would sell my soul to Satan himself to rid my memory of. Nonetheless, the fog in my head had all but subsided. All the psychotic thoughts that had ravaged my psyche earlier were gone. I had shifted into survival mode.

I couldn't see a thing. With every step, I could feel my body breaking fallen twigs. Any chance of stealth flew right out the preverbal window. I was basically moving through that woods with the grace of a panicked hippopotamus in a crowded death-metal nightclub.

I heard three rapid steps to my right that were not my own. Before my head could turn in that direction to investigate the source, I felt an extreme pressure on my chest. Someone or something had crashed into me. My heart was nearly exploding. All I could see was a gray blur over top of me as I fell flat on my back from the impact. I managed a half of a shout before I felt a hand cover my gaping mouth. I nearly lost consciousness as the salty palm prevented me from taking in air while in that hitching, panicked state. The hand slowly loosened its grip, and I was finally able to see the source of it. It was not one of the things. It was just a man. Before I could register any details about him, he spoke: "You think you could make any more fucking noise, numb-nuts?"

He let his hand go so I could reply. "What in the fucking hell, pal!" I shouted.

His hand returned over my mouth again, tighter than ever. I honestly considered biting him and trying to fight my way out of his grasp. At last, I was able to see him standing over me. He was around five foot ten and maybe 160 pounds. He had to be at least sixty years old. He had shoulder-length gray hair jutting from underneath a very Elmer Fudd-esque crown cap. His face was almost completely covered with craters, likely from a lifelong, losing battle with acne. He had a ratty, sparse goatee around his mouth with a rattier, sparser Fu Manchu hanging from his chin. His beady, squinting eyes were either chestnut brown or black. I couldn't tell for sure in the darkness.

I could tell that his tackling me and subsequent holding of his hand over my mouth had taken a lot out of him. He was gasping for air. He wanted to say something but was working his way up to it. Seeing an advantage, I rolled to my left while gripping his hand and forearm. I yanked him downward as I stood, sending him barreling headfirst into a pile of twigs, dead brush, and leaves.

"You fuckin' idiot," he shouted as he landed. "Go ahead and try to find that crying baby."

"You hear it?" I asked.

"Of course I hear it. I ain't deaf, dickhead," he replied.

He was still catching his breath, lying in the damp brush at my feet. "So, what should I do, nothing?" I asked. "Would you rather just leave an infant out in the woods to die?"

"That ain't no dying infant, dipshit. That there is how they get you. All I'm trying to do is keep yer stupid ass from getting killed."

"You certainly have a funny way of doing that—tackling me to the ground and nearly suffocating me with your old, liver-spotted palm. Ever heard of 'psst' or 'hey you'? Typically, when trying to break the ice with another human being, trying to physically restrain them is frowned upon."

"My god," he replied, getting back onto his feet and brushing the dirt from his red flannel and blue jeans. "You really have no idea what it is you're dealing with out there, do you?"

"I'm not from here. I just got here today. And I have seen plenty of what's out there—enough for a lifetime. And if you're telling me that's not really a baby? Then I am more than happy to go back to my car and get the hell out of this town. So, if you'll excuse me? This has really been nice. Thanks for the memories." I shouldered through him, walking back in the direction of where I had entered the forest.

"It's sad, watching the new ones come here. How long it takes all of you to realize just how screwed you really are."

I stopped and turned back to face him, not knowing what to make of his statement. "I'll send you a postcard from my mansion in Boston. Feel free to write me back. Let me know how screwed you think I am then. You certainly seem like a fellow who has things figured out."

I didn't usually throw affluence or entitlement around like that. Only when I really wanted to hurt someone's feelings. Up to that point, that guy had earned it. He looked down dejectedly and continued to brush himself off. I turned again and headed back toward the car. I came to the gap in the trees where I had entered the forest and jumped down a small yet steep swale onto the roadway. My car was still parked just off the bridge but was now surrounded by at least a dozen of those things.

They were almost dancing around the Malibu. Their disgusting, rail-thin, nude bodies flowed in a hypnotic fashion. Their movement was a controlled chaos. They demonstrated human as well as animal locomotion—examples of dexterity that could not be found anywhere else in nature. Each exhibited incredible coordination while using their arms and legs in equal parts to move around. They could maneuver on their hands as though they were feet, their bodies completely inverted, never interrupting their normal gait. Some used both their hands and feet at once, like dogs. Some walked upright, normally. Others slithered horizontally, inches from the ground, arms and legs bent unnaturally, allowing them to travel beneath the car.

Their heads were all massive, stressing the flesh around the skull almost to the point of it bursting open. Each had the same facial deformities—missing eyelids, lips, noses, ears. They were all thin to the point of obvious starvation, although it did not seem to affect their energy levels. The only noises they made were breathy, long-winded exhales and an occasional high-pitched moan. At no point did one of them touch another, even though their movements around the same car seemed so enchantingly chaotic. There must have been some coordination involved between them, but they clearly were not communicating verbally.

Despite their obvious similarities, each one was unique; each had its own distinct characteristics. Some of them were definitely male, and others, female. The idea of breasts still bulged above the exposed ribs of some, obviously female. The shoulder blades and backs of others were more pronounced and muscular, suggesting males. Normally, one could easily tell by identifying their genitalia, however, any of the things I had figured for men appeared to have had theirs ripped away long ago.

It was as though they were observing the car, unsure what to make of it. They were studying it, devouring as much information about it as they could. They were utilizing a hive mentality—a coordinated, collective information-gathering operation. I'd never seen anything like it outside of insects. My body felt calcified. I could not get myself to leave the middle of that road, no matter how much I needed to hide. I was legitimately terrified beyond any ability to move my own limbs. I felt a sharp, sudden pain on the side of my head. An instant later, I saw a rock approximately the size of a matchbox car fall at my feet. My hand flew up to my head, feeling for blood, already able to feel another lump forming inches from the one that was still there from Big Bear's earlier strike. Turning, I saw the man from the woods, just into the tree line. He had obviously thrown the rock to get my attention. He was frantically motioning for me to rejoin him in the woods.

The rock, however painfully, knocked enough sense into me to get me moving. Methodically, I made my way back to the faux-path that was cut into the trees and joined my new colleague. He signaled for me to lie down just over the top of the swale. In one motion, he rolled underneath some netting that had been covered over with brush and leaves, perfectly matching our surroundings. His hand was all that was left that I could see as I followed him. It was uncanny how well camouflaged his setup was. I rolled on my back and slowly made my way underneath the netting and next to him.

"What in god's name are those things?" I whispered.

He let out an ever-so-quiet chuckle and replied, "Yer startin' to see just how fucked you are now—ain't you, boy?"

23

The man and I walked about a quarter of a mile through the forest, away from the wretched, massive-headed creatures, and arrived at a cabin. There were no lights on in the structure, and it blended in to its surroundings remarkably. If you weren't looking for it, you could walk straight by it and never notice the modest abode. It was just as much a shanty as it was a cabin. It looked like something that had been put together over the course of a weekend, perhaps by someone more concerned about obtaining shelter than anything having to do with style or durability. The exterior consisted of plywood nailed directly to four-inch-by-four-inch beams and headers, all of which had been stained a taupe shade of deep brown, rendering the entire exterior almost black. The roof was black-painted tin that overlaid more plywood. The entire structure had one, solitary window facing out toward the direction we approached from. It was positioned about a foot to the right of the only door. Despite its many apparent shortcomings, it looked well maintained, as though it had been built within the year or two.

"Gorgeous. This your house?" I asked sarcastically.

"I know it ain't up to your lavish standards, Daniel. It will have to do. Less you wanna go take yer chances with them melon-heads."

"How do you know my name?"

"Saw yer show a few times."

"Really? You've got cable in this thing?"

He replied with a note of snark, "As difficult as it may be for a city boy like yourself to believe, I've not lived here for my entire life."

"Melon-heads. Is that what you call those . . . things?" I asked.

"That is the preferred nomenclature."

We walked in the door into pitch blackness. I heard a couple of clicks, and suddenly, the single-room structure became flooded with light. My new friend had turned on a couple of battery-powered LED lanterns. The man quickly placed a prefabricated, black-painted piece of plywood over the one window, not wanting any of the interior light to bleed outside. For the same reason, he rolled the floor mat up and placed it at the base of the door.

The cabin was a single, cluttered room but was surprisingly organized and well kept. There was a closet just inside the door. It held several pairs of boots, coats, and other clothing items. The right side of the cabin consisted of a dining table, couch, and recliner surrounding a pellet stove. Straight ahead was an indoor outhouse complete with a small sink, mirror, and incinerator toilet. The far-right wall was completely hidden behind bookshelves surrounding a relatively nice, executive-style, wooden desk. It was far cleaner inside than I had expected. The floors were not only pristine but came complete with hardwood flooring that had clearly been polished recently.

"Lemonade?" the man asked.

"Sure. What's your name, anyway?"

"The name's Andy Moncrieff," he replied, grabbing a plastic cup from a cabinet above the kitchen table. He filled it with water from the sink and mixed in a tablespoon of lemonade mix.

Taking the beverage from him, I asked, "So, what's your story, man? What in god's name are you doing out here?"

"Think you ran into some of my friends on the way in, no?" he replied, pouring a clear liquid from a flask into his glass of lemonade.

"That vodka?"

"Yep."

We sort of stood there silently for a moment. He stared at me. I stared right back at him. He knew what I wanted. Without any further uneasiness, Andy stepped over and emptied a generous amount of vodka into my cup. Now it was a good, old-fashioned, two-man vodka-and-lemonade party.

"Thanks. So, you're with the feds? You know those people we saw in the blacked-out Yukon on the way in?"

Andy began laughing. It started as sort of a soft chuckle and over a period of about ten seconds evolved into a full-blown belly laugh. Eventually, he hunched over and began laughing as hard as I had ever witnessed a man laugh. There was a moment where I legitimately thought he might piss in his pants.

Finally catching his breath, he came back to reality and replied, "The feds!" Another chorus of laughter ensued, and he continued, "Them fuckers ain't the feds, my friend."

"Okay, fine. Why is that so hilarious to you? They sure as hell looked like federal officials to me."

Still catching his breath, "Well, they ain't."

"Then who are they?"

Shaking his head, he seemed as though he was trying to figure out how to answer. Finally, wiping some drool from his chin that had dribbled from his mouth during his fit of uncontrollable laughter, he managed, "What religion do you fancy yourself there, city boy?"

Confused and well beyond annoyed, I replied, "I'm nothing. I make fun of religious people. I call them 'churchies.' Sometimes right to their faces. Why? And why do you keep calling me city boy? I live in a suburb of Boston."

Previously, he had come off as moderately amused. The conversation was difficult yet lighthearted. Then, without warning, a hateful scowl took over his face. He took several steps toward me and barked, "I choose to lump all of you East-Coast dickheads into the same class of city-boy pussy. Y'all are like a bunch of spoiled brats—living in the lap of luxury—thinking you got a set of balls in yer pants but you've never proven a damned thing in yer worthless fuckin' lives. Yer a bunch of grown men who've never gotten yer asses kicked and good-lord-in-heaven does every one of you ever need it. Rats with credit cards is all you people are. Only adversity you ever overcame was when yer daddy didn't buy you the exact type of Mercedes-Benz you wanted."

It was my turn to laugh. I couldn't help but chuckle at his misguided viewpoint and incredibly inappropriate way of explaining it. "Tell me how you really feel, Andy."

I didn't get a chance to start my next sentence before he had his hand on my throat and I was on my back. My head slammed against the door behind me as I crashed to the floor. My lemonade and vodka mixture flew behind me, ricocheted off the door, and saturated my face and hair. My eyes temporarily went crossed. The attack wasn't completely unexpected, but the sheer violence behind it was. My vision blurred, my ears rang, and I immediately became nauseous. His hand was still on my throat with the full brunt of his weight pressed down onto my stomach and chest. I couldn't take in air. He was barking more lunacy at me as his saliva poured onto my face with every revolting word.

"You got a lucky shot or two in on me in them woods, boy. But yer in my fuckin house now. What'd you think? You were gonna be the first city boy to win in a fight against a country boy in human history? You keep tryin' me, boy; keep testin' me. What do you think is gonna happen? They gonna find yer body out here, in them woods, in a town that don't exist? How are they gonna identify you when yer bones are picked clean by them melon-heads?"

"Dental records?" I suggested sarcastically with what was just about the last ounce of air I had in my lungs.

I'd had about enough and didn't get the sense that he was planning on calming down anytime soon. I grabbed a nice, big handful of his balls, picked one of them out, and squeezed as hard as I could.

I have never fancied myself as much of a fighter, but I had been in a few scraps in my day. One thing I had never understood about fighting was the so-called fighting-like-a-man etiquette. If I must fight someone, the absolute last thing in the world that I'm worried about is following some set of unwritten rules. I will happily go directly for the balls if offered the opportunity. Hell, I'll bite someone's ear off if I have to. After all, the object of any fight is to win. I feel like how you arrive at that victory is meaningless. The entire act of physical altercation is barbaric. So, who's to say what level of barbarism is okay and what isn't? Trying to draw lines or create a code of conduct for two men who are fighting each other makes about as much sense to me as trying to impose rules on a monkey shit-fight at the zoo.

Anyone or anything, for that matter, that has ever been earmarked for a set of nuts throughout the eons of evolution shares the same horrible vulnerability. It is odd, after all, that so often men are the ones getting into fights when we are the ones with the most easily exploitable organs, dangling clumsily off the bottoms of our bodies, in perfect punching or kicking proximity to our opponent.

It is the ultimate equalizer. Any normal man could conceivably win a fight against a professional cage fighter by connecting on a single, lucky nut-shot. That same average man, if afforded the opportunity, could theoretically eviscerate a polar bear using the same strategy. It truly doesn't matter. If you have a set of balls, you also have the ability to become completely debilitated at any moment.

Unless you've experienced it, you have no concept of that level of pain. I often argued with my wife about it. She explained that she felt childbirth was obviously more painful. I disagree. I honestly do not believe that childbirth would be survivable if it hurt worse than having a nut squeezed. Having one of your balls in that situation is completely debilitating to the point of instant desperation. You go from normal to complete, crippling agony in the blink of an eye. Nothing in this world compares.

Andy's eyes rolled back in his head, and he let out a high-pitched whimper—a far cry from all his tough talk moments before. I felt his weight lift from me as he rolled onto his side. He let out a long, disgusting fart. The extraordinary pain I was inflicting on his nether regions was causing him to lose all semblance of control of his body. My hand was still firmly grasped onto his testicle. I wasn't letting go of that thing for the world. I had that thing secured like it was the winning Powerball ticket.

His hands flew back, and he began screaming like an old woman. "Stop! Stop! Stop!"

I growled back at him, right into his whimpering little face: "Oh, I am never letting go, Andy. I'm gonna pop this fucker."

He was lying on his back next to me. His breathing was positively frantic. He wailed like a baby with a soiled diaper. His legs kicked. He had absolutely no control over his motor skills. Finally, after about five seconds, which I'm sure felt like an eternity to him, he looked me directly in the eyes. His face was pouring sweat and radiating torment. In a childish and completely helpless tone, he whimpered "Please . . . please stop."

"You gonna stop acting like a crazy hillbilly if I do?"

He nodded his head. At that point, I honestly don't think he had the ability to vocalize another word.

I let go.

His hands immediately went down his pants, grasping his jewels. He lay there moaning, still in horrible pain for several minutes. He let out a peculiar, yet disgusting, series of coughing, whimpering dry heaves that I can't say I've ever heard from another human, before or since. A moment later, he began to cry like a baby. Realizing that I had the floor, I got on my soapbox.

"You know something, Andy—I am not your typical Boston, trust-fund baby. My daddy wasn't exactly buying me luxury cars or anything else for that matter, seeing as the last time I saw him or my mother, they were dropping me off at the police station in a box. Don't remember it much. I was about four hours old at the time.

"Shortly thereafter, I became property of the Commonwealth of Massachusetts, which comes complete with bouncing from one foster home to another, not having legal guardians who give any sort of shit about you, fighting kids twice your age and size for meals, fighting kids at school who make fun of you for not having real parents, inevitably revolting in your teenage years since nobody ever taught you how to behave, and getting tossed in and out of juvie five times.

"I always got good grades, though. So, I went to college. But since I didn't have anyone to put me through it, I had to go to school all day and work at a lumberyard in the evenings, unloading trucks by hand, one after the other, well into the night. The only reason I worked there was because they let me sleep in the office at night. I would wake up after three hours of sleep and get on the commuter rail back to school and do it all over again.

"That went on for about five years, Andy. Only then had I earned my degree and begun doing gainful work. When I got my show—which, apparently, you've seen—it was literally the one and only good thing that had happened for me throughout the course of my entire life. I met my wife and had my daughter since, but before I got my show, my life was about as terrible as they come. My wife has, on many occasions, had to explain to me things I should buy with my own money because I honestly had no concept of material possession. I hadn't ever owned anything. Forgive me, Andy, but fuck you if you think I'm some sort of East-Coast imperialist. I am probably further from that than you are."

Andy had since rolled over and was facing me. His voice was still several decibels too high. His hands were still firmly secured to his junk. "I think you might've done some real, permanent damage to my balls, you asshole."

24

Andy poured us another couple of rounds of his special "lemonade," sans the water or lemon mix. Basically, just two big cups full of vodka. Any ice that would have, under normal circumstances, gone into our beverages had been previously stuffed into the Ziploc bag that rested atop Andy's testicles. The mood had calmed. Andy was still breathing heavily, flustered, whining and moaning occasionally. But we were sitting comfortably across from each other at what I assumed was his kitchen table.

"Throw out everything you think you know about religion," Andy sort of barked at me from across the table, suddenly.

Slightly taken aback by his idea of a conversation starter, I replied, "Okay, why?"

"There is one way and one way only that it works, and all the rest of it ain't nothing but a load of tree-humpin' hippy crap."

"Okay, Andy," I replied. There aren't many situations where I am utterly at a loss for words. It appeared that he was incapable of getting to his point, either out of sheer ignorance or the fact that he simply didn't have one. Either way, I had the impression that I was dealing with a fully grown man who possessed the conversational abilities of a toddler.

The conversation that is about to take place goes a long way toward explaining the single largest problem I've had while attempting to explain myself to my team of psychologists here at the mental hospital. To this day, I believe everything Andy told me that night. However, due to my doctors' misguided beliefs, it's often dismissed as heresy or a series of nonsensical ramblings. As hard as it may be for them to believe, I do not *hate* religion—if believing in something like that, in some way, helps you out . . . fine. There is, however, plenty of nonsense that occurs around religion, and only religion, that I do find strongly disagreeable.

Here is my god's-honest (no pun intended) view of major religion. Religion needs to, but subsequently and by its own design cannot, exist within a vacuum. One of the main focal points of every major religion is that its members should go out, into the world, and convince other rubes to climb on board their weird, little religion trains. This is a concept that completely flies in the face of basic human nature. Nobody on the planet enjoys having complete strangers tell them that their belief system, however bat-shit crazy it may be, is wrong. So wrong, in fact, that you should believe my idea instead. My idea is just as bat-shit crazy as yours, but never mind that. So, right off the bat, religion, at its very core, fosters conflict.

I have also never been able to understand why nothing else from the Bronze Age has made it through every advancement that we as a civilization have made other than every major religion. Nothing provable has happened to change, advance, fortify the argument for or suggest the existence of any major religion in over two thousand years. Yet, every week, gaggles of people show up for their worshiping exercises. As if everything that occurred a world away, thousands of years ago, in a time when people honestly believed that rubbing donkey shit on themselves repelled evil spirits, should define their entire spiritual lives.

Why stop there? Why not go back to how everything was in those days? After all, what a terrific time that was to be alive. If you weren't getting your head chopped off in the middle of a desert, you were probably dying of leprosy. Medicine was frowned upon because if you got too good at it, you ran the risk of being ostracized and labeled as a wizard. If someone committed a crime, it was not uncommon for the citizens of the community to gather and fire rocks at the accused criminal until he or she died—which I'm sure was not quickly. People were honestly worried about sea monsters. Sorcery was a very real civic concern. Medicine and celestial events were based on and subsequently dismissed as magic. The people of that time were a baby step above cavemen, yet millions of people still interpret their writings, quite literally, as gospel. It baffles me.

I often wonder if a thousand years from now, some far more advanced civilization might dig up a long-lost, well-preserved copy of *Peter Pan* and maybe Pan will be interpreted as a deity. Maybe Hook will be the devil. Maybe the Lost Boys will be Pan's apostles. As ludicrous as that sounds, it's not far from what's already happened countless times throughout human history.

All of this combined with the fact that it's impossible to have any sort of an adult conversation with people who fancy themselves as religious. Unless you believe the same thing as them, it will quickly become an argument that is impossible for either side to win. You're never going to convince someone who has molded their entire life around their personal belief in a fairy tale that they are wrong. But when you take that into context, it is hardly surprising. Wars have been fought over such disagreements. Wars are still being fought over the same disagreements. Ten thousand years from now, whatever five dozen, brain-damaged humans still exist, clinging to life on our irradiated planet, will still be fighting wars over these same disagreements. After all, every major religion that exists today would collapse without such conflict. It's that us-versus-them attitude that is the basis for every one of their brands—creating that bunker mentality throughout their congregations which manufactures more counterfeit justification for everyone's continued involvement and financial backing.

I took off my cap and rested it on the table in front of me. I rubbed my eyes and let out a calming exhale. I leaned forward in my chair. "So, what the fuck are we talking about here, Andy? I'm sitting here. Elaborate—for the love of Christ. Why should I denounce religion in favor of whatever you think you know?"

Andy tapped his fingers on the table and licked his lips. There was, indeed, some kind of hamster-wheel spinning around up there in his head. Finally, he replied, "The entire reason I have been here for however many years it's been is because I don't have the ability you have, and I want it."

"What might that ability be?" I asked.

"We call you a Bridge," he replied.

"A Bridge? What the hell is a Bridge?"

"That's right. As in, a person with the ability to bridge this world and The Overworld."

"Wait, what? The Overworld?"

"The Overworld is where we go when we're in between assignments."

"Assignments? As in lives?"

"That is correct."

At this point, it was taking every bit of me to keep myself from laughing. I feared pissing Andy off again and invoking another physical altercation.

"Okay, and why do you think I'm a Bridge?"

He looked at me like I was the one who was insane. "Their interest in you, of course. Isn't it obvious?" He pointed behind me.

"Who, the melon-heads?"

"Yes, sir. You can live here yer entire life and never catch a glimpse of one. Suddenly, here you come fuckin' around, and it's melon-head city out there."

"So, they're attracted to me because I'm a Bridge?" I asked.

"Maybe. Maybe not just them. Maybe their leader is as well."

"And who is that?"

"Crowe," he replied.

"As in Roderick Crowe? The guy from this book?" I took *The Memoirs of Kenneth Harvey* out of my back pocket and tossed it onto the table. It slid toward him.

"Holy shit!" Andy shouted, quickly thrusting a hand over his mouth. Obviously, he wanted to keep from making noise. "Where the hell did you get this?"

"Guy named Lance Filner gave it to me."

"Never heard of him." His eyes crept from excited to solemn. "All these years, I've been looking for this."

I was a little surprised by his genuine reaction to the book. I'd found it creepy, boring in parts, certainly nothing profound. Yet, here was this man, gazing upon it as though he had just witnessed the unearthing of the Holy Grail.

"Lance Filner is the one who brought me and my crew to this town in the first place. He keeps bugging me to read this book. He says that I'm somehow the key to solving the problems around here and that reading this book will somehow help me out with it."

"Let's back up a minute here, Danny." He had taken on a more serious tone, bordering on professional. His hillbilly dialect had even vanished, which is not something I knew people could turn on and off. "Other than melon-heads, have you experienced anything else paranormal since you've been in town?"

"Oh, sure, how much time you got?" I replied. "On the way in, I got incredibly angry for no good reason. I tried to bite my friend in his face and was subsequently knocked unconscious by my other friend. While I was out, I had a nightmare about flying around through fractals. Do you know what those are?"

"Yes, believe it or not, I know a lot about complex geometric shapes."

Trying to cloak the shock on my face at the fact that Andy knew how to add or subtract, let alone that he knew about advanced geometry, I continued, "As I'm flying through these fractals, I feel this overwhelming sense that the shapes I'm seeing somehow describe me, my sense of self, my soul. Even though they are just incredibly complex shapes, floating about in space, I feel as though I'm being guided through them purposefully. I look to my right, and there is someone or something else in there with me. It was this white, floating, iridescent entity. It had these elongated bands of what I thought to be pure energy swirling around it. I felt comfortable with it, familiar, as though I had known it for all my life." I looked up and found Andy smiling. I looked behind me, then back to Andy. "What? What are you grinning about?"

"I just cannot believe I am sitting here with you," he replied.

"Why?"

My heart skipped a beat as Andy unexpectedly slapped his hand against the table, hard enough to disturb our beverages to the point that some of our vodka sloshed out of the top of our cups. He shouted, projecting an unreasonable excitement, "Because you're a fucking Bridge, man! A real Bridge. Right here, in my cabin!"

"Is that like a rare thing?"

With a low-pitched chuckle, "Is that like rare thing, he asks me. Does the Tin Man have a sheet-metal cock?"

"Okay, I get it, Andy. It's rare. Anyhow, Lance has been telling me that I'm the key to saving this town. How could he know that I'm a Bridge? I only met him a day ago."

"Who knows how anyone knows anything. Hell, I didn't know he had this book. Either way, he was right about you being a Bridge. What else has happened to you since you've been here?"

"So, I'm floating around with this familiar entity, through the shapes. Suddenly, I hit this clearing and in front of me appears this . . . city. The Black City is what I've been calling it. It looked modern, glassy, enormous. As far as I could see from my left to my right were massive buildings—all completely black. As I'm floating there, taking this all in, I feel these hands on my shoulders, and I feel myself suddenly being dragged backward at a break-neck speed. I fought one of the hands off and turned myself around to face whatever it was that was pulling me. It was another entity, but this one had no discernable features. For everything it lacked in appearance, though, it more than made up for in raw emotion. It was evil—pure, raging hatred personified—in a single being. It uttered this phrase to me in Sumerian. We managed to translate it when we arrived at Lance's place: 'The demon warrior, the destroyer, the god of the deep, commands you unto the realm of the death gods.'"

Andy was shaking his head at me and smiling, his grin bigger than ever. "Fantastic, man, that is absolutely spectacular."

"Wait, what part?"

"So, let me take you through what's happened here. This is more evidence as to why you're obviously a Bridge. Firstly, you were indeed traveling through yourself—a journey into your own soul, I guess you could say. That's why everything seemed familiar at first. Those shapes you saw, the fractals, are what make you, you. They represent your mannerisms, your ideals, your thought processes, your underlying philosophy toward everything. Think of them as the computer code that your entire sense of being is written in."

I had gone from amused to enthralled. A lot of what he was telling me jived with my experiences up to that point. "Right. That's exactly how I felt about them when I was seeing them."

"And your familiar entity," he continued, "is what we call a guide. There's a lot involved with explaining guides and spirit groups and the evolution of souls. Basically, we all have guides who assist us through our various assignments or lives. They usually exist at a higher level of soul development than ourselves. Think of them as your spiritual guidance counselors."

"So why does this make me a Bridge?"

"I don't care how badly knocked out you were. Nobody, and I mean nobody, gets to see their spirit guide and remember it well enough to describe it. Nobody gets to see the inner workings of their own being while still alive and in their earthbound form. Only those rare few whose souls exist in their earthbound state as well as the higher realm simultaneously could possibly describe such a vision. That vision could have only been had and subsequently remembered by a Bridge."

"What about the evil entity? What about The Black City?"

I could tell by his expression that he knew the answers. He just didn't know how to put them into words for me. Instead, he replied with a question of his own. "You gonna finish reading this book, or do you want me to tell you what Roderick Crowe really is?"

25

The Deposition of Rick Voss: (First Session):

Agent Roy: *Ricky, when you managed to get back to the house, and you found the Yukon waiting for you. Were these the same officials you told us about earlier?*

Mr. Voss: *No, they only looked like federal officials, but they weren't.*

Agent Roy: *Tell us what happened when you were confronted by these . . . officials.*

Mr. Levine: *If I could just jump in here. I would like for you to keep something in mind as you continue, Ricky. Several people are dead. People with families and friends. Real people. Do them the justice of being truthful. So far, all we've got to go on are a series of happenings that took place in a town nobody can find.*

Mr. Voss: *All I can do for you people is tell you what I know. Ultimately, it falls to you to decide what to believe. Hook me up to a polygraph machine for this deposition if you think I'm lying to you.*

Mrs. Miles: *I am going to act like I didn't hear that. Just explain what happened when you got back to Lance's house. Disregard Doug's suggestion to keep anything he asks in mind. Those of us who managed to pass the bar in fewer than seven attempts call that leading a witness.*

Mr. Levine: *Now, I don't have to put up with this, your honor.*

Judge Stokes: *If you keep leading witnesses, you sure as hell do. Do yourself a favor and stop trying to influence testimony and Sarah might stop belittling you.*

Mr. Levine: *Just get on with your story, Rick.*

Mr. Voss: *Whatever, Doug. We pulled into the driveway and then onto the grass, around the Yukon, and parked. Big Bear got out of our truck first and approached the SUV. He took about two steps before all four of its doors swung open. Out came three men and one woman. The man who had been in the driver's seat was older. He was the one who seemed to be in charge. The woman who had been in the passenger seat, I assumed, was the second in command. She was younger, about my age—attractive, blond, great legs, big blue eyes, nice facial features, curves in all the right places, none in the wrong places.*

Mrs. Miles: *Okay, Ricky. We get the point. She was hot.*

(laughs throughout the room)

Mr. Voss: *The other two guys from the back seat were the muscle, I presumed at least. They both carried rifles. All four of them were dressed in black suits, black shoes, black ties. The men wore black sunglasses. The woman wore red-tinted sunglasses with gold rims.*

Big Bear introduced himself and extended his hand to the older guy. The man brushed passed him, barely acknowledging his presence. The two clowns with the guns hung back near their vehicle while the woman and the old man walked to our right, into the front yard, and began staring at the house. They just gazed at it in sort of an odd, inquisitive fashion.

After pushing out a long, disappointed-sounding breath, the old man spoke. "Lance, old friend, what did you do?"

Lance sort of looked around with a befuddled look on his face. Everything about his body language suggested to me that he was genuinely terrified of these people. "What? What do mean, Michael?" he whimpered.

"How the hell do you know their names?" I shouted. I had reached a point with Lance where I was no longer willing to tolerate his bullshit. Clearly, to that point, we hadn't even come close to getting the complete story out of him. I am trapped in some town that I agreed to visit because of a series of lies fed to me by him. And to complicate matters further, I am surrounded by shadowy officials who don't seem to approve of my presence.

"Where is he, Lance?" the older one fired back angrily.

"Where is who?" Lance replied.

I swear to god, faster than a knife fight in a phone booth, the female approached Lance and had her hand around his throat. With one arm, she managed to lift him two feet off the ground. I looked at her face, and she wasn't even putting forth any effort to accomplish such an incredible feat of strength. Lifting the dead weight of a grown man off his feet by his throat with one arm was apparently nothing to her. Lance immediately started choking. Big Bear tried to rush the woman, but somehow the older man, fast as a blink, flashed from the middle of the front yard to the driveway. He must have traveled a solid twenty yards in a quarter of a second. He positioned himself between Big Bear and the woman and executed some sort of a double-fisted punch to Big Bear's chest. Big Bear was knocked off his feet by the colossal blow. He wound up flat-assed on the driveway with the wind knocked out of him. It was quickly established that these people were not normal human beings. Sam is a former Navy Seal. He is nothing short of a physical specimen—a mountain of a man. No normal old man on the planet could have knocked him down like that.

The man stood over Big Bear and shouted behind himself to Lance, who was still suspended by the throat by the woman. "You know exactly who we are referring to, Lance. Where is Daniel Hallowell?"

The woman lowered Lance back to his feet and eased her grip on his throat, allowing him to speak in between hitching, panicked coughing. "I don't know where he is. He saw something, something in the backyard. Right after that, he threatened us all and took off in his car. He went south. Why don't you go find him and leave us alone?"

The other two with the guns just sort of stood there, stoic. Their faces were completely devoid of expression throughout the entire ordeal. The woman locked eyes with Lance. Her face was a portrait of intensity. "You knew this would happen. You knew that if you brought one of them here, we would respond. You knew we would be forced to respond. Have you any concept of what you've done? Any concept of how dangerous he is?"

"Whoa, whoa, whoa!" I shouted. "Let's everyone take a breath. First off, who the hell are you people? And Lance, why do they think Danny is dangerous? It is high time you come clean about all the shit you're keeping from us."

The old man looked me dead in the eyes as he spoke. "Yes, Lance, why don't you explain to these people exactly what it is you have gotten them into? Why don't you tell them who their friend really is?"

"It's t-t-too m-m-much to explain right n-n-now," he replied, stammering and holding back tears.

Big Bear had since caught his breath and shouted, "You better figure out how to fight your way past that stutter and start talking. You don't want me to have to come over there and make you."

All eyes went over to Lance. He looked at the old man as though he were seeking his permission to tell us what we needed to know. The man obliged with an upward hand motion in Lance's direction as though to say, "Get on with it, moron." Lance took a series of deep breaths, wiped the tears from his eyes, composed himself, and began to talk. "Danny is what is referred to, as a Bridge. That means he can bridge the gap between this life and the realm that exists between lives. Basically, he is a very unique soul who exists in both realms at the same time."

"How could you possibly know this about him? You met him about twenty hours ago," I asked.

"There are only two such people living anywhere in the world at the moment. I found this in the house, alongside Harvey's memoirs."

Lance pulled out his wallet. From inside of it, he produced a thin, yellow, folded-up piece of paper. He unfolded it and handed it to me. It was a photograph—terrible resolution. It was a black-and-white image of what appeared to be a rock or a brick or something. Carved into it were about a dozen names. Each name had a city and date next to it. Daniel was near the bottom. **(Daniel Hallowell – Boston – 10/15/1978)**

"What the hell is this, Lance?" I asked.

"That is a list of all of the people who are earmarked as Bridges. It's their name, city of birth, and birthdate. It is a picture of the keystone that survived the fire at the old Ashford Hill Lunatic Asylum. The carving was only exposed after the building collapsed. It was not facing inside the building or outside, just another large stone. The other stone somehow became dislodged during the fire and toppled over, exposing these carvings. Nobody knows who or how those inscriptions were made. The face of the rock, where those carvings were made, would have been completely inaccessible."

I read the name below Daniel. *(Meng Xu – Shanghai – 4/7/2059)*

"How is this possible, Lance? The person below Danny isn't born for another forty years," I asked.

"The photograph of that keystone was taken in 1931. Danny wasn't born for another forty-seven years at that point. Somehow, whoever created this list had the ability to transcend time. They were somehow able to catalogue Bridges in the present as well as those in the distant future. All in all, the list appears to cover a span of about 250 years of past, present, and future Bridges."

Mr. Levine: Did Lance give you any indication as to how he acquired this photograph? Any idea of its whereabouts now?

Mr. Voss: I told you already that he found it in his house, in the same place where he found Harvey's book. Apparently, it was another artifact, left to him by his long-lost grandparents. I have no idea where it is now. I gave it back to Lance that night.

"So, what if Danny is a Bridge. Why does that make him dangerous?" I asked.

Lance replied, "It has long been rumored around Ashford that Roderick Crowe, the head doctor from the asylum prior to its devastation in the fire, was himself a Bridge. Allegedly, he used the vast power associated with that gift to create an incarnation rift here in Ashford."

"What the hell is an incarnation rift?" I asked.

Lance shook his head in a frustrated fashion. "We are getting into some subject matter here that I'm not sure I can explain to you. Or that I should explain to you. These guys would be better than me at explaining this further." He pointed in the general direction of the officials.

The woman stepped toward me and spoke. "Lance knowingly brought the one type of person into Ashford that we've worked for decades to prevent from getting into this town. Your friend Danny, if he falls into the wrong hands, has the power and potential to take the cancer that Crowe created and spread it to a point that is beyond our control."

I couldn't help but laugh. She was, after all, talking about Danny. I had known him for years up to that point. She was talking about the same guy who once knocked himself out cold at a nightclub because he got wasted and tried to do the atomic dog on the dance floor. Somehow, the combination of alcohol and his body position caused him to lose his balance and topple forward. The top of his head slammed flush into the hardwood. It's one of the damnedest things I have ever witnessed a human being do. He regained consciousness about a minute later. We all had to physically carry him out of the club and into a taxi, all the while laughing our asses off. But then, there I was, listening to some bionic woman describing Danny as though he were a god. It truly just came off as hilarious to me, initially.

Her head sort of tilted to the side in an inquisitive fashion, as though she'd never been laughed at before.

"Look, gorgeous," I said to her through my laughter, "I really don't know who you think my friend is. But I assure you, you have him pegged very wrong, and furthermore, you watched us all drive in here. Why not stop us then and turn us around if Danny is such a danger?"

She rolled her eyes at me in an annoyed fashion as she replied, "We watched a bunch of men in a truck and a rental car drive in. We didn't know who you were or what Danny was until we had had a chance to test you."

"Test us?" I asked.

"Those loud bangs over Lance's house that you might have noticed, that had you all screaming like girls. Those were a result of a device that we use to triangulate and understand identity across timelines. Only then were we able to determine the nature of Daniel's . . . condition."

"Wait, what?" I was growing more confused, but at least we had solved the mystery behind the horrifying crashes while in Lance's study.

"Do you still believe he is the same person here, in Ashford, as he is elsewhere?" she replied. "Do you believe that any of you are? Aren't you curious as to why you can't find your way home? Have you no concept of what this place is?"

"Well, I sure would love to know. All we've gotten so far are half answers and fallacies from numb-nuts over here." I pointed to Lance. As I finished talking, another fully blacked-out Yukon pulled into the driveway, seemingly out of nowhere.

The older man stepped away from Big Bear and spoke. "Come with us. It's in all of our best interest to locate your friend as quickly as we possibly can." He motioned for us to get into their vehicles.

Gary finally spoke up. "How do we know you're not going to drive us off someplace and chop our heads off or something, man?"

For the first time, the agents demonstrated some emotion other than stoic ultra-seriousness and laughed loudly at Gary's remark. The older man replied once his genuine amusement had subsided. "Where would you think we'd take you if we intended to kill you? There is no better place than where you stand now. It isn't like we could drive you off to a more remote location than Ashford."

"Fair enough," I said. "So, if we go with you, are you going to answer some of our questions?"

The woman replied, "If you come with us, it will be a mutually beneficial exchange."

"I like the sound of that," I replied with a snicker.

At that point, I didn't see a choice in the matter. These people, whoever they were, were our only ticket home. We all piled into the Yukon's and drove off. I rode with the blonde, naturally.

Mrs. Miles: Let's take a break. We will pick this up again after lunch.

Judge Stokes: Granted. I think we can all use a break to digest this . . . information.

26
Andy's Cabin in the Woods of Ashford, Ohio – 4:15 a.m.

"Should I even bother reading this book?" I asked Andy. "It seems to me that you know a hell of a lot more about this place and what goes on here."

"Not nearly as much as you'll get out of that thing."

"How so?"

"I'm a normal guy, Danny," he replied. "My interaction with Ashford has always been unique, but compared to you, pedestrian. What you've got there would fill in a lot of the gaps you're looking for. Hell, it would fill in a lot of the gaps I've been trying to fill for decades."

I was getting a horrible headache to go along with an ever-tightening knot in my stomach. "Why don't you explain to me why being a Bridge is so important around here? I mean, I've been a Bridge my entire life, right? Why is it suddenly such a big deal?"

"You've never been to Ashford. You have to understand a little bit about where you are."

"Okay, where am I?"

Andy's eyes wandered up toward the ceiling. He was trying to figure out how to answer me. He shifted the ice bag around on his crotch a bit and spoke. "Does it say anything in that book, however far you've made it into it, about a lunatic asylum burning down?"

"Yes, it does!" I replied, excited. "Harvey receives a letter from the sheriff of Ashford explaining it. Sheriff Williams, I think his name was. He says there were some strange goings-on around town—people vanishing. The townsfolk were growing increasingly anxious, and the burning of the asylum was sort of the straw that broke the camel's back."

Andy allowed my explanation to sink in for a moment before formulating his response. "Sure, sure. Here's why it was the straw that broke the camel's back. Prior to it burning down, it was run by Roderick Crowe. As I told you before, he was the head doctor for all the crazies they had pent up in there. The rumor is that he had developed a new therapy that awoke normally dormant parts of the human brain in his patients. Some gene therapy, chemical compound, mumbo-jumbo. It has been explained to me that it not only unlocked previously unused sections of the brain but also triggered horrific deformations to the physical brain. Prior to it burning down, there were reports of family members going to visit loved ones at Ashford Hill. When they were dropped off there, some of these people were mentally incompetent to the point of being dangerous to themselves and society. Others were mentally impaired to the point that literacy wasn't even possible, any sort of arithmetic was completely out of the question, they were unable to even feed or bathe themselves. Essentially, what is now referred to as severe mental impairment. However, after being administered Crowe's therapy for some time, these people not only became more intelligent, but their IQs ballooned into the genius scale. One case, which I think is mentioned in that memoir, is Margaret Peirce."

My eyes lit up. "Margret, yes. I just got to her."

"One of the few Ashford locals who I maintain contact with dug into her past using the Interweb or whatever you East-Coast, intellectual queers call it. She was originally committed to an asylum in Pennsylvania when she was five years old, after killing all her siblings in their sleep with a pair of scissors. She cut up three of them in all, two younger sisters and an older brother. She said that the demon Beelzebub told her to do it. She never went to any school, never had access to anyone who could have taught her much besides how to live in incarceration. However, she somehow survived the fire at the asylum. When she got out, she spoke and wrote in an incredibly advanced manner. She understood levels of mathematics and physics that college professors struggled with. She accurately described what, at the time, was a conceptual idea of nuclear fusion that has since been proven to occur in the center of stars—and it didn't stop there. She was able to accurately predict the future—near-term, long-term, future world events, future local happenings. She could look at a stranger and describe the entire history of their life to that point, what would happen to them later that day, days later, years later—even when and how they would die—and she was never wrong."

"Was she a Bridge, like me?"

"No, she was merely a normal person. But she had received Crowe's therapy. She was able to unlock and utilize every nook and cranny of her brain. She was how we all likely would be if we had the same reaction to Crowe's treatment."

"Okay, I'm still not seeing where I come in here."

"Your power, which you have no idea how to use. That is where you come in. Consider this, Margaret and the other patients at Ashford Hill were given some sort of medicine that made them more intelligent than Einstein. Yet, even with such an incredible level of brainpower, Crowe still managed to convince them that he was a god. They called him The Divine Father. These aren't your average misguided nitwits that would follow some lunatic to South America and drink his Kool-Aid. This was a group of people who were smart enough to comprehend the inner workings of quantum mechanics. Yet, at the same time, they absolutely worshiped this guy as though he were the second coming of Christ. That is a level of power that all of the gold in the world cannot buy."

My head was pounding. "So, what you're saying is——because I'm a Bridge like Crowe, I am as powerful as he was?"

"Precisely! You just have no idea how to awaken that power."

"Okay," I said with a chuckle. "How do I awaken it?"

"So, you're a Bridge, right? You are only different from everyone else when you're in an area where you're able to establish a connection to The Overworld. In your present circumstance, that's Ashford. Think of it logically. On much of the planet, we have no access to the other realms of existence other than the one that is right in front of our faces, all the time. Think of most places on earth like islands in the dead center of the Pacific Ocean. Where are you going to build a bridge to? Nothing but open water, right?

"Sure. Makes sense," I replied.

"But there are other places, Danny. You're sitting in one right now. Extraordinarily rare places where The Overworld is close enough to reach out and touch. But I can't touch it. None of your friends can touch it. But you are a Bridge. Not only can you touch it, you have the power to transcend consciousness and actually exist within it."

"So, why are those melon-heads all over my ass?"

"We'll get into that shortly. You like Chef Boyardee?"

"No better food to pile on top of a stomach full of vodka than precooked, canned pasta," I replied.

He stood, opened a cabinet above his head, and came away with two cans of ravioli. He emptied their contents into a saucepan and placed it atop the pellet stove. He tossed into the stove a couple scoops of wood pellets and some newspaper and fired it up.

"You know, as someone who behaves in an incredibly socially inappropriate fashion, leveraging the full menu of horrible, insulting, and homophobic words to describe others with, when you actually get to a point where you're explaining something you're interested in, you are incredibly eloquent. You're a fascinatingly interesting contradiction, my friend."

He looked at me, seemingly puzzled, and then pointed at his crotch. "What, do you want to make out or something, city boy? You're already intimately familiar with what I'm packing down here."

"I was just trying to make small talk. You're a tough nut to crack. No pun intended."

He continued, deflecting my attempt at a subject change, "You have to at least understand the CliffsNotes version of how the spirit world operates if you're ever going to truly harness your power."

"You know about the spirit world?"

"I do. The real spirit realm. Not some haunted house like you're accustomed to."

"So, there's a difference?"

Again, he began laughing. Only this time, he was holding his back, still trying to recover from the effects of our earlier skirmish. "Oh, yes," he replied. "It's very different. It's what I was getting at earlier. You need to throw out everything you think you know about religion. It is all nonsense. Here is how it all really works. I'm sure you've heard of the concept of a soul?"

"Of course."

"Not only do we all have one, but every living thing has a soul. Every animal, every plant, every tapeworm, every bacterium. Even in some rare cases, nonliving things can temporarily possess one. There is only one source of souls—a singularity that exists within The Overworld. The same realm that you have access to but can't yet consciously reach. Each of our souls is a sliver of that source. Some might refer to that source as god.

"Earth is only one of the innumerable places that exists beneath The Overworld. All beings that inhabit those countless planets get souls from the same singularity. Our souls are infinite. Our current bodies are only our current vehicle. Think of your body like a car: eventually it will die, and you'll get a new one. The purpose of each soul is to embark on a great conquest throughout the course of countless lives, on countless planets, as countless beings. At the end of the conquest, the soul will achieve an incredibly elusive level of perfect spiritual balance. Only then can that soul rejoin the singularity in The Overworld and participate in the creation of new worlds, new realms of reality, new matter, and new souls.

"Ultimately, it's a means of progressive and infinitely improving knowledge attainment, experience trending, and information gathering that contributes to and enriches the singularity itself. The better and more powerful this singularity is, the more balanced and knowledgeable our collective universe becomes. It is a constant, evolutionary cycle that, over eons, is designed to produce a celestial perfection through countless, natural, living experiences. For my money, it's a system that was put in place by a species who were billions of years more advanced than us. Maybe it's how every new universe becomes terraformed on a celestial level. I don't think there is a god, per se, rather an all-encompassing, indescribably powerful being in the form of that singularity, and we are all a part of it."

"What you're saying is that my soul, your soul, my friend Gary's soul, and everyone else's, is cut from the same cloth of the same singularity?"

"That's right."

"And that this life is just one of countless lives I've lived and am yet to live, all toward the betterment of my soul?"

"Precisely!"

"So, what happens if my soul doesn't get better in a life? What if I'm Hitler and I use my life to carry out unspeakable atrocities?"

"For most of us, there is a selection process for your next life. In a way, we all choose the lives that we take on in advance. Choosing a next assignment that best fits whatever state of soul development you're at, at the time, is one of the principal responsibilities of your soul group. That choice is a team effort. If you do poorly in one life, you reconvene with your soul group and elders in The Overworld and decide upon a better course of action for the next life. You can choose a life that has the best chance of further advancement. There is, indeed, another place where souls like Hitler end up, but that is a completely different conversation altogether."

"Lovely. So, why am I a Bridge to this realm and nobody else is? Why me?"

"Anybody's guess. Remember, we are all random shards, trimmed from the same singularity. Every shard is a little different. Everyone has different abilities, different mannerisms, different inherent values, different inherent motivations. In your case, along with everything that makes you . . . you, your soul has the rare ability to bridge this world to The Overworld while in this town. Think of how fucking rare that is, Danny. Try to comprehend the level of power that represents."

"Sounds more like dumb luck to me. I still have no idea how to utilize it."

"You've already caught a glimpse of The Overworld," he suggested.

"Is that right?" I asked.

"I believe you called it: The Black City."

27

The conversation dragged on. I felt the vodka taking hold. I hadn't realized how drunk I had gotten until I stood to take a piss. It was as though I had to correct for the rotation of the entire earth before I had my bearings and managed to aim my stream into Andy's incinerator toilet. There was absolutely no barrier between him and me as I pissed a mere three feet from him. Andy barely missed a bite of his ravioli. He remained completely unfazed, as though random men went to the bathroom within arm's length of him all the time. It occurred to me that I needed to understand Andy himself a bit. He certainly seemed to know a hell of a lot about me.

"How is it that you know all of this, Andy?" I finally asked. I was surprised to find that a thick slur had taken up residence in my voice.

To that point, Andy had been blathering through some very circuitous concepts that denounced all major religion and replaced the idea of god with some sort of penultimate singularity from which all our souls originate. His theories also replaced the idea of heaven with a temporary realm that we visit between the thousands of lives that we are apparently incarnated into. This happens until our souls become fully baked, for lack of a better term. Finally, at long last, our souls get to rejoin the original singularity.

In my line of work, at that time, I'd heard it all. On a normal day, had I been approached by some guy who was convinced that I was a human bridge between earth and the ethereal plains of the afterlife, I would probably back away slowly with my hand in my pocket, dialing 911. This was, however, far from a normal day. It had long since occurred to me that Andy was a little more than met the eye. It began to worry me. I am typically a very good judge of character based on first impressions. I had Andy pegged for your typical Kentucky-fried hillbilly, right up to the point that he began explaining all these incredibly fascinating theories to me. His confidence in the subject matter combined with his eloquent method of explaining it all constructed a human being who was a complete and total contradiction of the person I'd suspected him to be.

That really worried me. It's not every day you find yourself in a secluded cabin, sitting across a table from a stranger. A stranger who, an hour ago, you wondered whether he could read or write. Only to find out that he has mastered Euclidean theory and the geometry behind fractal dynamics. To boot, this man had somehow formulated his own set of theories that addressed some of the most fundamental questions of the human condition. Such as, what happens after we die? What is the purpose of our existence? Look no further for such answers—Andy is here, and he's got all of them. Fair warning, he's liable to snap at any moment, call you a queer, and try to beat the living shit out of you.

I kept running into the fact that what he was explaining to me would be impossible for any person to know with any level of certainty. The only chance that normal human beings get to experience the celestial side of their spiritual evolution is when they die. As Andy had explained, he was just a normal guy. I was the only Bridge in that room on that night. Therefore, however eloquently he may have been explaining his stance, it was still just speculation. However, I am a Bridge. I somehow knew he was right about me being one. That scared the shit out of me as well. That familiarity I had felt while looking at that blackened city, flying through those fractals and observing the apparition who guided me, had seeped back into the forefront of my mind. That same creeping familiarity that had taken me over as I'd investigated the eyes of the spectral man in Lance's backyard. His plastic-like perfectness hung thick over my head as I listened to Andy talk about all of it. It was as though Andy had triggered my own memories of the places and situations he described. He was bringing my subconscious to the forefront and converting that cached data that had long lay dormant in the deep recesses of my brain upward and into primary memory. A lot about myself started to make sense.

For example, I had essentially been forced to go through Catholic grade school. Being an orphan in Boston, good luck getting around that. I can clearly remember, even in the first grade while learning about religion, how incredibly nonsensical I found it. I was in the first grade; most kids that age believe in Santa Claus and the Easter Bunny. They believe pretty much anything any adult tells them. But for some reason, even then, Catholicism seemed about as logical to me as driving your car off a cliff in the off chance it would fly. I just, for some reason, knew that every nun or priest or deacon that was up there talking was feeding me bullshit. I got into major trouble once when I asked one of the nuns how she could possibly be an adult who "believes this shit." That was in the fourth grade. Even at that age, I characterized the people who pushed that material onto me as unstable lunatics. I am in my forties now and still do. Only now, it doesn't bother me nearly as much as it did then. Believe whatever makes you feel better is my stance. Just keep it to yourself and don't try to impress your scared, confused values onto me.

But I wasn't exactly in the majority. Most of my classmates ate it up. Many of them probably still do, to this day. While I never adopted any of those teachings in anything approaching a serious fashion, I did wonder about myself. Why was I seemingly programed to not believe? It seemed like everyone else was. I had wondered about that throughout all the years of my life up until that night. As Andy explained his hypothesis, it occurred that he was really filling a large gap in my sense of being. I was a Bridge, and because of that, I knew how things really worked. Most everyone else wasn't and were, therefore, open to suggestion. I was closed from day one. I knew, at least on a subconscious level, that at no point in human history had a brother and sister, likely somewhere in Iraq, talked to a snake who kept trying to get them to eat apples. It all sounded to me like someone free-writing their thoughts out on paper while in the final throes of a heroin overdose.

I was getting the complete opposite feeling on that night. I knew Andy was right. I could feel in my bones that it was the complete truth. Thoughts of previous lives that had occurred to me in years past but had been dismissed as fleeting vestiges of my subconscious began crashing into the forefront of my mind.

One moment, I was a soldier in a red coat, running through a thicket. I remembered feeling a piercing, unbearable pain in my back and then watching a mist of blood escape from my chest. Falling to the ground in front of me, I could recall understanding that it was all over. I had been shot through the heart, on some long-forgotten battlefield. That life, that assignment, had run its course.

The next moment, I was in a magnificent gown, dancing atop a half-finished pyramid. Palm trees swayed in the distance below, and a thousand slaves toiled in the sultry evening heat. The Great Sphinx was to my back, and I was overcome by a great sadness. This was my day of sacrifice before the pharaoh. I could recall watching the crowd dance below me in wild and feral celebration as my decapitated head rolled down the limestone stairs toward them. That life, that assignment, had run its course.

I could even recall nonhuman lives—forms of life, galaxies away, that even the wildest poet's imagination could not have conceived of. In one, I swooped through the clouds of a surfaceless planet. I was able to genuinely remember that I had to, throughout the course of my entire life, maintain a certain altitude for fear of never being able to escape the crippling gravity of my super-massive home-world. I grew old and eventually weakened. One day, when ready, I allowed myself to become doomed to the crushing atmosphere within the depths. That life, that assignment, had run its course.

I conjured another fleeting thought of being a conscious, energy-based life-form. I thrillingly bounded, at the speed of light, across my metallic, conductive planet. The ability to make decisions at that velocity was positively spellbinding. I was consciously aware of the fact that to move, I had to jump from one metal-rich planetary plate to another. All the while, I had to avoid the certain death that came with accidently encountering the rogue, magnetic iron deposits that dotted my lands. After what, relative to me, was a long, magnificent existence (in human terms, probably about ten minutes), my electrical signal weakened, and my energy evaporated from the rocky face of that home-world. That life, that assignment, died with it.

In each life, I remembered dying. One way or the other, I became deceased. It seemed that the concept of life and death was a shared, universal certainty. Perhaps immortality was an omnipresent, cosmic impossibility. Being unable to live forever did, after all, jive with Andy's take on things. If souls had the ability to exist forever, inside of a single incarnated existence, they would never return to and enrich the singularity.

Andy was smiling across from me. He was still talking, but I could no longer hear any of his words. I stole a glance at my cup. It was still three-quarters of the way full. I could handle my liquor. I hadn't had nearly enough to be blacking out. But it seemed that I was, for some reason. As I gazed back up from my beverage and my eyes again met Andy, I found him laughing hysterically. I could see him trembling, red-faced, in uncontrollable amusement. For a moment, I knew something was wrong. Then the entire world turned black.

I found myself thinking of the fractals. I began to remember dying in previous lives and what would happen just after my terrestrial consciousness would cease. I tried to wrestle myself awake, but my eyelids were lead weights, my arms and legs were jelly, the gravity of the earth had increased by a factor of a million. I was too deep into my own thoughts. I punched my ticket again, back into the chaos of my own subconscious.

I somehow knew my way around, although I never controlled where I ended up. As soon as I would arrive, however, it was as though I had driven back into my old hometown. I knew every landmark, every iridescent flash or flicker against the flowing, liquid, glassy background. I'd seen it all a thousand times before. I would eventually end up surrounded by my dearest, oldest, most-beloved friends——my soul group. A group of souls, like me, who were all cut from the same quadrant of the singularity. We were grouped together to assist one another along our journey throughout all our lives. We pointed out the failures and accomplishments in our most recent incarnations and helped one another select future lives. All of this was to collectively advance the souls within our group to that pinnacle of enlightenment, where we would all be able to rejoin the singularity.

The concept of love is universal, and it stems directly from that place. The members of my group, or any soul group, rarely incarnated together into the same terrestrial location and time. Therefore, we hardly ever crossed paths in a living form. Even if we had, we would likely not have known it. But as soon as I reunited with them in that awe-inspiring celestial nirvana, I felt as though I were home. I was surrounded by my real family——my universal family. A group of souls who had been with me and guided me through thick and thin for eons upon eons, since the beginning of time.

I looked around, my heart and mind filled with a near-overwhelming sense of euphoric joy. All my friends were around me. Gishgim and Shesa stood to my right. Ahead of me were Amki and Hazi—the funniest of all of us in the group. In the middle was Penzer, one of the more advanced souls among us. Most of them glowed a dim yellow or a dull to mildly flickering orange, but Penzer was a shimmering blue-gold—many lives and many experiences ahead of the others. I, however, was on a completely different echelon, emitting a shimmering molten-purple hue. I was an extremely advanced soul, far closer than the rest of my group to rejoining the singularity.

Suddenly, the smile eroded from Penzer's face. He looked upon me in genuine horror and shouted, "Urbarra, who did you bring?"

I recentered my gaze to my left and was met by The Perfect Man. The same man I had faced eye-to-eye in Lance's backyard. He was still smiling at me with that sinister, salesman grin. I could feel my heart pound within my earthbound body as soon as I saw him. He had invaded my most intimate of haunts. Nothing about him belonged there among my soul group. I looked away from him and back over to Hazi and Amki. They had begun backing away from us, as had the others. I sensed their fear. I had put them in grave danger by introducing this entity into their midst. This was a realm that was not supposed to be infiltrated by such an abomination.

Evil permeated from him. It had become obvious that his outward appearance was simply a façade for the horrifying reality it concealed. As I looked back at him, his smile was gone, replaced by a gaping lower jaw. He stood stoically, mere feet away. His reflection glistened off the glassy backdrop with his lower jaw at least a foot below the upper. Inside his cavernous mouth was blackness. A blackness like I had never seen before—a thousand times darker than a cloudy, moonless night. He wanted me to look inside it. He was showing me something. It was the absence of life, devoid of anything pure, completely vacant of all joy or comfort.

The Perfect Man was before me, and he represented everything that was evil throughout all known realities, transcending all space and time. As were the fractals a representation of my inner soul, he was a representation of Satan himself. I say that with a tinge of disfavor for the term. Satan is a Biblical character, after all, and I have spoken ad nauseam about my feelings toward that train of thought. However, as I witnessed the pestilence who had stalked me through a physical town in Ohio and clear into the recesses of my very soul, I remain at a loss for a better descriptive.

There was no concept of fear in that place. There was no concept of judgment, no social status, no economic status, no representation of guilt or even disappointment. It had been a refuge from such earthly emotion since the creation of the universe. But on that night, there was a cancer ripping apart the very fabric that held my dearest group of souls together. A malignant calamity that I knew would follow me to the end of everything, pressing the weight of its heinous agenda down upon me and everything I dared to love.

As he walked closer, he seemed to inexplicably grow several feet in stature. He towered over me, looking down with his horrible jaw still stretched down past the middle of his chest. He managed to speak to me without any use of his mouth. "Urbarra, I wish to show you how to exist outside of time."

I was petrified. My mind raced, grasping for an appropriate response. After a fleeting panicked moment, I managed to vocalize the only thought that could gain a foothold within my vacillating mind. "How? How are you here? What is your purpose here?" I shouted in The Perfect Man's direction.

He was right on top of me, his face not two feet from mine. As I looked at him, his immaculate facial features became abstracted. It was suddenly as though I were observing him through an invisible sheen of frosted glass. His disgusting, gaping chasm of a mouth melted upward and over the middle portion of his face. I could no longer make out a single, discernable facial feature.

Through the middle of the fog that had become of the spectral monster before me arose something far worse. It was as though it were approaching from a distance, through the haze that had become of him. It was getting closer. His face had melted away into a murky compound of plasmatic material that hung clumsily in the air, dancing to the now-hammering drum of my pounding heart. I could hear my pulse inside of my own ears. I knew I was getting close to being taken over by shock, to succumbing to the indescribable dread that I felt in that moment. The beast beneath his façade of perfection had just then come into view.

Out of the obscured vapor that remained of his cloak, the demon emerged. With it came the storm—a flood of impassioned rage detonating in that higher realm of consciousness as an ineffable barrage of electrical discharge. The monster was projecting its wrath into my Overworld. With it came raw, unbridled emotion, manifesting as the raging tempest I found myself trapped inside of. There was no longer any sign of the other members of my soul group. The pristine shimmer of my nirvana was rendered all but a myth among the whipping gale that surrounded the nightmare before me.

It was here.

Before me, I beheld the most shockingly terrifying entity that my mind could have possibly conjured. Its general form was humanoid, but that was where the similarities ended between us and it. It stood no more than five feet tall, was desperately thin, and hunched over slightly to its front. Its white-gray skin glistened in the opaque half-light produced by the still-raging electrical bombardment that accompanied its presence. Its thoroughly exposed body was coated with a clear, oily substance that produced a sheen over its entire dermas. The ectoplasmic substance, whatever it was, seemed to have been baked onto it as though the demon had been basted with it as it broiled in the flames of Hell.

It was looking directly into my eyes. The face was something half skeletal with the last vestiges of paper-thin flesh stretched over. Its nose was a mere point of cartilage with a bisecting strand of skin at its bottom, segregating its abnormally large nostrils. Otherwise, it was a black hole in the dead center of its face. Above its nose were its beady eyes, completely absent of a discernable pupil or iris. They were impossibly black, as though each were comprised of nonvisible matter, producing the complete absence of anything that could possibly reflect light. They were sunken deep into the sockets. Around the eyes, a more concentrated mass of sludge had accumulated, creating a mirror-like radiance that, for reasons I cannot explain, glowed a neon yellow. It produced a raccoon-like effect around its eyes, surrounding the endless blackness of them with a halo of vivid jaundice.

There were no teeth in its mouth, however; the shape and absence of lips and rigid boniness of its jaw and chin gave it a beak-like chasm in the middle of its face that appeared perfectly capable of cutting its way through flesh. Its mouth was a similar black hole, devoid of teeth or gums of any kind. Not unlike its original form, it hung open in an unnatural, horrendous fashion.

Its arms and legs were a flagrant, unwelcomed contradiction to the rail-thin trunk that made up its torso. It had the shoulders of a wrestler—defined and muscular. The shoulders continued downward to equally chiseled arms. The tone was as impressive as it was objectionable. Still matted in the glistening, gray-white paste, still covered-over by a meager, single layer of decaying flesh, however the muscles that comprised its arms and legs were more perfectly defined than those of Michelangelo's David. Its fingers appeared more as grossly elongated talons than anything resembling human appendages. Scaly, charcoal-colored fingers, each a foot long, terminated into razor-sharp, blackened nails that curled downward. Each was a perfect weapon, honed and sharpened over centuries of acrimony in whatever torturous realm it called home. Its feet were equally as threatening.

It brought with it everything I'd felt when I'd previously been dragged toward The Black City by the phantom. The same paralyzing fear mixed with mind-altering ire. I had seen a lot in my time investigating the paranormal. I'd even, on occasion, been physically and emotionally affected by disembodied spirits and poltergeists. Nothing came close to the unbearable, psychological impact that this uninvited hijacker pressed upon me on that horrible night. It was not a slow creep this time around. It was as though a switch had been flipped and I was immediately inundated by concentrated malice.

My fear of it melted away, although I don't think I became less terrified of it. It was as though it forcibly transformed my fear into rage. My dread evolved naturally into fury. It sensed my fear, knowing I was looking at something so unnatural to the human condition that it might push a man to levels of panicked horror, driving him irreversibly out of his mind. Sensing this, the demon pushed the fear from me. In its place, it filled me with the one thing it knew: evil.

"What are you!" I shouted. My voice was barely audible over the thunderous whipping of the battering storm that it rode into my realm.

Its voice was deep and monotone, slow yet methodical. It cut through the heavy atmosphere like a razor in a controlled, animalistic growl. "I've been given countless names by countless beings on countless worlds. Your hunger, Daniel. I can smell your hunger. A rare bird you are, to experience such a divine hunger."

It paused a moment. Its gaze turned upward, as though it were sensing the murderous animosity within me through the air above. Its sharpened claws dangled below its waistline as though it were pushing the atmosphere around in an effort to gain additional knowledge from its surroundings. A moment later, it returned its eyes to mine and continued, "Countless beings on countless worlds, Daniel. I've eaten every kind. Your hunger—the only way you will make it go away is to satisfy it!"

It lunged forward as it screamed the last sentence. A thousand storm clouds discharged blue streams of electricity as it did. Its horrible mouth shot a wake of vile sputum in my direction. The wind around us in that moment reached hurricane force. I was thrust backward, thrown a thousand yards from my previous perch. The disorientation quickly induced a sense of panic. I was spinning with no ability to control myself or arrest my momentum. I closed my eyes and began to scream.

Slowly, as my voice ran hoarse, the spinning subsided. For the first time in what felt like hours, I could sense the existence of my arms and legs. I was back in my human form. When my eyes opened, I was temporarily blinded, but my pupils quickly dilated as sunlight penetrated the forest canopy above. I was sitting in the same chair as I had been, but Andy was no longer anywhere to be found.

I was absolutely freezing, likely in the preliminary stages of hypothermia. The cabin around me was in ruins. I could see the remnants of the pellet stove and the shattered pile of porcelain that was once the incinerator toilet. One wall of the cabin was left standing, but barely. The others had been reduced to a few rotting studs. The makeshift tin roof had fallen forward and rested before me as a rusting pile of scrap. The floor of the cabin was reduced to a mound of soggy lumber, coated with patches of moss. I picked up a can that I found nestled against my foot. The wrapping was sun-drenched and waterlogged, and the inside had long since accumulated moisture and mildew. The label was still barely visible: Chef Boyardee – Beef Ravioli.

This was, indeed, the cabin I had begun my soul-ravaging journey from. The same cabin I had been comfortably inside of what seemed like hours before. However, it was obvious that there had not been a cabin there for a very long time.

28

The Deposition of Rick Voss: (First Session):

Agent Roy: *So, Ricky, you just got into a car with these super-humans? No questions asked?*

Mr. Voss: *To be quite honest with you, I don't know what other choice we had. We attempted to drive out of town only to discover that we couldn't, at least not how we drove in. My best friend had lost his mind and gone missing. These people, however strange, shared our goal of finding Danny and getting him, along with the rest of us, the hell out of there.*

Mr. Levine: *Where did these people take you?*

Mr. Voss: *They took us on a very short trip to what used to be a transfer station on the outskirts of town. Obviously with so few residents, there was no longer any garbage collection or recycling service. So, they repurposed the facility and were using it as their base of operation.*

Mr. Levine: *Take us through your time there.*

Mr. Voss: *We pulled down a long, rock driveway that was wide enough for two lanes. It was fenced on both sides with woods beyond the fence. It was so dark. If it weren't for our headlights, we wouldn't have been able to see anything. Mind you, I had been in rural areas before and driven around them at night. But up until that point, they had all been domesticated—active areas where people lived. There were typically other cars, lights from surrounding homes and businesses. You take for granted even that sort of minimal illumination. The normalcy you get when you live and travel around active areas seems commonplace until you get into a place like Ashford. The darkness at night there is disorienting. It makes you cling to the people you're with or any new people you can find for fear of finding yourself alone there in that sort of desolation. I can't really explain it any better. We were all to a point mentally when we ran into those people that we were willing to take every chance that could help us find our way out.*

The forest broke open into a massive clearing after about two minutes on that dirt road into the transfer station. Ahead of us were two buildings. To our right was a massive steel structure like an aircraft hangar. The other, dead ahead of us, must have been the old administrative building. It was something right out of the seventies—yellow plaster, tall and rectangular with recessed windows. In between the two sets of windows was an entryway which consisted of a green, fabric canopy over a glass door. I couldn't see any lights on inside of the building despite it having such large windows.

We got out of the vehicles. The surrounding environment felt ominous; we could all immediately sense it. There weren't any animals making noise or crickets or lightning bugs. The whole town just seemed . . . dead. The four with the guns took up a position that faced outward, toward the woods we had passed through on the way in. They were guarding our perimeter from something. We continued to the one door, and without anyone doing anything, what looked like a tablet slid out of a slot in the wall next to the door. It rode along on some sort of umbilicus. It snaked approximately five feet out of the wall, oriented itself so the screen was facing up and outward in front of the boss man. This was not something that had been there when these people took the building over. Quite frankly, it didn't look like something that should've existed anywhere. The entire apparatus was shimmering chrome, except for the paper-thin black tablet it held.

After it made a series of different pitched beeping noises, the boss man placed the palm of his hand on the screen. As he did so, an odd lighting effect appeared on and above the screen. The light from it projected beneath and around his palm, giving off the illusion that his hand had penetrated the screen, as though he had reached inside of the tablet. Once his hand was inside, an electronic voice came from some hidden speaker above. "Eribu, sut Resi," which I have since translated to: "Enter, Commander."

Agent Roy: *What language is that?*

Mr. Voss: *Sumerian.*

Agent Roy: *Commander of what exactly?*

Mr. Voss: *I'm getting to that, Martin.*

Anyhow, the boss man's hand was still within the light effect given off by the future iPad thing. He seemed to move his hand around in a rehearsed, orchestrated fashion. Then he pulled his hand out, the light shut off, the thing went back into the wall, and the door unlocked.

We all walked inside, and the door closed behind us. We were inside of an entryway. In front of us was what looked like a vault door like you would see at a bank. The glass from the first door was tinted black and covered over with another layer of black film, making it impossible to see outside or, likely for good reason, inside.

As soon as the door shut behind us and locked, a panel lit up to the left of the vault door. This time, the attractive blonde stepped forward and placed her palm on top of it. No light effects this time, just a different series of beeps and blips. A new, electronic voice from the heavens filled the room. Again, in Sumerian. "Eribu, Etlu Ilati." This translates to "Enter, Warrior Goddess."

Mr. Levine: *Why are these people's computers speaking to them in a language that predates the birth of Christ by nearly three thousand years?*

Mr. Voss: *This is all far easier to understand if I explain it in chronological order and as thoroughly as possible. If I must keep stopping and answering questions, we will be here all night.*

Mr. Levine: *Is it necessary that you take us through the entry into this facility step by step like this?*

Mr. Voss: *You tell me, buddy. I'm not in any position to determine what is or is not necessary. You're the ones asking the questions. You told me to take you through it, and that's exactly what I'm doing.*

(Sighs from Mr. Levine)

Mr. Levine: *Fine, Mr. Voss. Please carry on.*

Mr. Voss: *You bet.*

So, the computer talks, and Miss Warrior Goddess takes her hand off the screen, and as soon as she does, a series of loud bangs go off, one after another. The vault door was unlocking. One of the gun-wielding guys approached it and clutched its two handles and swung it open. That door must have weighed five hundred pounds, easy. He swung it open like it was the door to his pantry.

We entered. The room was vast—soaring ceilings at least twenty feet above our heads. It was near complete darkness, only a single, infrared lamp above our heads illuminated the area in an eerie red glow. As we passed that, the rest of the lights in the room flickered on, temporarily blinding us all. It took several moments for our eyes to adjust to the brightness. As our pupils came back down to their normal size, we found ourselves in a large room. The entire interior of the administrative building had been gutted and converted into one boundless space. There were dozens more of the people who'd brought us there toiling away, working, doing whatever in the hell they did all day and night. Everything was white—the walls, the furniture, the doors, even the tile on the floors. The ceiling above had been stripped to the girders, and each was lined with odd strips of what must've been LEDs. They didn't seem like they should have been powerful enough to illuminate the room, but they packed a hell of a punch.

"How are all these people working without any lights?" Big Bear asked.

The boss man answered, "We owe you a bit of explaining. For now, let's just say, we don't require light nearly as much as you do."

A bunch of the others who were in earshot stopped and smiled. Everyone seemed friendly enough, just very weird. None of them were speaking to one another. They all seemed to be going about their tasks completely independent of one another. I still don't understand their organizational structure, but it seemed to be working for them.

We were led through a series of desks, down a walkway that perfectly bisected the room down its center. Some of the desks were occupied; others were vacant. The ones where people were working glowed from underneath in an infrared, crimson-colored light. There weren't any computers or keyboards or monitors. I didn't see a stapler the entire time I was there or a tape dispenser or a little jar of pens and pencils or paperclips. Instead, each one of them sat at their desk, basking in the infrared light. Each of the workers wore what appeared to be chrome headphones over their ears. Leading beneath the desks were clear, fiberoptic wires that seemed to contain a more concentrated stream of the red light. The light traveled upward from underneath the desk and into their left ear-cups. From the right ear, it traveled in the other direction and back underneath the desk.

"What are all these people doing? And what are these headphones they're using?" I asked.

The blonde sort of giggled as she responded, "It would be very difficult for you to comprehend. It is a level of collaboration that your kind will someday, far into the future, begin to understand."

I was baffled. She explained it as some technology that didn't yet exist. But there it was, inches away from me, clear as crystal. And what did she mean by 'my kind'?

"Can you expound upon that? What am I looking at here?" I asked.

Nobody bothered to reply. The boss man led us to the far wall of the room. It was flat-white, like everything else in that place. To the naked eye, it just looked like a normal plaster or sheetrock wall but suddenly, once again, another one of their iPad version eight-thousands appeared out of nowhere. The boss man performed some more of his magic, and a door manifested out of nothing and opened into a conference room. There were about a dozen, white, sleek, bucketed seats attached to a metallic-white table. The wall-slash-door shut behind us. Somehow, we were still able to see out into the facility, as though there were a normal glass window between us. The lights flicked on, and at the same time, the facility outside went back to complete darkness. All that could be seen outside of our room were the red lights emanating from the various workstations.

The muscle had not come into the room. It was me, the boss man, the blonde, Gary, Big Bear, and Lance. We were all deep into some combination of horror, confusion, and curiosity as we sat down in random seats around the table.

Gary was the first to say anything. "Tell me you guys have some food in this place."

The blonde asked, "What is it that you would like to eat, Gary?"

"A double quarter-pounder with cheese, large fry, and large Coke," he replied, with a chuckle.

She looked at Lance, who was more terrified than anything else.

"The same. I would like the same, I guess," Lance said.

She looked at me.

"So just any old thing I want, and you can produce it?" I asked.

"Probably," she answered.

"Fine," I replied with a chuckle. "Put me down for a twelve-ounce filet, medium-rare, with a twice-baked potato on the side and an ice-cold can of PBR."

Finally, she looked at Big Bear, who, without hesitation, proclaimed, "I would kill a grown man for a big old bowl of Texas chili, some garlic bread, and about sixty ounces of ice water to wash it down with."

Seemingly as soon as Big Bear had finished his sentence, the faux door to the room swung open and one of the suited eunuchs entered, pushing a cart. It contained exactly everything we had ordered. My filet was sizzling; Big Bear's chili was steaming hot. My twice-baked potato, despite my not specifying, had all the fixings preadded—butter, cheddar cheese, and sour cream. My steak was cooked to medium-rare perfection, exactly how I would normally have taken it. Lance and Gary got their McDonald's sans any of the packaging and sort of looked at me and Big Bear disappointedly, clearly jealous of our choices. Big Bear got a giant glass that appeared to contain exactly sixty ounces of water.

We all dove in headfirst. None of us had eaten much since breakfast, and quite a bit of shit had happened since then. It occurred to me, somewhere between my third and fourth mouthfuls of my incredibly delicious steak, that there was no explainable, conceivable way that anyone should have been able to produce the food we were ingesting so quickly. None of us cared. We dug into it like a pack of bears who had just roused from hibernation. The boss man and woman sat and watched us eat for a while—both appeared disgusted.

"I am hoping you aren't judging us by our eating habits," Gary said. "We just haven't eaten much today. I get low blood sugar."

The woman replied, "And what better food to get that blood sugar back to optimal levels than a double quarter-pounder with cheese. Enjoy it, Gary. Afterward, we need to get down to some business."

I spoke up in between bites. "The tech in this office is decades ahead of anything any of us have seen. You can produce food out of thin air. I think before we get down to any sort of business, we need to understand a little bit about who in the hell you people are. None of us are going to be very comfortable working with you until we do."

The woman began to speak, and the boss man quickly cut her off. "Allow me. Firstly, my name is Aniku." He pointed to the woman as he continued, "And this is my longtime colleague, Anunit."

"What language are those names derived from?" asked Lance.

The man shook his head and replied, "Sumerian to you, as that is the civilization from your timeline who used our language. We refer to our language as Vu. Your distant ancestors spoke Vu because it is the language that all new species are first given at the time they are ready to begin communicating among one another in such ways."

Big Bear replied, "Wait a minute, you people gave us the Sumerian language?"

"That's right. We give Vu to our children species at a very specific time in their enlightenment. It is standard protocol for all earth-like species. There are other types of life-forms who are given different, early types of communication, but any humanoid species, such as your distant ancestors, with oral communications capabilities, are given Vu."

"Why?" I asked.

"These questions that I am answering for you were answered based off trial-and-error experiments that predate the existence of this entire universe. We found, a very long time ago, that a fledgling species, having been left to their own devices, will fumble around for millennia before they establish a workable language. Without a workable language, said species will obviously not communicate well. They will, therefore, spend thousands of years fighting one another over basic misunderstandings. It was found that simply introducing language to them and allowing them to take it, advance or transform it into whatever works best for them, greatly accelerates that species's ability to begin collaborating, advancing technologically, socially and spiritually."

"So, you're like, what, aliens?" asked Gary.

The man seemed to be considering the term, unsure exactly how to respond. After a moment of thought, he explained, "From your perspective, 'alien' may be a fair term but is still quite a bit off the mark. Traditionally, the human species describes aliens, as beings from another planet. We don't exist on any planet specifically. It is very difficult for me to explain what we are without using terms that you might perceive as arrogant or blasphemous."

"Trust me, Aniku, you won't offend any of us," Big Bear replied.

"Do try your best to follow along. I will explain from your perspective, as it greatly differs from ours. We do not conceive time in the same way your species does. There is a very ancient philosophy—and by ancient, I submit there is no human simplification that can be applied to describe how old it is. This protocol effectively governs the realm that you exist within. It is known as the Deshcarn Mode. The Deshcarn Mode is the all-encompassing protocol that describes the process that governs the circle of life and consciousness across all realities. By all realities, and using your terms, every form of life on every planet in every solar system in every galaxy within this universe and beyond.

"At its most basic core, the Deshcarn Mode is a game. It allows beings of the upper realm, once we reach a very enlightened state, to create new universes. Within those universes, we gain the ability to sow the seeds that will eventually produce life. Once that life is produced, we can assist it, with as little influence as possible, to advance. Once our creations are advanced enough to conceive of their own consciousness, we begin to implant them with genii or what you refer to as . . . a soul. Each soul is carved from our singularity—our great storage of knowledge. An infinitesimally small fragment of that singularity is passed to each of our created at the time of their first consciousness. To answer your question—are we aliens? Well, in the sense that we are not indigenous to this planet, sure. But, keep in mind that we aren't indigenous to what you conceive of as space and time, either. We didn't show up here in flying saucers, we don't abduct people to experiment on them, we don't mutilate cattle or leave circles in cornfields."

Anunit let out a brief giggle as she listened, finding humor in Aniku's attempt at explaining who and what they were.

Aniku continued, "The idea of aliens as imagined by humanity is, for lack of a better term, naïve. It demonstrates . . . and please excuse me if you find this insulting . . . a systemic inability for humanity to extrapolate. You've, long ago as a species, figured out that if you ever wanted to travel the stars, you would first need to invent a way of getting from point A to point B in such a way that doesn't involve you having to burn an accelerant. The distances are too far. Such a journey would, therefore, require more resources than you could possibly mine from your own planet to reach your closest celestial neighbor. However, for some reason, you seem unable to apply that same logic while imagining aliens. Stories of them arriving within the very types of ships that you know are woefully inadequate and desperately inefficient abound throughout your cultures."

I spoke up. "Okay, we get it. You're not little green men from Mars, but who exactly are you, and where exactly do you originate from?"

"The closest term that human beings have conjured up to describe us with, throughout all of your millennia on earth, would be . . . angels. Please understand, we ultimately are your creators. Well, not us personally, but we stem from the same overarching civilization who did create you. You must also understand, I am attempting to explain who we are to members of a race who have not yet developed the appropriate language or mathematics to describe us with. It would be akin to one of your neurosurgeons of today attempting to explain what he does to a caveman. I truly mean no offense to any of you. It is the truth."

"None from me. Every time I talk to Gary here, I feel like I'm talking to a caveman," I shot back, getting a few chuckles from around the room.

I pressed on, "To me, angels are beings from our spiritual culture, be it Christianity, Buddhism, Islam—most major religions have some concept of them. They are often guides of sorts. They are said to assist those who have lost their way back onto whatever path that particular religion says that people should be on."

Aniku smiled. "Certainly! You've hit the nail on the head, my friend. Obviously, we are in no way affiliated with any of your major religions. Your religions are based on concepts completely dreamt up by human beings and ultimately have no bearing whatsoever outside of your own planet. Religion is not a concept that we pass on to the species we create. They do tend to come about, though, nearly without fail. Typically, the moment one of our species develops the ability to think on a celestial level, religion inevitably becomes established. Religion is far more of a species's reaction to the idea of celestial loneliness teamed with an inherent fear of death than anything else."

Mr. Levine: I'll have you know, Mr. Voss, I am a devout Christian. I haven't missed a week of church in forty-two years. All of this is becoming very difficult for me to listen to.

Mr. Voss: Would you like for me to leave out the parts that I think might be difficult for you to listen to?

Mr. Levine: If this is indeed relevant to the chain of events that cost people their lives in this town of yours, then carry on. If it isn't, please skip to the relevant details.

Mrs. Miles: Mr. Levine, you have asked my client several times to take you through these events as he remembers them. He is in no position to determine what is or is not relevant to your case. If you would like for him to give you specific details about specific events that you may find more relevant, please feel free to ask more pointed questions. Thus far, he has given you exactly what you've asked for.

Mr. Voss: *And stop referring to Ashford as "my town". As I've previously stated, you and the rest of these suits in here may or may not believe me, but all I can do is tell you what I know. One more insinuation that I'm somehow making this all up, and I swear to god the next guy to depose me will be asking me questions about the time I kicked seven shades of shit out of a state prosecutor.*

Judge Stokes: *That's quite enough, Mr. Voss. Might I remind you that you are obligated to be here via an official summons from the State of Ohio. You are going to sit there and answer these questions to our satisfaction. And Mr. Levine, either assist your subject with more pointed questions or quit bitching about what he is explaining. You can't have it both ways.*

Mr. Levine: *I will tell you one thing, your honor. I am not obligated to be here, and if this is how I am going to be talked to, I will happily leave.*

Mr. Voss: *Works for me. Door's right over there.*

Agent Roy: *Judge, might I just state that I personally am finding the subject's explanation extremely informative. I feel as though he is telling us what he knows in a lucid series of chronological events as he witnessed them, which is what I am ultimately after.*

Mr. Voss: *Well, hey, thanks, Martin.*

Mr. Levine: *Is there much more about their ideas around religion, Mr. Voss?*

Mr. Voss: *Tons.*

(Sighs from Mr. Levine)

Mr. Levine: *Fine. Let's just get on with it.*

Mr. Voss: *So, anyhow, I was pressing Aniku on why he described his kind as angelic. He continued, "We are only angelic in the sense that I am a protector for your species and many others. A protector against certain events that may undermine the Deshcarn Mode. An incarnation rift, such as the one happening right now, in this very town, is one such event."*

"Sounds more like a god to me," Big Bear said. "I mean, you claim to be our creators, early influencers, and you are obviously over-watching us."

"Gods, at least the ones you've created for yourselves, typically want something back from the ones they create. We simply want to protect our own interests. We certainly do not require anyone to worship us. In fact, we go to incredible lengths to remain unknown in the eyes of our created. Forgive me again if this offends you, but we have completed a great deal of research to prepare an answer to this very question, and the closest we can come up with that you would understand is, indeed, 'angel.'

"A hint for you and your race to take with you when you eventually leave here. While your kind is inimitably early in your research of such topics, advancements in your fields of metaphysics combined with continual evolution and understanding of quantum theory will eventually lead your kind to the correct mathematics. Once you understand that, you will eventually be able to demystify the behaviors of light and what time truly is and where it comes from. This will help your kind reconcile the weakness of gravity in relation to the other physical forces and allow you the ability to develop the necessary language to describe who we really are. So, perhaps now, you understand the difficulty in my attempts to explain this to you?"

"That certainly was a mouthful. Sounds a lot more like physics than it does metaphysics. I am fairly well studied in metaphysics," I stated.

"Your kind has barely scratched the surface of how those two worlds need to function as one or how to demand answers to your most puzzling questions. Eventually, someone will question whether the human brain could conceive of a mathematical simplification for many of your great questions. Eventually, that research will conclude that the human brain is indeed capable of finding a simplification for those questions; however, it is deprived of the necessary calculus, as it does not yet exist on your planet. Your ability to philosophize has already begun to outpace your scientists' ability to prove or disprove questions that the philosophers are posing to them. You are ever close. But you simply do not have the resources to prove anything out. The idea of looking within yourselves on a metaphysical and quantum level will eventually show you the path forward."

"You mentioned that there was a rift happening here? What exactly is that, and why is our friend wrapped up in it?"

"Your friend Danny, as I mentioned before, is a Bridge. And the event we have been referencing is an incarnation rift. The Deshcarn Mode dictates what souls are assigned to what hosts. An incarnation rift is an indescribably rare event. One may only occur when a host who is a Bridge manages to manipulate the process of soul assignment. Which is exactly what Crowe managed to accomplish here."

"I'm sorry, I don't understand," I said. "You are saying that some psychotic doctor, decades ago, managed to gum up the works of a system that your kind have been fine-tuning for billions of years?"

"Roderick Crowe was and still is a Bridge, like your friend. You must be an incredibly advanced soul to possess such an ability, perhaps one or two incarnations away from being ready to rejoin the singularity. There is an inherent risk, as well as an inherent trust involved, which we are very aware of, in allowing such souls to incarnate at all. We typically trust that once a soul has managed to reach such an echelon, then that soul, no matter what circumstance they may incarnate into, is trustworthy and will be able to navigate any scenario we could conceive. However, there is a risk. Being a Bridge, allows the host the ability to transcend its own reality within its own conscious mind. From completely within themselves, they can consciously travel between their incarnated realm—in this case, earth—and our realm. Other non-Bridges can also, in chemically induced circumstances, travel to our realm, but only within their unconscious minds. Therefore, their experiences are dismissed as dreams or hallucinations, and no specific details are remembered. A Bridge is as conscious as you or me as they make the journey, able to absorb detail and memories. A Bridge can, however, only travel from very specific and disparate points in space and time. Therefore, the risk is ultimately low. They must exist in the right celestial location, out of innumerable galaxies containing an infinite number of celestial locations, during an appropriate and relatively short time frame to make the inward journey into our realm.

"Crowe, in this case, defying incredible odds, managed to inwardly travel outside of his earthbound realm and gain knowledge that would have been otherwise impossible for him to acquire. He then used that knowledge to, up until now, permanently link this point of space-time with the dimension where he gained that knowledge. He created a pathway of sorts between dimensions. A link that we have yet to figure out how to sever. He then produced a primitive chemical compound made from roots of plants that he imported from South America. He injected his patients with his compound. This allowed them, for short spells, to unconsciously travel through the rift he created. He played on his patients' unconscious minds, causing them to expect to unconsciously experience certain things. He would then give them his potion, and they would inevitably dream through the exact scenario he had described. They would commemorate some detail from the experience—about as much as human beings manage to remember from an average dream. To them, in their eyes, this validated Crowe's previous predictions. This eventually led to them viewing Crowe as a deity who possessed the ability to take them to a higher realm where he conceivably ruled. Which, ultimately, was not untrue. He was, indeed, allowing them to transcend to a higher realm, just as he told them.

"The side effects of his potion are horrific, to say the least. They would cause his patients' heads to grow to extreme shapes and sizes. The patients would experience missing time in many cases. They would become highly intelligent; far above your genius scale. This may sound like a benefit, and in the short term, it is—but in the long term, as their reality sets in, they grow increasingly volatile and dangerous. Because Crowe effectively severed the point in space-time where Ashford sits from the realm where the singularity exists, he trapped the souls of Ashford within their host bodies. Imagine a town full of dead bodies whose souls have no means of escape and nowhere to go if they could. Eventually, the brain will die as well as the body, but the soul will remain trapped within. Therefore, you are left with physical beings being controlled by only what the trapped soul allows for.

"In the case of human beings, the soul works in conjunction with the brain to render what you refer to as cognoscente reality. This communion gives humans the ability to interface with their environment. In an incarnated state, such as earthbound as a human being, a soul without a brain is akin to a computer without a formatted hard drive. It will still run, but it won't know how to do anything. There is no physical outlet for the input it is trying to push. You are, therefore, left with highly aggressive, highly confused, completely unpredictable beings who have no concept of pain, discomfort, hunger, fatigue, right or wrong, or any other human brain-driven concept. They exhibit superhuman strength and stamina since they have no ability to detect when they are doing damage to themselves through overexertion. Their nervous systems no longer have a living brain to feed pain signals into."

"This is some heavy shit," I said. "I understand Danny is a Bridge, like Crowe. But why is he so dangerous? Call me crazy, but I don't think Danny knows how to make chemical compounds that create zombies or manipulate space-time. He's a bit of an asshole, but a relatively normal guy. He means well."

"Under normal circumstances, it would be a mathematical impossibility for two such Bridges to exist in the same space-time location within a mere hundred years of each other and both have the ability to transcend between realms from the same place. The Deshcarn Mode was designed around tens of thousands of fail-safes designed specifically to prevent such a scenario. What makes this scenario so unique is that Crowe managed to create the persistent link between realms. In doing so, it allows any Bridge, including your friend Danny, the ability to consciously transcend. I guarantee you, Ashford, Ohio, is not Danny's normal area of transcendence. For all we know, his point in space-time where he should be able to travel between realms isn't even in this galaxy. But because of what Crowe has created here, he can. This makes him dangerous, as it allows Danny the ability to consciously travel to and from Crowe's current place of residence. Because he can consciously do this, he can remember details of his journey. He can gain knowledge like Crowe did, conceivably carrying on his work. Your friend Danny is now a tool that Crowe can potentially manipulate in order to take up his vicious agenda."

Lance finally spoke up. "In what way? Didn't you say that Ashford was locked into some other point in space and time? So, wouldn't that inherently contain the problem to Ashford?"

Anunit answered, "If you are grasping for ways to validate your bringing Danny here, then do us a favor and stop. You've made a potentially grave miscalculation. Until Danny arrived, Crowe's agenda was, for all intents and purposes, contained. Our first action, to initiate that containment, was to eliminate Crowe's earthbound form and anything he may have documented about it. We did this by burning down Ashford Hill Asylum. A dozen of his patients were outside at the time and managed to survive, but Crowe himself was incinerated, eliminating his earthbound host. In doing so, we cut off his ability to physically interact with this realm. However, as my colleague has explained, his soul remained here and retained the ability to travel through his portal between realms. But, without a physical host who is also a Bridge, who he can consciously manipulate from within his realm, he had no chance of expanding his operation outside of Ashford. If you look at Crowe's body of work, it is not hard to imagine a scenario where he manages to use Danny to spread his area of control beyond the borders of Ashford. Once he figures out how to do that, we do not have a way of stopping him that would allow for your race to continue its participation within the Deshcarn Mode. Please do humor us and at least try to understand the gravity of the situation you've brought upon us, Lance."

"Wait, wait, wait!" I shouted, "What do you mean by our species' ability to participate in the Deshcarn Mode?"

She continued, "If the cancer that Crowe has seeded here in Ashford is allowed to expand, every human host that dies will be unable to pass its soul back to the realm of the singularity. The entire purpose—the entire inherent, underlying protocol defined within The Deshcarn Mode—is knowledge attainment and universal, celestial betterment via tangible, applicable experience. Souls such as yours inhabit life-forms; those souls interact with those life-forms on a metaphysical level, gaining experience, gaining knowledge and understanding. Once your souls have done so sufficiently, they are returned to the singularity, ultimately adding to its vast, unmeasurable, singular power. As this happens over and over again, the quality of souls that come from it gets better and better. They are better equipped to gain knowledge. They can gather different and new types of competencies. The power of the singularity must always move forward within this cycle. It cannot go backward. Doing so would have the potential to thrust the entire protocol into a negative feedback loop that would quickly become irreversible. Eventually, the entire universe would be seeded with genii who are weaker and less prepared than their predecessors. Billions of years of celestial advancement across innumerable worlds would be destroyed. Our entire universe would eventually die.

"The souls within the human beings who die within this town no longer have the ability to obtain tangible knowledge. They only obtain knowledge of the disjointed experiences that they have while existing within their dead hosts. Experiences that are based in evil and hatred. These are souls that have become tainted. They must never be returned to the singularity. They are the very type of genii who possess the potential to poison it. Crowe has essentially rendered anything that dies within Ashford useless in the eyes of the Deshcarn Mode. If his agenda were to spread or go global, our only recourse would be to cut earth off. We would have to sever the ties between our realm and yours. Sending new genii to your civilization, knowing that when they came back, they could potentially lead to our destruction, is not a risk we will ever be willing to take. Danny is the perfect tool to allow Crowe to set that chain of events into motion."

Gary asked a very sensible question. "I don't get this at all. How is it that this asshole managed to travel to your realm and gain information that he could use to affix this town to your realm? Do you just sort of leave those type of plans lying around for any old dickhead Bridge who shows up to find? Seems to me like you guys should have done a better job of concealing those plans."

Anunit and Aniku sort of looked at each other, unsure who would be best to address that particular query. Finally, after a few uncomfortable moments, Anunit spoke up. "Where Crowe linked his portal to does not seem to be a part of our realm that we are aware of."

"What the fuck does that mean?" I asked.

She continued, "There is another realm besides ours that we do not control. And Crowe, as a Bridge, was able to transcend between both our realm as well as this other one. I've told you of our realm. The more religious of you might refer to it as Heaven or Paradise. We believe that Crowe created a portal to what you might refer to as Hell."

29
The Woods of Ashford, Ohio – 1:45 p.m.

I rose from my rusted chair that had apparently been sitting abandoned in that forest for quite some time. There was no sign of Andy anywhere. I somehow knew that his existence must have been invariably linked to the cabin that sat in ruins before me. I wasn't really expecting to find him. I questioned whether he was even real. Had I really been conversing with him the previous night? Had I been sharing drinks with him? At what point had he slipped his knock-out potion into my vodka? I had been watching him like a hawk the entire time I was there. He was pouring himself drinks from the same flask. Did I ever actually see him take a sip? At that point, I doubted that any of it had happened. The state that the cabin was in, in those frigid, mid-afternoon hours, suggested that it had decomposed naturally, over decades. What I was observing was not something that could have happened over the course of a few hours.

It is exceedingly difficult for me to properly describe how cold my body was. As I stood, I was able to feel the hypothermia-induced stiffness that shot through my back, midsection, and lower extremities. It was a struggle just to get myself upright. I had no idea of how long I had sat there, exposed to the elements. My body screamed that however long it was, it had been entirely too long. I needed shelter—somewhere to take refuge from the brisk northern Ohio fall. I could sense that I was in trouble. I was defenseless. If I were to happen upon a situation that required physical effort, I would be helpless to perform.

I stood and made my way back in the direction of my Malibu. I had left it the previous night, parked just off the one-lane bridge. The last time I had seen it, it was surrounded by melon-heads as they crept around it, studying every microbe of its detail.

Every step was a battle. I wasn't ten feet from my chair but already desperately out of breath. I found myself needing to plan and account for every diminutive muscle movement. The act of extending one foot in front of the other required a conscious signal to be sent from my brain to the necessary muscles in my crotch and legs to push my legs forward. It was at that moment that I realized I was in real trouble. I needed to get warm, and if I didn't, I would be dead in minutes. If I were to collapse, there would be no getting up. That horrible town, that place I should have never entertained the idea of traveling to, would become my tomb.

I wasn't about to die there. Not without a fight. After a five-minute personal war through the underbrush, I stumbled down the steep swale and onto the road, not a hundred yards from the one-lane bridge where I had last seen my car. It was nowhere to be found. The bridge itself sat empty, in a state of complete disrepair. The military-green paint that lined its steel side beams was all but gone; only a few mildew-covered flakes remained stuck to the structure. The rest of it was brown with rust. Much of the concrete base had given way, seemingly long ago, and fallen into the rushing creek below.

Even the road I stood on had aged a hundred years since I had last seen it hours before. I could break apart the crumbling asphalt with my own feet. It was a challenge to distinguish its surface, as most of it lay buried in an age of tree-born debris, pebbles, and dirt. Vines hung overhead, bridging the towering ash trees on either side. It was mid-day but already dark and impossibly cold.

I began to trudge up the road. My feet were completely numb, which in a way I was thankful for. I had a feeling that frostbite had sunk in. When they were to thaw, the pain would be far too excruciating to bear. I shoved my hands down the front of my pants. My crotch became the last bastion of warmth that I could muster. I was a dead man walking, and I had no destination.

Somehow, in what seemed to me as a couple of hours, decades had passed around me. I clearly remembered the night before, on the way into that dead-end corner of Ashford. There were no houses then; therefore, I didn't expect to see any on that trip. I didn't have a plan. I was walking for the sake of not having any other option. I just understood that sitting was not an option in that condition. Rest would have meant certain death.

Defying all odds, I managed to reach the stretch of road where I had been forced to stop on my way in. The last time I was there was my first encounter with the melon-heads. One had approached the front of my vehicle while the other had snuck onto my rear bumper. Their presence spooked me farther down the road and set in motion the events that had led to my being in that predicament. There were no signs of the repugnant creatures on that walk, though. The only sounds were my own struggling respiratory system and my jeans rubbing together with every step, no doubt chapping my inner thighs. Every time a breeze would kick up, I became impossibly colder. My clothes were damp from exposure, offering absolutely no resistance to the bitter elements.

I reached a turnoff in the road. It was to my left and onto a dirt path that I had no recollection of passing on my way in. I knew there was nothing for miles ahead—at least nothing I could recall. I struggled to shift my weight to my left, dragging my exhausted feet. I took the turnoff.

Not three feet down the hazardous, pockmarked road, I came across a wooden sign. It had not been upright in years and was lying interwoven in the feral underbrush. It was a street sign from long ago. The letters were carved into the wood with painstaking detail. The paint on the sign had long since worn off, leaving only a dim shading of its previous glory behind. Its inscription was still simple enough to distinguish: Whistler Road.

This was the road I had been told about. Lance had mentioned it the first time we talked. This was the road that Roderick Crowe called home. The old sheriff had also mentioned it in Kenneth Harvey's memoirs. This was also where the Ashford Hill Lunatic Asylum once stood.

I continued down Whistler. I had no other choice. At least I knew that at some point there were buildings and houses there. Perhaps there was still somewhere for me to take refuge. I was making slightly better time than when I first started on the trek. The act of walking had gotten some semblance of blood pumping through my system, but I was still in mortally dire straits.

The road was dirt and barely wide enough to accommodate a single car—clearly designed at a different time in our history of commerce. The trees on either side of the road were massive but somewhat evenly spread apart from one another. They left large gaps between them, allowing me to see into the forest over vast distances. This further added to my sense of desolation. Between the trees, I could see at least a mile to either side of myself, yet there were no signs of civilization, only more trees and frost-covered hilltops. Patches of white pines, clumsy ash, and the occasional weeping willow completed the panorama around me, in all directions.

A sense of eeriness hung over that road. It was the mid-day, but the feeling in the air was midnight on Halloween. Something was in those woods, just out of sight, watching me from where I could not see it. Chills shot up my back, through my frozen neck, and terminated at the base of my scalp. The eeriness was beginning to evolve into ripe, pure dread.

I pressed on, latching on to the idea that if something was indeed stalking me from within that wilderness, and they intended to do me harm, it would be over quickly in my terribly weakened condition. I caught the hint of something. It was an unmistakable odor. I knew it immediately. Every New England town I had traveled through in the winter months had familiarized me with that smell. It was a fireplace. The fresh smell of dried, burning pine became thicker as I moved along. My steps became faster, more motivated. I needed to find the source of that scent. Wherever it was coming from, there was fire, and where there was fire, there was warmth, survival, salvation.

I tripped over top of an unnaturally steep dip in the surface of the road and found my source. It was a log cabin just off the road to my right, down a rock driveway and into the forest. The one-story, simple structure stood defiant to the decay that plagued everything else I had passed on my journey. It appeared well kept—two windows in the front, a front door, redwood logs still tied together and sturdy. To the right side of the cedar shakes that covered the roof, glorious plumes of white smoke billowed from a brick chimney. The structure was otherwise unexceptional in every way. But from my standpoint, in my condition, it was as beautiful a sight as I could have imagined.

I approached the front door. The address was just to the left: 1551 Whistler. It sounded familiar. I didn't care. I didn't bother knocking. Thankfully, it was unlocked. I barged in and made a beeline toward the smell of the fireplace. I burst through a small foyer, passed an opening to what might have been a kitchen, through the shadow of the person in the kitchen, and into the living-room area.

I fell in front of the red-bricked fireplace. The fire was roaring. I immediately began to gag from exhaustion. I was lying in the fetal position, relieved to finally get myself warm but terrified of the pain I was sure to endure as my body defrosted. There was no blood in my feet or hands; my veins had constricted. If you've never been cold like that, you don't understand what it feels like. It feels like someone is cutting open the tips of your fingers and toes while at the same time crushing them inside of a vice-grip. The process isn't exactly quick. An adult male body has something approaching 100,000 miles of blood vessels, veins, capillaries, and arteries. All of which require warm blood. When they become deprived of it and suddenly start to get it back, it is a very gradual, unimaginably painful recovery process.

I managed to take off my shoes, sweater, socks, jeans, and underwear. I needed the damp clothes off my body as quickly as possible. I was completely nude save for a t-shirt. It was the only article of clothing that I had on my person that wasn't utterly soiled. I moaned and grunted, fighting the misery that my body was putting me through. My fingers and toes were a dark blue and were slowly turning a pale white. It occurred to me later that I was lucky they weren't black. I was maybe fifteen minutes from full-blown frostbite. In many cases, frostbite kills the tissue to the point of no return, requiring amputation. I couldn't think about that. Thinking about having a body part chopped off while in the agonizing grips of defrosting appendages is not a pleasant or productive thought.

Every minute that passed, the pain dulled slightly more. I wasn't leaving the front of the fireplace for anyone or anything, but I had begun to regain control over my thoughts. Animalistic desperation had begun to give way to more lucid, civilized introspection. It occurred to me that I had made no effort to determine if anyone else was in that house. I had barged in, completely out of my mind, had taken off all my clothes, and had parked my naked ass in front of the fireplace. I had then proceeded to moan like a baby for a solid ten minutes. I hadn't been confronted, so either they weren't in the immediate vicinity, they simply didn't care, or they were in a state of shock brought on by my behavior. *But someone had to make that fire*, I thought. It was still roaring. I investigated it, and judging by the condition of the top two logs, they could not have been inserted into that fireplace more than a few minutes prior to my arrival.

Had I seen someone when I'd rushed through the front door, through the foyer, past what must have been the kitchen and into the living room? It was such a blur, and I had been so desperate. My brain was not properly accepting input at the time. Anything I may or may not have seen on my way to that fireplace couldn't be trusted while my mind and body were in such a fragile state. There was a fleeting spark in my mind, though, of a memory. Unmistakably, it was there. Somewhere on the edge of my periphery, I'd seen someone around one of the corners when I'd entered. I'd rushed right past, never acknowledging their presence. Some obscure, still-functional part of my reptilian brain indexed the vague memory for safe-keeping, to be continued once warm. The pain had subsided, but suddenly I was petrified. Some part of me knew I was going to have to deal with what I had previously seen, and that time was rapidly approaching.

What sort of person would allow a stranger to rush into their home in the manner with which I had and make no effort to confront them? Not a gasp, a cry for help, or a shout in my direction. No questioning who I was or what my business was for being there. Why I was naked, wailing like a madman in front of their fireplace.

I rolled over, out of the fetal position, and onto my side. I faced the front of the log cabin, toward the front door through which I had entered.

I could see into the kitchen from my vantage point. It was just across the room, not fifteen feet away. Floating there before me was a woman, three feet off the ground. She wore a summer dress. Long-dead strands of hair blew wildly in all directions from her scalp. A smiling scowl that epitomized sinister, murderous intent roamed her wretched face. Her eyes were locked onto me. Her hands and unnaturally long, blackened fingernails extended fervently in my direction. Her arms were at least a foot longer than any normal human being's. Not a single part of her was touching the ground. The front half of her levitating torso was through the door, into the living room where I sat, horrified, while the rest of her remained behind, in the kitchen.

Her body managed to stretch and disorient itself, contorting into a seemingly limitless collection of repulsive shapes, sizes, and lengths. She was frightening to the point that it is difficult for me to put into words. My ears popped as the atmospheric pressure in the room rapidly disappeared. She floated along the crest of the ever-thinning air. She was moving closer.

30

My mind latched onto a curious memory as the wretched woman levitated toward me. I was still immersed in the aroma of burning pine as the frigid pain subsided throughout my extremities. I had already been through so much, and my mind must have found it necessary to take me away from it all, however briefly. Despite the horrors around me, it was the smell of the fireplace wherein I found myself getting lost, latching onto.

Ellen and I had taken Annie on a weekend trip to Killington, years ago. She had been learning to ski at a smaller, glorified foothill outside of Boston for a few years, and we wanted her to experience a true mountain—really test her mettle on some formidable slopes. She had begged us to take her for years. We had always concluded that she was too young, bound to get hurt. Finally, we caved and took her up to Vermont for her eleventh birthday. For a solid two years, she had been easily handling the local slopes and was growing bored. She was more than ready.

I vividly recall Annie reading the brochure on the ride up. She called out the names of the hills one by one: Vertigo, Superstar, Double-Dipper, Escapade. Ellen grew annoyed with her overly excited banter. To me, it was awesome. She was a kid in a candy store, and so was I. I would give anything sacred to me to see that look in my baby's eyes once more.

Annie had set her mind on conquering one particularly ludicrous, double-black-diamond slope while on the way there—The Crucible. Ellen emphatically forbid it. Originally, I agreed with Ellen. Not allowing our eleven-year-old onto a hill designed specifically for professional skiers, professional snowboarders, and adrenalin junkies would have been the responsible decision for everyone involved. Then we got off the gondola after a long, thrilling day on the slopes and just happened upon the entrance to The Crucible. Ellen had since retired to the lodge after a long half day of bitching about her boots being too tight. I looked at Annie, and Annie looked at me. We both knew what needed to happen. We needed to defeat The Crucible.

I grabbed Annie's face at the crest of the slope, atop a forty-five-degree, endless trail of craters and moguls as far down as either of us could see. I gave her what had to have been the worst parental advice of my life. "Annie, if you get hurt, whatever you do, don't tell your mother that I let you on this hill." She rolled her eyes at me and giggled.

I was far more terrified of the impending decent than she was. "Let's go!" she shouted to me before I had had a chance to completely build up the courage to push myself over the crest of the hill. Before I could blink, she was twenty yards ahead of me, bounding through the moguls.

"Annie! Hang on!" I shouted.

I was after her, but there was no catching up. An instant later, I hit a particularly icy crater that sent my left ski about three feet too far to the left, stretching my groin muscles to the near-breaking point. I managed to balance on my right ski for an additional half second before hitting the next mogul, which subsequently twisted my body backward, facing back up the hill. My skis flew off and soared over me, above my head. I hit the ground flush on my back and came to rest atop a powdery swale. I was shaken and a bit embarrassed but fine nonetheless. More than anything else, I was scared shitless for Annie. I had been skiing most of my adult life and considered myself something of an expert in the craft. If I had taken such a vicious spill ten seconds into the run, surely eleven-year-old Annie was in serious trouble.

Annie, now fifty yards down The Crucible from me, caught my still-watering eyes. Her ponytail bounced perfectly from left to right as she bounded through the moguls. She was in complete control. Her form was sublime. Her balance was that of a ballet dancer. She even caught the eye of a group of teenagers on the lift above us, ogling her abilities. Surely it wasn't every day that they saw an eleven-year-old utterly dominate such an advanced trail. She was born for this. She was perfect.

I couldn't help but let out a tear and a proud whimper. When I was eleven, I was bouncing between foster homes. I was already intimately familiar with the streets of South Boston. This was South Boston before it was trendy and before the movies made it into a tourist attraction. Before all the douchebag yuppies would drive in from Metro-West, have one beer at Murphy's Law, and fancy themselves as "tough Bostonians" for the rest of their hoity-toity lives. This was back when South Boston was called Southie and if you referred to the neighborhood as South Boston instead of Southie in the wrong company, you probably weren't going home with all the teeth that you left with.

Most days, I would shoplift my dinner from one paki or another—a convenience store to people outside of Boston. I had about an 80-percent success rate of not getting caught. When I did get caught, I would get picked up by the ever-empathetic South Boston police, who would typically slam my head into the trunk of their cruiser before kicking me into the backseat. They would then take me home to my foster parents, who would notice the welt on my head and promptly add three more the moment they were sure the police were out of earshot.

The next day, I would go off to school and tell the nuns that I fell down some stairs. On a normal day, thirty other kids who took the same shit the previous night would use the same excuse. Nobody of authority within the school or diocese ever seemed in any position to question the systemic run of hopelessly uncoordinated children, all of whom just couldn't seem to approach a staircase without falling down it. Must have just been a coincidence.

That was a million miles away. The great thrill of my life, the single thing I am proudest of, was watching my daughter just get to be a kid. I never got that chance. For all intents and purposes, I've been a hardened, calloused, shithead of an adult for my entire life. I got to be a kid through Annie. It was days like that, experiences like that, seeing the world through her eyes, watching her be thrilled as she motored down that hill, where I could have died happy. I could have closed my eyes and never woken up just knowing that she was happy and safe and getting to have fun.

I did manage to pop my skis back on and coast down the side of the double-black-diamond, avoiding further self-inflicted damage or embarrassment. I caught up to Annie about three minutes later, waiting for me at the bottom of the mountain. Her grin was a perfect mix of *That was the most fun I've ever had in my life* and *That's right, who's a badass now?*

I managed to pizza-wedge my old aching body up to hers, and we hugged. My little girl had conquered The Crucible. She looked at me straight in my eyes and told me, "Don't worry, Dad. I won't tell Mom that you hurt yourself on . . . that hill." We both laughed, but I'd be lying if I told you her remark didn't sting my pride just a little. I passed my wiseass mouth to my daughter.

We headed into the lodge and met Ellen. We all sat by the fireplace and enjoyed some always-nuclear-hot, ski-resort cocoa. Our pact to keep our jaunt down The Crucible secret lasted all of five minutes before Annie spilled the entire can of beans to her mother. She was far too excited and proud of herself to keep it under wraps for any longer than that. I remember just sort of gazing into the roaring fireplace as Ellen read me the riot act. How could you allow your eleven-year-old daughter on a hill like that? I thought we talked about this. What if she had gotten hurt, Daniel?

I just basked in the aroma of that smoldering pine. I loved that smell. I loved that day. Not a single thing in the world was going to wipe that smile off my face.

31

That same fragrant smell of roasting pine enveloped me. I was thrust back into my horrible reality as the nightmare closed in. The woman's eyes glowed lavender like nightshade. They were locked, dead onto mine. She was the stuff of my most fantastic nightmares. Obviously, it was not something of this world—it was not even something native to our realm of consciousness. Surrounding her was a barely visible yet unmistakable shroud of electrostatic energy. She was four feet off the ground, hovering five feet from me, and she was inching ever closer.

She was a contradiction—wiry, rotting, tattered yet still powerful, forceful, and terrifying. The anger behind her glowing eyes, that scowling face, and her rigid, shuttering jaw evoked something beyond demonic. The specter of the woman hovering toward me on that awful day may have been that of a deceased woman, but whatever haunted it, whatever animalistic rage possessed it, was not something that had ever walked this earth in human form.

The savory aroma of burning pine was suddenly replaced by an acrid, sulfuric, rotting-meat stench. I was not two feet from the still-raging fireplace, but I could suddenly see my breath in front of my face. The temperature in the room dropped by fifty degrees in the blink of an eye. I wanted to fight but was absolutely petrified. I was so goddamned tired. I had nowhere to run, and I was still half naked. To boot, I was still recovering from my most recent brush with death by hypothermia and frostbite.

The atmosphere in the room was replaced with a veil of unfathomable anger. A shadowy, distorted blackness crept across the room as the figure contorted toward me. Wherever this thing came from, whatever heinous dimension of origin it crawled into our world from, was a domain bound in chaos. I somehow sensed it as easily as I sensed the heat at my back from the fireplace. This thing was from somewhere where pain was comfort, dark was light, torture was order, suffering was peace. I began to submit. I just wanted it all to be over, even if it meant death.

All the hair on my body stood on end as her shimmering, electrostatic cloak replaced the atmosphere. My eyes watered from her stink. Her tattered, dirt-covered dress hung down and had begun caressing my exposed legs. I cringed and moaned. Her face was inches from mine, and I could hear her low, purring growl.

The woman's arms were five feet long from shoulder to wrist. Her hands stretched downward another foot. Her decaying fingernails descended an additional six inches. Her body hovered above me, but her arms dragged behind her along the floor of the cabin. Her nails irritated the wood floor as they scratched wells into the varnish. Her nightmarish growl grew louder as her head tilted back and her shoulders flexed. She began moving her hands over my feet and up my legs. Despite my still half-frozen state, I could feel her nails slowly scratching over my legs. I knew that she was drawing blood, digging in, but I couldn't bring myself to take my eyes away from the lavender glow that surrounded her face. I was horrified beyond all words or action as her tremendous hands slowly wrapped around my neck. She began pulling me upward by my throat, forcing me to stagger to my feet.

The moment her hands touched me, I suffered the most intense static shock of my life, which was quickly replaced by a violent burning sensation that shot throughout my entire body like a lightning bolt. Half was due to the pressure she was putting on my throat; the other half was just because she, for reasons I cannot explain, was piping hot to the touch.

For an instant, I caught a glimpse of the petrifying realm where she originated from. It was as though she had wired directly into my brain, forcing her horrendous vision upon me. There were bodies, naked bodies of men and women, for what seemed like miles. They were stacked impossibly deep. The area around them was red and sandy—Mars-like. They filled a crater between four massive, endless swales of sand and gravel. There was an abrasive, corrosive mist to the air that would periodically condense into droplets of boiling, acidic rain that fell onto the damned souls below, immediately scorching their skin.

I squinted my eyes as I felt her grasp on my throat begin to thrust upward and noticed that the bodies were all moving. Despite all their horrific injuries and devastated, traumatized bodies, they were still alive—ever conscious of their agony and torment. The air was filled with screams of men and women alike. One lesson, which I now can't unlearn, is that under those levels of unimaginable misery, there is no discerning a man's high-pitched wailing from a woman's screams. I had a bird's-eye view from the perspective that she was forcing upon me. The people—hundreds of thousands of them—squirmed like maggots. Each fought desperately to escape, however impossible. Along the edges of the pit, below an ocean of writhing arms and legs, sat a mixture of sand and gravel that had been crushed over the ages into a powder. It was about the consistency of twice-milled flour. There was simply nothing for any of them to grab onto—no conceivable way of gaining any sort of purchase. They all grunted between their agonizing yelps and howls. The noise of that many people in that sort of deplorable circumstance was deafening, like a stadium that had been thrust into frenzied turmoil.

Along the sides of the sandy walls were what appeared to be enormous rodents jutting from the hills, going directly into the human lake of desperation. Every few moments, as the tide of people would flow toward them, the beasts would begin tearing them to shreds, thrusting back and forth, sinking their dull but powerful teeth into any human appendage they could seize. The hulking rats would then proceed to mow through the hopeless, horrified souls with impossible violence. The trapped would slowly become shredded and consumed without so much as a moment's consideration for their agony. After several gruesome thrusts, the beasts would spit the still-breathing, horrifically injured people back into the middle of the pit. Once there, they appeared to regenerate their mangled appendages only to begin the heinous cycle all over again. At no time did I see one of those people stop moving. It was as though they were damned to struggle and suffer, flowing through an endless sea of torment, being torn to pieces and slowly eaten by the mammoth, ravenous vermin for all eternity.

The raging, disembodied woman pulled my body upward, slamming my head against the ceiling. As though there were a positive to take out of that situation, the jarring blow to my head thrust my consciousness out of her vision and back into my own horrifying reality. Her head had drifted through the ceiling above me as her body, unlike mine, was not required to interact with earthly matter. My head, however, was still being squeezed upward against the ceiling of the room. Her hands were still wrapped around my throat. I lurched and gyrated, struggling to free myself. But my flailing arms and legs just passed straight through her as though I were punching air.

She ever-so-slowly tilted downward, bringing her warped face back through the ceiling and directly next to mine. Had I been allowed to have taken in any air, I would have screamed. The violence painted all over her face keeps me up nights to this day. It gleamed with an evil that I only dreamed possible from the devil himself. She truly was indigenous to the depraved hellscape that she had forced me to witness inside of her horrible vision. I somehow knew in that moment that this thing wouldn't ever stop. Even after it had choked the life out of me completely, it would squeeze and squeeze my throat until it severed my head clean off my shoulders.

I felt myself beginning to lose consciousness. Curiously, just before it all turned black, I had an epiphany. This thing was the eventuality of the emotion that had swept over me earlier. Had I given in to that rage, that unbridled hatred toward humanity—had I submitted earlier to it, given in to The Perfect Man, fought away from Big-Bear and murdered Gary in the tow truck and lost myself within that raw tempest of emotion—this monster is what I would have become. It was all over her face. She had the same aggression in her eyes. I knew that kind of anger—that raging, agonizing hatred that only blood could possibly satisfy. I just hadn't given myself over to it, but that woman, that animal, clearly had.

My ears began to pop as my face began to swell. My mouth closed, but my tongue, for the first time in my life, dangled out involuntarily. Moments from death, I heard a muffled voice wail from below me. "Put him down, Margaret! Now!"

I fell, crashing into the floorboards, completely unable to break my fall. I was agonizing for clean air, bleeding badly from the neck and barely conscious. After a moment, I managed to look up. The woman was still hovering above and gazing down angrily. In the blink of an eye, she inverted and thrust herself toward me again. Her face was still riddled with hatred and intensity. Her arms extended out as her electrostatic cloak exploded around her and into a massive discharge of magenta-colored energy. She was moving in for the kill as I cowherd on the floor. I was helpless to defend myself.

At the last moment, a man leapt over me from behind, putting himself between me and it. She stopped and met him eye-to-eye. I saw him whisper something to her that I could not make out while in my badly damaged condition. A moment later, the man turned around to face me, and the atrocious woman was gone, having vanished into thin air.

I managed a couple of dry heaves, clearing the bile from my swollen throat. Afterward, I was finally able to take in a normal amount of desperately needed oxygen. I felt the man reach underneath my armpits, pulling me backward, away from the fireplace. Until he had, I had not realized that I was mere inches from the still-raging coals and they were beginning to do further damage to my already wracked body.

"Good lord. Good lord. Are you all right?" the unidentified man shouted from behind me.

I specifically remember thinking, *Am I all right? Is this jackass fucking kidding me?*

I turned around and locked eyes with him. I was still far from regaining my abilities of speech. A long, disgusting strand of mucus hung from the corner of my mouth, clear down my chin, and dribbled onto my chest. The man reached out a hand, and instinctively, I grabbed it.

"The name is Kenneth Harvey. You must be Daniel Hallowell."

32

The Deposition of Rick Voss: (Second Session):

Judge Stokes: *I will open here. Now, Ricky, I am here to oversee your deposition. Make no mistake about it, I will ensure that your friend and colleague Mr. Daniel Hallowell receives a fair trial that's based on the facts. For me to deliver that, we need the facts of what happened to you and your friends over in Ashford. I am not going to abide any more outbursts out of you that are directed toward anyone who is present here today. If I hear you threaten Mr. Levine again, you are going to be held in contempt and I will throw you in jail. Do you understand my terms, Ricky?*

Mr. Voss: *Yes, your honor.*

Judge Stokes: *Mr. Levine . . . as a state-appointed prosecutor, you are expected to be able to drive this deposition in such a way that gathers the absolute maximum amount of information from Ricky regarding these . . . happenings in Ashford. Now understand, Doug, some of it is gonna be religious in nature, and some of it might negatively touch whatever sort of delicate sensibilities you're carrying around with you. But you are going to find a way to overcome that. You're going to do your job, and you are going to maintain your professionalism here. Do you understand my terms?*

Mr. Levine: *I understand, your honor.*

Judge Stokes: *And that goes for everybody in here. This is a legal proceeding, and it is going to be treated as such.*

(Nods in approval throughout the room)

Mrs. Miles: *As was discussed in private yesterday, your honor, my client and I motion for a statement of participation and intent from Agent Roy. His presence at these proceedings is being called into question for several reasons. He was in no way involved with the FBI's investigation into the Daniel Hallowell case. Nothing in his record suggests that he holds any sort of criminal investigative function within the bureau. Neither Mr. Levine nor I have requested his presence or have called for him to serve as witness to any of the events described herein.*

Judge Stokes: *Martin, I have your documents and should have shared them with the room yesterday. You specifically asked me not to share them. I am of no legal obligation to share them unless a motion is brought about. We now have such a motion that I must grant. Mrs. Miles, your motion is granted. Agent Roy, care to tell us all what it is you're doing here?*

Agent Roy: *Certainly, your honor. Allow me to quickly apologize, I should have made my purpose and intentions here clearer. I am, for lack of a better description, very loosely affiliated with any of the criminal investigative bodies that exist within the Federal Bureau of Investigation. I am a member of a much smaller branch of the bureau. We don't work out of Quantico; we work out of the Pentagon. I have been with this branch, quite literally, since the moment I graduated from Dartmouth. We have one focus, and that is information gathering. Not to put too fine a point on it, but I gather information that very senior members of our government view as critical to our national security. I am here under written order of the NSA and am tasked with gathering as much information as I can. Please make no mistake about it, I am in no way present to disrupt or alter the case of the State of Ohio versus Daniel Hallowell.*

Mrs. Miles: *Excuse me, Martin, but I hardly see how these proceedings could possibly have anything to do with national security.*

Agent Roy: *Like I said, I am here to gather information. I then bring that information back to my superiors so that we can make an educated decision on that very subject. Trust me, we are all delighted when a case is found that poses no threat to the homeland. However, the only way to definitively arrive at such a determination is to investigate it.*

Mrs. Miles: *Wonderful. Judge Stokes, I motion for the immediate dismissal of Agent Roy from these proceedings, pending a jurisdictional grievance to be filed, by me, immediately following today's proceedings.*

Judge Stokes: *State your grounds for the record, Sarah.*

Mrs. Miles: *On the grounds of this being the* State of Ohio versus an individual. *No federal charges have been filed against Mr. Hallowell. The FBI did assist various state agencies with the initial investigation but have since closed their case file. They cited, in their own words, "clear intent, motive, and evidence implicating Mr. Hallowell." Therefore, I must conclude, with no open case file and no federal charges on the table, that Agent Roy, as an admitted member of the FBI, has no jurisdiction over any of these proceedings.*

Judge Stokes: *Just so I am clear here, Sarah, your argument is that the FBI, who are here under the authority of the NSA, doesn't have the right to bear witness to a deposition here in Wahoga County, Ohio?*

Mrs. Miles: *Quite frankly, your honor, he shouldn't have been allowed in this room yesterday, and something tells me you know that.*

Judge Stokes: *The lady has a point, Martin.*

Agent Roy: *Now, let's all keep our heads. I am authorized to explain a bit more about my purpose here. Give me a chance and hear me out.*

Mr. Levine: *Great, now we're deposing this guy.*

Judge Stokes: *That's quite enough, Doug. Okay, Martin, I am going to allow you this final chance to explain your reasons for being here. After which, unless you can provide something germane to these proceedings, I am inclined to order your dismissal on the grounds brought forth by Sarah. Do you understand these terms?*

Agent Roy: *I do, your honor. As I attempted to explain before, I am not here regarding case number 8087644, which was the FBI's criminal investigation into Daniel Hallowell. As Sarah explained, that case file has since been handed over to the State of Ohio authorities and closed on our end. If you want me to further explain the reasons for my being here, then you are going to have to sign some extensive non-disclosure agreements or leave the room while I explain to those who do sign them.*

(Everyone signs the forms)

Agent Roy: *I am present on the grounds of NSA case number 1487, code named Sapphire Gates. As stated in your agreements, this is a highly classified case, and nothing can be repeated outside of this chamber about it. I take it that I don't need to inform you all of the reach and incredible depth and breadth of resources at the disposal of the agencies involved here?*

(Everyone nods in understanding)

Agent Roy: *Terrific. My intentions here have never been to pull rank or exercise any authority or in any way disrupt these proceedings. With all due respect to you and your client, Sarah, if you were to file a jurisdictional grievance, it would be denied by a federal judge via fax and I would be right back in this chair within fifteen minutes. By no means am I obligated to explain my case to you. I am, however, happy to do so. I think it is going to put a lot of what Rick has explained into a proper context.*

Mrs. Miles: *We all signed your paper. Get on with your explanation.*

Agent Roy: *Fair enough. Sapphire Gates is a case that was thrown our way decades ago by the CIA. The formation of the NSA occurred, and they began working closely with the bureau. Together, both entities managed pools of resources that better aligned with this case. In other words, the CIA couldn't figure out what in the hell was happening and thought we might have better luck. I am holding in my hand the 1928 Census Results for Wahoga County, Ohio. Front and center here on page one: Ashford Ohio – Population 8,658 – Mayor Douglas LeRouche, Sheriff Frederick Williams – 99.6% White Caucasian – .4% Other.*

Judge Stokes: *Martin, I am going to be sixty-one years young next week. I've set foot outside of Wahoga County for maybe sixty days throughout that entire sixty-one years. I didn't go to Dartmouth, but I do fancy myself a higher-educated individual. And I can tell you, with absolute certainty, that there isn't a street, avenue, road, goat path, deer trail or goddamned gap in between two trees anywhere in Wahoga County that I haven't ventured through at least a hundred times. Furthermore, as the highest-ranking judge in this county, I am tasked with reviewing the census results annually and have never seen or heard of an Ashford. I've never overseen a case regarding Ashford in any way shape or form, which certainly seems strange as a judge of its county for going on twenty-five years.*

Agent Roy: *There would have been no way for you to have known of Ashford or for you to have stumbled across it, your honor.*

Judge Stokes: *Just what in the blue hell is that supposed to mean?*

Agent Roy: *It seems that someone, not us or any other government or law enforcement entity, did an impeccable job of wiping away all evidence of Ashford's existence. Whoever it was managed to do so in an impossibly thorough fashion. They managed to alter all your records here in Wahoga County, and that was just the start. They also wiped clean all correspondence, on a planet-wide level, originating from Ashford. Basically, any letter ever mailed from that town ceased to exist along with every birth record of anyone who ever lived there. Same goes for death records. On the federal level, and we are talking about the Library of Congress here, there is absolutely no record of Ashford having ever existed.*

Judge Stokes: *Okay, we get it—there is no evidence of the town. So, what makes you think those census results you've got there hold any water?*

Agent Roy: *Great question, your honor. Several reasons. This census form is a copy. The original was lifted from what was described as a stunningly beautiful blond woman who was detained in 1947 for vagrancy in Cleveland. She was processed, and she never spoke a single word to any member of authority. They locked her in their holding cell, but when they glanced back up from the lock a moment later, she was gone. She had completely vanished without any trace or any conceivable way of getting out of her locked cell. The Cleveland authorities involved the feds, who dispatched the CIA. At the time, the CIA was Truman's shiny new agency, so they would get the first crack at anything and everything. They came to town to find this fugitive, all the while sort of half-believing the yarns that the local cops were spinning about this disappearing woman.*

Truth be told, the CIA provided some very key insight. Ultimately, the information they did manage to gather led to their opening the Sapphire Gates case file. But by the time they got their hands on the census results, anything they might have relied upon to cross reference the information it contained had been inexplicably torched— for lack of a better term.

Due to an incredible stroke of luck, however, one of the guys on the case had allegedly attended some sort of hunting camp on the outskirts of Ashford, when he was in grammar school. He swore he could retrace his path there. Apparently, it wasn't all that complicated of a trip—a couple of turns off the highway, and you were basically there. He brought a team of officials out here to Wahoga County, and, lo and behold, the town that he remembered was no longer where he expected it to be. They got off the highway and onto subroute 46, made a right after a couple of miles onto what is now US-613. According to this census, that road used to be known as County Line Road. Several of these phantom people on the census declared addresses on County Line Road. Today, however, if you take that right, down US-613, you drive for about five minutes, and suddenly, you are smack in the middle of Hunters Valley Township. But everything that they were seeing on the census in conjunction with their witness's recollection screamed—there should be a town here somewhere.

For years, the case went cold. They dismissed the woman's disappearance as an anomaly, citing some sort of screw-up by the officer charged with properly incarcerating her. They dismissed the census form as a hoax or ruse. Their colleague who claimed to have gone to hunting camp there even withdrew his testimony, claiming his memories got scrambled somehow from the stress of his job.

The case was dusted off and heated back up in the 1950s. At the time, reliable clocks were starting to go into the dashboards of every car. People around Wahoga County started taking their cars in for service, claiming that their clocks were periodically jumping over brief stretches of time. These claims were initially met with scrutiny by the auto manufacturers. The clocks were always reporting the correct time when the cars were brought in to be checked. But the customers were adamant that they would be out driving; they would look at the clock, look back at the clock again a few seconds later, and it would have jumped ahead by ten minutes. All the while, their pocket and wristwatches would corroborate the dashboard time as accurate. So, they would assume that the dashboard clocks were lagging for ten minutes and then suddenly jumping ahead to the correct time. Which, in the words of the manufacturers, would have been mechanically impossible. There were no time-synchronization mechanisms in the fifties. If a clock were to lag back then, it would remain behind until a human being manually set it to the appropriate time.

However ridiculous it sounded, the mystifying reports kept flooding in. Finally, after about a year of this, Ford sent out a team tasked with doing nothing but driving around Wahoga County while closely observing their dashboard clocks. Wouldn't you know it, five members of their team found the missing time anomaly two minutes after turning right onto US-613. It always happened about halfway between the turnoff from subroute 46 and the township limits of Hunters Valley. Somehow, ten minutes were going by in an instant as they rolled over what, relative to them, was about one foot of asphalt, at fifty miles per hour.

Judge Stokes: *Hell, I remember that craze from when I was a boy. I specifically remember my parents taking me down there to see it happen. It was an urban legend. It stopped happening after a few weeks if I recall correctly.*

Agent Roy: *It doesn't happen anymore. We surmise that whoever is responsible for cloaking Ashford has figured out a way to clean up that chink in their clandestine armor.*

Mr. Levine: *I'm sorry. You think people are cloaking Ashford, Ohio?*

Agent Roy: *It is a veritable certainty, Mr. Levine. About ten years ago, new utility lines were strung down that stretch of US-613. We had half the brains in the bureau paying close attention. They put in new fiberoptic cable lines and refurbished the old power lines. Secretively, once the work was done, we sent teams to run tests. Several of our technicians managed to intercept the fiberoptic cable on either side of the suspected location of Ashford. They sent very rudimentary pings to each other, knowing exactly how long their pings should have taken to travel from the agent at the source to the agent at the destination. On average a ping, over fiber, over such a short distance, should return in a matter of milliseconds. Their pings, however, were taking longer—and consistently longer. They sanity-checked by infiltrating other like-distanced stretches of fiber running the same ping tests, always getting their expected return times. But over an entire year, anytime they would clock the pings between where Ashford was suspected to exist, they would take a considerable, quantifiable amount of extra time.*

It wasn't, at that point, difficult to calculate how many extra, invisible miles seemed to lie between their two ping points—roughly, 8.3 miles. Even more interestingly, almost exactly ten minutes of driving in a car, at fifty miles per hour, appeared to lie between the two ping points. Even though the two teams of technicians on either side were within shouting distance of each other throughout the experiment.

Similar tests were conducted to calculate the rate of energy decay over the same stretch of road on the power lines. It was determined with absolute certainty that power was indeed being lost along the road and being drained by invisible consumers.

Finally, the water mains were tested. One of our engineers did the math and figured out the exact rate that the water flowed down the US-613 main. Again secretly, we cracked the main open and poured in some harmless dye. The dye was engineered to remain purple for exactly nine minutes within the volume of water in that specific water main, over that distance, while traveling at that known rate. After that nine-minute period and under those exact conditions, the dye would degrade and turn yellow. Basically, we were dying the water on one side of where we believed Ashford should have been. We were then observing it, within the same water main, on the other end of where we thought Ashford should be. Being only a few feet down the road, by the time the water that we had colored upstream reached the observers on the other end, it should have still been purple. However, every time we have conducted this test, the water on the observed side comes back bright yellow. Not only that, but the colored water takes ten minutes to show up on the other end at all.

Mr. Voss: *Wait a minute. Why didn't you just send something down the pipe and wait for it on the other end and see how long it took to get there? Why mess with all this dye stuff?*

Agent Roy: *Great question, Ricky. By the time we got around to this particular experiment, we were working with the data we had already gathered from the previous observations with the fiberoptic cable and the power lines. We needed to calculate the missing distance as precisely as possible. Objects in flowing water, over a distance, will never travel from point A to point B in a consistent amount of time—they bob around, they get hung up, sometimes they never reach the other end at all. By tinting the flowing water and figuring out the rate with which it was flowing through the main, we found a method of calculating the exact distance between point A and point B that we knew was accurate and measurable. Basically, we created a word problem that would allow us to measure missing distance. We knew how long it should have taken for the flowing water to travel X meters at Y rate between points A and B. Therefore, it was easy to extrapolate. When the water took longer to traverse the distance, within the Ashford experiments, we were easily able to calculate how much farther it had traveled. Wouldn't you know it, our calculations proved repeatedly, the water that we were tinting had to have been traveling exactly 8.3 miles. It was shocking. We were standing within shouting distance of each other and observing water take ten minutes to travel between us at a rate of nearly fifty miles per hour.*

The experiments have never stopped. We have yet to figure out how to infiltrate Ashford, and rest assured, it is not due to a lack of brain power. Every resource of the government, over the years, has been enlisted to help. Hell, we once tried to send Navy Seal HALO skydivers down there, thinking maybe if we hit it from above, something different would happen. They just landed smack in the middle of US-613, precisely on top of their mark, not any closer to Ashford than you or I sit right now.

That is what brings me here today, folks. This town exists. It is invisible, but it's there. It is exactly 8.3 miles across. As far as I know, only god, Ricky and the people he traveled there with know what in the hell is going on inside of it. Many, many people, over decades, have gone to their graves trying to unravel the mystery of Ashford, Ohio. Since none of us have ever been able to get in, we have never been able to properly assess the potential threats to national security that such an anomaly might pose. I am here to understand how they got into that town and to see if it is a process that can be replicated. From the standpoint of your federal government, any sort of ingress into Ashford is impossible. And he (Agent Roy points to Mr. Voss) is proving all the best scientific minds this country has had to offer, over decades, wrong.

33

Judge Stokes: *Thank you, Martin, for that thorough, eye-opening, yet incredibly difficult to believe explanation.*

Agent Roy: *I am obligated to, once again, remind everyone present that you all have signed non-disclosure agreements. Absolutely nothing you've heard from me here today can be repeated outside of these walls, even to immediate family members.*

Judge Stokes: *I think you can trust us, Martin. If I go home and start talking to my wife about any of this, she's liable to put me in a home. Sarah, how'd our friend from the FBI do? You still want to file that jurisdictional grievance?*

Mrs. Miles: *I withdraw my intent to file a jurisdictional grievance, your honor.*

Judge Stokes: *Seems like you and Ricky here found yourselves an unlikely ally. I will tell you one thing, I sure as hell never expected a representative from the bureau to come in here and corroborate some of the yarns Ricky's been spinning our way. How about you, Mr. Levine? Any objections?*

Mr. Levine: *None, your honor. I am anxious to get back to hearing Ricky's testimony.*

Judge Stokes: *Fair enough. All right, Ricky, you're up. The last you left us, you were eating a magic dinner in the enchanted exchange station with the angel people who were grappling with something called an incarnation rift. Why don't you take it from there?*

Mr. Voss: *Sure, your honor. At that point, we had finished our dinner and were all just sort of sitting around the table digesting. We were happy to have eaten such a delicious meal, but it was not sitting well. We had just been informed about how Crowe had punched a hole between the town we were sitting in and, for all intents and purposes, Hell. Lance had billed Ashford as "The Town Satan Calls Home" when he was trying to sell us on coming. We sure as shit didn't think he meant it literally.*

Big Bear drove the next bit of the conversation with Aniku and Anunit. "So, there is some sort of celestial rift sitting open somewhere in this town? And it has poked a hole between Ashford and Hell? Is that what you guys are telling us?"

Anunit answered. She seemed to pounce on the opportunity. "To be clear, we don't call it Hell. Hell, to be frank, is a term made up by ancient religious human beings who needed to scare people into being decent throughout the course of their lives, to keep order and civility. Your soul or genii will not be damned to that realm after you've lived an unsavory life. In all but the most exceptional cases, no matter what you do in your earthbound state, your soul will only travel back to our realm. The reason we described it to you as Hell initially was because it is the closest description that you, as humans, have created to describe it. If you were to find yourself there, you would immediately find our describing that realm in such terms to be accurate."

"But you just said," replied Big Bear, "that no matter what we do here on earth, we can only wind up in your realm, right?"

"In all but exceptional cases. Dying here in Ashford would represent one of those exceptional cases. If you die here, then your genii go to the other realm."

Big Bear's palms both slapped down atop the table. He was clearly upset by the revelation. "What? What in the fuck are you telling me?"

At that point, we all nearly shit in our pants. Anyone who really knows me knows I have never been mistaken for a saint. I do, however, like to think that I have lived my life mostly aboveboard. Sure, there's more than a handful of women traipsing around various cities who might disagree with some of my methods, but I've certainly never done anything horrible or seriously hurt anyone. Yet, suddenly I'm sitting there being told that if I just happened to die in that town, because it's locked into some horrible catharsis with this other realm, I would automatically go to Hell. I've been to some shitty weddings and social events in my life. I was once convinced by a group of friends to go watch Eddie Money perform at the Suffolk County Fair. But never have I been so desperate to claw my way out of a situation than the one I found myself in then. I needed to get out of that town at any cost.

This was the first time I seriously considered abandoning Danny and saving myself. I've struggled with that thought process since, but I honestly don't think he would or could have blamed me for it. If a tree branch in that town had decided to fall over top of me at the wrong time, I was going to Hell. Try to imagine that for a moment; put yourself in my shoes. I am trapped in a town that I know jack shit about and wouldn't even be there to begin with had I not been lied to, repeatedly, by Lance. Now I find out that the truth is far more terrifying than anything Lance had conjured up in his attempt to coerce us all into showing up there in the first place. I don't know what's true and what's bullshit, but I trusted the alien-angel people over Lance. To that point, the story Lance had given us barely passed for a CliffsNotes version of what was really going on. My goal became very clear to me——I had to do anything I could to get myself out of that town without dying.

Aniku spoke up as that realization began motoring through all our heads. "That is correct. The point in space-time where Ashford currently resides is bound to the other realm. It cannot be bound to that realm and ours simultaneously. It is one or the other, but never both."

"Why not both?" I asked.

"You have to understand the Deshcarn Mode," Aniku replied. "It is one of several celestial protocols. Think of earth like a property. Earth is one property in a universe-sized metropolis of fantastically diverse properties. Those properties are viewed as assets—not only by us, but by other factions as well. We are all trying to accomplish the same thing. We all want as many souls underneath our protocol as we can get. Our goal is to constantly enrich our singularity, as I've stated previously. Therefore, the more genii we manage, the better. If we were to keep our link open while this rift is also open to the other realm, we would effectively be linking our home to that unwieldy, phantom realm, using Ashford as the gateway. We would essentially be leaving our front door wide open to be infiltrated by some of the most sinister genii imaginable."

Big Bear replied, "This other realm we are all pasted to right now here in Ashford? It's just another realm like yours, with another singularity, competing for genii?"

Aniku and Anunit stole a quick glance at each other before responding. Neither seemed to want to be the one to explain what they told us next. Finally, Aniku took the reins and started talking. Anunit sort of uncomfortably slouched down in her chair.

"To answer your question, Sam, this other realm is absolutely nothing like ours. There is no singularity there like we've previously described. It is a far more malevolent location on the astral plain. The genii that find their way to this realm meet one of two distinct fates. They are either repurposed and sent back out as agents of that realm once they are purified. Which, to put it bluntly, means they are put through a cleansing process that is bound in unimaginable misery and suffering, over the course of millions of years. Every moment a soul spends in that realm consists of incomprehensible torture the likes of which cannot properly be communicated to you in your language. There are simply no earthly words to describe it. Conversely, the purpose of our realm is to enrich souls when they come back to us after an incarnated existence. We go to incredible lengths to nurture our genii. We place them into groups that assist and guide one another over eons upon eons of incarnated lifetimes—constantly improving, constantly building upon wisdom, learning from mistakes, bettering our collective singularity.

"The realm that we are sitting below here in Ashford, however, is subservient to a completely different doctrine. There is one single ruler of this realm. You would call him the Devil or Satan or Lucifer. We call him Enki, which roughly translates to "God of Death." His realm exists mainly for the purpose of absorbing genii into himself. Instead of bettering a singularity like we do and continuously redistributing souls across the celestial landscape as our Deshcarn Mode dictates, Enki keeps his souls for himself and his own contemptible attainment of power and knowledge. Most of the souls that end up there just end up being continuously tortured for eternity for no other purpose other than Enki's own perverse amusement."

"So, what do you call this place?" I asked. "What is your word for it?"

"Again, we don't have a word for Hell because there is no such thing as Hell in our realm. We tend to use religious terms to explain things to humans since you can relate to them. We simply call the situation here a 'Rift.' For example, we are not really angels. The name of our civilization is 'Du Agaden,' as in 'The Agaden.' We refer to this realm as 'Du Ki Ashford Perasu,' which translates to 'The Earth Ashford Rift.' It is named based on an ancient cataloguing system. There is absolutely nothing theological about it.

"To us, as interdimensional beings, an incarnation-rift is a trivial circumstance. To your race, it is nearly impossible to wrap your minds around such a link between your planet and some other dimensional point in space and time. To us, it is nothing more than traveling on a rarely taken road that leads to an unsavory part of town."

"If it's so trivial, then why don't you just close it down? Blow up the road?" barked Gary with a tinge of annoyance to his voice.

"We tried. To effectively sever the rift, there are several steps that need to be carefully taken in a very specific order. Firstly, you must isolate the affected area. In this case, we isolated the town of Ashford, Ohio, effectively cutting it off from our realm. You must then disconnect the affected area from the astral plain, segregating it onto its own slice of space-time that then becomes isolated from the rest of the earth. By doing this, we prevented Crowe's scourge from spreading outside of Ashford. Finally, you must eliminate the Bridge. The person acting as the Bridge, while alive, acts as the physical link between your world and the other realm. Once the Bridge is eliminated, the affected area can typically be relinked to our realm and continue to participate in the Deshcarn Mode."

"You burned down the asylum decades ago, killing Crowe. Shouldn't that have severed the gateway between earth and the other realm? Why has Ashford remained off the grid for so long?" I asked.

"As I said, we typically can reestablish the link between our world and yours once the Bridge is eliminated. Ashford has proven to be a unique case. Somehow, Crowe managed to gain knowledge of other Bridges while he was still alive. He even managed to document their names, future locations of birth, as well as dates of their birth. You've seen the evidence of this in the photo Lance shared with you. It was immediately obvious to us that there were plans set in motion for years to bring other Bridges to Ashford as a kind of fail-safe. If something happened to him, these other Bridges would be able to come to Ashford and pick up where Crowe left off. Even worse, despite the death of his physical body, Crowe's genii, for reasons we do not yet understand, managed to transcend into The Bulk instead of the nightmare realm that Ashford is linked to."

"The Bulk?" asked Gary.

"The Bulk is the term that we use to describe the area between two realms of consciousness. It is a void or limbo existing between two dimensions. While existing within The Bulk, some genii can consciously interact with either realm. The soul, or in this case Crowe, can only exist physically within the void and must rely on other means to project his influence into our realm here in Ashford. For these reasons, we are forced to keep the link between our realm severed until we figure out a way to either destroy Crowe's genii or force him completely through the rift and out of The Bulk and into the nightmare realm. This would prevent him from interacting with earth at any level of consciousness. But now, thanks again to Lance, the waters are even more muddied with a new Bridge running around."

"What are you planning to do, kill Danny? Because a few of us in this room might have a slight issue with that approach," I asked.

"Your friend is a Bridge; however, he has not yet established himself as the Bridge to their other realm. They no doubt want desperately for him to become that gateway for them. Make no mistake about it, there are forces that you cannot even imagine outside of these doors. They are after your friend, and they will stop at absolutely nothing to convince Danny to establish himself as the second coming of Crowe's living gateway. If they succeed, then a flood of genii from the nightmare realm will cross through it and into this town. At which point, there is very little we could do to stop them. It would be nearly impossible to contain such a calamity to Ashford. The genii that would flood through that gateway would be purified in billions of years of agony and torture. There would be no reasoning with it or negotiating. It would be a hostile force beyond anything your kind has ever encountered—bound in hatred, forged in the fires of pure evil.

"First, they would hijack any living being they could find, replacing their genii with their own. You refer to this act as demonic possession. They would then use their hijacked hosts to kill us all, immediately transforming anything they possess into perfect killing machines that are driven by unthinkable hatred and an ancient, masochistic aggression that there is simply no strategic answer for.

"To make matters even worse, Ashford just so happens to have a ready-made army of hosts waiting in the wings for the gateway to be opened. Some of Crowe's patients are still out there in the woods, hiding, stalking, observing, existing consciously in Crowe's realm and physically in yours. The locals refer to them as 'melon-heads.' In addition, Crowe's ex-patients have been abducting people around Ashford, on a consistent basis, since their escape from the fire. Those persons, once abducted, are brutally murdered, and in turn, their souls join the ranks of the melon-heads— trapped in their earthbound hosts. They then, over time, through a process we still do not fully understand, develop characteristics of the melon-heads. They, themselves, post-mortem, go through a transformation. It is as though they evolve into melon-heads themselves. All in all, we estimate the total number of them to be around two thousand. Two thousand host bodies who are ready, at a moment's notice, to be implanted with earth-conscious, evil, merciless genii from the nightmare realm.

"Your colleague is the last piece of the puzzle that Crowe needed to assemble in order to effectively charge this army with his calamitous genii. Danny is all that Crowe needs to produce an army of demonically possessed, hyper-aggressive, hyperintelligent brutes whose physical limitations are not bound within earth's laws of physics.

"Therefore, to answer your original question, Ricky. We do not seek to kill Danny; however, if he is to succeed in bridging this world with their realm, none of us will have a choice in the matter. We need to find him quickly and get him as far away from Ashford and Roderick Crowe as we possibly can. If he establishes that link, then we won't hesitate to kill him. I assure you, Ricky, one human life is well worth taking compared to the unimaginable nightmare that would cascade over your entire planet if Crowe were to succeed."

We briefly had a chance to collectively exhale and allow all this complex, confusing, and terrifying information to sink in. Not two minutes later, a brilliant flash of crimson light beamed into our conference room, then another and another, brighter each time. It was coming from the massive row of cubicles we had passed on our way into the room. We all turned and faced the source. All the other Agaden were standing at their desks with looks of dread thickly painted over their faces. It was the first authentic emotion of any kind that I had witnessed from the Agaden since encountering them. One approached the invisible wall through which we had entered the conference room. Aniku had already opened the doorway, allowing him to enter. They spoke English to each other, and I could barely overhear their conversation.

"What is it? What's happened?" Aniku asked.

"We've received a strong, unmistakable spike from our instruments monitoring the Whistler Road area."

"Meaning what, exactly?"

The Agaden was breathing heavily, near hyperventilation as he replied, "Ashford Two and Three have somehow found their way out of The Bulk and into Ashford, near Whistler Road."

Aniku fell backward into his chair. He was intensely distressed by the revelation. After a moment of sitting in an uncomfortable, disconcerting silence, he barked back to the man, "Get Biru and Nenza armed, and get the trucks ready. We have to meet this head on!"

I stood. "Will someone please explain to us exactly what is going on?"

Aniku looked at me. With a slight shake of his head and in a melancholy tone, he explained, "Two of Crowes most dangerous accomplices have just come back through from The Bulk. We call them Ashford Two and Ashford Three. Ashford One is obviously Roderick Crowe. Ashford Two is Kenneth Harvey, and Ashford Three is Margaret Peirce. They are Crowe's highest-ranking subordinates. Now we know where to find your friend. Who's up for a really interesting ride over to Whistler Road?"

34
1551 Whistler Road – 5:35 p.m.

I just sat on the floor a while, unable to believe that the man crouching a foot away from me was Kenneth Harvey. My neck was throbbing and gashed, both of my legs were riddled with cuts and scratches from the spectral woman who had, moments before, attempted to pull my head from my shoulders.

The only reason she stopped is because a guy who wrote a book roughly ninety years ago—a book that, coincidentally, I'd been reading in my downtime recently—told her to. Even though I had been reading this man's personal memoirs that took place in the 1930s, there he was, right as rain, in 2018, and he didn't look a day over thirty-five. I honestly just wanted to be dead.

"Can you get me the fuck out of this town?" I muttered to him, barely having regained any ability to speak.

He gazed into my bloodshot eyes and shook his head no. I stood and began putting my pants back on, finally.

"Then do me a favor, pal, and fuck right off." I felt a bulge in my back pocket. "Oh yeah, and here's your book. Just a little constructive criticism. It sucks." I threw his own memoir at him only to watch it pass directly through his torso and skid across the floor. It came to rest against the adjacent wall.

He watched me dress awhile. I did everything in my power to avoid any sort of communication with him as I put my clothes back on. Despite retaining my stench of body odor mixed with fireplace smoke, mixed with nature and a slight but unmistakable tinge of man-ass, my clothes had had a chance to dry to a crisp next to the fireplace. For that, I was thankful.

I stole one last look at Kenneth Harvey as I buckled my belt. I wanted no part of whatever he wanted to sell me. I knew he was not of this earth, and I had spent the entirety of my adult life chasing after things like whatever he was. But at that point, I didn't care. I was going to get the hell out of that town however I could. My plan was to find the setting sun and walk toward it, in a straight line, due west, until I either found my way out or died. Either outcome would have been welcomed as a sweet release.

"Danny, I might be able to help you find your way out of this town if you would just give me a few minutes to explain," Harvey shouted as I walked by on my way to the door.

Even though I was pretty sure both of my wrists were badly sprained from being dropped to the floor by the monster, I managed, however painfully, to flip him the bird as I stumbled by. I reached the front door a moment later only to watch it slam shut on its own, then lock itself. I then felt a hand on the back of my neck dragging me away from the door. It was Harvey. He said nothing as he pushed me into the kitchen. He was far stronger than I was, rivaling the woman whom I first encountered in that very cabin. I was helpless to fight back. He brought me to a window over a sink that was straight out of the 1950s and finally spoke.

"Take a look outside, and you tell me if that's where you want to be."

I blinked several times, focusing my attention outside. The sun was already beginning to set. There was only a sliver of orange and magenta painting the horizon through the towering ash trees in the distance. It was that half-lit point of the evening where it wasn't quite dark, but everything was beginning to distort. Immediately outside of the window stood at least a hundred melon-heads. My skin crawled as they looked on at me. Each of them more horrible than the other. Each shared the same astonishing deformations of their skulls. They had an intensity to their eyes. They stood looking at us in an aggressive stance, each ready to pounce at a moment's notice. You could feel their malice, almost taste their hostility. In those numbers, their power brought about the feeling of an impending hurricane just offshore—a storm so severe that one's only recourse is to board up and get out of dodge. This was a highly motivated infantry battalion forged in pure evil, tempered within the sadistic fires of Lucifer himself. Ashford truly was the town that Satan called home, and I felt at that moment that I was meeting him face-to-face in the form of his legion. It was apparent that the only reason I was still alive was because Harvey was allowing me to be.

"Those are my friends, Mr. Hallowell," Harvey whispered into my ear, still grasping the back of my now-shuddering neck. "You know what happens when you meet my friends, Danny?"
"We all play a really gross game of erotic Twister?" I asked.

He released me, knowing full well that my escape route was completely blocked. He smiled. He even let out a brief chuckle at my remark. He was hardly threatening—in appearance, at least. A normal, almost unhealthily slender build. Perhaps five foot ten on his tiptoes, 140 pounds soaking wet with a rock in his hand. The front of his black hairline was slowly receding into the middle of his curiously small, peanut-shaped head. He donned a pair of spectacles like something you would expect to see on a printing press worker from the Wild West. His clothes matched the part as well. He wore what I am guessing was a bygone-era leisure, five-piece suit, complete with pointed shoes, stirrups, suspenders, a vest, a jacket, and an eggshell-colored button-down shirt. Every inch of clothing was starched to the point where the edges were sharp enough to slice though rawhide. A pocket watch that likely belonged in a museum bulged from his pocket complete with the chain that linked it to his waistband.

Maintaining a slight grin, he replied, "Not exactly, Danny. Not exactly." His grin suddenly disappeared. "You see, my friends," he continued, pointing toward the window, "you can't outrun them. They aren't bound to physical limitations in this world. Their bodies exist on this earth, but their consciousness exists in a different place—a far superior realm of space and time. They are being controlled, Mr. Hallowell. They are instruments to be used to do The Divine Father's bidding here on earth. They are beautiful. You should see them in action. They can invert themselves and run on their hands faster than any human can on their own two feet. They can leap a hundred feet in a single bound. Well, most of them can, anyway. To be honest, each one is ever so slightly different. But they do have one thing in common. Do you know what that is?"

"Excellent credit?" I asked.

My snarky remark failed to elicit any sort of response from him this time. Instead, he just carried on with his diatribe. "They're all hungry." His face had taken on a more sinister scowl. His teeth clenched together as he continued in an overbearingly aggressive tone. "You see, they don't get to eat very often. Remember, they aren't alive in an earthbound sense. So, they do not *need* to eat. They don't require carbohydrates or electrolytes or protein like you do. They *want* to eat because when they taste blood, it brings intense pleasure to their master. Oh, but they won't kill you—no, Danny. A dead body doesn't bleed nearly as much. They will keep you alive for as long as possible, a nibble here, a bite there, a finger, a toe, an eyelid, a tongue. But your heart will remain beating, forcing every drop of fresh, warm blood down their throats, quenching his thirst, powering him, arousing him."

"So, just so I understand correctly," I interrupted. "If I leave, they're going to eat me slowly because their douchebag freak of a boss gets off on it? Is that about the half of it?"

"I certainly wouldn't call him that. But that is the crux of your situation, yes."

"Who is him?"

"He goes by the name Enki."

"So, not Roderick Crowe? I thought he was your Divine Father?"

With another chuckle, "Roderick Crowe is indeed—he is the one who came before you—also a Bridge. He is the one who originally broke open our pathway to Enki's realm. In doing so, he was gifted more knowledge than anyone could ever fathom. Roderick Crowe is the great apostle, The Divine Father who taught us and ultimately delivered us all into Enki's salvation. Enki, however, is the god of gods, supreme master of the entire realm onto which Ashford is affixed. It is his desire that our friends outside fulfill."

I wandered back into the living room and sat back down atop the mantle, sensing that my only recourse was now to engage in a forced conversation with Kenneth Harvey. It was either that or be eaten alive by melon-heads.

"What is it that you want from me, exactly?"

"I want you to meet him."

"Okay," I said with a blatant tinge of annoyance to my voice. "Where is he?"

"He doesn't exist on this plane of consciousness; however, you have met him already, several times. The first time, you were overtaken by his power at Lance's house as you met him outside the window in the backyard. The second time, our friend Andy gave you a special elixir that allowed you to transcend into his realm. There you met him again, but not in his true form. He appeared to you in the form of a demon because you subconsciously made him that way."

"Andy? You know that son of a bitch? I knew there was more than vodka in that disgusting beverage."

"Yes, Andy and I are cohorts of sorts, stretching back to my time in Ashford in human form. Had you finished reading the book you tried throwing at me, you would have been able to figure that out for yourself."

"Okay, so I made Crowe into the creature I saw in The Black City after your old pal roofied me?"

"That's right, Danny. You and Crowe are Bridges. You both possess the same gift. You have yet to figure out how to harness your transcendent capabilities within the confines of your conscious mind. You have, however, figured out how to transcend unconsciously. And as you must at least be moderately aware, the unconscious mind is a chaotic, overly creative, overly fantastical state of human **cognizance**. The unconscious mind is the same place where your dreams and nightmares come from. You unconsciously control what you see in that state. And you unconsciously conjured up a Black City that doesn't really exist in our realm. And you made our Divine Father into something that appeared to you as a monster."

"So, he isn't a demon? He's really that perfect, game-show-host-looking guy I saw outside of Lance's window?"

With an exasperated exhale, Harvey answered, "No, not at all. The form you saw in Lance's backyard is quite frankly not something you want to know about."

"Do you honestly think anything is going to surprise me at this point, Harvey?"

"How do I put this? About a week ago, a man named Riley Sherborn went missing here in Ashford. About once a year, another man or woman goes missing around this town. I trust that Lance explained the disappearances to you? They've been going on since before I was summoned here by the sheriff in the 1930s, since immediately after the asylum burned down. As I stated previously, Crowe does not exist within this plane of consciousness. The only way for him to interact with this realm is for him to possess a host, either alive or dead. What you witnessed in Lance's backyard was the dead body of Riley Sherborn being controlled by Roderick Crowe."

"Well, fuck. Why does he have to do that? Why can't he just come back here in his original form, like you and Andy do?"

"He was present in his office when Ashford Hill burned down. He burned to death that night. But all the while, he was not alone. He was trapped there by the Agaden."

"The who?"

"The Agaden. Clearly, you barely touched my book. There is an opposing force here in Ashford. You've seen them, on your way into town. Lance described them to you as the feds. However, they are an ancient race known as Du Agaden. They saw what Crowe was doing here on earth as a threat and decided to kill him. And in doing so, they inadvertently forced him into The Bulk."

"The what? Speak fucking English, will you?" I barked.

Now Harvey was growing annoyed. "The Bulk is an area that is not of this world, and it is not of the next. It is a void in between both realms. And since this limbo is his current place of conscious residence, he cannot manifest in his previous human form here on earth. I can and Andy can because we died here after the Agaden had isolated Ashford from the rest of earth and from their realm. And Crowe has allowed us to remain here ever since. The only other place we could go and exist consciously is through the rift, past The Bulk."

"Why don't you go there? Why wander around an isolated town for all of eternity, full of giant-headed monsters that want to eat people, answering to some idiot doctor who is trying to play god?"

"We don't have to pass through. We exist here, and we exist in The Bulk with our Divine Father. Our motivation is not something I can explain to you. It is something I would have to show you. Being there with him in his presence is a sensation you wouldn't be able to comprehend via spoken word."

"Not a chance, pal. So, I began reading your book. And I meant what I said about it. Worst piece of shit I've ever read. But when I left off, you were interviewing Margaret, and you thought what she was explaining to you was nonsense. You thought she was insane. But now, here you are, explaining much of the same nonsense to me, and you believe it? What happened? Peer pressure?"

"I wouldn't have to explain this to you if you had just read the goddamned book."

"I've been a little busy here, guy. I haven't exactly had a lot of time to kick my feet up and dive into a novel."

With another exasperated groan, he continued, "Margaret and I quickly began to make a great deal of progress in her therapy. She became more and more lucid on a daily basis. Her intelligence was off the charts, demonstrating mental abilities I couldn't have imagined before meeting her. I had never seen anything like it—nobody had. We would sit in the sheriff's station, just looking out the window together, and she would be able to predict everything that would happen outside of the station moments before it would happen.

"'A robin is going to perch on the third branch from the top of that tree.' Sure enough, ten seconds later, it would happen.

"'Mrs. Carter is going to trip slightly coming out of the grocery store and drop exactly one apple out of her bag. She is going to bend over and pick it up with her right hand, put it back into the bag, only to have it fall out again after three more steps from the store.' Then, the entire complex scenario would play out before our eyes, mere moments later.

"Over time, our relationship evolved into more than a doctor-patient sort of arrangement."

"Kenny, Kenny . . . you dog," I said.

"Shut up and listen, Mr. Hallowell. Despite our blossoming love affair, there was always one ten-thousand-pound elephant in the room between us. There was always one thing that I could not, for the life of me, get past with her. She refused to let go of the belief that Roderick Crowe was not dead.

"I once took her to the police station and demanded that the sheriff show her his teeth, which they had recovered from the rubble of the asylum after the fire. Even then, even after seeing them for herself, she remained undaunted in her belief, positively rigid that her 'Divine Father' still existed, despite his human form being so obviously deceased.

"One evening, not unlike this one, she convinced me to accompany her to the location where Ashford Hill had burned. By that time, it was mostly cleared out—open field, only the foundation of the asylum and a few random piles of stones and bricks strewn about. She brought me atop the remains of the foundation and asked if I wanted to meet her Divine Father. I sort of laughed and said sure, not really believing her, thinking she was pulling one over on me.

"She kissed me. We stood there a moment, just kissing. And behind her, I saw a group of what you refer to as melon-heads slowly emerge from the tree line, not twenty yards from us. She turned and saw them, and she smiled and sort of motioned for them to come closer. Mind you, I was absolutely horrified. To that point, I had never seen anything like them. As they began moving closer to us, Margaret pulled me into her and began furiously, ravenously kissing me. She ripped away the bottom of her dress and pulled me down on top of her. As we made love, right there on the cold concrete slab, the beings surrounded us. She told me not to worry and to just keep doing what I was doing. I entered her, and as I did, the world transformed around us, melting at the speed of light. It is hard to explain it to someone who has never seen it, but she brought me with her into The Bulk. We transcended together, and while I was there, I looked around, and the monstrous beings had transformed, along with our surroundings.

"Replacing the open field and the disorganized piles of rubble were glorious sloping constructs of pastel-colored matter, the likes of which do not exist in this realm of consciousness. There was no distinguishing where the matter ended, and the sky began. The horizon was infinite, melding together into one unimaginably beautiful, incredibly vast landscape.

"The moment I entered that place, the only emotion that registered was pure bliss. It was as though someone had extracted all the dopamine in the world and injected it straight into my heart. The monstrous beings that had surrounded us previously were still present but had transformed into remarkably brilliant strands of luminescent vapor. Each distinctly different from the next, they hovered and flowed around one another, each its own phosphorescent entity, each possessing its own unique yet bewitching beauty. In their presence, you could feel the energy they gave off within their light. You could bask in their brilliant radiation. You could feel their emotion, their sense of being. And it was pure love—an infallible love, a thousand times that of a mother to her newborn child. I looked down at myself and Margaret and found our own bodies had been replaced as well. We were exactly as the beings around us were, a sort of molten energy, yet still our conscious selves. We were wrapped around each other; our souls intertwined, floating together on an ocean of indefinable euphoria, and I knew right then, that was where I wanted to exist for the rest of time.

"As we finished making love, another of the beings approached. As it did, all the other shards of light parted way, making a path for it. This being was not like the others. As brilliant as they had registered to us, this one beamed with the brilliance of a star gone supernova. It was a distinct purplish shade that none of the others possessed, including ourselves. It was rounder; it had the feeling of a perfect sphere of pure energy, yet an impossible elasticity that set it apart from the rest of us. It needed no introduction. This was The Divine Father.

"The moment I found myself in his presence, everything Margaret had been trying to tell me since the day we had met in the sheriff's station was proven truthful. He emitted an energy that was far stronger than anyone else in that realm. And while the overpowering sense emitted from the other beings was love, The Divine Father projected knowledge. Knowledge of, for lack of a better term, everything. Just by being in his presence, I could feel his sense of awareness. This was how Margaret had gained the ability to execute her psychic stunts and predict things and maintain an IQ that put everyone else on earth to shame. Because she had basked in the same light I found myself in then. It was like being immediately implanted with every line from every encyclopedia in the universe, instantaneously. Human knowledge was a small part of him. Without him even having to speak to me, I somehow deduced that he was in possession of every deep, celestial secret since the beginning of time.

"The best way for me to describe him to you is ultraconscious. You see, Daniel, consciousness is something all living things take for granted in their incarnated states, as you are now, for example. Some of us have the chance to rise above that. You have the gift to do so. You can't properly appreciate consciousness until you reach new levels of it. I spent my life studying the animal brain—racking my own, trying to unlock its secrets. Thirty seconds in his presence taught me more than a lifetime of my own experiences on earth ever could. You see, consciousness at those levels transcends space and time. There is no concept of past, present, or future. On those levels, you are distinctly aware of all things, all possibilities, every possible scenario on every plane of existence. You are totally unbound from your earthly limitations. To put it as simply as I can, you gain a more sweeping view of all things.

"And you, Danny, you are one in a trillion. You get the chance to go there consciously and in your human incarnated form."

"Jesus, man. And you want to take me to this place?"

"That's right."

"We don't have to fuck, do we?"

"Be serious for a moment, Mr. Hallowell, and attempt to understand what I'm offering you. Forget about Crowe for a moment, and think about your own life. Think about what you've spent your life doing, what you've chased. You have spent your entire adult life running around to locations where you would be lucky to find one confused, disembodied spirit of an old housewife or listening to recordings of static hoping for one barely audible phrase to come through. If you were extremely lucky, you might catch one half of an apparition on camera, upon the rarest of occasions. I am offering you a chance to stand in the presence of a god. A god who can instantaneously implant you with the answers to every question you've ever pondered the answer to. All your questions about everything pertaining to life and death and everything in between would be answered at your demand. And any all-knowing being who could answer such questions could surely offer up some advice for getting yourself out of this town. Imagine the insights you could gain? Imagine the knowledge you would leave there with? They called you 'the man who proved the afterlife' once. How would you like to be known as the man who got to describe it to humanity? Daniel Hallowell—the man who met god."

"Do I have a choice?"

"Of course, you always have a choice, Danny. I just honestly have no idea how you and your friends are going to get out of this town alive without meeting him."

35

The Deposition of Rick Voss: (Second Session):

Mr. Voss: *We weren't exactly asked to leave the Exchange Station. We were forced out the way we had come in and back into the vehicles. On the way out, there was a flurry of activity. All the Agaden were up from their workstations and rushing about the facility; most were armed. As a species, or people—whatever in the hell they were—they didn't show much emotion. But at that point, each wore an immediately noticeable cloak of anxiety.*

The next twenty or so minutes are hard for me to talk about.

Mrs. Miles: *Just do your best, Ricky, and be truthful.*

Mr. Voss: *We tore away from the station in a convoy of vehicles, all fully blacked-out GMCs. It was me, Lance, and Anunit in the rear vehicle. In front of us, Big Bear, Gary, Aniku, and two Agaden riflemen. There were another two vehicles ahead of them, both filled with more Agaden with even more guns. Things were weird from the moment we began to move. I glanced out the side window, and something, in the woods grabbed my attention. I could see these people . . . or things, running alongside our cars. They were in the trees, naked and running on all fours. Somehow, they were managing to keep pace with us, and we had to be moving at over sixty miles per hour.*

About thirty seconds into the trip, the radio in our vehicle screamed to life on its own. It was on a broadcast of a baseball game from the 1930s. Goose Goslin was batting, and Mel Harder was pitching. It was blaring—mind-blowingly loud. The sheer noise of it was disorienting.

Anunit was driving; the shock from the radio threw her off for a moment, and she nearly swerved into the ditch. At our speed, any incident would have likely killed or severely maimed us all. She fumbled a minute, trying to turn off the radio, but it would not turn off. Finally, after a few more intolerable moments of the bygone broadcast nearly blowing out our eardrums, Anunit, as fast as I've ever seen anyone move, formed a fist and punched a gaping hole directly through the radio into the dashboard, absolutely demolishing the radio. As she did so, a few sparks flew from the dash and one last astonishingly loud pop blew out all the speakers. Save for the roaring engines of the Yukon and the ringing in our ears, we were again thrust back into a welcomed silence.

"What in the hell is going on?" I shouted at Anunit. "That baseball game was from eighty years ago."

"Eighty-two. Kind of busy right now, Ricky!" was the only response I received.

I leaned forward and looked out the window. I saw something outside.

Mr. Levine: *Something? Care to elaborate?*

Mr. Voss: *It was rail thin, maybe five foot ten, completely nude, and moving alongside our vehicle within our dust trail. It was easily keeping up with us, and we, at that exact moment, were traveling at seventy-five miles per hour. It had scabs all over its body to the point that it looked tan. It was missing its ears, eyelids, lips, genitalia, and nose. The worst thing about it was the head. Its head was at least three times larger than it should have been. It was like a horrific caricature.*

It was using absolutely no energy to keep up with us, and the entire time, it was running on its hands with its legs dangling above its head. It twisted its neck in such a way that should have severed its spinal cord. Instead, the unnatural contortion served to keep its wicked gaze on our car. The moment it noticed me looking at it, it shot back into the tree line and disappeared.

I looked ahead of us into Gary and Big Bear's car. The interior lights were blinking on and off as fast as a strobe light. When they were on, they seemed to burn incredibly bright, illuminating the inside of their vehicle with brilliant explosions of radiation. Aniku was driving their Yukon, and I could see he was struggling to maintain control, as I'm sure he was being repeatedly blinded. Finally, I saw Big Bear lay down on his seat and kick the overhead lamp with his steel-toed boot. As he did, it dimly flashed once more and then was permanently extinguished.

"We will be at Whistler Road in three minutes!" Anunit yelled back to us.

Just as she finished speaking, we heard a massive crash that was quickly followed by an abrupt burst of automatic gunfire. Another moment later, out ahead of us we saw the lead Yukon fly sideways into the trees. It crashed thirty feet up and split completely in half against the trunk of a massive ash. It had been moving down the road at seventy-five miles per hour, leading our charge. Something had managed to hit it from the side with enough force to completely stop its forward momentum and fire it thirty feet into a tree. The force was so intense, it ripped the five-thousand-pound, steel-reinforced cabin in half as though it had been made of tin foil.

We slowed as we passed the wreckage. "Aren't we going to stop and see if we can help them?" I shouted.

Anunit answered without a tinge of hesitation, "They're all dead already. There's nothing we can do for them."

Lance had begun crying next to me. He was so terrified that he couldn't handle it anymore. I wasn't far behind him. It seemed like there was a good chance I was about to die within mere minutes, and when I did, I was going straight through the rift and straight to Hell. I was powerless to do anything about it. I was caught in a vehicle in the middle of a war between two powers eons more advanced than my species.

I managed to steal one last glance at the destroyed Yukon to my right. It was wedged into the tree thirty feet above us. It had since burst into flames and was split open on its side between the first and second sets of doors. One of the Agaden was still alive but completely coated in flames. He was hanging upside down in the scolding wreckage desperately trying to free himself, but his leg was horrifically broken and wedged underneath one of the crumpled seat housings. A moment later, at least a dozen of the things emerged from the woods below the smoldering vehicle. They all shared the same disgusting deformities of their heads, and they were all hideously skinny with paper-thin, scarred flesh stretched over their bodies.

One of them somehow, in a single bound, leapt thirty feet into the air and grabbed the trapped Agaden. In a single motion, the creature pulled what was left of the still-alive man apart from his crushed leg, severing it at the hip. I heard his blood-curdling scream through my window over our still raucous engine as what was left of him fell to the ground. As he hit the earth below, he was immediately descended upon by the things. They moved toward him with their razor-sharp nails and teeth, primed and ready to finish him off. As they descended over him, they appeared in no hurry to put him out of his misery. Just before he disappeared behind us, I saw the creatures slowly kneel over his cowering body and several began taking slow, meticulous bites from him, as though they were savoring a long desired meal.

Our remaining three vehicles came to a turn a minute later, and we all flew around it, nearly going up on two wheels as we did so. The road was paved and in relatively decent shape compared to what had basically been a series of horse trails to begin our awful journey. On the better pavement, the engine noise was quieted, replaced by the smooth humming of the tire treads on the pavement. We were all nearly hyperventilating, including Anunit.

"Is this like a normal fucking day for you people?" I shouted to her.

"Not exactly," she replied. "This is quite an unusual day for me as well. We've got to get to your friend, and we've got to get him out of here before Ashford Two and Three get him to transcend."

Very faintly, as Anunit finished her thought, I began to hear what sounded like a baby crying. It was coming from outside of the car and could just barely be heard over all the other noise. As we moved along farther down the road, the crying became louder. After another minute of driving, it became positively unmistakable. It was deafening—a veritable chorus of wailing infants nearly as loud as the screeching radio anomaly we had endured moments before.

"What the fuck is that?" Lance shouted. He was nearly hysterical.

Anunit answered, "It's the melon-heads. They emulate the sounds of crying human infants to confuse, disorient, and terrify their prey."

"Well, it's fucking working! Melon-heads? That's what those things are called?" I shouted.

Suddenly, there were brake lights in front of us. We slammed on our own brakes and skidded to a stop. After a minute of not knowing what was going on, we pulled up next to the other two vehicles. We were three-wide across the entirety of the darkened roadway. Anunit rolled down her window, as did the other Agaden drivers, and they began conversing.

Big Bear and Gary were in the vehicle next to me. They both looked absolutely horrified. Gary, in typical Gary form, had his camera out and was rolling on the entire operation. I sent a confused look at Big Bear, and he motioned for me to roll my window down. I obliged.

"Why the hell are we stopped?" I asked.

"Roadblock!" shouted Big Bear. He pointed ahead. I contorted my body between the two front seats to see out of the windshield. Ahead of us, about fifty yards up the road, at least fifty of the melon-heads stood, seemingly in formation. Their positions were designed specifically to block our path. Their forces were stretched completely from one tree line, across the entirety of the road, and clear to the other tree line. There was no getting past them.

"Oh, fuck me!" I heard Lance cry out suddenly. Only Lance wasn't looking ahead like the rest of us were. He was looking behind us. I turned around fast enough to crack my own back. There were at least another fifty melon-heads to our rear, in the same formation, completely cutting off any retreat we might have had in mind. We were trapped by an army of possessed, giant-headed, demonic, hyperathletic monsters.

Aniku and Anunit hastily exited their two respective vehicles along with the Agaden from the remaining lead car. The two unnamed Agaden simultaneously fired what I initially thought to be gas canisters from a grenade launcher at the two crowds of melon-heads. In reality, they were probing flares. Their rounds stalled and exploded in midair above the two herds of creatures, illuminating them in a bright reddish hue. The melon-heads were bathed in a fiery vividness that, above much else, added to the horror of their nightmarish march in our direction.

The two groups were undoubtedly inching closer, slowly pinching our position. As the flares exploded above them, they became stirred up and immediately began yipping and wailing. The unthinkable noise of a hundred distressed infants filled the air. It is impossible to describe how inconceivably frightening it is to witness such a mass of fiendish beings like that making such noises. Noises that we, as human beings, associate with the most vulnerable of ourselves were booming from the most threatening, hyperaggressive brutes that any of us could have imagined. A hundred crying babies howled all around us from an army of psychotic abominations now drenched in a deep-red incandescence from the flares.

Without lips or eyelids, their faces projected unbridled intensity. They were ultrafocused on us. Their lack of lips produced the illusion of them grinning in our direction. Each of their sharpened teeth were intact and exposed all the way to the jawline. They were ready to devour us at a moment's notice, and there was nothing in their bulging, psychotic eyes that suggested any idea of mercy.

Most of them were standing upright as we would, but some were crawling toward us on all fours. Others were walking on their hands with their heads bent impossibly backward to keep their focus on our trapped convoy. They moved about one another in what I can only describe as a hypnotic fashion. They were packed in together like sardines, but at no time did one touch another. They flowed and shimmied and seemed able to predict one another's movements. It was a hive mentality, as though they shared a singular source of control over all their collective motion.

"Oh my god," I heard next to me from Lance.

I quickly turned to look at him again. He had his eyes fixed out his side window. Not five feet from our parked vehicle stood two of the melon-heads, staring threateningly into our car. They stood upright, shoulder to shoulder. This close, I was able to make out the utter disgust that they projected. The entirety of their vascular systems could be observed through their paper-thin skin. Every bone jutted out to the near point of rupture through their yellow-brown dermis. Their nails and teeth were razor sharp—perfect weapons. Their heads—the skin on them was stretched so far that on one of them, it had burst open, exposing the back of its oblong skull. Since it had once been stretched over such a large area, the skin over its face dangled clumsily in a glob of puss-covered flesh near where its chin should have been. It looked like a bad mask of a human face that someone bought for Halloween, only to find out it was five sizes too big.

"That's my grandma and grandpa," Lance yelled in a disconcertingly high-pitched, panicked, and childish tone as he reactively reached for the door handle.

"Lance, those are not your fucking grandparents anymore. Do not open that fucking door!" I screamed.

It was no use, and it was too late. He already had the door half open. The two melon-heads didn't flinch as the door swung open in front of them and Lance jumped out. They just sort of craned their heads to one side and then the other like a couple of curious dogs hearing a cat on the television. They almost seemed amused by Lance's approach. I screamed for him to stop, but he wouldn't listen. As I continued shouting in his direction, it got the attention of the Agaden, who noticed the situation and immediately began shouting at Lance and moving toward him.

I turned back and saw Lance still approaching the two melon-heads. The female thing reached her arms out to Lance, as though to hug him. Lance glanced back to me. The crazy son of a bitch had an ear-to-ear smile on his face. In his warped, frenzied mind at that desperate hour, he had finally found his long-lost grandparents. He turned back toward the outstretched arms of the monstrous woman and hugged her. They embraced a moment. For a fleeting instant, it was Lance hugging his grandmother or whatever sort of psychotic construct remained of her. He had finally vindicated his entire reason for being in Ashford. He had finally found out what had happened to them. I like to think that in that moment, the massive weight that had been haunting him for so long, thrusting him into a crippling level of depression, was finally lifted. I like to think that he, at long last, felt some sense of relief, however briefly.

An instant later, the nightmare that was once Lance's grandmother unhinged her jaw and sank her razor-sharp teeth around the entirety of Lance's head, completely ripping his face in half from top to bottom. The unspeakable act left a gushing chasm from above his forehead and clear down below his chin. A final, desperate, high-pitched, hitching squeal was all Lance could muster as his legs buckled underneath him. The other melon-head, his grandfather, had begun thrashing at Lance's lower body and stomach with his claws, instantly spilling his intestines to the ground. His body was stood up, still in the grips of his grandmother's impossibly powerful jaws. Lance's legs kicked a few times. He tossed around a few final semiconscious arm movements and then went completely limp.

Automatic gunfire rang out as Anunit and Aniku reached him. The melon-heads flew apart in dozens of pieces, their bodies proving brittle and easily vulnerable to gunfire. All that was left of them after a couple of seconds was a pile of gore at the edge of the tree line. Among the carnage, however, lay Lance's brutally mutilated corpse. He had finally found his grandparents, but finding them meant finding his own demise. The gunfire had stirred up the herds to our front and back. They were moving in on us, and there was nowhere left to hide.

36

I need to take a moment here to reflect personally a bit. I want to make sure my reasons for writing this are clear. I don't want anyone—mainly the staff here at the institution—getting any wrong ideas about why I'm doing this or about the way I'm detailing these events. Basically, I don't want anyone thinking I'm trying to clear my name by documenting this series of events. Nothing could be further from the truth.

As I write this, I know that whoever reads it isn't going to believe it. I know it will be of no help whatsoever toward shortening my stay here in this psychiatric facility. I firmly stand by my assertion that the "professionals" tasked with helping me through my "challenges" are completely inept. They have taken the stance from day one that I'm delusional, that I'm simply making all of this up, and that I am therefore exactly where I belong.

It has never mattered to them how Ricky corroborated everything I've told them through his own deposition. Never mind how Agent Roy declared that the very town I've told them about exists and has been a focus of shadowy sects of our own government for decades. Since no part of that deposition was admissible in court, it held no weight within our badly broken legal system. It therefore had no bearing on my eventual sentencing. I find it vexing, to say the least, that for that same reason, it has also not been allowed to have any bearing on the state of my mental health. At least, according to my pecker-headed therapists, it doesn't.

I do feel somewhat better by having written what I have thus far—better than when I started writing it down. Prior to my writing this, I had explained these events, these three days in Ashford, in clips and flashes, out of order, foggy, confused. Now that I've managed to piece it all together chronologically, it is registering far more clearly to me. Perhaps it will make my story more convincing.

I really don't care if these people ever believe me. Perhaps I *am* right where I belong. Not because I'm lying or fabricating this story. Not because I suffer from delusions or hallucinations. But because of what I went through during my last hours in Ashford. Because of what I became. I want Annie to read this. I want her to believe me. It is up to yourself, and only yourself, to choose the world you see. I would soon come to find out just how fickle my own truism could be.

37
1551 Whistler Road – 6:45 p.m.

Harvey opened the front door. I exited, and he followed just behind me but quickly brushed past and began to lead the way. Outside the door, the army of melon-heads waited. They were packed into the front of the property shoulder to shoulder for as far as I could see. The stench of them was agonizing to walk through, like month-old ground beef forgotten in the trunk of a warm car. My eyes watered. I was petrified. Any one of them at any moment could have ended me in the blink of an eye. Their hideous nails were sharper than steak knives. Their teeth were like razorblades jutting from their enormous skulls.

There was a path cut through them, leading us back behind the cabin. I knew this was Whistler Road. I knew where we were going. This was the site of the old Ashford Hill Lunatic Asylum. This was the heart of what had haunted this town for nearly a century. Out in front of us, lurking in the trees, something caught my eye. It was Margaret, in all her horrific glory, an hour removed from nearly choking me to death. She was floating through the trees, a spectral nightmare with her magenta eyes illuminating her path. She whisked and flowed through the forest with the grace of a black panther, stalking us along on our trek.

Time was behaving strangely, and my head was swimming in an ocean of confusion and lethargy. I was fully conscious of what was going on, but I could feel myself becoming disconnected from the normal cycle of the natural world. When we departed, seemingly moments prior, the sun was just beginning to set behind the towering ash trees to the west. Even though mere moments had passed, relative to me, it was somehow already pitch black. The only sources of light leading our way beamed from the ghostly apparition of Harvey's body and Margaret's haunting eyes. I felt the entire sense of my consciousness being pulled somewhere against my best wishes. I felt myself being manipulated on a spiritual level. My very soul was being inextricably joined with the menacing atmosphere around us.

I thought of the ride into town. Not as we were entering, but before that. Back to when it was just me, Big Bear, Ricky, and Gary. Gary smoked a bowl, and I got angry. We would go through the same scenario at least once a week with him. It is amazing how simple, everyday annoyances and problems come to seem so trivial when you find yourself marching toward what is very likely your death. I would have died for any one of them, and they for me. I felt so sorry for what I had gotten them into. I had no idea where they were or how they were or what they were going through. I began to cry. It wasn't a few tears running down my cheek. It was a full-blown wail, as though I had just lost my most beloved relative. I was losing everything—all control over myself. My mind was being ripped away from me by a force I didn't understand and likely never would. Harvey continued alongside of me. He maintained the calloused composure of a heartless prison guard, ushering a dead man on his last walk to the electric chair.

I was never going to see my wife again. I was never going to see my friends again. Then I thought of Annie, cruising down that double-black diamond with a smile from ear to ear. I spoke to her on the phone a couple of days ago. I gave her the last fatherly advice I would ever give her—to do her report on Diane Fossey. I should be with her, finding out how she did on the assignment, hugging her, taking care of her, being there for her when she needed me. Not here, not now, not with my soul being stolen, not giving up everything for a cause I wasn't even capable of comprehending.

I desperately latched on to those thoughts, getting the sense that as soon as I let them go, they would be ripped away from me forever in the metamorphosis that was being pressed upon me on that journey through the forest. I was supposed to die someday long into the future, holding Ellen's hand in a warm bed somewhere. I was supposed to die after having watched my baby graduate from college, having made something of herself, having walked her down the aisle. Not like this. Not so hopelessly alone.

The sun was impossibly beginning to rise in the east, even though we had only traveled for what felt like ten minutes. We entered a clearing approximately an eighth of mile into the forest. The clearing was massive and completely overgrown. Every type of ground cover— grass, weed, shrub, sapling, and vine—was well represented throughout. The large trees that dominated most of Ashford, however, were completely absent from this space. The area was wide enough to accommodate a factory—massive—more than enough space to have been where the asylum once stood. The only semblance of a structure was just ahead of us. Harvey and I, with Margaret not far behind, moved toward it. Behind her, the army of melon-heads followed. We came to the last remnants of Ashford Hill Asylum. It was a single slab of badly decayed concrete flanked on one side by the remains of an exterior wall that sat atop a single cornerstone. In total, the wall was perhaps five feet wide by four feet tall. If the wind had kicked up the wrong way, I would have fully expected for it to topple over, joining the rest of the grounded ruins for all eternity.

Harvey and I climbed atop the foundation and became enveloped within the still-darkened, predawn twilight. He turned to face the legion of disgust that had stalked us all the way there from the cabin. Without warning, he began to shout to them in an utterly inhuman volume. His vocal tone registered completely different from anything I had heard from him previously. He sounded synthesized, blaringly loud, deep, authoritative, god-like.

"Now witness, my brothers and sisters, the coming of Enki. Witness the fulfillment of the prophecy of The Divine Father. Give yourselves over to it. Allow yourselves to be saved. Participate in the cleansing. Embark in the great devouring."

I had lost control. I was present and aware of where I was and what was happening, but I was being rendered into a mindless construct of a raw soul. I had no opinion and no thoughts or power over what was happening. Before I could formulate a sentence, each of the melon-heads dropped to their knees. They bowed their heads, and in unison, hundreds of the repugnant creatures laid their elongated, clawed hands on the ground in front of themselves. Margaret hovered through them, straight through the middle of their ranks like the commanding general of evil that I assumed she was. She took her place in the front and center of her kneeling battalion. She, too, floated down to ground level and morphed her elastic, phantasmal body into a kneeling position before us. I felt a hand on my shoulder that slowly began to slide down my back. I looked to my left and found Harvey taking a kneeling position at my side.

"Am I supposed to kneel?" I managed.

Harvey smiled up at me. "We are kneeling for you, Daniel. Behold your army. Witness the beginning of your reign."

"Let's just get this over with," I whispered to him with a final tear dropping to my chest from my chin.

Harvey stood and moved in front of me. I was facing the army. His back was to them. He placed both of his hands to my chest. Immediately, I felt a massive electrical discharge emitting from him. It began violently jolting me backward. He followed me, pressing his hands ever stronger to my chest. A moment later, I felt a second set of hands on my back. I turned my head and found Margaret behind me. I was sandwiched between them with all four of their hands savagely pushing their supernatural force through me. Every instant that went by, the more intense it became. After a few more moments, the smell of burning ozone filled the air around us as my entire body began to shimmer with a radiant yet diffuse tangerine brilliance. Through the abruptly growing haze, I could barely see the melon-heads leaping up and down. They were in celebration of what was becoming of me. The unbridled power of the two nightmarish phantasms shot through me with blue streams of statically charged energy. It began to shoot from me as well. I had become flooded with their spirit. It seemed to seep from every pore.

Another moment passed, and the three of us became completely enveloped by it. The world around us exploded in a perfect sphere of potent, ethereal brilliance, a power so intense that I knew it was only meant for certain souls and it would instantly kill anyone who did not belong.

Another curious sense of familiarity washed over me. In such an unprecedented situation, something that completely flew in the face of all known laws of physics and philosophy, to feel déjà vu, as I did then, registered to me as horrifying. I felt the last bit of Daniel Hallowell leaving me, and I felt something else taking his place. It wasn't the unbridled rage that had taken me before, but something every bit as evil. I instantly gave myself over to it. I began to feel a sense of arrogance, as though this were all somehow meant for me. This was where I belonged, and nobody was going to stop me from taking my place atop my throne. This was my coronation.

The entire clearing exploded in a booming flash of luminescent brilliance as our turbulent sphere of supernatural energy reached its critical mass. It was an explosion that, relative to me, burst with the force of an atom bomb, instantly enveloping the entire area into its blaze of stunning light. I felt Margaret and Harvey struggle to pull their hands from me. I instinctively raised my clenched fists toward the heavens. I became everything in that moment. I was the way, the truth, and the light. I was the answer to every riddle. I was the missing variable to all unsolved equations. I was an undiscovered force of nature. I was a presence above all matter, all understanding, all science, all philosophy. Everything I demanded would be given. Everything I wanted altered would change. Everything I wanted dead would die.

I raised my head to the heavens as the roiling remnants of the towering detonation sucked all the oxygen from the clearing and back toward me. As the wave of the infernal blast reached me, I began to travel with it. I left the ground and exploded like a rocket into the clouds. I was on my way to meet my master—to meet my brethren—to claim my rightful place alongside my fellow gods.

38

The Deposition of Rick Voss: (Second Session):

Mr. Voss: *I just sat frozen in the back seat of the Yukon, gazing through the still-open side door at what remained of Lance and his grandparents. At no point had I pegged Lance for an intelligent man, but good god, nobody deserved to die like he had.*

The frenzied horde of melon-heads was closing in on us, moments from overtaking our position. I could hear their horrible crying getting louder and louder. It echoed around our vehicles and through the trees to our sides. When their screeching, infantile moans finally came to rest on my eardrums, it shot through the nerves along the sides of my neck. It registered as abrasive to me as metal scraping against a chalkboard. My focus from the steaming pile of gore to my right was quickly ripped away as I heard Big Bear shouting to my left. He had exited his vehicle and was barking out orders to the Agaden. What are the chances? *I thought. All our travels that we had been through, all the roads we had ventured down, so many memories of the investigations, the drinking, the fun, at some point, years prior, had led us down to Charleston, West Virginia, to some hole-in-the-wall bar. A snide remark toward a woman by Danny introduced us to Sam Millbury. And we've since come to know him as Big Bear. He came to be our friend, our comrade, our brother. And how lucky we were to have a former Navy Seal in our midst on that night. Who better to instruct the Agaden? Who better to prepare us for the fight of our lives?*

Big Bear had removed his shirt. He was one massive muscle jutting from a pair of black, boot-cut Levi's sitting atop a pair of steel-toed Caterpillar boots. He had taken his shirt and torn it in half and tied one of the sleeves around his forehead to act as a sweat barrier. Even though he was obviously ready for war, he approached the Agaden in a perfectly calm fashion and told them: "Give me the biggest gun you've got."

A moment later, one of the Agaden threw open the rear hatch of one of the vehicles and produced a gas-operated, fully automatic, Israeli Tavor Tar-21 assault rifle. It was complete with a night-vision, red-dot, optical scope; ten fully loaded magazines; and an American-made, under-barrel M203 grenade launcher. Big Bear took a moment to take in his new piece of hardware. "Yeah. That'll work," he whispered with a sideways grin.

He pulled the group of Agaden together and shouted for Gary and me to join them. There was a total of six Agaden, including Aniku and Anunit. It was them, Big Bear, Gary, and me against at least a hundred melon-heads. Big Bear barked out the orders. "How many grenades do we have, including under-barrel?"

Aniku answered, "Sixteen in total, among all of us."

"Okay, let's use them now while we've got a little bit of distance. They'll be useless once they get in close to us. Gary, Ricky, you guys stay close to my hip. We're taking the group behind us."

Before Big Bear could finish, Gary and I were handed rifles of our own along with one, ten-inch tactical bowie knife each. I had no idea how to use any of it. I stuffed the knife into the back pocket of my jeans and forgot about it, choosing to take my chances with the rifle instead.

Big Bear continued, "Aniku and Anunit, I will head the charge back here. I need one of your men, and the rest of you guys take the group in front. How's that work?"

Aniku responded, "That works for us, Mr. Millbury. Remember, their minds are not controlled from within this realm, so headshots are useless. They are possessed. Best to render them completely immobile."

"You're telling me to cut these motherfuckers to pieces, sir?" barked Big Bear, having mentally transported back to his Rambo days.

Aniku sort of smiled, charmed by Big Bear's newfound moxie. "That would be the advisable approach, Mr. Millbury."

"Why don't you guys get a room?" Gary hollered in Big Bear's direction. I sort of giggled nervously. There was no reaction from Big Bear. He was somewhere mentally that stretched way beyond joking. We all snapped to it. The horde was not thirty yards to our front and back. They were pinching us in.

"Shoot for their fucking kneecaps, boys!" were the final instructions we received from Big Bear as he fired off the first grenade, launching a forty-millimeter-high explosive round directly toward the center of their formation. The melon-heads, in an inconceivable display of hive-like coordination, managed to create a gap at their center with cheetah-like quickness. The grenade shot directly into the hole within their formation that they had formed. At the exact moment of detonation, each of them—all fifty or so of the god-awful creatures, leapt into the air. Each of them easily cleared twenty feet off the ground in an absolute flash. In doing so, the grenade only caused minimal damage to a couple of them. Even the ones who were grazed by the explosion moved back into their original formation, creeping ever closer. Their cries had grown so deafening that I expected blood to begin flowing from my eardrums at any moment.

"Fuck me!" I shouted. "What in the fuck are these things? The satanic X-Men?"

I was surprised to find Big Bear smiling next to me. "No, it's perfect. I have an idea."

Just as he said that, the Agaden to our front began unloading on their half of the attacking force. The entire area exploded into an absolute warzone. Automatic and semi-automatic gunfire and grenade explosions became intermingled with the repulsive, ear-splitting sobbing of the melon-head army. I had heard of what many veterans refer to as the fog of war. I was never able to grasp its meaning until that night. So much frenzied activity and so loud that you can't even hear yourself think. Meanwhile, all of this is happening at light speed over the backdrop of yourself knowing that you will probably die at any moment.

Big Bear quickly huddled up with our group. He had pulled out two grenades and removed their pins and was holding both fuses down with his thumbs. "You guys each get one of these," he shouted. "When I say throw, Ricky, you toss yours high and to the left of their formation. You be sure you put it about twenty-five feet off the ground and about fifteen feet from their center. Gary, you put yours high and to the right, same deal. You guys got it?"

We understood.

"Throw 'em, boys!" he shouted.

Gary and I tossed our grenades as instructed, with mine high and left, Gary's high and right. An instant later, Big Bear fired another round from his launcher directly to their center. The melon-heads again saw Big Bear's round approach and jumped to either side, forming another gap at their center, only this time, Big Bear had anticipated it. As his exploded, they again leapt into the air, this time directly into Gary and my grenades. They exploded simultaneously in the dead center of two bulbous masses of gruesome melon-heads while they were suspended in midair to the left and right of their original formation.

There were so many of them packed into the two confined areas that the combustion of our grenades was muffled from within the midst of the horde. Within the flash of the explosions, the twin, egg-shaped masses of them jerked wildly in all directions. In the next instant, everything turned red. They exploded into a thousand pieces. The burning shrapnel from our explosives reduced them to boiling liquid in the blink of an eye. Another instant later and we were rained down upon by pieces of them. It sounded like hail hitting the vehicles behind us as pulverized pieces of teeth and bone impacted our position, riding the crest of the returning shockwave at an impossible velocity.

My eyes were bulging. I hadn't blinked in a solid minute. I was absolutely amazed by what we had just accomplished. I felt an incredibly rude and brutally aggressive slap to the back of my neck, snapping me back to reality. Big Bear was shouting down at me. "You think we're fucking done, boy? Start shooting!"

Gary and I, along with our friendly Agaden representative whose name I never got, stood on either side of Big Bear and began firing at anything that moved. We were the ones moving in. We had gone on offense. We were taking the momentum for ourselves. I do suppose I was helping, but I couldn't help but watch Big Bear. Every time he pulled his trigger, another of them would fly apart at the waist, completely in half. For every round that he ejected from the muzzle of his rifle, something on the receiving end died. He was a magician with his firearm; it was truly an extension of himself. He had managed to go from the gentle giant we had grown to love over the years to an absolute killing machine in a matter of minutes. Even the melon-heads began to cower in fear of his advance. He truly was their worst nightmare. Every muscle in his upper body glistened with perspiration and was honed and flexed in the most intimidating display of testosterone I have ever been witness to. His focus was fervent and impassioned, like nothing I've ever seen. His entire sense of self had transformed into a single-minded, single-bodied machine whose only purpose was to exterminate its enemies. Gary, on the other hand—I'm pretty sure didn't hit a single one of them. I felt compelled to keep checking to make sure he hadn't accidently shot himself.

There were maybe five of them left on our side as the battle raged on behind us. The blood-red luminescence of the flares was quickly wearing off, and the night was growing darker by the instant. We were running out of time to kill them.

"You guys get up front and help the Agaden. I got the rest of these fuckers back here," shouted Big Bear.

Gary and I raced back, past the vehicles, and found the rest of the Agaden in a line. Their faces were all incredibly calm as they fired into the approaching horde. We joined them. This time, the melon-heads were right on top of us. Aniku and Anunit had obviously not thought of our grenade trick, having barely thinned out their half of the psychotic invaders.

As the nightmare closed the final few yards, the monsters moved fast enough to dodge our bullets latterly from one side to another, yet one never touched the other. It was like they were electronically superimposed in front of us—able to manipulate their position in space and time in the blink of an eye, at will. The idea of quantum superposition shot through my head for a moment; it was as though they could exist in multiple points of space and time simultaneously. We were thoroughly fucked, I thought.

I began to move backward. They were right on us. Aniku turned and without warning shoved Anunit backward into me, away from the swarm. I caught her as she screamed back to Aniku in a language I did not understand. Aniku's eyes closed as he looked at her, ignoring her desperate plea. He began to move as they moved, faster than any mortal could possibly ever hope to. He was a churning blur as he mowed through their front lines with the violence of a wedge tornado. Behind him, he left a blood-soaked wake of remnants of the melon-heads who were unlucky enough to have crossed his path. In the first five seconds alone, he took out at least ten of them with his bare hands and an iron will. Another instant later, he was brought to a complete stop with his throat caught in the clawed grips of one of the monsters. He shimmied and gyrated wildly for a moment as the creature began to squeeze his throat harder. The beast's talons wasted little time gauging a bloody hole into his throat. Aniku's body went limp as his hand reached into his pocket and pulled out a grenade. The melon-heads, in the grips of their unquenchable bloodlust, did not notice as they swarmed over top of his rapidly dying body.

Somewhere under that pile of blood-curdling aggression, Aniku pulled the pin from the grenade while he was being ripped apart limb by limb. A few seconds later, that grenade exploded, enveloping him, along with at least thirty of the freakish beasts, in a seething ball of flames and burning metal. Another barrage of gore showered down from above, coating us, along with our already disgustingly filthy vehicles, in another fresh coat of melon-head stew. My ears rang, as the fire had halted for a moment, and the remaining melon-heads on our side of the battle had halted their approach, seemingly in as much shock as all of us.

Anunit was inconsolable. Clearly, the two of them had been more than just colleagues. I remembered how they had explained to us how old they were and how long they had been collaborating. I could not comprehend what it was like for her to lose someone who, for all I knew, was her only confidant on this side of the known universe. The tears streamed from her eyes as I rested her limp body against one of the still-parked vehicles.

The Agaden were finishing up the remainder of the melon-heads to our front. There were perhaps ten of them left, and they had begun retreating. With all their supernatural abilities, even they were smart enough to realize that there was very little they could do against our firepower. I turned and found Big Bear walking back toward us with an ear-to-ear grin pasted on his face. He had mowed through the remaining melon-heads behind us with minimal difficulty. We all joined the Agaden in front of the Yukons and watched the last of the feral strays leap into the woods and out of sight. We were left only with the sound of crickets and an intense yet constant ringing in our ears, as the warzone had left us on the verge of permanent hearing loss.

I turned to face Anunit, who was still sobbing against the vehicle. "I am so sorry for your loss," I told her. "He was a great one. He saved all of our lives here tonight."

She looked up at me, and her sobbing gaze, in an instant, transformed into complete terror. She was looking at something behind us. We all turned, and not two feet from Big Bear stood a particularly intimidating melon-head. Big Bear was easily six foot five, and this thing looked down upon him. It breathed into his face with a growl accompanying every exhale. Its lidless eyes peered into Big Bear's with absolutely nothing behind them but murderous intensity. Its razor-sharp teeth ground and gnashed against one another in a despicable display of misguided fervor. I glanced to my left and saw Big Bear's weapon resting against one of the tires of the Yukon. He was completely unarmed. Before he was given a chance to completely inspect the sheer size of the monster in front of him, Big Bear was lifted off the ground by the hulking abomination. The melon-head had punched a hole directly through Big Bear's torso and then used its own arm as a lever to violently jerk him from his feet, all 250 pounds of him.

Gary and I began screaming and rushing toward him. Blood poured down the small of Big Bear's back, drenching his jeans. The beast's hand remained exposed, gripping upward along the spinal column with its immense and gruesome talons. One thing that I see every night when my head hits the pillow is Big Bear in that horrible moment. It is something I refuse to let go of. Not because it is a problem for me but because I don't want to let it go. I want the memory of Big Bear's last moments to serve as an example for how I approach conflict. I want to remember it until the day I die.

The man was a marvel. Knowing full well that he had been mortally wounded, that he was in his last moments on this earth, knowing that his soul would be forced into their Hell having died in that town at that time, he didn't even make a sound. He was caught in a situation and in a level of unimaginable agony that would have sent even the toughest of us into a crazed fit of hysterics, yet he did not so much as breathe heavily. His face was as calm as a mountain lake on a windless morning. His gaze remained razor sharp, scorching a hole through his colossal opponent. At no point did he give the monster the satisfaction of seeing him in any sort of distress. With the tempered precision of a surgeon and the last bit of adrenalin he could muster, Big Bear gripped both sides of the beast's tremendous, elongated skull, and, with one final smile into its revolting face, he twisted it to the left with enough force to decapitate any mortal being. The melon-head immediately collapsed to its knees and clumsily dropped Big Bear at its feet. It crumbled backward, seized violently for a brief time, and was dead a moment later. Blood shot from an open fracture at the base of its skull dripping from its exposed spinal column courtesy of one Sam Millbury.

(Pause)

Mrs. Miles: Ricky, if you need some time. I think everyone here would understand.

Mr. Voss: Let's just get through this.

I was hysterical, as was Gary. We dropped to our knees atop Big Bear's mangled body. I shouted to Anunit, "Can you help him?"

"He is already gone, Rick. I am sorry," she answered.

Gary approached her, screaming. "What fucking good are you people? You're so advanced that you can produce food out of nothing, but you don't have any doctors?"

"We've both lost someone tonight, Gary," she snapped. "There is no bringing a corpse back to life. No matter how advanced a civilization might become. Once the genii leaves the body upon death . . . it's just over."

I cried for what felt like an hour. I didn't even want to live any longer. I feared making it out of that town knowing I would have to explain to Daphne that the love of her life was gone and how he went. Big Bear was simply the best man I've ever known. He was taken from us under such incomprehensible circumstances that it called into question for me the point of everything. If this was life, and if this was how the universal protocol that governed over us all operated, then you can count me right the fuck out.

I've still not gotten over Big Bear. I see a therapist twice a week, to this day. If there was ever a man who didn't deserve to die the way he did, it was him. If you could create a perfect human being with a machine, he is what you would end up with—— an absolute warrior with the intellect of a scientist and the heart of a lion and the temperament of a monk. In a way, I wish we had never met him. I wish we had never walked into that fucking hole-in-a-wall bar in West Virginia that night and discovered him and Daphne and investigated Old Foolish together. He would have never gotten dragged into the paranormal business with us. He would have never joined our crew. Above all, he would have never been there on that awful night, meeting his demise at the hands of some possessed nightmare of a dead human being.

I have grown since then. I came to reconcile the fact that just knowing Big Bear was a blessing. The time I did get with him was, in a way, worth it. I am a better man for having known him. All of us are. He was a rare soul who had the ability to draw the best from everyone around him. That part of him will never die, and it's sure as hell not trapped in Ashford or some other evil realm.

I sobbed another few moments atop him when, out of nowhere, I felt a breeze that quickly grew into a hurricane-forced gale. It hit my face with the force of a speeding freight train and began blowing past us. All the trees on either side of the road jolted in the wind and bent dangerously over top of our group. An immense deluge of dead leaves and sticks began pelting us and blowing by at an awe-inspiring velocity. We all began struggling to maintain our balance against the obnoxious wind, latching onto the vehicles for support.

Over the trees, to our right, a bluish bulb of brilliant light began to rise toward the heavens. I didn't have time to decipher what it could have been before the atmosphere exploded above us, drenching the sky in a tangerine cloak of hellfire. I began to think that a hydrogen bomb had gone off nearby. It was the half-lit darkness before dawn, but the event had pushed the night sky away in all directions in an instant. Our eyes were forced to abruptly adjust to our suddenly luminous surroundings. In the trees all around us, we began hearing the remaining melon-heads yipping and screeching. Several of them darted straight past us and across the road and back into the woods. They were heading, without hesitation, directly to the mysterious source of the blast. We suddenly were not a priority of theirs any longer. Instead, they seemed to have shifted their attention to celebrating the supernatural detonation.

I looked down at the Agaden, still shielding my eyes from the angry sky. "What the hell do we call this? In a term that we humans would understand?"

Aniku looked at me with a somber or perhaps even terrified look painted over her face. "It's Danny—he is transcending. We are too late."

39
The Bulk

I could feel the crystalline water particles boil away instantly the moment I shot through them. I was no longer a man; I was a stream of boiling energy rocketing through the atmosphere unchecked, unabated. My arms and legs were replaced by crimson and fuchsia-colored flames. I was controlling my ascent into the heavens using their thrust.

Ahead of me, somewhere into the thermosphere, was a light—a faint yet unmistakable dot of orange in the distance. It wasn't as though anyone told me to go there, but I somehow knew it was my destination. I propelled my esoteric self toward it. It got larger and larger the farther I climbed toward its fixed point in space. The tiny, orange dot grew into a shimmering, metallic sphere, bursting with all colors on the red and yellow scale. It appeared as a miniature sun, exceedingly larger than when I had originally acquired it. Even while on my way, I could feel its power. This was where I belonged; this was the realm where gods ruled from. From this grand vantage point, I would look down upon the lesser, insignificant beings who worshiped me.

As I approached the sphere, I found myself no longer needing to control my ascent. I was doing nothing—putting forth no effort whatsoever—yet I was still being drawn into it. It began to glow in a hypnotic but somewhat organized fashion. It was communicating with me via gamma-ray bursts of luminescent radiation. And I somehow understood, as though it were speaking to me in plain English. It was as though I had been communicating in such a fashion for all my life.

"Daniel, you are welcome here. You are not to be harmed here. You are home."

It repeated that phrase to me within its soothing, mesmerizing light. It flashed its message to me more and more rapidly as I grew closer to it. It was a beacon that had been programmed to ensure its message was received, in its totality, no matter my relative distance from it. The closer I got, the faster I traveled. I was being pulled into it at an incredible velocity. The elastic form that my body had taken stretched for miles as it approached the speed of light. I could not see the end to my fiery self as I stole a glance backward. Where my legs once were stretched a stream of broiling electricity. It extended like an immense pillar of organized lightning the entire way back to the earth behind me. After another minute, I began to wind around the sphere at an impossible clip. I was traveling around the massive, moon-sized object fast enough that I was lapping the trail of myself. I began stretching my own spectral halo around the mass.

I was not frightened by any of it. The experience brought about a sense of perfectness, as though I were traveling home after being away for far too long. This was the process of me taking my place at my throne. I knew while I was spinning at an incomprehensible speed around that sphere that I was obtaining a critical mass. At no point did I ever decelerate. It was one gear, ever forward, ever faster.

Eventually, the universe around me started to shatter. Faster-than-light speed brings about a spectacularly different flavor of reality. One would think that it's so fast your head would explode but traveling at that speed felt normal. It was what I was built for—what I was designed for. The sphere was an object for me to use to propel myself into what I was supposed to have become all along. A brilliant electrical discharge exploded all around me like ten thousand lightning strikes crashing at once. The explosion was massive, igniting the atmosphere all around me. At the incomprehensible speed that I darted through it, it appeared as a tunnel of billowing flames. It occurred to me, just as I began to scream through the fantastic light show, that I had been the cause of it. The explosion was the result of me having reached my critical mass. I was ripping a hole in the very fabric of space and time. My transcendence was nearly complete. I could only see blinding white for the briefest of moments before I punched through a layer of what looked like electrified ozone. As it cleared, I found myself floating at a normal rate of speed. I observed my body again as I touched down on the surface of the sphere.

In that new reality, I had retaken my original form. My arms and legs were as they normally were. I instinctively reached for my face, finding my features exactly how they should have been. My baseball cap was long gone, along with all my other clothes, but I was not naked. I found myself wearing a brown robe tied at the waste by a sheath of pure gold. Every seam was stitched with a shimmering material that I could not identify, but it glowed in the half light of that world with the luster of just-polished diamond. I was barefoot, but that realm did not seem to require shoes. My focus was not quite there. Everything in front of me was bright yet cloaked in a visually impenetrable haze. I reached up and rubbed my eyes, allowing my pupils to dilate. As I regained focus, I found myself walking slowly into a state of pure magic. The ground below me looked like liquid glass comprised of every color of the known spectrum and others that I'm certain have never been observed by man. Despite its glassy appearance, the ground was forgiving; it had a mossy feel. There were no discernable peaks or valleys anywhere in sight, only flowing, polished slopes of unimaginably beautiful terrain. Everything glistened as though it were forged moments prior at the hands of the most gifted celestial artist. There was no discernable horizon anywhere in the vast distance. Instead, the landscape appeared to melt perfectly into its own atmosphere, forming a single yet infinite and exquisite dimension.

All known laws of nature and physics that were familiar to me no longer applied. It didn't matter if I was walking uphill or down, I put forth the same level of effort. It occurred to me that I was only breathing out of habit. There was no oxygen flowing into my body. To prove the theory, I stood still for several minutes and held my breath, receiving absolutely no ill effects. I decided to see what running was like. I could feel my feet being propelled beneath me, pushed along by the rubbery bounce of the forgiving ground. I must have been able to run a hundred miles per hour without breaking a sweat or needing to catch my breath. I was completely free—the best possible version of myself physically and mentally.

I felt unstoppable beyond all human comprehension. I began to feel things within myself that can only be described as natural, inhuman forces. The closest I can come to properly explaining that state of mind is that of a raging forest fire that had become self-aware, knowing that it had defeated all attempts at stopping it, knowing that there was nothing standing in the way of it engulfing the entire earth. It was an ultimate sense of domination and indestructibility.

I could leap a thousand feet into the air and land a hundred miles away. I only had to land if I wanted to. I could glide over the surface like an eagle. There were absolutely no physical limitations. I was totally lost within myself, completely immersed in my personal nirvana, bounding from one amazement to another.

I was suddenly thrust out of my fascinating romp by a voice speaking softly behind me. "Daniel Hallowell, I presume?"

I turned to find a man about my height with long, brown hair parted down the center. He had a thick yet well-manicured goatee. He, too, was barefoot but wearing a white robe very similar to my brown one. He was smiling at me and seemed anything but threatening. He looked like Jesus, had he purchased his robe at Barney's.

"Who are you?" I asked.

"My name is Roderick Crowe," he replied.

"You're Roderick Crowe? You're the one they call The Divine Father?"

"They call me a lot of things, Danny. But not unlike you, I once walked the earth, worked a job, had friends, fell in love, and wound up here. The difference is, I have honed and mastered the powers that you've only discovered moments ago. I have drunk from the endless fountains of all knowledge, all intellect, all discipline."

"Where is here? What is this place?"

"This is your slice of The Bulk."

I took another amazed look around before responding. "So, we're in between realms right now?" I finally asked.

"Precisely," he replied with a slight chuckle. "By now I'm sure you've felt it. I'm sure you have the sense about you that you have transcended. You are of divinity now, an idol who exists on a plane far superior to all animals and all things created under all false prophets."

"Am I dead? As a human being?"

"You are no longer alive, but you are far from dead, Danny. Everything about you has multiplied in ability by a factor of infinity. You are harnessing the complete power of your unconscious spirit at a level that is impossible for all human beings, save for a select few, one per trillion perhaps. You've taken a journey inward, within your incredibly gifted mind, and managed to impose your unconscious will upon physical reality, bringing you here, now. What is a god but one who can alter and shape reality through the power of their own will? Welcome to your kingdom, Mr. Hallowell."

I kind of looked around again. "It truly is incredible, but I sort of wish I had a say in some of the decorating."

Crowe let out a laugh. "I assure you, Daniel, you do. All of the landscapes you see before you now are but a construct, a template to be molded into anything your imagination can supplicate."

I could no longer hide the elation in my voice or avoid wearing it on my face. "What do you mean?"

He circled around me. "What do you desire most in the world? What would you most like to possess right here, right in front of you, right now?"

I let out something of a conniving laugh. "How about a bottle of Parker's Heritage Collection, twenty-seven-year-old, small-batch bourbon?"

Before I could even properly articulate my request, it appeared out of thin air, directly in front of me. The bottle was uncorked and a fresh glass of the $3,000 bottle of bourbon had already been poured, ready for my consumption.

"Are you fucking kidding me?" I shouted in amazement. "This is the most sought-after bourbon on the planet!"

Crowe was laughing heartily as I reached for the glass and chugged it down like it was orange juice and not the most expensive bourbon known to humanity. "What planet do you speak of? What currency are you referencing?" Crowe replied. "Earth, dollars? In time, you will come to realize how insignificant earthly pleasures truly are compared to what has become available to you. You will come to understand currency as something you control and create over something you desire and need. From your new perspective, such human-based concepts are but breadcrumbs to ants."

"Let me get this straight," I said as the impossibly smooth, charcoal burn of the whiskey crept its way into my belly. "I can just produce things with my mind? Anything I want?"

"That's correct, Mr. Hallowell. This *is* your kingdom. Here, you are the almighty. You are the constructor of this entire reality."

I began turning and flailing my arms in circles and lines, constructing anything I could think of. My mind was racing so fast that I ended up with something resembling a half rollercoaster, half skyscraper. Crowe observed my handiwork. He appeared far from impressed. "It takes a little time. You'll get the hang of it once you've settled in a bit. And don't forget," he suggested as he pointed out ahead of us, "you can create *anything* you want here."

Just as he finished his thought, the most stunningly beautiful woman appeared in front of us. She was completely nude with silky blond hair and the body of a dancer. Her round, perfect eyes and olive-colored skin gleamed like a beacon of sexual energy against the shimmering backdrop of my newly inherited kingdom. She approached with a stare that screamed ravenous desire. She pressed her incredible body to mine and began nibbling my earlobe. "I will see you soon, Danny," she whispered longingly as she floated away and faded off into the oblivion from where she came.

I was completely awestruck. I couldn't quite fathom that I had the power to conjure up anything my mind could dream of. Anything that could be imagined was mine simply by thinking of it. Even my wildest fantasies could be fulfilled in that place. Crowe just sort of watched me, smiling. He must have once been through that same level of wonderment—giddy as a schoolboy as I was then. He put his arm around my shoulder and sort of tossed his left arm in a sweeping motion from left to right. As he did so, the entire landscape shifted to that of a beach in the late evening, under a completely cloudless sky. The heavens were filled with more stars than any man could possibly count in a thousand lifetimes. The sea was a perfect shade of cool, electric blue and was gently flowing against the albino-white sands of the beach, which stretched as far as I could see in either direction. There was an oaken deck curiously placed in the middle of the beach. Atop the deck sat a wooden table with two chairs.

"Shall we have a chat, Mr. Hallowell?" Crowe asked, pointing to the table.

I sat across from him, facing the sea. There was a perfect, cool, salty breeze billowing off the water. This was obviously no earthbound location. It was far too beautiful and perfect to exist anywhere on our overcrowded planet. If this beach existed anywhere on earth, there would have been a hotel right behind us with a thousand screaming children running in all directions from their deadbeat, inattentive parents. There would have been at least fifteen articles of trash strewn about the landscape. This place had never been touched by man; it was completely virgin, as it was when time began.

"I sense that you like this place," said Crowe from across the table.

I let out what must have been my tenth completely unnecessary exhale in the last five minutes. "You could certainly say that, Roderick."

"Well, it is yours. Anything you could ever desire for all eternity."

"What about my family?"

"You can conjure them as you can anything else; however, they will not be your actual family while they are alive down there on earth. Your wife and your daughter are but normal human beings. They are, unfortunately, not of our ilk. Normal human beings cannot transcend from earth inwardly and travel to a place like this while alive. It is one of the great impossibilities of the cosmos. It is also what makes you so incredibly unique—such a miracle." He pointed toward the ground.

I could see the earth. Crowe had cleared a space at our feet, making it completely transparent. Through the void, I could view the vast blue sphere that was the only world I'd known up until moments prior. It was far enough away for me to take in its entire circumference. It was also beautiful and absolutely humbling to observe from such a distance. A home to so many people, yet small enough to cover over with the palm of my hand.

"If your family were to die—and by no means do they have to for any reason—they would immediately meet you here in your kingdom."

I felt horrible even thinking of it, *killing my own family*. This was certainly never something that had crossed my mind for even a moment. But I had obviously never been made aware of what happens to us after we die, until then. Based on how spectacular my slice of The Bulk had proven to be, the thought of allowing them to live out their lives on that soiled, slowly choking, war-torn, mismanaged, prison of a planet we call the earth was quickly beginning to feel like the crueler option.

"How could I do that? That's crazy," I barked.

"By no means are you obligated to do anything. This place does come with a cost, though. There is one simple task you will be asked to fulfill in exchange for all of this. There is a price to every crown."

"What price?"

"We are both Bridges, yet you are the only one who is still technically alive in your earthbound state. Make no mistake about it, we are both cut from the same elite cloth; however, we do answer to one supremely higher power."

"Let me guess: Enki?"

"That is right. Enki is far more powerful than you or me, and he is the overseer of the realm beyond our bulk, just over these shores. The only reason we are permitted to keep this area for ourselves and our loved ones is because he allows us to."

"Your old friend Kenneth Harvey told me about Enki. He said he controls your ex-patients back in Ashford. He makes them eat people for his own personal amusement."

"He does what he has to do to advance his own interests, the same as every other faction that exists on his level. And that includes the Agaden. He wants the genii of the earth for his own, just as they do."

"Why?" I asked.

"For all intents and purposes, it is a celestial game that predates the very existence of time or our known universe. There are dozens of factions who want souls from various planets. They all have their own reasons for wanting them. The earth currently resides under what is known as the Deshcarn Mode, which is a cycle invented and managed by the Agaden. They want our souls for their purposes. Conversely, Enki wants our souls for his purposes. And I will tell you this—when we die, despite the lies that the Agaden have peddled to anyone who will listen to them over the eons, our soul does not travel to anything that even remotely approaches what has been described by humanity as heaven. Our souls are trading chips for civilizations billions of years more advanced than our own. Think of them as currency. Our soul, once detached from our earthbound body, upon our death, is stored, catalogued, and effectively warehoused in one unsavory fashion or another. Whether the ownership of our soul falls under the management of the Agaden or Enki, it isn't going to be an enjoyable experience either way. It is what makes this opportunity so profound. You are one of an incredibly rare few who can make your own heaven and join the ranks of radically advanced beings like Enki, the Agaden, and myself.

"So, what does Enki want from me?"

"He wants you to become the Bridge between his realm and earth so he can destroy the Agaden and bring the earth's genii under his control. Without you, he cannot get there."

"Why me? Why didn't he just use you?"

"My body is long dead. I burned to death at the hands of the Agaden a long time ago. A Bridge must be a living being who exists on the other side. You effectively bridge your own unconscious mind on earth to your conscious mind within Enki's realm, acting as a conduit for him to travel through to do his bidding."

"Why would I do this? If Enki wants everyone's souls so bad and if he is as powerful as everyone says he is, wouldn't I effectively be condemning the entire human race to his hell?"

Crowe again began to laugh and flail his arms around. "Because of all of this. Because of this personal paradise you have secured for yourself and your family. Because you are a god. And *if* you do this, you get to remain a god for the rest of time. You simply cannot be offered more than that, Danny. He is offering you and your family everything you could possibly desire or even imagine. As for humanity, the despicable animals they are, they're already condemned. If they are not condemned to Enki, then they will remain condemned to the Agaden. Humanity is but a failed experiment. They've been given every chance to thrive on a perfect world that was served up to them on a silver platter, and they can't even make it through a calendar year without murdering hundreds of thousands of one another.

"On a celestial level, humanity is not exactly a great prize, nor would their being handed over to Enki be viewed as much of a loss. Think of Enki as a method of liquidation for a failed asset. A liquidation that, let's face it, Mr. Hallowell, humanity has had coming since the moment they began trying to exterminate one another. Human beings are a race that has proven time and time again, they cannot coexist among one another and cannot accept subtle differences within others of the same species. These are fatal flaws that cannot be corrected and, therefore, will damn humanity to centuries of war, plague, famine, and eventually extinction. Enki would provide them salvation from such horrors. Enki would waste no time taking them away from their tainted existence."

I shook my head, annoyed at his incredibly dismissive viewpoint toward humanity. "At least the Agaden aren't planning on killing them all as soon as possible. Humans at least get to live out a life, however misinformed they might be. They get to believe what they choose to believe about dying and where they go afterward. With Enki, you're saying he would take them immediately, just so he can add another deposit of souls to his bank. I can't, in good conscience, go along with a decision that would kill every man, woman, and child on earth."

Just then, a massive crash of thunder rocked the world around us. In an instant, the sea became a tempest of rolling whitecaps. The wind accelerated tenfold, and a thousand electrical discharges fired all around us. A deep, threatening, growling male voice boomed from the heavens so loud that it blew our hair back. "If you refuse, everything you love will be purified through a billion cycles of pain."

The voice faded as quickly as it had arrived, and the world flashed back to how it had been prior to the horrifying interruption. "What the fuck was that, Crowe?"

"That was Enki. Please try to keep in mind, Mr. Hallowell, that he is ultimately in charge here. You might be the god of this world, but he is the overarching titan that controls this entire region of space and time. To refuse him would mean your certain death, on earth and here. It would bring about the death of your family. And when that happens, you will not get to come back here. You will go to his realm, and he will torture you for all eternity in such ways that you cannot possibly comprehend.

"Please, Daniel, I made this same deal a long time ago, but my body on earth was killed by the Agaden before I could form the gateway. Enki allowed me to remain here, knowing that you would come about. You are our last chance. Your refusal would mean the end of this bulk and the end of our reign as gods of this place. I am truly sorry that this burden fell to you; however, his will must be satisfied."

"What kind of gods have a boss?" I asked with a conniving note to my voice.

"Please try to understand the gravity of the situation." He was begging. "This is not a negotiation. Consider your friends, down there, in Ashford. If you refuse, then you are effectively sending them to Hell and depriving your family of an eternity of bliss here with you."

Just then, he flipped his hands around in a curious motion. He formed a window in midair that I was able to see through. He showed me Annie, asleep soundly in her bed, dreaming of everything ahead of her, everything to come, completely oblivious to what had become of me. A tear rolled down my cheek. I felt weakness for the first time since arriving in that place. To her right, drenched in the dim light from the lamp on her nightstand, sat a paper. The headline atop the first page read: "Dian Fossey – Savior of the Mountain Gorillas."

Just to the right of the headline was her grade for the assignment. She got an A. I knew she was keeping it there to show it to me the moment I walked in the door from my trip to Cleveland. I knew how much she loved me and how much I meant to her. The earth was still so beautiful to her. That was how I'd taught her to see it. That was what my phrase that I had repeated to her ad nauseam meant. Her world was still an endless dreamscape of opportunity and wonder. She existed there on earth as I did in my incredible slice of The Bulk with the same level of unbridled enthusiasm and fascination. I loved her far too much to just rip away everything she might ever get the chance to experience. My destroying her future would have completely flown in the face of everything I'd ever taught her. The tears were rolling down my cheeks as I stood from the table. I looked at Crowe, knowing full well that I was about to make a decision that would lead to my death.

"You tell Enki he can go fuck himself."

Crowe looked up at me; the smile had completely vanished from his face, replaced by an evil scowl. "Tell him yourself, Mr. Hallowell."

I turned around, and behind me, my beautiful realm was completely gone. In its place was a frozen wasteland. There was a path cut up the center of one of the most horrible scenes I had ever laid my eyes upon. I was being pulled toward something by a force completely beyond my control. On either side of me were thousands upon thousands of bodies. All of them were still alive, each half in the ground and half out. In their freezing state, they were thrashing from one side to the other. Their mouths hung open, suggesting an unimaginable level of suffering, but they were far too cold to scream. Walking among the damned were what looked like enormous rats. They would approach the people at random, and they would eat them. I observed one of them eating a man. The poor bastard only managed a series of breathy gasps as the creature devoured him. As quickly as it would eat him, he would regenerate. He was cursed to endure the torment of being eaten alive for all eternity. I was petrified and disgusted beyond all comprehension.

I was finally able to see what I was being pulled toward. It was a massive altar perched in front of a miles-wide sheet of blue flame. The immense blaze was engulfing what must have been thousands of men and women who were damned to burn forever, never realizing the sweet release of death and never burning thoroughly enough to allow their nerve endings to die. They were trapped in a horrifically perpetual state of incomprehensible agony. The immense altar was made of pure diamond. A throne sat at its center. The throne was made of bone, but not purely human. Several perverse constructs of skeletal structures, completely alien to me, contributed to it.

Atop the throne sat what must have been Enki. He was a brilliant, white figure. His arms and legs were the entirety of him. Where his arms ended, his legs began, completely devoid of any sort of torso. He perched atop the throne like a four-legged spider with his elongated, ghostly appendages folded in all directions underneath him. A slender, lurching being at least a hundred feet tall if he were to stand. His face jutted out from the rest of him, far enough away that it was no longer over the altar. Instead, it was approaching mine. It was the face I had seen when I was knocked out, inside of the tow truck; the face of the red figure that had tried to drag me into The Black City. It was a portrait of pure evil. This being, this thing, was the source of all malice, all hatred, all terror across the universe. He did have features—a mouth, nose, colossal eyes that were black as midnight—but it all somehow remained indescribable. When the sight of his face hit me, it did not register as a face or a figure of a being. Instead, it registered as a paradoxical emotion. His face, simply put, was the personification of pure rage and unimaginable depravity.

All I could do was scream as soon as I saw him. As I did so, he reached to my left with one of his massive, spectral arms. His arm stretched at least fifty yards into the sea of tortured bodies. He didn't even move from his perch or take his eyes from me as he snatched one of the unlucky prisoners from his frozen perch within the tundra. He hoisted him into the air, his legs kicking wildly, desperate for any escape.

Enki had pulled a particularly large man, seemingly at random, from the pile and tossed him down at my feet. The man was half eaten by the rats, already in an unthinkable level of misery when Enki grabbed him by the hair and pushed him farther toward me. He lifted his face to mine. My eyes were closed. I refused to look at what was left of the revoltingly mutilated person before me.

"Danny, is that you?" I heard in a hoarse whisper just in front of me.

I opened my eyes. I jumped backward. I lost all control of my emotions. Enki had not chosen a person at random. This was what was left of Big Bear. He had obviously died on earth and been brought here by Enki to be . . . purified, as he would call it.

I cried out to him. "Oh no. Oh, god, Sam. What's happened to you?"

He was barely able to speak. The entire left side of his face had been chewed off. The bottom half of his body was badly burned while the top was black with frostbite. The only words he managed to me were a stuttering attempt at, "Can you kill me?"

Before he was able to finish, Enki tossed him unceremoniously behind his throne and straight into the endless curtain of blue flame. I watched as Big Bear tossed and writhed around in frantic, psychotic desperation. He was damned to continue his purification, burning to death for the rest of time. I was beyond tears, having reached a state of complete shock. I finally managed to speak, overcoming the uncontrollable rage and disgust I felt in that moment. "I will be your fucking Bridge to earth, but you give me Sam back. How he was before you got to him."

Enki nodded. He was considering my offer. He stood, towering over me—over everything in that realm. His legs were fifty feet long; his arms stretched farther than I could see in any direction. His face was so high that I could not physically crane my neck enough to observe it, soaring somewhere into the blood-red sky.

With one of his hands, he reached behind himself into the curtain of flames and pulled Big Bear back out. He was horrifically burned.

In his next motion, Enki enveloped his smoldering body in his other enormous hand. As he pulled Big Bear through his fingers, Big Bear emerged, naked, but perfectly intact, as he would have looked prior to enduring the atrocious torture he had been put through. He was picked up and placed at my side.

Big Bear looked at me yet was still unable to speak. I looked at him, unable to come up with anything to say. I was glad he was intact, but that didn't make us any less screwed. I think he was just as aware of that fact as I was. Enki leaned down and positioned his horrible face mere inches from ours. As he spoke, his words were so loud and so deep that they pushed us backward and off our feet with the force and energy of a hurricane.

"A world of which you have loved. A world on which you will watch me feast."

We lay on the ground and watched Enki in front of us shrink his enormous, spectral figure down into a perfectly spherical ball of energy that glowed with a blinding shade of brilliant red. I looked at Big Bear and managed one final statement: "I have a plan. Stay with me, whatever happens."

A moment later, the roiling sphere that Enki had become shot into my chest, completely flash-burning everything I was from existence. In my last moment of consciousness as Daniel Hallowell, just before I was completely replaced, I grabbed Big Bear by the arm. He latched on to me. In the next instant, Big Bear, my body, and Enki were traveling at the speed of light.

I had been possessed by Enki's calamitous genii, and we were on our way back to earth.

40

There are pieces I can remember, but, by and large, it is a disjointed blur. After Enki took me, there was a sensation of freefall, like in a bad dream. I knew we were traveling back to earth from his realm, but somewhere along the way it all darkened. My body had become a vessel. I was no longer in any control. I was conscious of my surroundings, but nothing registered. My memories were no longer my own. For these reasons, I am relying on Ricky's testimony to take us through this crucial part of my story.

The Deposition of Rick Voss: (Third Session):

Mr. Voss: The lightshow above the trees had subsided, leaving only a single streak of what appeared to be electrified smoke billowing into the sky. It extended clear into the upper atmosphere and likely beyond. It was impossible to see the top of it. We stood among the shredded corpses of at least a hundred melon-heads. Gary was still lying atop Big Bear, sobbing uncontrollably. I quickly felt my sadness turn to anger. That anger quickly turned to rage. Anunit had found her way to her feet, and I met her the moment she did. I grabbed her by her pressed lapels and slammed her with everything I had backward against one of the vehicles.

"How in the fuck did Lance get out of this town so easily to find us, but you couldn't get us out? Why did he tell us your name was Victoria? You watched us drive into this hell. How could you knowingly allow us to come here?"

My initial shouting evolved into hysterical screaming at her. Just as I was completing my tirade, I felt a pair of hands on my shoulders. A moment later, I was literally flying backward. I landed on my back fifteen feet into the forest. One of the other Agaden had pulled me away from Anunit and tossed me clear across the ditch and into the trees. I had the wind momentarily knocked out of me. The underbrush was so feral and thick that it braced my fall enough to prevent significant injury, but it still hurt like hell.

I was seeing red. I immediately bounced to my feet despite the best efforts of my body to get me to stay down. I began running back toward Anunit. As I bounded over the ditch and back onto the street, she raised her right hand. As she did so, I was immediately paralyzed in midstride, completely frozen in place. My body was effectively turned to stone. It felt like there was the weight of a mountain in every possible direction, hindering any physical motion.

"What primitive ants you are," she shouted; her tone had suddenly become dark, threatening. "Only you could value something as feeble as an incarnated friendship so highly. How are you so powerless to comprehend the gravity of what is happening here? Do you honestly believe that we wanted any of this, any more than you do? What you're a party to, here tonight, might very well be the end of all human existence. An entire race, a young race, a promising race—wiped clean from the stream of time. Humanity is worth so much more than one man, but you can't see beyond your own primordial emotional attachments, even under such dire circumstances as these.

"As far as Lance was concerned," she continued, "until tonight, he thought we were just federal officials. I must have told him, at some point, that my name was Victoria—a decidedly more human name than, Anunit. We allowed him to leave this town believing that he was leaving for good. So that we would not have to worry about him poking around. We had gotten wind that he was in possession of Harvey's Memoirs and the list of Bridges. He was sticking his nose into dangerous places, so we were happy to see him go. We did not let him back in. Either Crowe managed to manipulate our security measures to allow your truck to enter Ashford, or Danny's presence alone, as a Bridge, allowed you to break through our barriers. We didn't engage you as you entered because we were more interested in trying to figure out how you had gotten in, ensuring that you were alone, and that our security measures were uncompromised. Had we known you had a Bridge in your party, I assure you, we would have acted immediately. I submit, not pulling you out of that truck immediately and sending you out of Ashford was a mistake on our part. Potentially a species-ending mistake for humanity."

I replied, enraged beyond all logical thought, "Is that right? It doesn't look like your mistake is working out terribly well for your species either."

She stole a glance over to the still-steaming pile of gore. It was comprised mostly of exploded melon-head, but there were still a few very recognizable pieces of Aniku strewn about in the mixture of horror. "Nobody was supposed to die because of this, Ricky," she said with a more calming tone returning to her voice. "Danny has transcended. And when he inevitably returns through the rift possessed by Enki, we must close it, trapping him here. Meanwhile, Ashford will remain separated from earth's segment of space-time. Only then might we eliminate the threat. Earth will become free from the possibility of Enki infiltrating its genii. Enki will become trapped here for all time, unable to return to his realm and unable to leave Ashford. And then we go home. We all go home."

"So, the plan is for Danny to remain trapped here, possessed by Enki, forever? Are you fucking kidding me?" I shouted.

"The moment he transcended, Ricky, we ran out of any humane options. Think about what we are arguing over. You are smarter than this," she pleaded. "If you could only see for one moment Enki's body of work, you would sacrifice all that is sacred to you to avoid the ungodly wretchedness he would bring down upon this planet. He is a god of torture. He knows no other discipline. One of his most cursed abilities is his power to keep his victims alive, even while under the most absurd levels of physical agony. When your human body would normally die or go into shock or drive you into unconsciousness to escape his brand of torment, oh, Ricky, that is where Enki really shines. He can block you from dying or passing out or going into shock. He can keep you awake and fully aware of your pain. You will be completely and consciously aware of every burn, scrape, and bite for the rest of time, and you will be completely powerless. There will be no possibility of escape or rescue. This is what would become of the entire human civilization. Perhaps this might help you understand our motivations in bringing this to as swift an end as possible?"

Her explanation began to resonate with me. I certainly didn't need her level of detail. I was already horrified beyond any rational thought. I found myself being lowered down to the ground and slowly freed from her hold. Another moment later, and I was back on my feet. I was stiff and sore but again able to move around at my own will. I approached Anunit again, careful to appear more docile. I was clearly no physical match for her and her friends, and the last thing I needed, in that state, was another ass-kicking. "Doesn't this all mean—win, lose, or draw, Danny is property of Enki? Big Bear, Lance—what about them? Aren't they stuck in his Hell now?"

She just shook her head. She knew I already knew the answer to my own question. After a moment of incredibly tense silence, she spoke up. "If you want to see Danny again, we really must get back on the road and meet him upon his return through the rift."

The Agaden got back into the vehicles. I didn't get the impression that they cared whether Gary and I went with them. They didn't need us. They were the soldiers, and we were just the useless tagalongs. Gary and I ran to Big Bear. We made one last desperate attempt to pull his body up off the freezing pavement. It was useless. There was no way we could hoist a man his size up from the ground. The idea of leaving him out there, however, was not something I was willing to live with. Unexpectedly, Anunit had made her way out of her vehicle and back to us. She leaned down and with ease managed to lift Big Bear completely off the ground. The feat of elevating the dead weight of a 250-pound man was incredibly simple for her. She didn't even change her facial expression. I opened the rear hatch of one of the Yukons, and she respectfully placed Big Bear's body inside. A moment later, we were back on the road, racing toward the gargantuan tower of light that had resulted from Danny's transcendence.

Anunit was driving, and I was riding shotgun. Gary sat behind me with one of the other Agaden.

"What exactly is our plan here, again?" I asked, gazing through the side window at the immense tower of light. "You're going to close the rift when Danny comes back through? How do you close something like that down?"

She reached down in front of herself and flipped on the radio; this was obviously not the same Yukon we had taken initially, as Anunit had pulverized the radio in that vehicle. She pressed a button to a preset station. Coming through the speakers was a melodic, almost circus-like tune. Suddenly, a man, who did not have a particularly good voice, began singing over the strange music. "Who's that little chatter box? The one with pretty auburn locks? Whom do you seeeee? It's Little Orphan Anniiee."

Anunit flipped the radio off and explained, "Right now, on the present slice of space-time that we have Ashford isolated onto, it is 1936. What you were just listening to was a broadcast of Little Orphan Annie. Since 1936, we've only allowed Ashford to exist within present time on a handful of occasions—mostly to allow people in or out, and even then, the process is painstakingly choreographed. On such occasions, this town is only joined to the normal continuum for a period of about two seconds. For example, we allowed Ashford to exist on your timeline for one second to allow Lance to leave."

"What the hell are you talking about?" Gary asked.

"It is how we keep Ashford segregated from the rest of the earth. We lock it out of time. It has been 1936 here for going on eighty-three years. Your friend, at some point, managed to jump ahead while still in Ashford to present time. Prior to his departure into Enki's realm, relative to your friend, it was 2018. Relative to us, it is still 1936. However, I expect that to change momentarily as we approach the cross-rift. When Danny returns and once we have verified that he is in possession of Enki's genii, we will again return Ashford to 1936. You and Gary will be left in 2018. Enki will be trapped in a town completely locked out of time for all eternity, and you will go home."

"How could we have witnessed the light show that Danny's transcendence produced if it happened in present time and we're stuck in 1936?" Gary asked.

"His transcendence produced a rift, and that rift cuts through all timelines. So long as you were within range, there was no avoiding it, regardless of what timeline you currently inhabit. It is one of the fundamental aspects of a rift. Time becomes abstracted as trillions of normally disparate timelines become melded into one section of space."

"I wish I hadn't asked. So, people outside of Ashford, the next town over might be seeing this, in present time?" asked Gary. Neither of us were fully understanding her explanation.

"It's possible, but highly unlikely for a number of reasons. Synchronizing Ashford to the specific slice of space and time as the rest of the earth is an incredibly precise and difficult process. Human consciousness controls human perception. And humans are only consciously aware of what is perceivable at the very tip of their stream of time, not a second before or after. We have designed it that way. While Ashford does technically exist at the tip of your time stream, you can't see it, because of other security measures we have in place. We have, essentially, erected a domelike veil around and over the whole of Ashford. When viewed from either side, the veil abstracts what the viewer perceives. It alters what they view into, what is essentially, a picture of what they are looking at from one day in the past or one day in the future, but never the tip of their conscious present. Unless Enki has managed to get around that secondary layer of our security, which is doubtful, the locals can't actually see what we are seeing."

"I wish I hadn't asked," Gary joked.

"And Danny? Is there really no other way?" I asked, even though I already knew the answer.

"Try to take some solace in the fact that your friend effectively died fifteen minutes ago when he transcended."

I sat staring out the windshield at the forest-lined roadway, allowing her explanation to sink in. I was suddenly thrust forward in my seat, slamming my knees into the dash. Everyone else experienced the same jolt. I had been sort of half-looking at the wooden guardrail that lined the side of our present stretch of road. In a flash, it appeared to rot completely out of existence. There was a willow tree just off the road to our right, and it vanished into thin air. It was suddenly replaced by a series of mature, towering pines. The lines on the road had appeared fresh and bright a moment before, the blacktop smooth and accommodating. Suddenly, though, the roadway became a lineless hazard. The smooth asphalt crumbled in an instant into complete disrepair. This is what ultimately caused our vehicle to dip forward on the unstable roadway, producing the jolt we had just endured. The pitch blackness of the night had given way to daylight. If I had to guess, it was just after dawn in our new timeline.

"We are there," Anunit shouted to us, her voice riddled with anxiety.

We had made the jump back to 2018 from 1936, and everything around us had aged eighty-two years in the blink of an eye. We had arrived at the rift. From our original distance, the towering stream of energy that stretched into the heavens appeared as a thin streak shooting into the clouds. From our present location, however, far closer to it, it had grown considerably, as wide as a city block. It formed what appeared as an ionized column of fire just through the woods in front of us.

We parked in front of a mysteriously well-kept cabin. The address on the front of it read: 1551 Whistler Road. The front door was wide open, and the remnants of a fire billowed from its chimney. Who in the hell lives here? I thought to myself as I exited the vehicle. We were handed more guns. Anunit and the other Agaden prepared themselves. They were gearing up for open war. They had all armed themselves with their own guns and what looked like the headphones we had first seen back at the exchange station. Their ears were completely covered by them, and that curious red light would fire from the top of the device and down into one of their ears. From the other ear, the red light would travel in the opposite direction, from their ear to the top of the device. It was clear that this was a nonverbal form of communication that the Agaden had mastered.

We were all properly suited up. We walked into the tree line behind the Agaden. I was far from thrilled to be participating, but it was my only ticket out of that town. We stumbled through the trees and underbrush for several minutes. It was the early-morning twilight, but our surroundings were blindingly illuminated by the hulking beam of electricity that we approached. It was so large in front of us that I feared we were going to walk right into our own instantaneous electrocution. We reached a clearing a moment later. The grass was waist-high throughout the massive swath of open prairie that comprised it. There were curious piles of rubble, random bricks, and oddly placed piles of wood fragments strewn about everywhere. I distinctly remember thinking that that clearing would be the perfect place for a tick infestation and immediately felt stupid for worrying about such a thing with so many higher-priority issues at hand. At that point, I would have happily taken Lyme disease in exchange for a bus ticket to anywhere.

There seemed to be one remaining structure. It was a crude slab of concrete, about five hundred feet to our front. It was engulfed by the beam of energy that shot into the heavens. Surrounding it was an army of melon-heads and the most horrifying ghostly nightmare of a woman I could possibly ever imagine. Their collective focus was fixated on the beaming column and away from us as we silently crept closer to their position. They appeared to be kneeling before it, worshiping it. They were as eagerly anticipating Danny's return as we all were.

Anunit whispered to me, "This is where Ashford Hill once stood."

"I kind of figured as much," I replied with an obvious shudder to my voice.

The sky exploded above us. My eardrums nearly burst as the sonic boom rocked the entire area. Every tree around the clearing bent wildly away from the rift as though they were suddenly hammered by hurricane-force winds. All I could hear was ringing in both ears. I could see the Agaden and Gary's mouths moving, but their words failed to register. My entire world had blurred. I felt concussed from the massive shockwave that had been thrust upon our position so suddenly. After a moment, I managed to focus again on the rift. The army still knelt before it as an eerily brilliant sphere of vaporous light descended from the skies within it. It reached the ground a moment later and paused. It just kind of sat at the base of the rift a moment, glowing and pulsing, drenching its worshiping legion in its indescribable brilliance.

A man rose from the ground just below the sphere. He was completely engulfed in it. In the shimmering backdrop, he appeared as a shadowy, black figure to us—a silhouette. He stood stoically a moment, just looking around and absorbing his surroundings. He walked forward out of the rift, and as he did, his army rose and began to rejoice. Hundreds of giant-headed monsters leapt into the air and squealed and hissed as their leader had returned, just as they had prophesized. This was the culmination of their singular goal, their one-track-minded agenda of evil. They had stalked the forests of Ashford for eighty-two years, being controlled by a master that they would stop at nothing to bring to earth, and now they had.

The leader emerged from the rift and came into plain view. He smiled as he looked over his idolizing congregation. The army was whipped into a complete frenzy at the sight of their long-awaited savior. The melon-heads were fiercely jockeying for position to see him—fighting, biting, and clawing their way to the front.

A moment later, another man in what looked like a suit from the Wild West emerged from the crowd and stood at the leader's right. Another moment later and the enormous spectral woman swooped up to the leader's left. As each of them took their positions at his sides, the army became even more franticly aroused. Just the mere sight of their leaders had stirred the legion into a riot of devious motivation.

Anunit whispered to me again, "The man to his right is Kenneth Harvey. The thing to his left was one of Harvey's patients and his lover. Her name when she was human was Margaret Peirce."

Another man emerged from behind the leader. He stood in front of the other three, intensely eyeing the battalion. As this man emerged, the melon-heads fell silent. They stood in awe of him. Some of them fell to their knees in worship. I made brief eye contact with Anunit.

"And that would be Roderick Crowe," she said.

Behind them all, their true ruler stood motionless, having taken his place at the forefront of his army. He slowly lifted his stare upward. He had spotted something beyond his legion of evil. His gaze had suddenly become fixed on us. He, in that moment, exposed our position to his battery of foot soldiers. The other leaders followed in suit. In an instant, all of them had become focused on us. The melon-heads had begun to twist themselves around to see in our direction, slithering over one another in an organized mountain of satiating aggression, creeping toward our position.

We had become the hunted. And the ruler of that incomprehensibly evil force, Daniel Hallowell, had become our hunter.

41

The Deposition of Rick Voss: (Third Session):

Mr. Voss: *Danny was wearing a brown robe. His hair was pulled back from his face, wild yet organized in a controlled-chaos kind of way. His normally baby-blue eyes had transformed. They'd sunk farther into his face, and the whites had gone black as midnight. His pupils, however, glowed a brilliant orange and were giving off so much light that we were blinded when he looked directly at us. His normally lax stature had been replaced in his new form. He stood proudly at the front of his army—statuesque, regal. Every one of his veins popped. Every visible muscle flexed. The expansion and contraction of his chest with each breath was far more pronounced than normal. His teeth were grinding, and his fists were clenched. He was barefoot, standing atop a crumbling slab of concrete, yet it was not bothering him in the least. His robe was tied with a diamond-lined strand of pure gold. Every seam, every diamond-inlayed stitch, shimmered against the glow of the rift at his back. Everything about him screamed anger, rage, hatred. It was indeed the body of Daniel Hallowell standing before us, but whatever it was that possessed him wasn't anything remotely approaching the Danny we knew. There was no part of my best friend left.*

The jumbled horde of melon-heads crept closer to us. I stole a glance over at Gary. He was backing farther and farther away, completely unable to take his eyes from the creeping flood of evil that approached us. Even Anunit and the rest of the Agaden were wide-eyed and clearly taken by surprise at the aggression and sheer volume of the enemy.

Danny began to address his army. His voice was not his own and had been replaced by a high-pitched growl that echoed instantaneously, producing an unnatural, synthetic reverb. It was far from human. "Come forth, my children, and receive your new life. Worry not for the enemies in our midst, for they are but dust in my palm."

The melon-heads obeyed and began to congregate away from us and back toward their leader.

"Oh shit," Anunit shrieked.

"What?" I asked.

"Come forth and receive your new life. He is preparing to implant them with genii from his realm—unimaginably evil genii, tempered in eons of suffering and depravity, demonic in nature."

"Okay then," I shouted back to her over the deafening chorus of celebratory screaming erupting from the mob. "Sounds like a pretty good time to work your magic and thrust him back to 1936, or, anytime but our present."

The glowing red light on her headset was dancing frantically from ear to ear. It had previously seemed organized and somewhat coordinated. The lights, however, had begun to shoot wildly in all directions. "I am trying, but it seems like Enki has accounted for it."

"What the fuck do you mean, Enki accounted for it?"

"We are somewhere else on the timeline. We are not in 1936 or 2018, and we can't find exactly where we are. We aren't fixed to any known point in space-time. Until we can figure out where we are, the continuum in inalterable."

"Okay, what's plan B? Because mine is to start running as far away from this nightmare as I can get. Find a nice cabin someplace, hide in the attic, hope for the best."

Before she could answer, the entirety of the sky above us ignited into a fiery red-and-yellow glow. It was as though someone had doused the atmosphere above us with kerosene and thrown a match. The glow above appeared as molten fire and was slowly condensing, flowing like liquid metal toward the rift. This was the cataclysm. This was the long-feared demonic army of tortured genii making their way into our realm.

"We have to kill as many of them as we can before it gets here," Anunit shouted.

Just then, the Agaden began to unload on the melon-heads with their assault rifles. The monsters closest to us went first, their bodies flying apart in the sudden hail of hot lead. At least a dozen more were taken out by a salvo of grenades that were lobbed into their ranks. Most of them had their focus completely fixed on the rift and were awaiting their new genii.

They quickly became aware of our advance. As they did, they became far more difficult to kill. They had the ability to dodge bullets in midair. They could contort themselves in all directions, morphing into all shapes and sizes to avoid any injury our bullets and explosives attempted to inflict. Daniel, despite the absolute warzone that the area had been thrust into, walked directly toward us through the middle of his maniacal legion. His face was a portrait of perfect calm, completely undisturbed. As he walked closer, not thirty yards from us, the Agaden began to fire in his direction.

Each bullet that approached him would suddenly, in midair, dart around him to one side or the other. Many of them would fly past him, missing him by millimeters, striking unlucky melon-heads to his rear. He was clearly able to manipulate the environment around him, altering the paths of the ballistics with his mind alone. I had experienced his sort of stoic facial expression once before. It was on the ghost of my mother when she had briefly visited me moments after having lost her life in a plane crash. It was a sort of distant look that's difficult to explain to people who aren't as intimately familiar with the paranormal. It is a look that does not jive with our reality. The emotions on their faces originate from another level of consciousness, one that we likely have no ability to comprehend while living.

I looked back at Anunit and the other Agaden. In between their bursts of gunfire, the three of them were still struggling to figure out how to alter time, which was exactly what we didn't have. Out of nowhere, Gary began marching forward, directly toward the chaos, from behind the Agaden. I shouted at him to stop, but he was completely out of his mind. He was petrified beyond all logic. He sensed that his end was coming, just as the rest of us did, and decided to do the one thing that made sense to him in some fleeting vestige of frenzied thought. It's the only rational explanation I can come up with for what I saw him do next—and that is not for lack of thinking about it. I have relived the next few moments every time my head has hit a pillow since.

Danny watched Gary march toward him, within mere feet. I heard Gary shout to him as he pointed back in our direction. "Danny, you've got to stop this! They're going to kill you!"

Gary stood in front of Danny a moment. He was desperately out of breath. I saw his face as he looked on at what had become of him. I don't know how it didn't register to him sooner, but right then, Gary realized that what he was standing a few inches from was not anything even remotely approaching his friend. As that reality hit Gary, he began to sob. He had become so unmercifully aware that he was standing inches away from, for all intents and purposes, Satan himself.

Danny rested his right hand gently on one of Gary's cowering shoulders. It almost appeared as an endearing gesture. As he touched him, Gary was thrust into a fit of tearful jittering, completely giving way to all his emotion. Danny placed his other arm atop Gary's other shoulder. He rubbed them a couple of times, almost like he was consoling him. For a moment, I thought perhaps there was some obscure piece of our Danny still living inside of a nightmare, trying to escape.

Before that thought had had a chance to a take a foothold inside of my mind, Danny reared his head back farther than any mortal human being possibly could without breaking their own neck. His eyes again exploded with a flood of the brilliant orange light. With an inhumanly high-pitched screaming growl, he thrust his head forward with the velocity of a passing bullet train and slammed his own forehead square into the bridge of Gary's nose.

A mist of blood immediately sprayed wildly from the crater produced by the blow. I could literally hear, from where I was standing, twenty yards away, the bones in Gary's neck and spinal column shatter. The strike was so unimaginably devastating and so sudden that Gary's legs immediately went limp, completely buckling at the ankles and knees. He fell to the ground and began to twitch and seize uncontrollably. I knew he had no chance of surviving such a ferocious blow.

"You motherfucker, Danny!" I screamed in his direction.

The last look on Gary's ravaged face was not pain or misery or fear. Just before he faded away, I saw heartbreak in his eyes. Heartbreak from being so horrendously injured at the hand of a man he had grown to love, a man he would have given the world for, a man he looked up to for as long as he knew him. I lost control and began unintelligibly screaming and crying. My fists were clenched. I was forced to watch another of my brothers die for the second time on that horrible day.

For all of Gary's shortcomings, all his problems, he was the gentlest, most nonconfrontational man you would have ever met. He was humble to a fault. He knew how to have a good time, but he also knew how to work. He was the best at what he did, period. He might have been a pain in the ass to be around from time to time, but he was our pain in the ass. And I wouldn't have traded a single minute I spent with him for the world.

I'm sorry, guys. This is just heavy stuff for me to be rehashing right now.

(Everyone nods in understanding.)

Mrs. Miles: *Ricky, again, if you need to take some time, everyone would understand.*

Mr. Voss: *I'm fine, I'm fine. Gary was just the best. Those guys were truly my family, and they didn't deserve any of this. I was trapped in some shit town, watching my best friend murder one of my other best friends, and there was nothing I could do to stop it. Watching Gary seize and bleed out, knocked completely out of his mind, on the freezing cold ground, twenty yards away, is not something I will ever figure out how to live with.*

(Mr. Voss pauses for twenty seconds)

Okay, sorry about that.

The fiery atmosphere of haunted souls had reached a critical mass of concentration at the mouth of the rift. They were on their way down and moments from infiltrating our world and possessing the army of melon-heads. In doing so, they would form a force of evil with no earthly limitations that no nation could possibly begin to combat. The Bridge needed to be destroyed before even one of them got through.

Anunit approached Danny. "What kind of a god needs an army?" she shouted at him.

He considered the question a moment and replied in his high-pitched, echoing howl, "What kind of human questions a god?"

She tilted her head and smiled back at him confidently. "I am no human, Enki," she replied as she tore her headset off and slammed it to the ground. She stood five feet from Danny, her arms extended to her sides, her face pointed upward toward the fiery heavens. She seemed to be engulfing an invisible energy from the world around her. The air distorted and streamed like wind feeding a newly blossoming cyclone. After a moment, her entire body began to glow in a brilliant, white light. The light overtook her human form completely, snuffing it out of existence. She had assumed her native Agaden form. They had clearly made themselves appear human while on earth for our appeasement. But now the proverbial gloves were off. She still had two arms, two legs, a torso, and a head. But all her features had melted away into a smoldering mass of frosted, white energy that comprised the entirety of her. Every motion she made left tracers of sparking, blue-green energy in their wake. It was difficult to keep track of her exact position as her brilliantly vibrant form existed within the translucent blur of exploding power.

The other two Agaden had followed her lead, assuming their own natural forms. They joined Anunit and engaged Danny, who just smiled, allowing the display of aggression to continue before him. "Agaden," he growled, unable to wipe the smirk from his face. "You will be a rare, delicious treat for me to devour."

Just as Danny finished his thought, he managed to completely disappear and then reappear an instant later directly behind one of the male Agaden. Another instant later and Danny had him in an armlock from behind the chalky glow of his head. Without warning or hesitation, he twisted the Agaden with the speed and force of a runaway freight train, pulling him completely apart at the waist. His legs toppled into a gleaming heap below him. Danny was still holding the upper half of his shimmering torso in the air. His arms were still flailing wildly. The unlucky Agaden was very much still alive, even having received what were sure to be terminal injuries. A sort of silvery sludge oozed from the bottom of him all over the ground below. This was clearly their version of blood. As it poured and pooled below him, the thrashing of his arms and head became slower and more lethargic. He was bleeding out. Danny carelessly tossed the upper half of him to the ground. He would be dead within a minute.

Anunit attacked. The moment she closed the distance on Danny, he caught her by the throat. He squeezed her neck with incredible force, incredible hatred. She shrieked, and just as he was preparing to rip her throat completely out, the other male Agaden who remained rushed toward Danny and belted him across the side of the face with the butt of his rifle. He dropped Anunit to the ground. She rolled and writhed around as her hands immediately grasped her damaged throat. Her light had dimmed several shades from the initial brilliance of her original form. The Agaden who had just died had gone completely gray. It was obvious that their glow had a direct correlation to how sentient their life force was at any given point in time.

A quick jolt of elation shot through me as Danny was stunned by the strike to his face. It was the first strike of offense we were able to inflict upon him. He might have been possessed by a god, but he was still bound to a human body. Where the rifle had cracked his cheekbone, a massive gash had formed, all the way down to the cartilage. It immediately swelled, and his left eye abruptly began to close under the pressure. I made my move and began to slowly approach the situation. We had but moments before the calamitous genii came through the rift and galvanized the army of melon-heads, along with Crowe, Peirce, and Harvey. We would soon be inundated underneath an entire army of hell-born, psychotic reinforcements.

Danny did not seem aware of my approach. Instead, he grappled with the Agaden who had struck him moments before. Whoever that Agaden was, he knew how to put up a fight. Their battle went back and forth for several moments, allowing me the time I needed to close the distance. As I drew nearer to them, Danny managed to get the Agaden in another of his arm holds, completely immobilizing him. This seemed to be his preferred method of dispatching his adversaries: get them into submission, then strike the death blow. But before he could inflict his final kill shot to the Agaden, I shouted to him, "Danny! Think about Annie. Think about what she would think of you right now."

He paused a moment, still holding the Agaden in submission. "Do not address me as though you know me, human. You are but an ant awaiting its execution."

"Do you remember anything, Danny?" I belted. "I know there is some part of you still in there. I know you can hear me. You talked to Annie three days ago."

He had become agitated. He released his grip on the Agaden and dropped him to the ground in a writhing heap. He stood with his back to me, seemingly considering my remarks before replying in a cold yet curiously more human tone, "To remember my incarnated life is akin to you remembering what it was like to be an infant. None of that is of consequence now, human."

I replied again as I continued inching even closer, "She did her report on Dian Fossey. You told her to. Do you remember? You've always helped her. I've watched you raise her. Three days ago, there was nothing in the world you wouldn't have given to ensure her security and happiness. And now here you are, ready to lead an army. An army that, make no mistake about it, will kill her."

"Shut up," he snapped. "None of that matters now." His voice was becoming more human again; it had lost much of its synthesized, supernatural quality. The end of his reply sounded almost completely like our Danny.

He turned and approached me. The orange glow from his eyes had dimmed several shades. He was slowly transforming. But he was still very much Enki's hostage.

"Ricky," he said, the first time he had referred to me by name. "You have no idea what I have become or what you are dealing with here. Get yourself out of here. Get as far away as you can."

I shook off his remark. "I believe you are in control here. And I believe you are able to fight whatever is inside you, whatever made you kill Gary. Danny, I know that wasn't you, and I know there's a part of you that's dying in there for having done it."

He cried to me; his voice had completely returned to that of my Danny—an emotionally broken version of him, but no doubt it was him. "I said shut the fuck up, Ricky! Get the fuck out of here. Don't let him hurt you too. Please, don't let me hurt you, Rick."

He sprung toward me. He was still capable of inhuman strength. He shoved me off my feet to the ground. I landed flat on my ass. Something in my rear pocket sliced a hole into my upper leg as I landed on top of it. It hurt like absolute hell, but it gave me an idea. Danny towered over me. He extended his arms in my direction, ready to rip me to shreds. I reached back, grasping the tactical knife that had been given to me by the Agaden back on the road where Big Bear had died. I looked Danny straight in his enraged eyes and screamed up to him, "It is up to yourself, and only yourself, to choose the world you see!"

He lowered his arms. The remark resonated somewhere deeply within him. I could see in his eyes that that phrase had brought forth the soul of my Danny, my best friend. That single phrase had completely suppressed whatever else was inside of him. In that moment, I was looking at my friend again, at long last. I could see the guilt in his eyes. I could see how aware he was of having killed Gary moments prior. I saw a man who had literally been to Hell and back and found himself locked into an endless dance with the Devil inside of his own head. I saw my best friend just wanting to die.

I grasped the handle of the ten-inch, tactical blade, and in one motion, I seized Danny's moment of weakness. I brought it around my body and thrust it into the dead center of his chest. Danny's eyes bulged, and a hint of the haunting orange hue returned to them the moment the blade penetrated his torso. Enki had returned just in time to find his physical host on this planet receiving a mortal wound. I rolled away and as I did, I cried out to him. "Goddammit, Danny! I had to do it. You know I had to fucking do it! Goddamn you, Danny. You were my brother, man. I am so sorry." It was all I could think to say to him. I was crying hysterically. I had no idea if my apology even resonated. Danny collapsed to the ground, and in that moment, I understood what I had argued so vehemently with Anunit over. I certainly would have never chosen to kill the best friend I have ever had or ever will. But there was simply no choice.

Danny fell to his back mere feet from where I was crouched on the icy-cold ground. He let out a gurgling gasp. He was spitting up streams of blood. A moment later, a flash of brilliant silver light beamed silently from near the rift, completely blinding us all. As my pupils recovered, I saw the rift beginning to break apart. The once sturdy, towering behemoth of electrified energy wobbled and gyrated. It had been a brilliant, fiery shade of magenta but was quickly fading in color and luminosity.

I watched Roderick Crowe, Margaret Peirce, and Kenneth Harvey leap into the rift, sensing that it was about to close. The melon-heads followed them in droves, one wretched body after another. Each of them desperate to catch the last train to their promised Hell and home to their long-prophesized torment. Within a couple of minutes, me, Anunit, Danny, and the other Agaden were all who remained. We were all grounded and gasping heavily, exhausted beyond words.

I glanced over to Danny. He was motioning for me to come closer. He was holding on to his last gasp of life, choking badly on his own blood. I crawled to him, placing my head next to his. He wrapped his arm around me and began to whisper in my ear. It was barely audible. He had to repeat himself through his hitching gasps.

"Big Bear . . . Big Bear . . . Sam." He was for some reason repeating his name. Finally, he managed a full sentence. "Don't let Sam go back through."

I had no idea what he was talking about. I figured he was delirious. Perhaps some last few synapses inside of his confused, dying brain were firing off and producing incoherent thoughts that he was spewing out to me in his most desperate of moments. Then Danny's eyes lit up; he was looking at something coming out of the trees, something that I could tell scared the living shit out of him. Suddenly, the entire clearing was cast into a massive shadow. I reluctantly looked up and was met by the most horrific sight I will ever have the displeasure of bearing witness to.

Enki towered over us. He had been forced out of Danny's dying body, but he was still very much in our midst. He was a massive, ghostly, lurching, white figure—at least fifty feet tall. His grotesquely elongated arms and legs made up the entirety of him, culminating in an "X" shape where his torso should have been. He had the ability to shape-shift, and he was rapidly shrinking himself down to something approaching our size.

As he shrunk further, we could take in his face for the first time. It was the object that all horror is born from. It was a humanoid face, but it radiated emotion as the sight of it hit you. It brought you completely to your knees with terror, something that not even the apostles of Christ himself could put into proper context. I have searched far and wide for a better way of describing it, but there is no scientific or theological justification for the level of hatred I found in Enki's eyes. We were all paralyzed with dread. He reached his monstrous hands toward us. He was going to drag us through the rapidly closing rift and into his nightmare realm, into his kingdom.

Suddenly and without warning, Enki let out a screeching gasp as his body was slammed into by an explosion of kinetic force. The monster was pummeled backward away from us and knocked completely off his feet. The sheer violence of the mysterious crash was only matched by the utterly dumbfounding look of confusion that suddenly riddled Enki's disgusting face. This unmerciful, devastating collision was no doubt a first for something who fancied himself as a god.

Standing above him proudly with his hands on his hips, taking in his achievement, was the unmistakable, spectral spirit of Big Bear. He was wearing a cloak similar to Danny's, but far larger and a lot less fancy. He was an absolute marvel of a spirit—a shimmering, translucent physique not even possible through Michelangelo's wildest imagination. He was our savior.

He looked back at us with a smile and quietly delivered his wish. "Tell Daphne that I love her."

The tears flooded down my cheeks at his request, but I mustered the strength to nod approvingly. Before I could respond further, he dashed toward Enki, who was still in a concussed daze from the initial knock-out blast that Big Bear had inflicted. Big Bear thrust his hideous squirming body completely off the ground. He then executed a piledriver motion to Enki, thrusting his limp body headfirst into a jagged corner of one of the bricks that once made up the foundation of Ashford Hill. Enki's neck folded backward unnaturally—even for him. Big Bear held Enki's torso in the air with his unconscious head still dangling awkwardly against the slab. Big Bear, with that familiar ear-to-ear grin on his face, stomped on the back of Enki's neck. Each time he did, more cracking and breaking could be heard. After five unmerciful strikes, Sam dropped Enki's lifeless corpse to the ground.

A moment later, a high-pitch scream could be heard coming from Enki's corpse. A vaporous, smoke-like entity could be seen squirming from the devastated mouth of its body. It was far more of a living, gaseous compound than anything remotely human. But for an instant, it seemed to be attempting to form the construct of an almost human-like face. I didn't get a chance to fully comprehend what I was looking at before Anunit shouted next to me, ripping my attention away from it.

"Genii of Enki—God of the Deep—the Destroyer—the Demon Warrior! I command you—be banished unto the realm of the Death Gods!"

It then registered that the smoky mass pouring from the throat of Enki's corpse was its soul. Enki had been killed in his earthbound form and would therefore be forced into his own nightmare realm through The Bulk. He would no longer control any intermediate slice of space-time between his realm and earth. At least, that was how I interpreted the situation.

Big Bear stood over Enki. He bent down, placing his mouth just over the top of the vapor that was Enki's genii. He began to inhale, seemingly with the force of a jet engine at mach-3. Enki's soul was sucked instantaneously into Big Bear's magnificent spectral mass. Big Bear stole one final glance in our direction and then ran, with Enki in tow, toward the abruptly fading rift. Just before it closed permanently, he leapt into it and shot into the heavens in a flash of brilliant, iridescent energy. He took with him the last threat to all of us. In one miraculous swoop, Big Bear had exorcised the phantasmal plague that had cursed Ashford for nearly a century. He had given his life to save us back on the road. An hour later, he sacrificed his own soul to save the world.

I need to break for the day.

Judge Stokes: *Granted.*

42
Daniel Hallowell - Present Day – 3:30 p.m.

Give me a reason to care. Tell me what I have left to gain. I killed the best of us. Two of the most beautiful human beings anyone could have ever had the pleasure of knowing are gone. And they're gone because of me. I am directly responsible for Gary's death and indirectly responsible for Big Bear's.

We drove into that town under false pretenses. Sure, we had been coerced into going there, and we can certainly hide behind the fact that there was no way of knowing what we would face there. But we never know what we will face when we go anywhere, especially in that line of work. That was the draw. That was why we did what we did—to unlock the mystery, to forge ahead of human understanding and come back having experienced something thrilling—something that compelled us and our audience. In the immortal words of Hunter S. Thompson: "Buy the ticket. . . . Take the ride."

I am never going to run away from my guilt. There are responsibilities involved with investigating the paranormal. It is easy to say yes, and it is exceedingly hard to say no. Sometimes, however, just saying no, no matter how compelling an argument might be, is still the right answer. I should have never dragged my team to that town. We should have stuck with the original plan and done our boring investigation of the Carnegie Mill in Cleveland. Their deaths are on me. Their being there was my mistake. I am exactly where I belong.

I wanted to die. There are plenty of days where I still do. I have been to places and witnessed things that no human mind should ever be exposed to. Through my travels, I have caused the horrible deaths of two of my greatest friends. I widowed a wonderful woman in Big Bear's wife, Daphne. Her husband, who, quite literally, is an American hero, will never have a real burial, his body having been left in that god-awful place. His soul will never find peace, imprisoned in Enki's Hell for all eternity.

Gary, despite all the shit I've talked about him, was another beautiful spirit. He never had much in the way of possession, but he would have given the shirt off his back to anyone who needed it. He never hurt a soul. He used to just talk to me—we could talk for hours. He would ask question after question about how I thought the mechanics of the paranormal worked or how he could do a better job or how I thought he should position the equipment to capture the best evidence. He didn't have to care about any of it. He was an equipment guy. He could have just come to work, done a half-assed job, and gone home every night. Plenty of people in our business do. But he genuinely cared enough about me that he felt like he owed it to me, for some reason, to go above and beyond. He thought the world of me, and I never gave it back to him, and I killed him in the most unmercifully cruel fashion possible. In that instant of aggression, I ripped away everything that Gary had looked up to throughout his entire professional life. Not only did I kill one of the most loyal, loving people anyone could ever have the pleasure of knowing, but I absolutely broke his heart at the same time. A heart that had been filled with wonder toward me. A heart that beat within a man that I spent half my life shitting on in return for his unending kindness.

In that instant, as far as I am concerned, I invalidated my own existence. There is no longer any reason to try. There will never be any crawling back from that act. If there is any, even semi-conscious part of me that is capable of an act that callous, that brutal, then I am left with no choice but to extricate myself from society at large. I forfeit my right to any affection or love or life outside of the walls of this institution, citing the moment my head crashed into the unconditionally loving face of my best friend.

I can remember the situation vividly from this point on, now that Enki was no longer on the premises and my mind was my own again. I can complete my side of the story.

The Ruins of Ashford Hill Asylum – 8:15 a.m.

I grasped Ricky's head as the blood flowed from my mouth. I remember watching Big Bear abduct the soul of the awful demon who had possessed me, moments before, and run with it into the rift, sacrificing his own soul to his kingdom in the process. I hugged Ricky as the rift broke apart and faded off into the sky, returning the roiling, stormy atmosphere to normal.

I could feel myself slowing down. I was no longer able to take in air as my lungs had filled with blood. The ten-inch blade jutted from my chest. More blood poured from my face. I had received a massive gash from the butt of the gun that the Agaden had struck me with. Both of my eyes were swollen to the point that I could only see my surroundings through a blinding sliver of light. I had another severe laceration in the center of my forehead that I had sustained while dispatching Gary. I was absolutely freezing—colder than I had ever been. *It won't be long now*, I thought. Maybe when we die, the ineffable guilt melts away. Perhaps I would be relieved of that agony. Maybe I would be given some insight into what truly happens after we die that would bring my heinous actions into some perspective that I would find some comfort in. Somehow, though, I doubted it.

Flying completely in the face of everything I wished for, the Agaden that Ricky referred to as Anunit knelt at my side. She placed her shimmering, silvery hand atop my abdomen, gripped the handle of the blade, and pulled it from my chest. As she did so, a fist-sized ball of half-congealed blood shot from my mouth and exploded all over my face. I was blinded by it momentarily as the warm liquid flooded my squinting eyes. I could hear her saying something to Ricky. Their words were murky and distorted in my state. It was as though I were listening to them have a conversation underwater.

She shouted to Ricky, "His lung is collapsed, and the other lung is filling with blood. He is suffocating."

I felt another blunt object pierce my chest. This time slightly left of center. The pain was excruciating. I glanced down and found a metallic tube jutting from my torso. It reminded me of a tire gauge for a moment. Anunit twisted the top from it, and as she did, a massive, whistling bubble of air shot through my nose and mouth and down into my body. As that rushing oxygen hit my lungs, a stream of pure blood began to shoot from the top of the metallic straw. As the liquid flowed from me, I found myself able to breathe again. I was no longer suffocating. She was saving my life.

Ricky was holding on to my hand the entire time. I looked over to him and said in a hoarse whisper, "No, no. Please stop. Just let me go. Set me free. I can't live with this."

"We've lost too much today, brother. I'm not going to lose you too," he replied.

I lay back and breathed. It became easier and easier as the blood emptied from my remaining lung. The other lung had been shredded by Ricky's knife. I was still in terrible shape, but I was becoming more and more stable by the minute. Ricky, sensing that I was going to be all right, stood and approached Gary. He took his pulse, but he was long dead.

Enki was long gone, but, to this day, I can still feel traces of him. He left remnants of himself behind, deep within me. There is an anger in me that wasn't there before. There is a darkness. There is a perverse knowledge of the universe and the mechanics of all things and all people. It is impossible for me to listen to people now—impossible to take them seriously. I rose to such greatness only to fall so quickly to such sickening depths. Human beings are so insignificant on a celestial level. We are but rats with credit cards—as old Andy would tell you, completely ignorant to the true powers that oversee us. Our souls are but a currency that is declining in value with every ignorant moment we infest our own planet.

I am trapped in a world now where I must listen to these intellectual insects lecture me on and on about god and how he wants us to behave. But I am the only one who truly knows how full of shit they really are. And because of this knowledge, because of this heinous gift I was unwillingly given, I am considered the crazy one.

43

The Deposition of Rick Voss: (Fourth Session):

Mr. Levine: *It has become apparent to me, having deposed Mr. Hallowell and now Mr. Voss, that we are never going to truly understand how Samuel Millbury and Gary Jenkins died. So far, all that we have to go on are these utterly ridiculous yarns about monsters and devils and gods. I don't know about the rest of you, but I've heard just about enough of this.*

Judge Stokes: *Free country, Doug. There's the door.*

Mr. Levine: *You can't be serious. You can't honestly be taking seriously any of these . . . fables. You know what, I have sat here for three days listening to this man shred everything I was raised to believe to bits. My job is to do the best I can to understand the circumstances that brought about two homicides in your county, your honor. It is clear to me now that I need to seek alternate means.*

Mr. Voss: *I understand you work for the families of Gary and Sam, but the absolute last thing they would have wanted was this. They both gave their lives trying to save Danny. They understood he wasn't himself while in that town. They would not be onboard with this witch hunt of yours for one minute. To be candid, neither of them would have given a whiny little shit-eater like you the time of day.*

(Door closes. Mr. Levine leaves the room.)

Judge Stokes: *There's that professionalism and maturity we've come to expect from you, Ricky. Now that everyone's favorite little whiny—what was it? Shit-eater?*

Mr. Voss: *That's correct, your honor. It was my personal assessment of Mr. Levine, and I meant nothing more by it. I apologize again for my language.*

(Laughs throughout the room)

Judge Stokes: *All right, all right, everyone. Now, I believe I speak for the rest of us here. I am not saying that any of us believe your story any more than Doug did, but I, for one, am intrigued and intend to hear the rest of it out. Would you be kind enough to take us through the remainder?*

Mr. Voss: *I would be happy to, your honor.*

"Is Enki gone for good?" I asked Anunit.

She stood from Danny's side and gazed toward the now-calm heavens. It was as though she were somehow drawing information from above. "I think so, Ricky. Obviously, we will do more testing before we call this a complete victory, but I no longer sense his evil. His being killed here should have forced his genii completely through The Bulk and back to his personal hell. He should no longer have any means of influence over this slice of space-time."

Enki was gone. Miraculously, I hadn't hit Danny in the heart when I thrust the knife into his chest. If I had, he would have been dead within a minute. He wanted to be dead. He told me as much. Anunit somehow knew that I had punctured his lung and that the other good lung was filling with blood. She had a stint, and she jammed it into his chest. The moment she did, it released the blood from his good lung, and he was able to breathe again.

I was totally lost, and my mind was swimming. I stumbled over to Gary and checked his vital signs. His face was completely obliterated—shoved downward when Danny had hit him and congealed into a gelatinous mass. The bones from the back of his neck jutted from his throat, having sliced through his esophagus. His head was basically severed in the strike. The skin was the only thing keeping it attached to the rest of his body. He was dead an instant after the blow.

The Agaden had faded back into their human forms. Anunit placed her hand on my shoulders as I stood over Gary, sobbing. "His genii is still here."

"What? Gary's soul is still in Ashford?" I asked.

"That's right. The rift was closed before his genii was forced through it. I will personally see to it that it comes back to our realm."

"Thank you," I said. "And Big Bear, what about Big Bear?"

The gentle smile from her face subsided. "You saw where he went. In doing so, he gave himself over to Enki's realm. There is no getting his genii back."

The sight of Big Bear tackling Enki flashed through my head. I sort of smiled for the first time in days thinking about it. "Kicked that fucker's ass first though, didn't he? Maybe he will be the new ruler of that kingdom?"

She smiled again. "Perhaps, Ricky—I would very much like that."

We stood in the field; a frigid October air danced through the trees. It was only midday, but that half-sunlit clearing was as warm as it was going to get. The sharp scent of soon-to-fall snow had begun to fill the air.

"What happens next?" I asked her, sniffling away another uncontrollable flood of tears.

She placed her other hand on my chest and whispered, "We go home."

The sky exploded in a completely soundless flash of light. I was blinded. The only thing I could make out before my pupils fully compressed was Anunit's beautiful face as she sent me on my way with a final remark. "Goodbye, Ricky. I am glad I had a chance to know you."

In the next instant, everything went black, and I could feel the most intense pressure on top of me. It was as though I were being pushed downward by an invisible force with the mass of the entire planet behind it. I felt like I was moving at an incomprehensible speed. Just before the terror could completely take hold, another silent flash flooded the entire area, cruelly contrasting the blackness.

I felt my ass hit something. My eyes adjusted, and as they slowly regained their ability to take in my surroundings, I found myself sitting on the side of a road. On either side were cornfields. Danny was next to me, and his wounds had completely disappeared. He was again dressed in the clothes he had entered Ashford wearing. We were both filthy, but we were alive. I could see into the field across the street. There was a farmer harvesting his crops, riding atop a massive tractor.

"Where the fuck are we?" I asked Danny.

He didn't reply, choosing instead to climb up to his feet from the lukewarm blacktop. I rose from my back as well. Danny and I made our way to one of the sides of the street. There was a sign that read: "US-613 – Now Entering Hunters Valley."

I pulled out my phone. It was long dead. Danny didn't have his phone. He did have a watch. I grabbed his wrist and looked at it. It was 11:30 a.m. on October 16, 2018. It made no sense. We had entered Ashford on October 14. We had spent three days there. It should have been the seventeenth.

In the next moment, I understood what had happened. The Agaden had purposely placed us one day behind present time. If they had placed us back into actual present time, Ashford would have suddenly been thrust back to the present along with us. At least, that's my theory as to why they did what they did. It would have caused quite a stir here in Wahoga County if an entire extinct town suddenly reappeared out of thin air. So, they kept it hidden in time, just one day behind. I believe Danny testified to you that his watch has been one day ahead ever since he got back from Ashford. I believe he was laughed at when he explained why it was that way. As the calendar goes, we only spent two days there; however, we jumped forward into that fateful third day the moment Danny created the rift and we raced down Whistler Road to meet it. Quite frankly, I have still never been able to fully wrap my head around the exact amount of time we spent in that town. Time worked very differently relative to me and Danny. There were periods where we weren't in existence on the same timeline.

Agent Roy: *Fascinating.*

Mr. Voss: *Danny had recovered, but he was far from himself. He was running down the street shouting for Gary and Big Bear. He was hysterical. I chased after him a while. Whenever I would catch up to him, I would try to grab him, but he would just fight away again. He was totally out of his mind, screaming, crying.*

I grew too exhausted to continue chasing him. He ran up the road, and I just sort of started walking behind him. I caught up with him about twenty minutes later. He had tried to break into a house and was shouting at the owner to let him use their phone. When the owner refused, he tried to choke him and force his way in. Two of the owners' sons managed to subdue him and call the police. The police came and began to question us. Danny, without anyone even asking him about them, completely incriminated himself for the murders of Big Bear and Gary. I shouted for him to, pardon my language, 'shut the fuck up and wait for a lawyer,' but he didn't care. He hasn't cared since. He should have been allowed to die in Ashford.

And here we all are, a year later. Danny is probably going to end up in the same type of asylum that stirred up all the events that haunted Ashford for nearly a century. We have told you the truth about what happened to us there. You don't believe any of it. To be completely honest, I can't blame you. I doubt I would believe my story had I not lived it.

Danny did not kill Big Bear. The melon-heads killed him. Danny's body killed Gary while it was possessed by a force so evil that I hope humanity never comes to understand it.

Know this, there is nothing you can sentence Daniel Hallowell to, including death, that is going to punish him more than he already has been. He has literally met the Devil himself. He has walked the earth as him, seen the world through the eyes of the antichrist. All that I ask is that you take some of this into account. Danny, despite the best efforts of everyone around him, has done an incredibly piss-poor job of defending himself. The entire unfortunate scenario calls into question the very integrity of our legal system. It is literally impossible for anyone to prove that Danny committed either of these murders.

As incredible a story as it is, it is true. These things happened. I am looking at you, Martin. The FBI knows about Ashford. You said so yourself. We can't talk about what you told us here outside of this room, but maybe someone can. It would certainly help a man who is incarcerated right now. A man who is one of the best people I have ever known. A man who is a father to a beautiful daughter and a husband to a loving wife. Help him become vindicated and possibly realize his freedom again, however little he claims to care.

Mrs. Miles: *Is that everything, Ricky?*

Mr. Voss: *That's everything.*

Judge Stokes: *In that case, I would like to thank everyone for attending. Ricky, allow me to personally thank you for your participation. This couldn't have been easy with the caliber of prosecutor you had to deal with. And Agent Roy, I thank you for your time and certainly hope the bureau can glean some useful information about Ashford from this proceeding.*

Agent Roy: *Thank you, your honor.*

(Conclusion of Transcript)

44
Daniel Hallowell – Present Day – 5:30 p.m.

That was six years ago. I do appreciate Ricky's pleading on my behalf, but I truly don't want to be saved. I do crave freedom from this place, but who wouldn't? I crave it, but at the same time, it terrifies me. What would my freedom look like? I am a man who was once a pseudo-celebrity who, as far as the rest of the world is concerned, went crazy and killed two of his best friends. For all intents and purposes, that is true.

There are two reasons I did not wind up in prison or worse. The first is because there is no physical evidence of my crimes. That's easy—it is locked away in time, by the Agaden, in a town that nobody will ever find. The second reason is because my story, however true, sounds so bat-shit crazy that only a total lunatic could have made it up. I couldn't even get through a quarter of the story with my own lawyers that the Museum Network was kind enough to provide for me before I was laughed at and told to represent myself because my story was indefensible. I was told that I should have never admitted to the crimes since there was no way anyone could prove them.

To that, I say this. What makes a bigger man? A man who kills someone and, knowing there is no way anyone could prove it, refuses to confess? Or would the bigger man, knowing he killed someone, knowing there is no way to prove it, admit his wrongs? Seems to me, that should count for something. Seems to me, that is the least I could have done for Sam and Gary.

I went into trial with my third-string legal counsel representing me. By that point, I was basically represented by several kids straight out of law school, hoping to make a name for themselves. I had admitted to the killings, so the entire trial was basically just a drawn-out sentencing hearing. By what I suppose you could call a stroke of luck on my part, the jury deemed my testimony so otherworldly insane that they ruled for me to be sent away to a hospital for the criminally insane. And I have been here ever since.

Annie is in college and doing well. She is majoring in psychology with a minor in parapsychology. I am not saying her crazy dad had anything to do with influencing those declarations, but maybe he did. I truly hope I did. She has always been able to see the world through the right kind of lens.

My wife, Ellen, and I, as I stated, divorced. It wasn't ugly. It was necessary once she realized what I had become. Who could have blamed her? Who wants to be married to a man who is trapped in a looney bin and who has no qualms about being there or aspirations to ever leave? She got most of the money, and she can have it. I have little use for it, and I never really got used to having it anyway. There will always be a place in my heart for her. She was the best wife I could have asked for. I abandoned her through my own horrible judgment and actions, however unprovable they might be. I truly hope she can find happiness and someone who can love her as much as I always will.

There is precious little to look forward to here. My life consists of an endless parade of therapy sessions and pills—Gary would have loved it here. They truly have a drug for everything. It is not completely without entertainment value, however. Despite all my issues, I am on the tame side of the crazy spectrum. I have always maintained that I do, indeed, belong here; however, some of the other people in this place (good lord) truly, without a shadow of a doubt, belong here. There is one guy who figured out the other day that he could take one of the chairs from the cafeteria and bring it outside the doors of our holding rooms. He then proceeded to, with a running start, use the chair as a launching mechanism. He ran, jumped atop the chair, leapt into the air off it, inverted himself in midair, and landed twenty feet down the hallway, directly on top of his own head. The last I saw of him was his unconscious body being hauled away on a stretcher. I presume he is either paralyzed or dead; neither result would surprise me.

My crimes will never be proven, but at the same time, they will never be disproven. My team of jackass mental health professionals will never get me to sing a different tune. They will never be able to invoke a different story out of me or any more information than has been written here. Someday, when they are unlucky enough to have died and they have a chance to look around themselves and see what truly happens, I hope, for a fleeting instant in time, they think to themselves: *You know something? That Daniel Hallowell knew exactly what he was talking about. And I refused to take him seriously. What a closed-minded sack of shit I am.*

Epilogue
Shade River Psychiatric Hospital – 2:30 a.m.

I am writing this last chapter to document another night that has, once again, altered the course of my life in a profound manner. This night has provided healing and the potential of closure around my feelings as they pertain to those three horrible days in Ashford.

I was in a deep sleep a few hours ago, in my room at the hospital, fighting off the nightmares that have plagued me since my time in that town. I am not certain of the exact time it happened, but three bangs on the steel door to my room abruptly thrust me out of my slumber. As I leaned forward in my bed, waiting for my eyes to adjust to the hallway light that began to seep into the room as the door swung open, I was able to make out two male figures.

I can remember thinking how this must be something important. It is a big no-no in psychiatric facilities to wake patients if they are sleeping. Trying to get half of these people to sleep at all is enough of a chore.

I recognized the man on the left as Dr. Michael Bukoski—the head of the team responsible for my psychiatric care. I had met with him a few times early in my stay. I have since been handled by his parade of underlings.

I had no idea who the man on the right was. He wore a black suit, black tie, black shoes and had a look on his face that appeared, for some reason, as practiced seriousness. While I didn't recognize him, I immediately recognized what he held in his hand. It was an electronic voice recorder—the same kind we used to use in our paranormal investigations.

"A little early for a threesome, doc," I joked, trying to get my voice out of sleep mode. My remark elicited a smile and chuckle from the mystery man in the suit. This was further evidence that his previous facial expression was forced seriousness. And, as expected, no emotion from Dr. Bukoski was evident.

"Sorry to wake you, Mr. Hallowell. I know that it goes against all our protocols, but we are going to play you a recording and we want to know your thoughts once you've listened to it. Would that be okay?" Bukoski said in his typical, patronizing tone. He spoke to everyone as though they were five years old. It bothered me at first, but I have since conditioned myself to not care.

"Well, I suppose that would be okay, Mike," I replied. He hated being called Mike and I knew he hated it. Therefore, every time he and I would cross paths, I would go out of my way to refer to him as Mike.

He nodded to the mystery man. The man pressed play on the electronic voice recorder. It started off as static for about ten seconds. Then, without warning a voice came through: "I'm okay Daphne."

My eyes lit up. I immediately recognized the voice. It was Big Bear. As I was preparing to shout about a thousand questions to the mystery man, he sensed it and held a finger over his mouth, requesting I listen further. The same voice came through after another few seconds: "We're in Ashford and we need to find a way out."

Who is we? I thought to myself as I continued listening. After another moment of static, a new voice could be heard—this time it was distinctly female. "Be the Bridge again." I did not recognize her voice.

By this point, I had tears running down my cheeks. I had begun nervously pounding my fist against the cinder-block wall next to my bed. Hearing Big Bear's voice again contorted every possible emotion in my head into something I had no choice but to act upon physically. Finally, a third voice came through with a single word: "Please."

That last word sent me into a fit of tears, the likes of which I cannot recall experiencing since early childhood. Unmistakably, the third voice was Gary. All the guilt, the self-loathing, the depression, the pain washed away for one fleeting moment, hearing that one word in his voice. For one moment, that mountain of suffering and everything that I'd grappled with, lifted from my shoulders. My sobbing got worse.

The mystery man looked over to Dr. Bukoski and said, "works for me. I am convinced it's their voices."

"Where did you get those recordings?" I asked, overcoming my crying for a moment.

"Mr. Hallowell," said the mystery man, "we received this recording a week ago on US-613 as part of an ongoing investigation into the potential existence of Ashford, Ohio. They are the first such recordings we've been able to capture in decades of trying. You are the second to corroborate our suspicion that they are the voices of Sam Millbury and Gary Jenkins. Your friend Rick Voss recognized the woman's voice as Anunit, a member of a faction that we believe are, somehow, concealing the existence of Ashford."

"I find it all very difficult to believe personally, Daniel. But we all have higher authorities we must answer to, don't we?" asked Dr. Bukoski.

I just shook my head, feeling the first semblance of true motivation in years flow through my entire body. "So, what do we do?" I asked.

The mystery man took a couple of steps closer to my bed and responded. "Well, that's very much up to you, Mr. Hallowell. I'm Special Agent Martin Roy. I work for a branch of the FBI who has been investigating Ashford for years. We would very much like to talk more about this with you."

For the first time in as long as I can remember, I felt alive. I felt like I had a purpose worth living for.

Made in the USA
Middletown, DE
10 October 2018